MW01518579

"A riveting pl   d
pseudoscientific concepts, it snowcases   on
of science fiction. *The Between State* stands out like a piece of diamond in a pile of rocks for its deviation from the usual sci-fi obsession with space exploration and alien worlds. Its dazzling combination of sleep science and time travel dives into the "what ifs" of interfering with time without boring you with all the related philosophical premises and scientific jargon. Detailed and entertaining, this novel packs a lot of information into its fast-moving and curiosity-piquing plot. Although *The Between State* is part of a series, its ending could not have been more satisfying. I wished it wouldn't end and was elated to discover the series' next instalment. Read this title if you want to discover the possibilities that abound in sleep science and dream life."

—Joshua Olokodana for Readers' Favorite.

"*The Between State* follows an IT guy named Jeff who keeps finding himself having hyper-realistic dreams about being in the body of a woman he's never met. After discovering that this woman is a real person and his visits to her take place in the past, Jeff must try to deduce what is happening to them and why. As he works to solve the riddle, the idea of using this opportunity to help her move forward with her life after a difficult past becomes more and more tempting.

I loved the way the narrative of this story constantly kept me off balance and guessing what direction it would move in next. At one moment, it was quite an analytical look at the scientific theory behind body-swapping and time travel, and the next moment a beautiful human story about caring for the wellbeing of a stranger. It's a testament to the dynamic prose of author Joseph A White Jr that this work manages to tell such a tonally diverse story whilst remaining cohesive throughout. I was particularly engaged by the way Jeff's characterization evolved throughout the story, moving from a logical and analytical figure to someone whose growing emotional attachment to his body-swapping partner causes a very natural development that was delightful to watch throughout the narrative."

—K.C. Finn for Readers' Favorite.

"Joseph A White Jr wraps his tale *The Between State* around a fascinating concept, for which he conducted substantial research. The titular "between state" is presented as the stage between REM sleep and wakefulness, which happens to facilitate lucid dreaming. Memorably, it also leads the dreamer to question not only the tangibility of his world, but the soundness of his mind. This phenomenon ignites Jeff's impulse to analyze every thread of his subconscious, giving its shapeless fabric a reluctant form.

The friendship between Jeff and Mindi is undoubtedly the backbone of the novel's narrative. Genuine enough to withstand the test of a slow build-up, as well as the central conflict between the empirical and the theoretical, it nevertheless flirts with an attraction that sows hope in the hearts of these two kind-natured adults." **—Indie Reader Review.**

" *The Between State* by Joseph A White Jr is an original science fiction novel that will make you question reality. Every time Jeff Marlen falls asleep, he has very realistic dreams in which he is inside the mind of Mindi, whose life is troubled. Believing there must be a reason for him to be inside the mind of another person while in REM sleep, Jeff begins to note his experiences to find the purpose for his visits. The moment Jeff leaves logic behind and allows himself to feel what Mindi feels is the moment his whole view changes. I loved the change in narrative and how author Joseph A White Jr created a sense of comfort even when

everything was in chaos."
—**Rabia Tanveer for Readers' Favorite.**

"If you are looking for a slow-paced character-driven story with light romance and a touch of science fiction, Joseph A White Jr's *The Between State* might be it. The author does a great job of developing his characters. Jeff Marlen is portrayed as an assertive, intelligent, and compassionate character. Mindi is portrayed as a strong-willed and inquisitive character. Joseph A White Jr gives vivid depictions of his scenes and characters, and this served to add color to my imagination."
—**Keith Mbuya for Readers' Favorite**

" I admire the author's level of imagination and creativity. Jeff's dreams were so vivid and realistic, while his search for answers was engaging. The book is educational in the sense that I learned a lot about dreams and their impact on the subconscious mind and mental health. I loved the storyline and word selection. I recommend *The Between State* by Joseph A White Jr as a good choice for sci-fi lovers."
—**Mariam Tijani for Readers' Favorite.**

THE
BETWEEN
STATE

JOSEPH A WHITE JR

AIA PUBLISHING

The Between State
Joseph A White Jr
Copyright © 2022
Published by AIA Publishing, Australia
ABN: 32736122056
http://www.aiapublishing.com

All characters in this publication are fictitious and any resemblance to real persons, living or dead, is purely coincidental.

All rights reserved. No part of this publication may be reproduced, stored in a retrieval system or transmitted in any form or by any means electronic, mechanical, audio, visual or otherwise, without prior permission of the copyright owner. Nor can it be circulated in any form of binding or cover other than that in which it is published and without similar conditions including this condition being imposed on the subsequent purchaser.

ISBN: 978-1-922329-37-0

For my wife and family.

To Helen,
I trust we will meet once
again in our dreams.
Love, Martin

To Helen,
I trust we will meet once
again in our dreams.
Love, Martin

CHAPTER 1

He fell—descending fast—seeing only gray. No inky blackness, no white-out, just total, featureless gray.

And it was silent.

This wasn't skydiving.

There was no rush of air,

No view of the ground.

In the gray silence—he fell.

His mind asked, *What? Where?*

Confusion turned to dread. On the edge of panic, he struggled to focus.

Relax, an inner voice said. He did, and the fall stopped. No g-force or sudden jolt as a parachute opens. Not even that slight dip when an elevator settles to a stop. He floated like a cloud. Still and gray. Panic gone. Comfortable now.

Then he awoke.

The bed supported his body. A car passed on the street. The dim light from the streetlights and the stillness of the bedroom was not the grayness or the total quiet of the dream. The dream was unlike any he'd had before.

He put his feet on the floor; the feeling of the throw rug

reassured him. He shook his head, but it did nothing to dim the dream's memory.

He stood, looked at the clock, and decided to get an early start. Even after he showered, dressed, and drank his coffee, the dream stayed with him, as vivid as when he first awoke. He seldom remembered his dreams. Usually they faded and were gone, but the memory of this dream did not evaporate. It irritated him that he did not have a logical conclusion, an explanation, a reference point for the dream.

Jeff turned on the TV to distract himself.

". . . that's your weather for the great Northwest. Get out there and enjoy your Friday," the announcer declared on this spring day in 2017.

While on his way to work, he smiled at the contrast between the cool Puget Sound air and the warmth of the morning sunshine that pushed through the broken clouds. His office was a short drive south on the Interstate, and as he approached his exit, he thought about the weekend and what plans he could make. He'd give Charlene a call and see if she wanted to go to dinner tomorrow night. Maybe he'd golf on Sunday.

Jeff Marlen had graduated from the University of Washington with a major in computer science and a minor in business, and immediately landed an entry-level job in Seattle. After nine years, he now headed his own team, had a decent salary, and worked in an actual office with a window, no longer in a cubicle in the bullpen.

He liked his job and enjoyed the analysis of the clients' needs and being able to model the software to satisfy them. Any problem could be identified and eliminated. Whether the bug was an issue with the software, training, documentation, or operator error, he and his team always found and fixed the issues. The job was gratifying.

He strode through the parking lot of SiLD^2 Software, Inc. Some called him athletic, but he merely thought of himself as fit for a guy of thirty-three. He jogged twice a week, but only when the weather was good. His chiseled physique and facial features, luxurious dark brown hair with matching eyes and long eyelashes seemed to turn many women's heads, but he was virtually clueless to their attention. He didn't ignore them; he just didn't seem to notice. He entered the office building and committed to go to the gym after work today.

"Mornin' Jeff," Craig Howe said as he pushed the elevator button.

"Hey, Craig." The doors slid open, and they stepped in. "Got plans for the weekend?"

Craig rolled his eyes. "Little League game for the twins tomorrow, honey-dos, work in the garden on Sunday. I'm hopin' for a sunny day. You?"

"Going to dinner with Charlene," Jeff said. He admired Craig's family and home.

Craig nodded his approval.

The elevator chimed as the doors opened on the floor where marketing and operations were located. Craig turned left. Jeff headed off to the right.

"Catch ya later," they said in sync, and again, together, "Jinx, you owe me a Coke." A chuckle and a wave and they were off to their offices.

After work, Jeff went to the gym, had a good workout, then stopped and bought a takeout for dinner. He called Charlene and they agreed he'd pick her up at seven tomorrow night.

Jeff and Charlene had dated for over a year, and they could always count on one another. They referred to each other as boyfriend and girlfriend. Jeff admired her. She was beautiful, smart, and self-sufficient, and he considered it complimentary to refer to her as "low maintenance."

~

That night Jeff dreamed again. Once again he fell in the silence. The all-enveloping gray was like last night with no point of reference for where to or how fast he fell.

He dreamed and knew it, but his mind was too busy to analyze. The sensation of falling continued. He relaxed and expected to float like before, but he continued to fall. Panic filtered around the edges of the gray, and he struggled for balance. He wanted control, but the gray turned darker—on its way to black.

As he twisted his virtual body . . .

. . . his cell phone rang and startled him awake. Drenched with sweat, he fumbled for the phone as he had for balance in the dream. He glanced at the clock: 8:32 a.m., Sat, May 6.

He found "accept" on the phone. "Hello?" His voice broke.

"Jeff?" Charlene said. "You okay?"

Jeff cleared his throat, struggled for normal. "Charlie? Oh, yeah, I'm okay. Just woke up. I did an intense workout at the gym yesterday."

"I didn't mean to wake you. I'm sorry."

"No worries. Uh. It's about time I got up." He stretched. "What's up?"

"Could we meet a little later tonight, say eight-ish? Gail's coming in from LA and asked if I could pick her up at the airport. I'll meet you for dinner after I drop her off and say hi to Mom. Is that okay?"

"Sure, sure. No problem." His head had cleared. Reality had returned. "Where should we go?"

"Oh. Hmm. How about that little Thai restaurant in West

4

Seattle? We liked that."

"Sure, I'll meet you there."

"Oh, Gail's beeping in. Stay in touch; otherwise, at eight, 'kay?"

"Great. Bye."

She clicked off.

Charlene Thomsen, a tall, leggy, natural blonde with a great figure, was the same age as Jeff and a local raised in Kirkland. As well as lovely, she was intelligent, efficient, and a natural leader, which made her a superb manager in her job as a senior account executive in a big advertising agency downtown.

Jeff sat on the edge of the bed, his thoughts turning toward his dream. He'd had no significant dreams since his mother had died when he was in college. For several weeks after she passed, he'd dreamed of his mother's stroke. The doctors put her in an induced coma to reduce pressure on her brain. She never regained consciousness.

But these dreams were unlike the ones about his mom's stroke where he repeatedly felt the fear of loss. The night before, Jeff knew he was dreaming and what was happening to him. *There's a name for that kind of dream. What is it?* The name came to him—Lucid. Lucid dream.

He took a drink of coffee, opened his laptop, and typed. One web page he found repeated the lesson in health class about dreams. It explained several levels of sleep: Stages one and two sleep are light sleep where the body processes slow down, then stage three is the deep sleep where restorative sleep occurs, and stage four, REM—rapid eye movement sleep—where dreaming occurs. You might cycle through all levels of sleep several times a night, and brain wave activity is different in each of the stages.

In light sleep, he read, your muscles relax. That's where that body twitch occurs as you fall asleep, the hypnagogic jerk.

Deep sleep is non-REM sleep, where your body restores itself as brain waves, heartbeat, and eye movements slow. But in REM sleep, your brain is active, your heart rate and eye movements increase, and normal dreaming occurs. In REM sleep, the mind is reenergized, and events of the previous day are sorted and filed away.

He read that full awakening during light sleep was easier than being awakened during deep sleep. If you awaken in light sleep, you usually have no recollection of any dream. Awakened during REM sleep, however, the sleeper is most likely to recall the dream for a short time after awakening, and then the memory of it fades quickly.

Jeff learned about research that had occurred since he'd graduated. It indicated another state of consciousness between REM sleep and wakefulness in which the dreamer experiences *metacognition*—they know they're dreaming while in the dream.

Each level of sleep has measurable differences in brain wave frequencies. REM sleep and wakefulness each have their own brain wave frequency, and the area between them has a completely different brain wave frequency which indicates a hybrid level of consciousness. The researchers nicknamed it the "Between State." Scientifically known as the hypnopompic state, the dreamer is neither fully awake nor fully asleep and may experience a lucid dream. Lucid dreams are not as common as normal dreams, are not experienced by everyone, and few experience them regularly. The article concluded with the suggestion that people document their dreams in a dream journal.

Jeff found a partly used spiral notebook and put it and a pen on his nightstand with the hope there'd be no more dreams and he wouldn't need it.

The rest of the day passed uneventfully. He vacuumed the apartment, ran errands, and tidied up in case they came back to his place after dinner.

Charlene had picked up Gail at the airport and taken her to their mother's before meeting Jeff at the restaurant, where the couple had a table with a wide view of Elliott Bay. The waves tossed reflections of the city lights across the water, creating colorful water sprites that danced for their entertainment. Charlene shared her sister's continued sadness over their father's death, which still lingered despite him passing over a year ago.

"How are *you* doing?" he asked, giving her a chance to talk about it if she wanted. The subject of her dad, of course, was a tender one. Jeff never talked about it unless she brought it up.

"Oh, fine. You know Gail was the baby of the family, and I think she's had a little tougher time than me. Mom's the one I worry about, though. She's still young enough and could date if she tried."

He noticed the deflection she made away from talking about herself and waited a moment before asking, "Are you okay with it if she dates?

"Oh, yes. I loved Dad a lot. But Mom needs a life. It's been over a year since . . ." Charlene looked away for a moment.

Jeff nodded in understanding, took her hand, and gave it a loving caress. After a moment, he said, "No one should be alone."

Charlene's dad, Richard "Rick" Thomsen, had been a senior member of the Federal Aviation Administration (FAA) Aircraft Accident Investigation Team. Ironically, his death occurred in a plane crash over the Mediterranean Ocean on his return journey from investigating an incident. The cause of the crash was listed as "inconclusive," and the investigation remained open, which delayed final closure for the family.

Drawing on his own experience of losing his mother—which had sharpened his compassion—Jeff had provided emotional support for Charlene right after Rick's death, and they'd forged a strong bond.

After they finished their meal, Jeff followed Charlene back to her place for more wine. They enjoyed a delightful evening together—good meal, pleasant conversation—and Jeff stayed the night.

~

They awoke to a glorious Sunday morning. Jeff gratefully noted that he hadn't dreamed. Charlene fixed a light breakfast.

"What time are you going over to your mom's?" he asked.

"We didn't set a time. I was going to call them—maybe a little before lunch."

"Let me help you clean up, then I'll take off and let you get ready."

"Thanks, Jeff."

Jeff playfully ambushed her as she turned from the sink, putting his arms around her and giving her a long, slow kiss. He leaned back, brushed her hair away from her face, leaned in, and kissed her again.

"You'd better stop, Jeff, or we'll get distracted, and I won't get over there until well after lunch," she teased.

"Can't blame a guy for trying." He stole another kiss.

On his way home, he stopped at the bookstore at the mall and browsed books on dream interpretations. Two looked good. The indexes had entries on lucid and falling dreams, and on being blind and deaf in a dream.

Few who reside in Western Washington take pleasant weather for granted, so he spent the afternoon on his deck looking through his new books and watching the neighborhood kids ride their bikes. Later, he walked down to the deli, bought a sandwich and a six-pack of beer, watched a movie on TV, cleaned things up, and then went to bed.

~

Grayness surrounded him, along with the falling sensation. *Why this again?* Panic threatened, but he kept it at bay by remembering that he'd read about how to wake himself up. *I'll be fine.*

The books said it might be difficult to separate reality from a dream during a lucid event. But logic assured him it would be easy to tell the difference. The real world wasn't gray or silent. He'd simply relax.

The moment that thought formed in his mind, he stopped falling and instantly transitioned to floating. His analytical mind needed data points, and he listed what he had as he floated in the grayness. *One: It's gray. Two: Falling. Three: Floating like in the first dream.* When he'd relaxed into the floating, he awoke. In the second dream, he felt panic but awoke when the phone rang.

Just now, though, he hadn't awakened when he'd relaxed. Why not? He tried relaxing again. Nothing. *Still here.* Still floating. What next? He took inventory. No panic, just on alert.

The book had said that lucid dreaming reduces the helpless feelings of nightmares because the dreamer knows it's a dream and may be able to control the action. The dreamer isn't as vulnerable as they would be in a regular dream.

In the first and second dreams, he'd thought he was having a nightmare and had experienced anxiety. Now he knew he could control the anxiety. That was a start.

But he should have awakened by now.

How to wake himself up? Use computer commands! *Wake up now. Uh, control S, stop. Control Q, quit.* Nothing. Still floating. *Where's the escape key?* No escape; no change. *Is there a reset button?* That was silly—his naivete amused him. He

9

chuckled, glad he had a sense of humor and could keep working the problem.

The book said that most dreams originate from experiences and knowledge of waking life, that "dreams help sort, file, and discard the waking experience, and prepare for the next day." As he floated in his gray world, he searched his mind for comparative floating experiences. Another inventory. He'd already dismissed skydiving. Maybe swimming? No. Scuba diving? No. Sensory deprivation tank? It'd been years, though, since he'd been in one. Even so, maybe these dreams were about being in a flotation tank.

He visualized stretching out his arms but didn't feel any walls. And a flotation tank wouldn't be gray inside. It would be completely dark, and he'd be floating in warm water saturated with salts. Also, he'd hear his heartbeat, the splashing of water, breathing. *No, not a flotation tank.*

His brain, trained to work as a computer, searched further into his mind's database for an answer.

What if I'm dead? The word "purgatory" appeared in his mind. He'd gone to church a few times as a kid. His family wasn't devout, and he'd never accepted the faulty logic of the existence of a Heaven and Hell. Those labels were just incidental social metaphors. He didn't care if others believed in them, but he didn't. But having grown up in a country with a church on nearly every street corner, his mind used religion to find an answer to this experience.

But he still floated.

Then, through the silence, he heard a distant sound, a faint voice. Instantly, his analysis, self-doubt, and concern stopped. Thoughts about death evaporated like mist. But the gray fog around him remained.

Jeff strained to listen, focusing on the unfamiliar voice as it grew more distinct. A female voice, professional and courteous, said, "Doctor will be with you in a few minutes. She's finishing up with another patient. Help yourself to a cup of coffee."

Even though his visual sense provided only a pervasive, gray nothingness, he imagined someone pointing when the voice said, "The coffee's over there."

The sound of footsteps, then all was quiet.

Jeff awoke. The dim green light of his clock read 1:45 a.m., Mon, May 8. Two hours since he went to bed, which validated the book's claim that it took about ninety minutes to get into REM sleep.

He listened for the sound of a TV or radio that his mind might have integrated into the dream. But only a passing car and a train horn in the distance punctured the silence of the night. He switched on the lamp, squinted at the glare, then wrote everything down before the dream faded. Once finished, he lay back down and fell asleep, dreamless, until he awoke with the alarm.

Monday morning. He felt great and looked forward to work. But during open moments of the day and into the evening, the dream demanded to be analyzed. He searched for the stimulus, the origin of these strange recurring dreams, but found none.

The next night, Jeff turned out the light at 10:30 p.m. Cognitive dissonance occupied his mind. While he didn't like the dream experiences and wanted them to stop, he wanted to know what was going on and why, and he'd only get answers if the dreams continued.

The sensation of falling returned. This time, he was ready. Gone were his earlier fears and anxiety. He felt in control. As soon as the dream began, he focused on relaxing and immediately transitioned to floating.

He floated for an immeasurable amount of time until familiar sounds of everyday activities slowly increased in volume and filled the pervasive silence. There, inside the gray envelope, he heard a TV announcer, but not one he recognized from Seattle stations.

"The traffic this morning on the 405 is again bumper-to-bumper." The announcer laughed. "And it's likely to remain so until early afternoon when the folks going home will just clog things up again going the other direction."

While the TV remained on in the background, water splashed in a sink, dishes and silverware clattered, water ran from a tap, and the sink drained. Cupboard doors clicked open and shut. Then soft footsteps on a hard floor accompanied the persistent TV, the sound of which became lower, as if in another room. The sound of someone walking on carpeting. Sliding doors opened. Hangers slid on a rod. Fabric swished. Sliding doors closed. Cloth rustled, then the sound of a zipper.

Someone's getting dressed.

Delicate footsteps in rubber-soled shoes squeaked on a hard floor. He sensed a woman moving back toward the TV. A soft click, then silence, except for footsteps. A door opened and closed. Keys jangled. A lock clicked. More footsteps down a hall, and the sounds of life in a building followed by outdoor sounds, quiet footsteps on concrete, and traffic noise.

Suddenly, total silence.

Then he awoke in the faint light of his bedroom. After taking a moment to center himself, he turned on the light and quickly wrote what he'd experienced. The clock showed 12:45 a.m.

Like last time, he listened, turning his head from side to side and tipping it at all angles to pick up any sound of a TV or a neighbor doing chores late at night. All was quiet, just the usual serene neighborhood-at-night sounds. As it should be.

Once again, the dream had ended two hours after falling asleep.

He tried to correlate what had happened in this dream with what he'd read, but nothing came to mind. He lay back down to sleep, curious if the dream would resume. It didn't. He slept dreamless.

The next morning, while Jeff shaved, the dream replayed in his head and he picked up a clue. "The 405!" he said to himself in the mirror. "That's down in LA."

He dried his face, finished dressing, and ate a breakfast sandwich on the way to work. Thoughts about his dreams once again replaced planning for the day. While at work, the dream analysis gave way to emails from East Coast clients who had already started their day. When he stopped later to get a coffee refill, he remembered a phrase from the dream interpretation book: *Dreams are subconscious messages to yourself.*

Two questions came to mind while searching for insight on the dreams' origins: *What am I trying to say to myself? And when was the last time I was in LA?*

A text message came in from Charlene: *How about lunch?*

He texted back: *Meet at Sub-Shop noon? [smiley face]*

She sent back the thumbs-up emoji.

~

At lunch, they shared a foot-long sub and a bag of chips. They liked the same sandwiches, even the sprinkled vinegar on top.

Jeff, still distracted by the dreams, asked, "What kind of dreams do you have?"

Charlene glanced over at him. "Just normal ones, I guess; although I don't seem to remember them much after I wake up. Why?"

"Do you ever have recurring dreams? Any scary ones?" He paused, looking sideways at her. "What're they like?"

"No, no recurring dreams. And no scary stuff either. Though when I was a kid, I had a nightmare or two. They didn't last. Never climbed in bed with my folks because of them, but you hear of that sometimes—in the movies, mostly. Why?"

"Oh, nothing, I guess." He didn't want to go into it further.

Charlene frowned. "Something's bugging you. What is it?"

"Okay." He hesitated, reluctant to share. "I had a couple of nights' dreams where I fell and kept falling. Everything was gray, no sight and no sound. Then I woke up. That's it—no biggie." He closed the subject with a shrug.

Charlene narrowed her eyes. "Jeff, it's fine if you want to talk about it."

"There's not much to talk about. It's nothing. Really." He glanced up at her and saw tenderness in her eyes. "Thanks, Charlie." He gave her a quick peck on the cheek, wishing he had said nothing. Then he checked his watch and, with a wave of his hand, signaled it was time to get back to the office. "Thanks for lunch. This was fun. Beats sitting at the desk with a vending machine burrito overheated in the microwave for lunch," he said in staccato.

"You're so funny." She gathered up the wrappers and empty cups and tossed them in the trash. They left the sub-shop and shared a quick hug and kiss before parting.

~

That night, as he brushed his teeth getting ready for bed, he wondered if he'd soon be falling again. Having no explanations for the dreams bothered him. He wanted to know what would happen next. Although he had a TV in the bedroom, he rarely turned it on, but tonight he chose a familiar comedian to distract his mind. He set the timer for the TV to shut off automatically.

He fell asleep and dreamed again. First the falling sensation, then floating while enveloped in the grayness.

A woman's voice with a South Asian accent said, "Do you think of this other person as being internal?"

A young woman with a SoCal accent replied, sounding shy and hesitant, "What do you mean *internal*, Doctor?"

Neither voice was the one from the other night.

"Mindi, you said her name was Shirley," said the voice of the doctor. "Was her voice in your head?"

Did Jeff know anyone named Shirley or Mindy? He searched his memory, but no one came to mind. The young woman, Mindy, who was apparently the doctor's patient, replied, "No, she doesn't talk. She's just there, but she's really strong when I feel her there. One time I lost a big part of a day. My friend Amy told me things I said, and, well, I said stuff that didn't sound like me." She paused. "The next morning when I woke up, I didn't remember anything from the night before." Mindi took a deep breath. " Doctor, who is Shirley? I-I'd like to know. It's scary."

"This only happened once?"

"Yes,"

"Had you been drinking or using drugs?"

"No. I haven't had wine or a drink for a long time. That's just it—it feels like Shirley doesn't want me to drink anything, even before she left the note. She scared me with the note. I kinda lost a whole day. I don't take drugs. I don't take chances."

"A note?" the doctor said reflectively, urging Mindi to elaborate, but she said nothing. "I understand," the doctor continued. "It must disorient you. Have you had conversations with her? Tell me again how you know her name."

"Like I tried to say, she doesn't talk, but she's in here." Jeff heard a sound that sounded like someone had tapped his temple. "I can feel her trying to control me," Mindi said. "It feels like she wants to shove me out of the way. So yeah, it's like she's in my mind, but no talking. Then I found the note, addressed to me, my name at the top and signed 'Shirley' at the bottom. It looked like my handwriting, but I don't remember writing it. She told me to be careful, that I'd get hurt if I wasn't careful."

"Hmm. Do you feel threatened?"

"Doesn't that sound like a threat? It sounded like a threat to me," the young woman said.

"Well, worded like that, it could just be a warning. It might not be a threat, just cautioning you to be careful. And you're showing care by being open with me. Are there other notes?"

"No, just the one."

"Do you still have the note?"

"No. I threw it away. It scared me."

"How long ago? Could you get it back?"

"I tore it up. Threw it away. No, Doctor, it's gone. I'm s-sorry."

Jeff heard writing on paper, then the doctor said, "Here's a prescription that should ease your anxiety. It's a very mild sedative. Follow the instructions on the label; take them twice a day. I'd like you to keep a record of strange feelings or thoughts. Bring it with you next week. If you find any more notes, keep them. Keep track of any voices, or if you feel you're being watched, write that down. If you need to talk, call my exchange. They'll reach me right away."

"Okay, Doctor, thank you—"

The conversation cut off, but Jeff continued to float in the silent gray, and then . . . awake. He opened his eyes and focused on the TV. The same comedian was doing the same comedy set as before he fell asleep. The clock said it'd been just twenty minutes since he'd switched on the tube. The timer hadn't yet turned it off. He must have fallen asleep immediately.

In his notebook, Jeff wrote every detail of the conversation between the doctor and the patient. He reread his notes, looked again at the clock, then added another line to the night's entry: *Why no 90-minute interval before dream started?*

Jeff's mind operated on logic. A natural observer, like a scientist, he wanted to know what makes things tick. Especially these dreams.

Could it have been dialogue from a neighbor's TV? He muted his television and listened for sounds from another apartment or outside. Nothing. Everything was quiet, which was not out of the ordinary. His neighbors rarely made sounds loud enough for him to hear. The TV schedule had no doctor or drama shows listed for that night, so he dismissed that theory.

REM sleep usually takes over an hour to start, but not this dream. Why? He expected cause and effect to operate for everything, and he didn't like the curse of not knowing. Dreams had their roots in the mind, both the conscious and the subconscious, so the answers had to be in his head somewhere. Jeff lay in the darkened room, wanting no more dreams. He fell asleep, remained dreamless, and awoke refreshed in the morning.

~

Mindi turned on the TV while making herself a quick breakfast of a fried egg, toast, and a bit of applesauce. *That should get me through the rest of the morning.* She'd get a meal after the lunch rush was over at Denny's. The free meal perk at work really helped her budget.

The TV announcer said the traffic on the 405 was clogged up as usual, then made a stupid joke about how the 405 was always that way. She didn't have to drive on the 405, though—the bus would drop her off near the restaurant in Gardena.

She cleaned up the kitchen, finished getting dressed, turned off the TV, locked the apartment, and headed for the bus. The twenty-minute ride gave her a chance to read her Danielle Steele novel, but before opening her book, she looked around the bus and let her mind wander. Wool-gathering, her grandmother had called it. Her vision blurred for a moment, then it felt as if someone was watching her. She looked behind her, but everyone had their heads down or looked out the window.

Someone had left part of a newspaper wedged between the seat and the bus wall. To distract herself from the feeling of being watched, she pulled it free and opened it. May 8, 2015, LA Times Sports. "Angels play Mariners at Seattle, Series Tied," the article headline read. She wasn't into sports but might be able to use something from it to talk with a customer. It might earn a better tip, and good tips got her through the month, so she read the article.

She lived frugally, trying to live on her tips and salary from the restaurant—with two exceptions: Mindi's father had died last year, and she'd been sole beneficiary of his life insurance. Feeling secure with that financial cushion in the bank, she decided she could afford to live in an apartment by herself rather than have to have a roommate, and she could pay for counseling to help her with her "problem." Paying for the therapy she'd needed for years was an investment.

An attractive man climbed onto the bus, but she didn't let her gaze linger. Though she'd dated a little, she'd never had a successful relationship with a man, rarely anything more than a first date. They seemed to want more from her than she was willing to give. The one guy she'd met that she thought might be Mr. Right had said he'd be patient, but he wasn't. They both sabotaged the relationship, but it'd been her problem that led to a fight which ended with him yelling, "You know, you're plain crazy! You need help."

He'd slammed the door as he left, and he never came back. She was glad he'd gone, but also angry and hurt. She'd called in sick the next day, which made her feel guilty, and then she'd worked a double shift the next day to make sure her paycheck wasn't short. More important, she'd needed the distraction of work.

The note from Shirley, and a gap in her memory one day, prompted her to ask a friend and coworker, Jeri, if she knew a doctor who might be able to help her. Jeri gave her the doctor's business card. Mindi was relieved when she saw this doctor was a woman and eagerly called her office for an appointment.

The feeling of being watched passed. She made some notes like the doctor had suggested, then read her book. A few minutes later, she stepped down from the bus and enjoyed the sun on her face on the short walk to her job.

Mindi picked up an apron in the locker area and tied it on.

Another server passed the doorway and offered a quick, "Hi, Minn, how's it goin'?"

Mindi smiled. "Good, Joanie. You?"

She picked up her order pad and pen from her locker, pushed the door closed with her hip, and stepped over to look at the bulletin board to see what section she had for the day. *East side. Good.* The sun was hottest through the windows on the west side during the after-lunch shift, and the glare played havoc with seeing customer's faces. That minor hazard of the trade, plus the persistent flirting of the young guys and old farts from the offices across the street, went with the job.

CHAPTER 2

On Sunday night, Jeff drove home from Joint Base Lewis-McChord near Tacoma after a weekend fulfilling his monthly obligation in the National Guard Reserve. His body told him he'd earned his Drill Pay. After showering, he grabbed a quick bite from his collection of entrées in the freezer, then glanced at the sports page from the Sunday paper until the microwave signaled his dinner was ready. After dinner, he read the rest of the paper, watched a little television, and retired for the night.

He hadn't dreamed all weekend, but tonight he fell again. Yes, he had been mildly interested in another episode, hoping to find an answer to the why of it, so he felt resigned to the experience. Given a choice, though, he would have opted out.

Jeff tested his theory by thinking about floating. Sure enough, he stopped and floated. To end the dream, he relaxed and thought about not floating anymore, but he kept floating. A bright flash of light pierced the grayness for a split second, after which his visual field returned to the familiar gray. Then the light flashed on and off again several times.

Sounds accompanied the flashes: city traffic, a diesel motor accelerating or braking, mingled conversations, more traffic. He floated there listening, hoping the flashing would quit because when it appeared he saw nothing but brightness. He recognized the familiar chime of someone on a city bus pulling the cord to signal the driver to stop. Another flash of light, this time accompanied by a brief view over the heads of people riding the bus. Then all gray again.

It was a loose circuit, a bad connection. Whatever it was, he found it irritating.

Let me see, damnit!

His vision cleared suddenly and he was looking at a newspaper being held by delicate, feminine hands with a small gold ring on her right hand, clear nail polish on well-trimmed nails, and a women's watch on her left wrist.

He read. The LA Times Sports. May 6, 2015, SPORTS, "Angels play the Mariners at Seattle, Series Tied—"

Before he could finish reading, the grayness closed around him again. *Damn.* He willed to see again, but instead . . . he woke up.

He lay in bed with streetlight creeping in around the blinds and focused on the dream images, then switched on the light and wrote about the brief experience. He hadn't paid attention to what time he'd lain down and reminded himself to note it next time. Why was his mind constructing these scenarios of other people in other places, a two-year-old newspaper and baseball teams?

He'd never followed the Los Angeles Angels. He was a Mariners fan, sure—he lived in Seattle. Nearly everyone has a tribal loyalty to the local team.

"May 2015," he said out loud. Did the Mariners play the Angels in May 2015? He'd check out the stats to see if those were real games or if his mind had made it up. After shaking his head to clear it, he turned out the light. As he lay there, he realized the eyes reading the paper hadn't been his eyes but the eyes of a woman riding on a bus. And he'd moved on from one part of the dream by thinking of the next change: falling to floating to hearing to seeing. He'd test that again, if he could.

~

After working part of the morning, Jeff took a break and met up with Craig in the lunchroom. His friend, eyes shining with excitement, approached him and waved something in Jeff's face.

"Hey," Craig said, "got any plans for Friday? The wife and I were gonna go to the M's game together—we're playing the Angels. But she decided she wants to go see a movie with her girlfriends instead. Sooooo, I've got an extra ticket." He kept waving the tickets as a temptation.

Mariners and the Angels? Jeff thought about the dream last night and gave Craig a puzzled look.

Craig frowned. "What's with that look? Do I have to speak more slowly so you can understand? F-reee ti-ickeet." He drew out the words. "I'll drive, cover the parking. Do you want to go or not?"

Jeff grabbed Craig's wrist to steady his view of the tickets. "Who are they playing? Angels?"

Craig nodded.

"Sure . . . Yeah. I'm in! Thanks, Craig. I'll buy the beer."

"Great." Craig shoved the tickets into his pocket and slapped Jeff on the back. "We'll work out the details Friday."

He left the kitchen, giving a quick wave as he turned into the hallway.

Jeff watched him leave, wondering about the coincidence of his dream last night with the LA newspaper, the Angels and Mariners, and a game this Friday. He returned to his desk, and after a few keystrokes on the keyboard, he discovered the Mariners had won the first game on May 4, 2015. Anaheim took the other two games of the series on May 5 and 6. Jeff stared at the computer screen. He hadn't made it up. It had happened. Then it hit him. He'd been reading the sports page last night and built those teams, stats and dates into his dream. *Craig having tickets to Friday's game, just a coincidence. Right?* His phone rang, bringing him back to the present. He was back to work. Thinking about the dream would have to wait.

On the way home, he called Charlene and told her he was going to pick up a pizza and he could upgrade it to a large if she wanted to share it with him at his place. They didn't have to discuss toppings; they both liked double pepperoni, double cheese on a thin crust.

She hesitated for a long moment, so he asked how the visits went with her mom and Gail.

"Mom really misses Dad," she replied. "Even after a year. We had a good cry."

"I understand, I do, and I'm so sorry for your family. Why don't you come over? We can watch a movie."

"Yeah, I'd like some company. But I've got an early day tomorrow, so I can't stay."

"No problem. Come over when you're ready. I'll keep it warm till you get there. Oh, I've got salad stuff, but if you want ranch dressing, I'm out, so bring your own."

"Will do. See you about six."

After dinner they watched an old movie, a love story, *Somewhere in Time*, starring the late Christopher Reeve. When the movie was over, Charlene announced, with reluctance, that she needed to go home.

"See you this weekend?" she asked as she put her cellphone in her purse.

"I'm off to the game Friday night with Craig."

She smiled. "Well, have a good time, and say hi to Craig for me. Saturday maybe?"

He nodded. "Sure."

She kissed him goodnight and gave him a warm hug. He stood at the door and watched her walk to her car. Dad had always done that to make sure Mom was safe, and Jeff had made it his habit too. As she pulled away from the curb, he closed and latched the door.

Now . . . what about the Mariners-Angels game? He dug yesterday's newspaper out of the recycle bin and found no mention of the 2015 series in the article. The paper went back into the bin, having provided no answer to the puzzle.

He fell asleep wondering about the dreams and coincidences.

~

Relax and float, Jeff told his dream-self. The falling stopped, and he floated, held in suspension in the gray, silent space. He tried to will both sight and sound to appear, but nothing. He remained floating. His recent conversation with Charlene about her dad's death came to mind.

What if I die here, in my sleep?

Thoughts about death ricocheted in his mind. How would Charlene feel if he died so soon after she had lost her dad? The thought that her dad would never walk her down the aisle made him feel sad. Marriage? He and Charlene had never talked about marriage. Is that what his mind was trying to tell him? Something about them getting married? The sadness he felt for Charlene and her family enveloped him, and the gray darkened. He then thought of his mom and dad. They'd been planning on taking a cruise to the Caribbean just before Mom died. The space grew even darker around him. Logic battled with emotion. He needed to relax.

He imagined taking a deep breath and exhaling long and slow, forcing himself to relax. The darkening vision turned a shade lighter. He took another virtual breath, and the gray got even lighter. Then, like someone had turned up the volume on a radio, his dream-ears picked up ordinary sounds. He strained to make them out: water running in a sink. But not like last time. No dishes being washed. This was different, but familiar. He focused.

It sounded like he was in a bathroom. The gray remained total, though the sounds were well defined. Was someone brushing their teeth? The running water stopped. Someone spat, something—probably a toothbrush—knocked against a sink, a cabinet opened with a complaining squeak. The toothbrush settled into a glass with a clink.

If he concentrated, could he control . . . ?

Let me see!

A flash of brightness as a bathroom appeared around him. Someone was about to stick something in his eye. He jerked his head back, and the young woman's face in the mirror jerked her head back at the same time. The woman in the reflection held a mascara brush in a delicate hand. He recognized the ring, the nails, the same hand that had held the newspaper on the bus. She withdrew the brush, and he saw her near perfect face with partially applied eye makeup reflected in the bathroom mirror. For a short moment, the image didn't move. He just looked at her.

She appeared to be in her midtwenties. Thick, dark brown hair fell in waves down to her shoulders, and those wide, dark brown eyes . . . They transfixed him.

She's beautiful!

The woman blinked and tilted her head sideways as if she'd heard something. She spun around to look behind her, giving Jeff a quick panorama of the empty bathroom. The movement didn't help him maintain his mental equilibrium. He already felt off-balance.

The woman closed her eyes, Jeff's vision blinked, and when she shook her head, he sensed the shake. She faced the mirror again and stared blankly at herself, giving him another look at the lovely face.

The brush moved to a mere centimeter from her vulnerable eyeball, then she applied the makeup to enhance her lashes.

Jeff willed himself to remain still.

She paused and stared at her reflection for a few seconds, then said firmly,

"Mindi, you've got to get a grip."

He'd heard her name and her voice in his dream the other night.

She blinked twice, shook her head, and with that shake, the gray again enveloped Jeff. He floated once more in the timeless gray suspension until he awoke in his bed.

The sheet and blanket remained as he'd positioned them earlier, and the clock indicated another non-stock lucid dream. Only ten minutes had elapsed since he'd turned out the light to go to sleep. *Ten minutes?*

He turned the light on and wrote feverishly. The dream persisted even as he flipped through his previous entries, counting out loud to himself, "One, two, three, four, five, six . . . tonight makes seven dreams!"

The sound of his voice startled him. "Seven times . . ." He counted the dates of each dream, still talking out loud: "All in just over two weeks. What's going on?"

He wanted to tell someone, but he couldn't tell Charlene,

or his dad, or Craig. "No, not yet. No. Never. They're just dreams . . . Should I see a shrink?" He tossed the notebook down on the bed and stared at it, realizing that he'd just talked to himself like a crazy person. "They'll lock me up."

The room was quiet, his mind busy. He needed logic and facts. It could have just been a coincidence with the baseball games. But that woman in the dream, the same one each time. Riding a bus? Talking to a doctor? Putting on makeup? Are those coincidences too? What should he do?

His dad had once advised him, "Son, if you don't know what to do, unless a train is going to run you over, of course, jump, but otherwise, do nothing. Answers will come in time if you ask the right questions."

But what questions to ask?

He took a deep breath, exhaled slowly and decided not to make a decision. That satisfied him for the moment. He switched off the light, adjusted his pillow, and turned over. *Let's just get to sleep and have no more dreams.*

But sleep didn't come as fast as he wanted. His mind again cataloged what he'd seen and heard in the dreams. Eventually, however, a deep, restful, dreamless sleep enveloped him.

~

The feeling of being watched came over Mindi again while she was putting on her makeup to get ready for work. Her head jerked back as if someone had pulled it, and she went blank for a moment, until a strong sense of not being alone compelled her to look around. Of course, no one shared the bathroom with her.

"Mindi, you've got to get a grip," she muttered to herself. And then the feeling passed.

Could it have been a Shirley episode? Mindi hadn't sensed Shirley's presence since she'd been taking the pills the doctor had given her. She wanted Shirley gone and not a problem anymore. But it hadn't been Shirley watching her on the bus—of that, she was sure—and this was like then, different from Shirley. Scary to think that Shirley might leave her alone only to have someone or something else arrive.

Her next visit to Dr. Singh was Monday. Talking to the doctor always made her feel better. She reminded herself to jot this down in her notes. After all, Dr. Singh had told her to keep track.

The number two bus was full, so she had to squeeze in and stand. With only a twenty-minute ride, she could endure the guy standing behind her pressed up against her back. She wanted to escape into her book. But with her shoulder bag slipping and having to hold on to the sticky grab bar, reading would have to wait.

CHAPTER 3

Jeff wondered if, and when, he'd have enough data points to solve the mystery. Meanwhile, he turned to the books to provide him with information on research and the observations of others. Apparently falling dreams were common and linked to anxiety. The dreamer, many sources said, wanted more control in their life and couldn't get it. According to them, people who had falling dreams felt out of control.

But Jeff didn't feel out of control—except for the damned dreams.

The book he'd been using as his main reference said: *Slipping and falling means a decision is pending, and if made wrong, could cause emotional distress.*

But that interpretation didn't fit him. So why was he falling? What decision did he have to make? He had a good job—no reason to change. Charlene and he were tight, and he had a good car and good health. He had thought about marriage in the dream, though. Was that the decision he had to make? Maybe. Except for that, he struck out with the dream book's interpretations of falling dreams.

According to that book, dreams involving floating were

also common, but their meanings were usually the opposite of falling dreams. Floating dreams, in almost all cases, represented a positive aspect to the dreamer's life. He read:

Floating represents new beginnings: a job, a friendship or relationship, a renewed life purpose.

But he wasn't looking for a new job or a new relationship, and considering marriage was just deepening his present relationship, so that angle didn't bring him any closer to an answer.

One of the books said that floating in dreams meant calmness and peace, that your emotions and life were in harmony. That information fit, and Jeff felt good about that. He was at peace— except for the dreams. He also read that to float in space meant success during confusing times, and that it was a symbol of freedom, independence, happiness, calmness and peace in the waking life. He liked those interpretations.

The dream researchers said REM sleep started an hour and a half or more after the sleep cycles began, but he'd had some dreams that didn't fit that pattern. Why this departure from the norm? He closed the book, his questions still unanswered.

Although not scientific, his intuition—his gut—told him that these dreams were *not* bad omens.

~

Jeff's workday passed smoothly, and nobody cut him off on the freeway on the way home—a good day. He ate leftover, deli-bought meatloaf with lots of ketchup on the top for dinner— still not as good as Mom's. The comfort food brought on a bout of nostalgia for the carefree time of his childhood.

He fell asleep and began to fall, but then, remembering that he could control the action, he relaxed and changed the fall to float. In that way, it *was* like the sensory deprivation tank. The total gray was no longer threatening. Disorienting, yes, and not at all comforting, but not threatening.

So what's next?

A voice, a little muffled at first, grew louder and clearer. Still no view, only audio.

"Dr. Singh will see you now, Miss Ketchem."

Jeff recognized the voice from an earlier dream—the doctor's receptionist.

In his mind, he repeated the last name, Ketcham. *Is that the pretty brunette with the wide brown eyes? Mindy Ketcham?* Wait. Wasn't that thinking like a stalker? No, he was just curious, he reasoned. Not a predator.

While Jeff analyzed his feelings, the gray dissipated and revealed a clear view—and matching sounds—from his host's point of view. They approached a door with a brass nameplate that said, Dr. Ananya Singh. The view panned down to the doorknob. A female hand grasped it and opened the door, and his host walked through, closing the door behind her. She turned toward the quiet of the room, and Jeff saw her reflection in a mirror on the opposite wall. Yes. It was the same woman.

The serene furnishings, drapes, and carpeting of the psychiatrist's office muted the sounds, and soft lighting completed the therapeutic setting. Jeff watched the scene as if through a Steadicam.

His view included Dr. Singh, a slender, attractive South Asian woman with dark hair cascading over her shoulders. She wore a stylish navy blue pantsuit, cream-colored silk blouse sporting a wide collar, and dark blue high heels. Her jewelry was conservative, a thin gold chain necklace and a single gold ring on each hand. She smiled warmly. "Good afternoon, Mindi. How nice to see you today."

Jeff felt his enthusiasm rise. Now he had a chance to get

more of the information he needed.

Mindi shook her head, as if annoyed by a mosquito. She sat opposite the doctor, looked down for a moment, then took a deep breath and raised her head. "Where would you like to begin, Doctor?"

"Well, Mindi, first, are you taking the prescription?"

"I am, yes."

"How is it working for you?"

She touched the side of her head. "Oh, yes. It must be. I haven't felt her here."

"Not at all?"

"That's right." She paused. "Not since I started taking them."

"When did you begin feeling better?"

"Oh, after a couple of days, I guess. I just noticed she's gone. I haven't thought about her much lately. Really, not until you asked me just now."

"Good, so you've found no more notes, no blank spots or missing days?"

"No. I wish I'd known sooner that a prescription would've helped so much." She lowered her head again. Jeff saw her hands back in her lap, nervously clasping and unclasping. She fidgeted with the little gold ring.

"Is there anything else, Mindi?" the doctor asked. "Are you nervous?"

Mindi reached into her purse and pulled out a folded piece of paper. She unfolded it and looked at the doctor, who waited patiently.

"I guess it seems a little paranoid since Shirley's not really there, but I sense someone is watching me sometimes. Even now it kinda feels that way. Could it be the meds you gave me? Do they do that? Make you paranoid?"

The doctor wrote something in her notebook and looked

up. "Tell me a little more about your feelings that someone is watching."

"It's not like when she was trying to bully me and push me out of the way." Mindi looked from her hands into the doctor's kind eyes and back down again. "It's more like there's someone behind me, even when I know I'm alone in my apartment. I asked a friend if I could borrow the detector she uses when she travels to look for hidden cameras, like in motel rooms. I didn't find anything." She gave a little shrug.

Dr. Singh made more notes, then looked up. "Is it all the time or sometimes? Does there seem to be a pattern?"

"Not regularly, just sometimes. And when I focus on it, it seems to go away. It happened a few other times—when I was washing dishes, putting on my makeup, getting dressed. Once, on the bus. There are always guys staring at me on the bus, I'm used to that. I ignore it. I try to ignore this, too, but it's different."

"Is it becoming more frequent?"

Mindi looked through the curtains at the trees outside and paused while she thought. "No. Well, yes. Oh, I don't know. It's not all the time." She looked back at the doctor.

"Mindi, let's not worry about it right now. Those may be leftover feelings, and they're likely to fade. Keep track, like you are now. Record the time of day and what you're doing. It's good that you're keeping notes. Even if you're not sure, make a note. Let's see if there's a pattern and if it's increasing, stays the same, or quits, so we can talk about it. Call my office if you feel a need to. Okay?"

Mindi nodded.

The doctor leaned forward slightly. "It's quite common for someone who has experienced the type of things that you experienced to have what we call 'dissociative experiences.' Part of one's personality is thrust forward, like it seems to have been in your case, to be protective of the self."

"But, Doctor, Shirley isn't my friend. She doesn't like me. She's a bully. She wanted to push me away."

The doctor paused a moment, letting Mindi's resistance subside. "Mindi, after your experiences with your father, people who feel powerless may need to assert their authority over themself by trying to escape from the threats. They create an advocate, a protector, a bodyguard of sorts to prevent assault from occurring again. From what you've told me so far, it seems that's what Shirley is to you. Her methods seem misplaced and unwelcome, I understand that, but I believe she is that part of you who has to make sure you are never betrayed again."

Mindi looked back down at her lap and kneaded her hands together, considering what the doctor had said. Eventually, she nodded and looked back at the doctor. "So you mean Shirley is part of me, but tried to control me?"

"In a manner of speaking, yes, Mindi. Except not to control, but to protect. That is understandable. Even though your father died, what happened to you, and especially after your mother passed, may still be affecting you. It's not uncommon to feel at fault and especially to feel guilt and shame. You shouldn't blame yourself. The strength of purpose that Shirley displays is part of you. But if that strength gets out of control, the part of you that is Shirley could overpower your admirable qualities."

Mindi, and Jeff, listened carefully to the doctor's words.

"I sense you are a strong person. You are allowed to set boundaries, but in a healthy manner. You can learn to live without guilt. You have the right to be free of fear. Your life can be one where you experience healthy relationships."

Mindi wiped at the tears filling her eyes. She nodded and tried to smile at the doctor.

Dr. Singh continued, "It took a lot of courage for you to

share your experiences so early in our sessions. For many of my patients, it takes months, even years to share their fears. You came in here ready to accept your past, which shows that you have enormous strength to face what happened to you and to move forward."

"Thank you, Doctor," Mindi said quietly.

"I recommend you stay on your medication, but we may reduce the dosage in time. We've used them to assure that your renewed confidence will keep your other self in control. Please follow the instructions on the label."

Mindi nodded again.

"Mindi," the doctor said, then paused, waiting until she had eye contact. "Your Shirley-self uses overt power to get her way. That strength might be a valuable skill to use if you ever need it. But you do not want to become her in order to survive." She paused again, allowing Mindi space to absorb what she'd just said. "You have many other positive personality traits you can use to thrive and be happy."

"You mean I could become a bully, be mean to others, like she tried to be to me?"

The doctor looked at Mindi with a steady gaze, only validating Mindi's conclusion with a slight upturn at the corners of her mouth and an almost imperceptible nod of her head.

"Talk to Jennifer on the way out. Ask her to set up weekly appointments for the next month. You're making good progress. Keep your journal."

Mindi stood, murmured a grateful thank-you to the doctor, then picked up her purse and left the office.

Jeff's view stopped as the door closed behind her. He floated in the grayness, then awoke in his bed.

Had the private conversation between Mindy and her doctor originated in his subconscious? If so, what was his subconscious trying to tell him?

The dream books were right; lucid dreams can be like real life. And that psychiatrist's session seemed real, very real, to him.

Jeff put every detail of this dream, and his feelings about it, into his journal. He finished his entry with the similarities and differences between him and the woman from his dream:

> *I'm keeping a journal; Mindy's keeping a journal. I'm a guy; she's girl. She's in therapy, has an imaginary enemy, named Shirley. I'm having dreams with an imaginary woman, and maybe I need therapy. She's in Los Angeles somewhere in 2015 trying to be happy, and I'm in Seattle, 2017, and very happy.*

He closed the notebook and put his head on the pillow, wondering when he'd need to see a shrink. If he did see one, the doctor would have a field day with all of this. He closed his eyes and told himself that he needed to sleep for the rest of the night with no more interruptions. And he did.

~

At work the next day, Jeff took a few minutes before the boss's staff meeting to google "Dr. Ananya Singh, Los Angeles" and "Mindy Ketcham." It only took a few seconds to get a result on the psychiatrist. The instant he saw on the screen the words "Dr. Ananya Singh, PhD, MD, Psychiatrist, 10438 West 182nd St., Gardena, California 90248," and the accompanying photograph of her, he felt the blood drain from his face. His pupils dilated with surprise and he winced at the extra light on his retinas.

"Holy crap." He hadn't expected that. Jeff said under his

breath, "She's real!"

Feeling shaken, he closed his browser and walked directly but uneasily to the restroom and splashed water on his face. He leaned on the counter and looked into his own brown eyes, groping for a logical explanation. None came.

Craig walked in, stepped over to the urinal, and glanced over his shoulder at Jeff. "You all ready for the meeting?" He paused a second, waiting for an answer, then finished up and turned back around, his focus on Jeff's reflection in the mirror. "Hey, you all right?"

Jeff lied. "Yeah. Yeah, just had a lousy night's sleep." He took a breath. "I'll be there in a minute."

During the meeting, Jeff was so distracted by his discovery that he had trouble focusing. His discomfort was unnoticed by all, except Craig, who made eye contact and mouthed, "You okay?"

Jeff nodded and gave a dismissive wave. Craig turned back to the presenter, but Jeff couldn't get out of his mind the thought that the doctor was real. Where did he get her name and face to put in his dream? And he still needed to google Mindy Ketcham.

Someone asked him a question. Being the consummate professional, he deftly answered and engaged in the discussion. Dreams, brunettes, and doctors' faces forgotten—for now.

After the meeting, back in his office, he googled "Mindy Ketcham" and found nothing. He felt disappointed yet elated at the same time. It would be so much easier if he'd just manufactured her from his subconscious. Unable to go further in his investigation, he turned his attention to his work, where he knew what he did would create predictable outcomes.

Jeff read the dream book he'd bought: There are downsides to lucid dreaming. One is dream-reality confusion, which is the difficulty, or inability, to tell whether an event or experience occurred during waking or dreaming.

Jeff had no problem telling the difference between his dreams and waking. His problem was that the doctor was a real person he'd never met or known existed, and yet she'd appeared his dreams.

Mindy seemed just as real. But not being able to find her on the internet made him doubt her reality.

His dream book suggested that dreaming about people that you don't know could be a signal that the dreamer is lonely and ready for romance but hasn't met the right person yet. But that didn't apply to him; he wasn't lonely. Charlene and he were close and getting closer. Although he found the dreams interesting, he wanted them to stop. With no answer to their reason, he saw no point to them.

He retired for the night feeling conflicted, and the familiar dream pattern returned. He found himself on a bus again, seeing through Mindi's eyes. As she read her book, he saw her hands with those well-trimmed nails, the thin gold ring, and her watch. He also noticed that she wore black slacks and a black shirt, like some kind of uniform, and he heard the bus and traffic sounds along with the voices of those on the bus.

She looked up from her book and turned around, scanning the empty seats behind her. Only one row separated her from the back of the bus. He somehow knew she didn't want anyone behind her, and he sensed she felt he was there. That made him feel uncomfortable.

She looked down and straightened the name tag pinned on the left pocket of her uniform. Though upside-down in his view, he read "Mindi" next to the Denny's restaurant logo. She rubbed her temples.

He hadn't expected her name would be spelled that way.

In one swift motion, she placed her bookmark, closed the book, and put it into the carry-bag that sat on the seat next to her.

Jeff sensed that she'd placed the bag there to discourage anyone from sitting next to her.

She looked out the window. The street sign read 183rd.

He heard her urgent thought: *Gotta get off. I'll be late!*

She stood, pulled the bell cord, and grabbed her things, then moved toward the door.

It was morning. The sun rose over the hills on the left side of the bus as it traveled south. Jeff watched through her eyes as she stepped off the bus, double-timed it up to the corner, looked left and right, and scooted across the four-lane arterial to the other side of the street. Looking left and right again, she crossed the side street and headed to Denny's, just half a block down on the left. She looked at her wristwatch: 5:45 a.m. She pushed through the front door, made eye contact and gave a nod to the server at the cash register, then hustled into the kitchen with Jeff still aboard.

Then Jeff awoke. He stared at his bedroom ceiling for a moment, feeling disoriented. The dream had just ended—no falling or floating. He switched on the light, rubbed his eyes, and, cursing the inconsistency of the dream endings, reached for his notebook to write everything he'd seen during that short bus ride with Mindi. The clock said he'd been asleep for over seven hours, so he canceled the alarm before it would go off at six, then got up and walked into the kitchen.

He made himself a cup of coffee, drumming his fingers impatiently on the counter while the Keurig filled his cup, then carried his cup to the table and opened up his laptop.

With the cursor anchored in the search window, he remembered the street sign: 183rd. She'd gotten off a couple of blocks later and walked another block. He typed "Denny's 186th." The browser gave him a single listing: Denny's restaurant—18620 South Western Avenue, Gardena, CA. He highlighted and copied the address, clicked on the Google Earth icon, and then waited a few seconds while it booted up and the view of the Western Hemisphere appeared. He pasted the address in the search window and clicked the mouse button. The view of North America zoomed in on Southern California and descended to just above the street and Denny's. He set the little-person icon onto the blue line in the middle of the street on the map. The camera panned down to street view.

Jeff's eyes widened as the restaurant materialized. He ran his fingers through his hair. "Shit just got real," he announced, staring at the same Denny's that, in his dream, he'd just entered with Mindi. Eyes still on the screen, he reached for his coffee cup and lifted it to his mouth. His tongue met the steaming hot black liquid. "Ow! Dammit."

The last line in his journal entry for this dream read: *Real people appear in dreams, right? That should be no big deal? But strangers who are real people? And places where I've never been?*

He set the notebook aside, feeling uneasy at the progressing mystery.

~

She left the doctor's office enveloped with a sense of comfort. She felt especially good after this visit with Dr. Singh. The episodes of feeling watched had been gone for a couple of weeks. Well, except those boys who always ogled her on the bus. She accepted that it went with living in LA.

Mindi, though flattered to have men think she was pretty, felt uncomfortable when they paid overt attention to her. She remembered her mother as being pretty. Her mom had told her, and told her often, "Mindi, you are a beautiful young lady."

Since she knew being attractive could be a threat to her safety, she kept a three-function rape alarm handy—the kind with pepper spray, staining dye, and a piercing alarm. Carrying it gave her confidence. She'd read a book about healing from sexual abuse, bought another about depression, and had considered enrolling in a self-defense class. No one would *ever* threaten her again.

CHAPTER 4

Jeff checked his journal. No falling dreams for three weeks as an unwilling stalker. Maybe the dreams had ended. But even with that consideration, he was still mystified by the unanswered questions of the why and how of unknown people and places in these unique dreams. Even weeks later, he remembered them as if they'd been real-life experiences.

He planned to go to Charlene's and grill up some hamburgers, be with a few friends, drink some beer, but after he'd showered and shaved, he had extra time before he needed to be there. He'd stop at that metaphysical bookstore near the specialty beer shop where he hoped to pick up a half-rack of a new craft IPA that Craig had talked about.

The combination of patchouli incense and the smell of old books set a gentle tone in the bookstore. He stood near the counter and looked around but saw no one in the store. A woman dressed as if she might have just come from a Woodstock reenactment quietly entered from the back through a beaded doorway. Jeff saw her when he took a step toward the bookshelves. Rather than surprising him, her presence reassured him.

She wore Birkenstock sandals, a long, full, colorful cotton

skirt and contrasting pastel blue blouse, beads, and a crystal on a chain around her neck. Gray streaked her long black hair, betraying her age.

Their eyes met. "May I help you?" she said in a soft voice.

Jeff felt at peace here—the result, surely, of the incense, the setting, and her quiet demeanor. He asked if she had any books about dreams.

She smiled and took a few steps toward him, moving her gaze from his left shoulder in an arc over his head to his right shoulder, then back to his eyes.

Jeff didn't know it, but her warm smile indicated she approved of his golden aura.

"I'm sure we have something here that might interest you," she said. "May I know more about why you are asking?"

Jeff realized his experience here would be nothing like being in the big-box chain bookstore. After a slow, deep breath, as if to savor the atmosphere, he took a small step toward the woman. With no shyness, he explained that he'd been having strange dreams and he wanted to understand them.

The woman nodded in understanding and moved toward a bookshelf. "My name is Ingrid."

"I'm Jeff."

She ran her hand over the spines of the old books as if caressing a cat, then pulled a book from the shelf and balanced it on her palm, then placed a second one on top and opened to the first few pages. Jeff watched in wonder, so graceful were her movements. He hadn't experienced this level of peace since being a child.

Ingrid looked up, signaled with her eyes and a slight movement of her head for him to watch over her shoulder. At first, she'd appeared larger-than-life to him, but now he realized he stood a full head taller than she and could easily see her finger trace a path down the table of contents, the brown print on pages yellowed with age. Pausing on a chapter listing, she looked back at him over her shoulder, then turned and handed him the book.

He understood her intent that he go to the page she indicated, one on lucid dreams. Jeff's eyes met hers with a question. He hadn't told her the type of dreams he'd had. Ingrid merely nodded. Jeff found the page easily as the corner had been previously folded over, leaving a silent signal the page had been important to someone before. Initially, as he read, he felt disappointed. The first paragraph merely repeated what he already knew. He looked at her again, and she offered a nod to the book that he continue. The next paragraph read:

Lucid dreams are a gift from the universe. Not all who dream are graced with the wonder of experiencing others' worlds, meeting other like-souls to enjoy the symmetry of their lives which are denied to the ordinary; thence to awake with a loving memory of their journey.

Jeff looked at Ingrid. She'd studied his face as he read. Now their eyes met, and she gave another nod of affirmation. He sensed she knew not only exactly what the passage said but also the impact that it would have on Jeff going forward.

He blinked twice, looked down, and reread the paragraph, then he closed the book and held it as if he didn't want to release possession.

"You don't need to purchase the book," Ingrid said. "Perhaps you have received what you were seeking." Appearing satisfied, she placed the other book back on the bookshelf.

Entranced, Jeff felt complete trust for her suggestion. Nevertheless, he said, "I'd like to purchase it."

Ingrid reached out and took it from him with another nod and a gentle smile. She walked to the counter, Jeff in her wake.

After wrapping the book in brown paper, tied precisely with

matching brown twine, she wrote briefly in a well-worn sales notebook and handed the slip to him with the package.

Jeff looked down at the price. *Twenty dollars?* He looked at her, astonished. "That's all? It's an antique; it must be worth much more."

She ignored his comment, just offered him another smile.

He opened his wallet and handed her two twenty-dollar bills.

She made to hand one bill back to him, but he refused, urging her to keep it by saying, "Please."

She nodded. "I, and others, appreciate your generosity."

Reluctant to leave, Jeff looked at his wristwatch and remembered his obligations elsewhere. After murmuring a thank-you, he turned and opened the door. The bell mounted on the door frame gave a bright little tinkle and rang again as the door closed behind him.

He paused just outside the door, grasping for a description of the experience. One word came to mind—enchanting.

When he arrived at her apartment, Charlie answered the door dressed for summer. They exchanged a quick kiss, then he stepped back and admired her bare midriff—courtesy of a cotton blouse tied up Fifties-style—and her long, tanned legs, revealed by short shorts. Delicate, fancy white sandals completed her outfit. He smiled his approval.

Back in his familiar world again but feeling underdressed, he joked that he should've invested in some new flip-flops and worn Bermuda shorts rather than cutoffs.

She slapped him playfully on the shoulder. "You look fine, Jeff." She took the grocery sack from him, glanced at the half-rack of beer he'd bought at the specialty beer shop two doors down from the bookshop, and signaled toward the cooler on the deck.

Good-natured conversations during the party centered on

the controversial national politics of the day, what the local sports teams were doing, and a news piece regarding nearby Mt. Rainier being a long dormant volcano that could come back to life at any time. No one took bets on the outcomes of any of the subjects under discussion.

With the party over and their friends gone, Jeff and Charlene enjoyed watching the sun dipping low over Puget Sound. Jeff helped clean up, and she suggested he stay over.

~

There he was again, free-falling in the total velvety grayness of another dream. He considered the passage in Ingrid's book and took the affirmation to heart, which helped him relax into the experience. His dream-self then resigned to go wherever the dream took him.

The answer came abruptly. He felt momentarily off-balance as the sound of conversations and clatter coupled with a panorama of inside a bustling Denny's restaurant revealed itself. *Mindi's work.* Her eyes provided Jeff's view, and the sight held him hostage.

Mindi, with Jeff a silent passenger, surveyed the room. People sat in booths, at tables, and at the counter eating their meals. Cooks worked feverishly on the other side of a tall counter, plating meals, putting them under the heat lamps, and calling out servers' names to get the food to hungry customers. Jeff felt unsettled and experienced visual overload. He fought to understand. *Why am I here?*

After a few moments, the disoriented feeling of seeing through someone else's eyes surrendered to genuine curiosity.

Mindi moved to a recently vacated table and cleared it. Jeff felt her balance the dishes in her grip and then deposit them in a bus tub at a wait station. She grabbed a clean towel, rinsed it quickly in a small bucket, squeezed out the water, wiped the table, then set it with fresh napkins and silverware.

"Behind you," he heard, as another server came up behind Mindi carrying two armfuls of plates full of breakfast.

Cars paraded back and forth on the busy street outside, and people came and went, while Jeff experienced the life of this server from somewhere behind her eyes.

Whenever Mindi had a moment's break—when not taking orders, talking to other waitstaff, making another pot of coffee, interacting with the customers, and other routine restaurant activities—she rubbed her forehead and closed and rubbed her eyes.

Jeff suddenly remembered that while his consciousness watched this common slice of life play out before his eyes, he slept next to Charlene in Seattle. He reminded himself to gather data. Through Mindi's eyes, he noted the date on the customer's bills: June 19, 2015.

Jeff marveled at her efficiency. She earned her tips as an excellent server. Everything she did had a routine smoothness. When the breakfast rush was over, she took her break. She gave a fellow server a briefing on the customers in her station, poured herself a cup of coffee, doctored it with some cream, and then selected a less-than-perfect donut from under its protective dome. She passed through the swinging door into the back kitchen and sat at the break table off to the side of the buzz of activity.

Jeff noted the integrity of her choice of donut. It showed consideration for her employer. He watched through her eyes as she sipped her coffee, took a small bite from the donut, and then pulled a folded sheet of notepaper and a pen from her pocket.

Mindi dated it and wrote: *Feeling watched, not like by a*

customer who wants something—she paused the writing for a long while—*but like a date with a guy who is infatuated with me and takes notice of everything I do.* Another pause as she looked around the room, then she finished the entry with: *Even now I'm watched.* She folded the paper and put it back in her pocket.

Jeff felt a pang of guilt for causing discomfort for this woman, even though she was only a product of his imagination. He realized he'd begun to like her.

After finishing her break, she pushed the swinging door open, deftly stepped back to let a busser carrying a full bus tub through, and turned right toward the restrooms.

Jeff realized her destination immediately. *Oh, no!* In his mind's dream voice, he screamed. *No, no, no, no!*

Mindi halted and looked around. Had she heard someone? She shook her head as if to clear it, then rubbed her forehead again and darted into the women's restroom. She passed quickly into the stall, pulled down her pants and panties, sat down, and peed.

Jeff had never felt so uncomfortable. Sure, he'd seen Charlie, and others, do this, but they'd been intimate. *I'm a voyeur. I don't mean to be, but still—a voyeur!* He tried to assuage his guilt by telling himself he didn't actually see anything, which he didn't, but it didn't work. He didn't enjoy sitting there with this stranger while she used the toilet.

It was agonizing. He didn't want to be there; he wanted to wake up. What was wrong with his mind that his subconscious created this situation?

When she finished, Mindi washed and dried her hands, then leaned forward to look at herself in the mirror. She peered into her eyes, and Jeff felt sure she would see him, the watcher. Yet her expression didn't show that she'd seen anything. She smoothed each of her eyebrows with the tip of her index finger and exited the restroom, heading toward the dining room.

Except for the restroom incident, Jeff enjoyed being with her while she worked her shift. He caught himself thinking of this morning with her as if it were real life, even though he knew it was just a dream.

Suddenly, like a shutter had closed, he was floating again in the gray world. Then he awoke.

Charlene breathed rhythmically next to him. The lights from the city shone through the windows and softly illuminated the inside of her bedroom.

Jeff gently pulled the covers back, padded to the bathroom, and closed the door quietly. In the mirror he saw, instead of a brunette woman, himself with unkempt hair and needing a shave. The juxtaposition of images he'd seen tonight motivated him even more to work to comprehend these strange, recurring dreams which had become more complicated each time. Still, he resented his subconscious making him watch someone from such a private point of view.

He used the toilet, wishing he could unsee what he'd just seen tonight with Mindi. As he washed his hands, he realized, by the date on the customers' bills, his experience had taken place two years ago. These dreams felt both real and surreal.

He drenched his face with cold water and watched the water swirl in the sink, imagining that his sanity exited clockwise down the drain.

~

The next day, when Jeff got home from Charlene's, he retrieved his dream journal and documented the dream. He'd been concerned that he might forget the details of being with Mindi at Denny's; however, his fears were groundless. He remembered everything with clarity. Though reluctant, at first, to write the part about the toilet—in case someone read it and thought him some kind of pervert—he included it as part of the dream. Even though he never intended to show it to anyone, he inserted a comment apologizing for his subconscious having manifested that scene.

However, the passage from Ingrid's book came to mind and reinforced his feeling that Mindi was real, rather than a construct of his mind. But that contradicted traditional research that said that dreams are the subconscious feeding off trivial or unconscious triggers from a waking life.

He had conflicting documentation now: the affirmation from the antique book versus the scientific source material of his dream books. The book from Ingrid sat on his kitchen counter, a brown paper package tied with string. Jeff smiled as he looked at it. It made him think of the song, "My Favorite Things." He untied the string, unfolded the paper—releasing the faint aroma of the bookshop—and set it reverently aside. The dog-eared page was easy to find again. He reread the passage, then smoothed the folded corner upright the way it belonged, and reserved the place with a proper bookmark. The feeling of grace he received from having reread the passage would comfort him if he did dream again. What other wonders were waiting to be read in the book and might provide him such comfort?

He rationalized this excursion into the metaphysical, a departure from the pure scientific method of his training, as being a part of his research into the dream phenomena he continued to experience.

~

No dreams for over a week. Charlene phoned him as he drove

home from work and told him she was leaving tomorrow to visit clients and prospects in Spokane, Boise, and Portland. They agreed to stay in touch, by text, at least.

"I'll be back in a week from Friday."

"Okay, when you get back, we'll celebrate on the town. But if you're sick and tired of restaurant food, I'll cook for you."

She laughed. "Sounds great. I'll hold you to it. We'll see which it'll be. But you know it's really no big deal. I'll only be gone a week."

"Yeah, I know. I'm already missing you." Jeff had become more attached to her over the last few weeks and felt uneasy that he'd shared that he would miss her. They rarely shared feelings like that. Would she be concerned he'd become possessive?

Instead, she responded positively to his comment and replied with warmth in her voice, "I know, Jeff, I'll miss you too. It's a date. We'll paint the town red. I'll text you when I get to Spokane to let you know I arrived safely." She'd never accounted for her safety like that before. It reassured him.

"Great," he said. "Thank you. Gotta run. Traffic's clogged up—wanna pay attention."

"Bye."

~

Jeff, an analytical thinker, could easily isolate a client's issue or a program's glitches. It was how his mind worked, what he'd trained to do. With Charlie gone, he had spare time to consider the mechanics of his dreams, but the more time that passed since the last dream, the more the diagnostic part of his personality diluted the magic of Ingrid's book. The dream-puzzles had invaded his life, and the solutions didn't respond to pure logic. Were the answers somewhere in between? Jeff's reluctance to give up on the idea that the mystery of his dreams could be solved using the scientific method caused a conflict in his mind. Ingrids's book suggested acceptance of things that couldn't be understood as "a gift of the universe," but Jeff was convinced that unexplained phenomena could be understood with enough data and observations.

The question was, are these more than ordinary dreams? Possibly actual time travel? Otherwise, how else could he have seen things in 2015 in such detail when he lived in 2017? He reminded himself that Dr. Singh, Denny's, and the newspaper article about baseball games were all real. But what about Mindi Ketcham? Was she real too?

But traveling in time wasn't scientifically possible. His research indicated it was only possible in the imagination and science fiction stories. Or was it? He began to have doubts. After all, he had data to the contrary—he'd seen detailed restaurant receipts and an actual newspaper dated 2015.

Time travel stories in science fiction were usually about large jumps of time. The hero traveled forward eight hundred thousand years in H. G. Wells's *The Time Machine*. In the movie he and Charlene had seen recently, Christopher Reeve's character, Richard, through hypnosis, goes back in time seventy years and falls in love with an actress in the past. The story's ending is bittersweet. But even seventy years is more dramatic than his two-year jumps into the past. Jeff found a novel by Jack London, *Star Rover*, where the protagonist, a confined prisoner, leaves his body to experience past lives. Even *Slaughterhouse Five*'s Billy Pilgrim, who became "unstuck in time," bounced around his entire life and traveled further distances. Still, none of this research provided any help in answering the questions of how, and particularly why he was having these dreams.

He began to consider that he should think of his dreams

as "time travel dreams" rather than, as he did at first, as "falling dreams." As mundane as the two-year time difference was, he still embraced the challenge of finding the answers to his questions.

These dreams hadn't faded upon awakening like the kind of dreams where dreamers play with a dog or cat that died years ago or bug-eyed monsters chase them. These dreams became clearer as the days passed and were more like reality than any of his previous dreams. The books warned of dream-reality confusion. Jeff unconsciously chose to be in denial of that possibility as he focused on a solution to the puzzle.

Jeff's self-image was that of a guy who lives a perfectly normal, better-than-average middle-class lifestyle in a real-life Emerald City, not in Kansas and the fantasy land of Oz with Dorothy's witches, flying monkeys, Munchkins, and talking animals.

With no apparent answers after sorting through the clues, he forced his attention back to his job at SiLD². Jeff felt grateful for his twenty-first century dream job where he combined marketing analyst work and duties as a customer representative. There, he could see patterns and trends, useful in marketing and program problems, and he enjoyed working with people, which was useful when solving their problems. He consulted with the software designers, with those who both beta tested and those that purchased the programs.

The relationship with his girlfriend had developed to where Jeff wanted to discuss the subject of marriage with her. He thought of "putting a ring on it" but then censored himself because that phrase more than subtly objectified a woman as property, chaining her to a man with jewelry. He'd first heard it from his grandfather, whose attitudes had been formed when patriarchy and overt chauvinism was the norm. His mother had counseled him to be cautious of microaggressions and unwittingly sexist phrases, so he tried to purge them from his vocabulary. Yet social tradition favored engagement rings as a solid demonstration of commitment, and that's how Jeff felt about the subject.

Charlene had commented once to Jeff that her biological clock was ticking, but she quickly added that she wasn't worried; she had plenty of time. Her thoughts at the time seemed to have been stimulated by the pleasant family memories that had surfaced when she'd talked about the loss of her dad.

Jeff, sitting with his back to the door, stared out his office window, thinking. He heard someone enter his office, rocked forward in his chair, and turned.

Craig stood there smiling. "Hey, Jeff. You look lost in thought. Can I interrupt and ask you about the Classic Program Update Synopsis?"

Jeff immediately stopped his daydreaming and engaged in a detailed technical conversation, thoughts of his curious dream world and the possibility of marriage set aside for the safer and more comfortable subject of his work.

~

Mindi got ready for her doctor's appointment, happy she'd not felt her "watcher" for well over a week. And Shirley had gone because her doctor had given her that prescription.

She paused for one last glimpse at her hair, putting a stray strand behind her ear. With that, she grabbed her purse, checked to see if her "paranoia notes" were in there, and left. She double-checked that she'd locked the door, then turned and headed for the bus stop.

Dr. Singh started the session with, "Well, Mindi, how are you feeling today?"

"I'm feeling well."

"Okay. I take it you've had no more of the feelings that

brought you here?"

"No, not really."

The doctor smiled. "Good. Any more issues with sensing you're being watched?"

Mindi looked down at her hands, not sure if she should ask her the question she'd been thinking about. "Well, Doctor, it hasn't happened since last visit. But to be honest, I wondered if it might've been Shirley watching me in a different way, you know. But then I decided it wasn't."

The doctor met Mindi's eyes. "Go on."

"Well, the last time I felt watched—it's there in my notes—I wasn't anywhere I could be in trouble, and I didn't feel threatened by the feelings. I was just doing my shift at work, and things were going well. No troublesome customers. Everybody I was working with was okay. Even the assistant manager, who can be a real jerk sometimes, was nice to me. She—I mean Shirley, not the manager—would've had no need to protect me. So that's why I don't think it's Shirley that watches me. And besides, it seems to have quit."

The doctor maintained her gaze, which urged Mindi to continue.

With a bit of hesitation, Mindi said, "Do you want me to keep taking the pills? I'm feeling pretty good. Like I said, things are good."

"Yes, things are going well for you, Mindi. No unwanted feelings for a while. Why don't we wait until next session, and we'll consider changing the dose? They're not making you sluggish or sleepy, are they? You're doing well at work? You're getting good rest at night, aren't you?"

"Oh, yes, Doctor. Things seem to be, well, more normal, I guess."

The doctor smiled. "Good. How about we settle on what

you said when you came in today? You're feeling well, and that is very good." The doctor looked at her calendar. "I'll be taking a few days off, so your next appointment will be in two weeks. I don't foresee any problems, but if there's an emergency of some sort, you can contact Dr. Shearing. You can reach him by calling my number and talking to the receptionist."

"Thank you, Doctor." Mindi gathered up her purse and left the office. Even though she'd told the doctor she felt fine, she now felt a little uneasy that she wouldn't be able to see the doctor for two weeks. What if she was watched again? Or the pills didn't work and Shirley came back?

CHAPTER 5

Jeff dragged something for dinner out of the freezer. He felt a little low toned but didn't analyze why. Charlene would be back in a couple of days.

Things'll be back to normal then.

He nuked the dinner in the microwave too long but ate it anyway, working absent-mindedly on the extra-chewy bites while he watched the local news. Nothing special there. The empty mind-calories of TV programming matched the empty calories from the cookies and milk he had for a snack.

He read a little of a mindless novel, more empty stuff for his brain, until he brushed his teeth and climbed into bed. Tonight, the dreams had slipped his mind, until . . . another of those dreams began. Initially, he didn't feel concerned. It started like the others, but soon he was falling much faster than before, and the gray was darker. That concerned him.

The fall ended with a physical jolt that startled him. No floating. Instead, he landed standing on a solid surface. He adjusted to the new situation and waited in the impenetrable gray. Uneasy anticipation replaced the relative peacefulness of the other dreams.

"What are you doing here?" demanded a husky female voice in a threatening tone. The voice, which he didn't recognize, came from directly in front of him, but he could see only gray.

Feeling cautious, he remained quiet.

"I know you can hear me," she continued. "What are you doing in here?"

He reminded himself that he'd handled everything else with these crazy dreams, so he just listened, trying to control his fear.

"You should be afraid. You don't belong here. What are you doing here?"

Startled at this voice's knowledge of his thoughts and feelings, his dream-self found its voice—though he hadn't known he had one. He answered with a defiant question, "Who are *you?*"

He couldn't answer her question because he didn't know where "here" was or why he was there. He waited, trying to control his confused thoughts.

He should be in control. *Where am I? And why is she so impatient?*

"Where you are is here," she said. "And yes, I am impatient for an answer. I don't have to explain. I want you to leave."

He felt her commanding him to comply. She had him at a disadvantage because she could read his thoughts.

"Damned right I know what you're thinking. We're here in the same place, and there's no room here for two of us. I'm telling you again—leave, or else!"

Jeff didn't like being threatened. His self-assurance returned. "Or else what?" he demanded. "I'll answer nothing until you tell me who you are."

Nothing but silence from the void.

Then with an unsure tone: "She's mine," the bully said.

"Who is *she?*" Jeff asked.

"You know who. You-you-you . . . you have to leave." Her

tone revealed a growing insecurity.

"I'll say nothing more until you answer my questions. Who are *you*? Where is *here*? And who is *she*?"

Silence.

He waited a long time.

Then, without warning . . . Jeff awoke suddenly without floating or falling in the gray. He stared into the darkness of his bedroom feeling quite surprised. The memory of the conversation remained clear, and he captured it in complete detail in his notebook. Nothing in tonight's dream contributed to enjoying "the symmetry of others' lives" though. He resented that.

The dreams were progressing, building to something, but to what, and why? He had a lot of questions, but no answers. At least he hadn't felt threatened by the voice in the dream. He turned over in the bed, hoping he'd get a full night's sleep and wake up rested.

He did.

~

Mindi rarely dreamed, and especially not since taking the medication to help her relax, but she awoke before her alarm with a vivid memory of last night's dream. A man and a woman had stood facing each other in a gray void—no walls, floor, ceiling, or props. They appeared to be arguing—though she couldn't hear them. The big-boned woman had short dark hair and wore blue jeans, a flannel shirt, and no makeup. The man was good looking, clean-cut, and wore slacks and a sports shirt.

Mindi watched them from a distance. The woman leaned toward the man, shaking her fist insistently. When he spoke— although the woman gave him few chances—his movements conveyed a sense of calm confidence.

Mindi lay in bed for a moment, wondering about the dream's meaning. Then she wrote a description of this silent movie in her notes for the doctor. The woman had to be Shirley. The man seemed to be someone she knew, but from where, she couldn't recall.

The dream hadn't faded like others had, which made it difficult to ignore. She struggled to understand it, but found no answers, except that the dream suggested Shirley wasn't gone.

~

Craig burst into Jeff's office with a cup of coffee in one hand and a stack of papers in the other. "Let me show you this, Jeff," he said, his eyes full of excitement.

Jeff wondered what had him so fired up. Software design and marketing was far from exciting.

Craig spread a bunch of photocopied sheets over the desktop. They looked like an organization chart. When Craig quit moving them around, Jeff recognized it as a huge family tree, printed on legal-sized paper.

"Did you get this from one of those genealogy websites?"

"No, no, no," Craig replied. "The guys down in development are working on a new product, and they asked if we could be the first beta test. They announced it in a staff meeting. Didn't you hear? I've found stuff I didn't know about my family from a public records search feature."

"So this is your family?"

"Yeah, look."

"Cool," Jeff replied with genuine appreciation. "You've done a lot of work on this. It looks great. Kind of interesting." He took in the detail, nodding his head in approval.

"Thanks. Yeah, you'll want to do it too. Look at this . . ."

Craig directed Jeff's gaze with his finger, which pursued a zig-zag pattern from the bottom of each page to the very top. "From now all the way back to 1620—see here, the Mayflower. I'm related to someone who came over on the Mayflower!"

Jeff acted impressed, but he'd never put much stock in blue-blood lineages, even though he, too, had an old European heritage. In fact, he reasoned that beginning with Columbus, thence to the Mayflower, and so on through to Ellis Island, the settlers of the Americas had, at first innocently, and later with full intention, caused a lot of pain to the indigenous peoples. Jeff wasn't militant about his feelings, but wasn't it arrogant, and just plain wrong, to erase cultures, to effectively engage in genocide? The natives were doing just fine before Europeans got here.

However, as Craig's friend, he didn't want to burst his friend's bubble of excitement, so he traced back down Craig's ancestors and stopped about two generations above where Craig and his siblings were arrayed at the bottom of the last page. What stopped him were the names of Craig's paternal grandparents, Alexander Howe and his wife, Craig's grandmother, her maiden name, Patricia Ketchem.

"Ketchem?" he muttered. The hair on the back of his neck stood up.

Craig put his finger between the boxes with those names. "Yeah, when my brothers and I were kids, we joked with our cousins, saying our grandparents should've been detectives." He paused, waiting for Jeff to comment.

Jeff looked up at Craig, puzzled.

"The name of their detective agency could have been Ketchem and Howe. Get it?" He laughed, but Jeff still didn't get it. Craig couldn't know Jeff's mind was somewhere else.

"Remember the puns of names that went around when we were kids? There were the lawyers, Dewey, Cheetham and

61

Howe. Our family could have been the cops that caught the crooks, Ketchem and Howe."

Jeff shook his head, slow to catch on, but Craig persisted, saying slowly, "Do-We-Cheat-Them-and-How? Catch-them-and-How. Get it?"

Jeff chuckled. "Yeah, yeah, that's cute. But isn't *Ketchem* spelled with an *a* instead of an *e*?"

Now Craig looked puzzled. Finally he understood, "Oh, yeah, somewhere along the line the *a* got changed. Let's see . . ." He looked over his charts. "Yeah, right here, 1774, around the start of the, uh, the Revolution. See where it changed from the British version *Ketcham* to *Ketchem*? Maybe it wasn't too cool to be British in some parts, huh? Don't know what difference it made, though. Still kinda looks the same."

Jeff nodded. "Interesting. You've put a lot of work into this. It looks good. How do you think it will hold up to the competition out there?"

Craig shrugged. "The project lead is hoping to find someone who's used the other ones to compare. I've logged a few hours on it. It's pretty intuitive. Say, why don't you do yours too? Beta test it. It could help the guys downstairs. Talk to Jackson down there. He can give you the password. Work on it here on your desktop. Code your timesheet, oh-two-five-development."

Craig's cell phone rang, ending the conversation about his genealogy. As he shouldered his phone and talked to the caller, he gathered up his papers and his coffee cup and headed to the door, taking with him a chance for Jeff to look below Grandma Ketchem Howe to see the names there.

Craig said into the phone, "Hold on a sec, okay?" He looked back over his shoulder at Jeff. "Want to get in a round of golf this weekend?"

Jeff's mind was focused on *Ketchem*, but Craig was waiting

for an answer. "Oh, oh thanks, Craig, no. Charlene will be back in town. We've got plans. Next weekend, 'kay?"

Craig nodded, returned to his phone call and walked down the hall.

Jeff added Ketchem to his list of clues, along with Angels playing the Mariners, the real Dr. Singh, and the real Denny's. The spelling of her name, *Ketchem*, might be the answer to why he couldn't find Mindi on the internet. If her last name was the same as Craig's grandmother's maiden name, maybe he could find her now.

He googled "Mindi Ketchem" but got no hit, just like with "Ketcham." He found, however, a newspaper obituary for a Ralph Ketchem, Torrance, who died August 13, 2014. Torrance was right next to Gardena. No next of kin mentioned in the obit. *Dead end?* If Mindi was a real person, regardless of how she spelled her last name, there was no obituary for her, so at least she hadn't died. She lived, or at least had lived, somewhere near Gardena, probably close to where the doctor practiced. Did she get married? Move? How could he find where someone lived two years ago?

He smiled to himself, thinking he should get the detective agency Ketchem and Howe to find her. Seriously, though, it wasn't important enough to pay for an internet search fee that would probably come up empty. Paying wasn't the issue. If he did find her, what would he do with the information? Sooner or later the dreams would tell him what he wanted to know.

The phone rang, jolting him back to work.

~

While waiting for her appointment with her doctor, Mindi looked back over her notes about her feelings of being watched.

She hadn't felt watched for a while. Today, she had something new to talk about.

She'd tell the doctor that she felt good, took her meds, and hadn't heard from Shirley directly. No customers had made a pass at her, and she was using the gym at her apartment building where she did fifteen minutes on the treadmill every other day. Those were the good things. However, she had had that strange dream with the beefy woman arguing with the nice-looking guy.

"You can go right in, Miss Ketchem," the receptionist said, breaking Mindi's reverie.

Dr. Singh validated Mindi's progress, then Mindi told her about the dream and her theory that the woman might be Shirley. Mindi had feared the doctor would think she was silly, but instead, the doctor listened patiently.

"Did you feel afraid of the woman as you watched them talking?" the doctor asked.

Mindi shook her head. "No. I wasn't afraid."

"Good. Since you weren't afraid, I suggest there's nothing to worry about, even if that is a visual rendering of Shirley for you." The doctor reminded Mindi that dreams are a way of sorting and filing things away, and that we rarely know what needs to be sorted and filed. "It may be your subconscious's way of filing her away. But remember, dream interpretation is not a science, but an art.

"Even if you were threatened in a dream, which you said you weren't in this one, remember, it's just a dream, and you can't be harmed."

Mindi agreed to continue to keep track of her feelings and dreams and to stay on her meds for now. When the appointment ended, she left the building with a lightness in her step and a strong feeling of progress.

~

Jeff and Charlene had taken advantage of the Independence Day holiday and made it a long weekend after she got back from her whirlwind trip. Now back at work, even though he'd been dream-free for a week, he was still puzzling out the clues.

Being a proactive rather than passive observer of the information from his dreams, he added the latest dream with that bully to his list of clues. *The bully must be Shirley*, he thought. But how did he know that? The answer that came to him was *logic*. When he'd traveled before, he'd been in Mindi's mind, and Shirley was in Mindi's mind. That was easy.

What about the coincidence of the last name of Craig's relative Grandma Ketchem? And did the deceased Ralph Ketchem somehow fit into the solution to the mystery of Mindi Ketcham, or is it Mindi Ketchem?

Midmorning, he ventured to Craig's office and sat down.

Craig turned to Jeff. "What's up, big guy?"

"Say, Craig. Your family tree's kinda cool. I might try that myself. May I see yours, again?"

"Sure, here ya go." Craig pulled the oversized sheets out from underneath other stuff on his desk and slid them across.

Jeff paged through one sheet after another, starting with the oldest on top, the ones dated 1620, down through to the present.

He wanted the latest sheet, the one with the name of Craig's immediate family, starting with Grandma Ketchem Howe.

From the dates in the little boxes, he saw that Craig's grandmother had a brother whose son, Ralph Ketchem, died in August 2014.

Craig's related to Ralph! Jeff couldn't get too excited, though. He'd seen nothing yet connecting Grandma, Ralph or Craig to Mindi.

Jeff looked up and caught Craig watching him poring over the sheets.

"You grew up in California, didn't you?" Jeff asked.

"Yeah."

"I don't think I know why you moved up here?"

"My wife's from Seattle. Met her at Cal State."

"Oh, which one?"

Craig laughed. "I only have one wife."

Jeff smiled. "Which Cal State?"

"Oh, yeah. Dominguez Hills."

"Dominguez Hills? Where's that?"

"Gardena. Family's from Torrance."

Things were heating up, but Jeff forced himself to remain cool. First there's Ralph, then Craig from Torrance, which was next to Gardena.

"And she wanted to come back up here to be with family?" he asked.

"Yeah, and I was kinda tired of the Southern California crowds and lifestyle anyway. Things have been pretty sweet up here." He patted his desk, referring to his job.

Jeff looked back at the paper and traced his finger below Ralph—one child, Miranda Jasmine Ketchem, birthdate March 17, 1991. If Mindi was a nickname for Miranda, he'd hit the jackpot! Lights and bells went off in Jeff's mind like a slot machine hitting triple sevens!

Could it be?

Jeff had what he wanted. He looked at his watch.

"Thanks a lot, Craig. Hey, who did you say to talk to about getting the password for this?"

"Jackson. Jack Jackson, down on two."

Jeff nodded and hustled back to his office. He sat and googled "nickname for Miranda." Result: *Mindy, alternate spelling: Mindi.*

Mindi Ketchem is a real person! He spun around in his chair in celebration. Then put his hands on top of his head as if it were going to explode. These were more than just dreams—he'd connected to a real person all the way back into 2015. *How impossible is that?* He had some answers but now even more questions.

His latest discovery made it hard for Jeff to focus, but he forced himself to work.

~

Jeff returned home still preoccupied with his dream problem. He got out his dream journal and added what he'd learned that day, found a 2015 calendar online, and started matching the dates in his journal with the 2017 calendar. Once finished, he felt disappointed because he had nothing more to investigate. "Damn," he said aloud.

That night he fell asleep promptly and welcomed the fall that quickly changed to float. While he floated, Jeff analyzed. First, these dreams met all the definitions of a lucid dream. Second, he now knew that Mindi was a real person.

Could it be that they were only dreams, nothing more? Intricate lucid dreams for which the memory didn't fade. But weren't these still just dreams? That seemed a more logical explanation than time traveling two years into the past.

How would he ever know if he were living a real-life science fiction story? How would he know if he was just crazy? Then, without the dream going any further in the grayness, he woke up—just twenty minutes after he turned out the light. For twenty minutes he'd been floating, thinking, analyzing, philosophizing. He stared at the ceiling thinking about what had happened and hadn't happened. Then he got up, opened his journal and wrote:

Journal Entry 7/5/2017: Controlled experiment #1,
First datapoint: System crash. Why? Too many inputs,
too much thinking.

Too much thinking was something that an ex-girlfriend named Marti—short for Martina—had once told him: "Baby, you think too much. Don't think, just feel."

Now that he was awake, he wondered what he could do to control his mind, which was the central processing unit in question.

Without realizing it, he was analyzing again, once more not in control of his CPU, because his mind was considering the similarity of spelling between Marti and Mindi. Both started with *M* and ended with *i*. Each had five letters. Did he construct Mindi's name from Marti's? Was Mindi really just a construct?

No, that can't be.

They looked completely different and had different personalities. Mindi could still just be a construct, of course, but not from an ex-girlfriend.

No. Mindi is a real person. Craig's cousin.

But the name similarity could be just coincidence. His mind circled back around, adding more self-doubt to the mix.

Marti had been into Transcendental Meditation—TM to those who followed Maharishi Mahesh Yogi's meditation technique. After paying a fee, he'd received his secret mantra and tried it for a couple of weeks without results. When he complained, the TM instructor told Jeff he was trying too hard. "Relax," he'd said. "Let the truth come to you."

His excursion into TM ended when his relationship with Marti ended, and several months later, an old ex-hippie who lived in his apartment building told him the same thing, for free. "Go with the flow, man," he said. "Chill out."

Thinking about the old hippie reminded him of the book he'd bought at Ingrid's bookstore. Maybe something in the book would show him how to be at peace with all of this.

His final analysis of the failed dream was that he'd overanalyzed it, overloaded the system with logic. The Marti-Mindi name thing kept returning to his mind, but he tried to stop that by reminding himself he was overthinking that too. Then it started up again, like a snowball that rolled downhill and couldn't be stopped. Finally, he fell asleep and remained dream-free until morning.

Jeff awoke refreshed. Even though he'd spoiled the experiment last night, he'd learned something. He had the falling/floating thing pretty well handled. He accepted that he'd lucid dreamed but had no control over the content or direction of the dreams. The dream book said that the lucid dreamer could sometimes alter the direction of the dream, but, so far, that eluded him.

Jeff resolved that the next time he dreamed, he'd relax into it. Satisfied with his conclusion, he got ready for work.

The days after Charlene had gotten back from her sales trip had been great. They were getting along so well that he continued to consider when would be the best time and place to ask her to marry him. He wished she'd bring it up first. But with that wish, he censured himself, cautioned himself to let it be and not to also analyze that too much.

~

That Friday night, he was surprised to have another dream. He'd thought the dreaming had quit after he tried to dissect it, that he'd analyzed it so much it was like the frog they cut into in biology class. After you were done with the dissection, it would never be a frog again. Perhaps he'd done that to his dreams. But no, here was another chance. As before, he fell. He anticipated seeing what would happen next and relaxed.

He floated. The gray parted. A woman with short dark hair, wearing blue jeans and a flannel shirt, stood in a vast gray area that had no horizon in any direction and no distinct ceiling. She clenched her fists and glared at him, looking ready for a fight, but he had no fear because he couldn't be hurt in a dream. Nevertheless, he didn't want a confrontation.

He glanced down and saw he was wearing a pair of dark slacks, a striped sport shirt, sleeves rolled up, open at the collar, and his loafers—his usual, casual office attire.

The woman stepped forward and Jeff looked up at the formidable woman now standing uncomfortably close to him.

Was this Shirley? The person who shouted at him last time? He wished he'd done more reading in the antique book and found a way to deal with an angry character in a dream.

She shoved her head forward, mere inches from his face, and shouted, "I told you to stay out of here!"

Luckily this was only a dream, because if she had bad breath, he would've smelled it.

She backed up a bit, then leaned forward again. "You don't belong here. I oughta kick your ass." She stopped, as if waiting for a reply.

"I don't know where here is," he replied in a soft, calm voice. She remained silent, so he said, "Please, tell me. Where are we? And where is here?"

Her posture remained confrontational. She said nothing.

He continued, "I don't know how I got here, and I don't know what I'm doing here." He lifted his jaw in defiance. "Tell me, please, why don't I belong here?"

The bully stared at him. "I'm all she needs," she said in a harsh voice. "She doesn't need you to protect her."

Jeff maintained eye contact and worked to keep his thoughts to a minimum, since she'd heard them last time. For a long moment they just stared at each other, neither one moving, swaying, or her even blinking. She seemed like a frozen computer image.

His mind wandered as he watched her, wondering how to find out what the date was. *Is this happening two years ago or now?*

Then the dream ended. No fall, no float. He just awoke.

He transcribed the dream, ending with:

> *When I considered the time difference, the dream shut down, even though we'd been standing there for a long time staring at each other. Is it a conflict in logic, a conflict of tense? Past tense/present tense, this makes no sense.*

He reread his rhyme and chuckled at the alliteration, then tucked the notebook down under the clutter in the drawer of his nightstand. Charlie would come over tonight and now wasn't the time to share his weird dreams. He hoped she'd understand, but surely there were limitations. On second thought, he knew Charlene wouldn't understand. Hell, he didn't understand. It would take much too much to try to explain the unexplainable, and it would, for certain, screw up their future. He looked forward to a pleasant future with Charlene with no unnecessary complications. He closed the drawer.

That day, he played eighteen holes of golf with Craig and had a few beers. After he got back home, he straightened up the apartment, took a shower, and was ready for his date.

CHAPTER 6

Jeff put steaks on the grill and pulled the cork from a bottle of a delicious red wine from a local winery. Later, they had popcorn and watched a movie. Charlie stayed over.

Once asleep, Jeff was falling, floating, and then front and center at another of Mindi's counseling sessions with Dr. Singh.

The doctor had just read Mindi's notes from her latest dream. She handed the folded paper back and asked, "How do you feel about that?"

"In the first dream when I saw her, I wasn't, uh, I wasn't concerned," Mindi replied. "But now, it's . . . disturbing. She sounded mean. I thought Shirley had gone. She hasn't been in my head for so many weeks." She blew her nose into a tissue, then looked at the doctor, who waited for her to continue.

"And that guy—the same guy as in the dream before—but this time I could hear them talking. Shirley told him to leave. She was acting like when she wanted me out of the way, but this time with words. The man was calm when he told her he didn't know what he was doing there and didn't even know where he was. Doctor, do I have more than one Shirley in my head? Y-y-you asked how I felt about my dream. It's disturbing. It's almost as spooky now as when I first saw you. I thought my pills were keeping it all away."

The doctor waited until Mindi had composed herself, then said with a reassuring tone, "Well, Mindi, you've kept Shirley from challenging you. This was a dream, not the same as voices, or rather the feelings you had of her when you were awake. Consider that she wasn't talking to you, she was talking to the man in a dream." The doctor waited a moment for Mindi to absorb what she'd said. "Like I told you, dreams have a way of, well, let's say sorting things out, letting the pressure off. It seems to me that the part of you that is Shirley is feeling threatened by your renewed confidence, and in your dream you have a surrogate to confront her. That seems healthy to me. I recommend you not feel threatened by the Shirley you see in your dream and assume this is a way your mind is flushing her out. How do you feel about that?"

Jeff considered the doctor's assessment of his presence in Mindi's dream and understood how that would make sense to her. But it didn't explain why he was there from his point of view. He continued to observe.

Mindi rubbed her forehead, and Jeff wondered if she'd heard him thinking. She clutched the tissue in her hand, looked down, then back up at the doctor and said, "If that's what it is, then I guess I don't have to worry about her. She won't push me around if that guy is there, right?"

The doctor looked at her desk clock. "That's right. I don't think you'll see much of Shirley in the future. If you don't have any questions or concerns, we're out of time, but I'll see you next week. If you have more dreams, we'll discuss it then. I'd like to leave your medication dose where it is. Now, still not using alcohol or marijuana?"

"Oh, no, Doctor, none at all."

"Good. Besides the prescription, I recommend you continue to stay away from anything stronger than Tylenol or aspirin. If you miss a dose of your meds, don't double up on them. Follow the dosage and schedule I prescribed. Keep on exercising, but don't overdo that, either. Okay?"

"Okay, Doctor. Thank you." She left the office, and Jeff sensed she felt better.

The dream ended there.

He awoke before Charlene and had coffee ready for her when she got up. They enjoyed a pleasant morning together. When Charlene left to run some errands that afternoon, Jeff made his dream journal entry documenting his dream and Mindi's feelings of discomfort at Shirley's resurrection.

Jeff admired how the doctor interpreted her dream to guide Mindi back to a comfortable place. He wished he had someone to interpret his dreams the way the doctor did for Mindi; it might make it easier to get some resolution to the confusion he felt. One thing was for certain, he didn't want to have to face Shirley again. Had he become more than just a minor player in Mindi's life? If so, why? He noted again that Mindi rubbed her head when he was with her, and it seemed she might be able to hear his thoughts. He wrote, *I have to be careful about what I think when I'm there*, then added, *How crazy do I have to get to be Dr. Singh's patient?* To amuse himself, he considered how many airline miles he'd get by going down to Gardena for his appointments.

Charlene returned from her afternoon shopping with ingredients for a special dinner she planned for them that evening. After dinner, they drove down to a local beach and enjoyed the evening while walking along the water accompanied by the peaceful sound of waves lapping on the sand. After returning to Jeff's apartment, they fell asleep in each other's arms.

~

Sleeping next to Charlene, he dreamed again. The fall stopped when he thought of floating, and the gray cleared just as he heard the familiar coarse voice in the undefinable distance of the gray space. But she wasn't speaking to him. She was yelling at Mindi.

"You are so weak, girl! We've been together since you let Father do those things to us. You didn't tell Mom. Why didn't you tell Mom? She would've helped us. You are going nowhere, and you can't pull yourself together without me . . ."

Jeff frowned, unhappy with the situation and feeling protective of Mindi. What could he do? Shirley was being verbally abusive. If allowed to continue, she could degrade the progress Mindi had made with the doctor. Mindi wasn't weak, but she was fragile. Jeff had to advocate for Mindi. But how?

Without warning, Shirley was suddenly uncomfortably close to Jeff's face again. "I told you to stay away!" she yelled, then paused as if expecting a response.

Jeff's anger rose, but then he looked into Shirley's cold, hard eyes and recognized their resemblance to Mindi's, as if she were a sibling. She was a hardened, hurt, and hurtful version of the young woman he'd come to like.

His heart lost its anger, replaced by compassion for the part of Mindi that had been hurt so much that Shirley had to exist to ensure that Mindi wouldn't be hurt again. Shirley, the sad facsimile of Mindi, wasn't a nice, considerate, hardworking, orphaned woman. Shirley was the result of the most extreme form of betrayal that could be done to a daughter.

Jeff was determined to avoid direct confrontation and not feed her anger. Ingrid's book spoke of meeting aggression with passivity, at least, and compassion at best—besides, Mindi might remember anything he said when she awoke. He faced Shirley, working to make his lucid dream face impassive to her aggressiveness. This being a dream, he knew she couldn't hurt him. Like most bullies, she'd try to use her bulk, the threat of physical assault, to intimidate him, so he tried to look like someone who wouldn't be intimidated. In doing so, perhaps Mindi would trust him, like she trusted her doctor, and Shirley would become powerless.

Shirley's expression continued to display frustrated rage. She ranted on, saying he was to leave, he was a trespasser, she would kick his ass! Her body trembled. In a few minutes, her facial expression changed to someone who sensed they were about to lose.

Jeff kept his mind clear of judgment and instead projected compassion and understanding to the image of Shirley shouting in his face. During a pause in the barrage, Jeff said, "I know you mean Mindi no harm, that you want to help her, but you're making her more afraid."

For a moment, Jeff thought he saw Shirley's anger diminish, but then the harsh look on her face returned with reconstructed rage. Jeff remained sympathetic to that part of Mindi who was expressing the hurt and anger that had fermented over the years.

Jeff said, "Shirley . . ."

But before he could continue, Shirley spoke. "How do you know who I am?"

Rather than answer her question, he said, "You must be in a lot of pain, but you can let go. Mindi is healing now, and she doesn't need you." He reached out his arms to offer Shirley a hug. When she didn't offer her arms in return, Jeff stepped forward a half step and put his arms around her.

Jeff hugged her a few moments, but she didn't respond. He stepped back and gave her a warm, loving look. After a moment,

Shirley's image shimmered like a hologram, then shuddered. Her expression showed she was struggling to maintain her presence. Then her image blinked out, gone. No sound, just gone; nothing left behind. Jeff had no time to consider what had just happened. Immediately, and with no warning, he found himself floating in the gray again. Quiet.

~

Jeff awoke, alone in bed. Where was Charlene? Why was it so dark? He was no longer in that gray dream room, but, he realized, it wasn't his bed in which he lay. Eyes opened, but not his. And the room was different. *I must be in Mindi's head.*

He saw what she saw: the ceiling, then her bedside clock. Jeff noted the time: 4:22 a.m. She closed her eyes, cutting off his view, and put her hands over her face. Her chest heaved with sobs that slowed as time passed. Eventually, her breathing slowed to normal, and the sobbing stopped, but the tears still flowed.

Jeff's heart melted with empathy for Mindi. He tried to remain detached but couldn't, because he experienced her emotions as if they were his own.

In her dream, Mindi must have witnessed them talking, followed by Shirley's disappearance. She'd awakened from a dream with the memory that her other self, Shirley, had vanished while confronting him.

Jeff knew the feeling that fed her tears wasn't grief but relief—relief that Shirley had been vanquished and would never return. Mindi dispelled any doubt Jeff had about that when she gave a deep sigh and her entire body relaxed. Shirley was gone along with the pain she'd caused.

So as not to intrude into Mindi's awareness, Jeff strained to keep his feelings in the quiet part of his mind, but the effort was exhausting. Would vanquishing Shirley complete his mission? The phrase surprised him, and his self-control slipped. *Is this a mission?* As soon as he thought it, he tried to isolate his thoughts from her, but he was too late. Her head jerked back.

She'd heard him.

Jeff's view through Mindi's eyes widened. She sat up straight and froze. Her gaze fixed on a shadow on the opposite wall, as if his "thought voice" had originated from there.

Not wanting to reawaken her fear that Shirley was still there, or worse, that the man who had vanquished Shirley might do her harm, he worked to stay quiet.

Mindi turned and swung her legs over the edge of her bed. She felt unsteady and used one hand on the night-table for support. The other, she used to push off the bed. As she looked down at her feet in the dim light filtering in past the blinds, Jeff saw she wore pink sweatpants. Her feet were bare, her toenails painted.

Cute feet! Once again, he'd neglected to control his thoughts.

Mindi looked furtively around the room, and Jeff admonished himself for thinking like a stalker. He had to wake up from this dream, leave her alone, especially because her first destination would be the bathroom! Jeff sensed her vulnerability.

Mindi turned toward the bathroom.

Jeff awoke next to the sleeping Charlene. *Phew! That was close.* He looked at the clock: 4:33 a.m. Back in his reality, Jeff felt grateful for two things: Shirley was gone, and he hadn't had to accompany Mindi to the bathroom.

Jeff thought like an analyst. If this happened again—and somehow, he knew it would—he had to find the pattern in the "dream program" that would enable him to leave the dreams at will. When they were both there in what he now called "the gray room," they were both asleep and dreaming, so their times of day would probably match-up—except for the two-year difference. When he slept and dropped into her head during her daytime, their clock times, of course, wouldn't match—an interesting datapoint, but it didn't explain the mechanism of the dreams.

He slid open the nightstand drawer, pulled out the notebook and pen, being careful not to make a sound, then went straight into the bathroom and shut the door. He needed privacy in which to organize his thoughts. The first item he wrote was his insight on how their times of day matched up.

The rest of his list, numbered:

2. Mindi can hear me if I think "out loud," but doesn't seem to hear if I make it a point to only think to myself. How does that work?

3. Shirley was there, confronted me directly. But now, gone.

4. Who can I talk to? What if I called Dr. Singh? NO! Consider the year difference.

5. Are these dreams only a product of my subconscious, or is this real time travel where I see real people in the past?

6. If this is reality and my mission was to help Mindi, have I completed my mission?

7. Who is in control of these dreams? Is this a programmed mission? Who's bidding am I doing?

He stared at his notebook. The conflict between believing the dreams to be reality or just intricate dreams started again. Once again, he ran the inventory of key datapoints of her as a real person, seeing a live shrink, working in a real restaurant. He paused, gathering his thoughts. *The time isn't real, though. The date difference doesn't make sense. Time travel just isn't possible.*

In this argument with himself, he'd lose one side or the other.

Movement sounded from beyond the door. Charlene was up. He stashed the notebook in the vanity under the towels, opened the door, and gave her a warm smile, which she returned. After a hug and a kiss, they fixed breakfast, got ready for the day, and each went to their respective jobs.

~

Tonight, as Jeff kicked off his slippers before getting into bed, he thought about how Mindi's trust in men had been hijacked by her father. Because they'd both been in the dream when Shirley had been yelling at her, he wondered if he'd eventually meet her in a dream face-to-face. He resolved if that happened, he would avoid anything that would cause her fear. In fact, he would like to help build her self-confidence.

As sleep overtook him, he began falling, and the grayness enveloped him. When he began to float, he heard Kelly Clarkson's "Heartbeat Song." He recognized the tune and the lyrics.

Mindi was wearing earphones. He saw the earphone cords as they swung in and out of view while she vacuumed the carpet in her living room—barefoot again. She pushed and pulled the small vacuum back and forth between the table and chair legs, singing along with the song, feeling alive and reborn and dancing to the beat while she vacuumed.

When the song ended on the iPod, she shut it off, and then the vacuum, and stood in the middle of the room surveying her work with satisfaction.

Jeff felt so pleased that he thought, *She seems so much better now Shirley's gone!*

Mindi must've heard him because she closed her eyes and put her hands over them. Then he heard her thoughts: *There it is again. Please, no.* She slumped in the chair, closed her eyes, and rubbed her temples.

Jeff quieted his mind, sorry to have caused her distress. He sat with her in silence and heard her next thought. *That was the voice of the man in my dream.*

That startled Jeff. He *had* to control himself.

Mindi centered herself with deep breaths, which quieted her thoughts. After a few moments, she opened her eyes and glanced at her wristwatch: ten thirty.

Time to get ready for the doctor.

Jeff noticed how fast she'd recovered from her previous mood.

She stood up and started for the hallway.

In the part of his mind where he could think and she couldn't hear him, he thought, *I hope she doesn't want to take a shower while I'm here.*

Mindi paused on her way to the bathroom, and Jeff heard her think, *I don't need a shower this morning. I'm fine . . . just wash up . . . put on makeup and go.*

Jeff realized that although she couldn't hear him from that space, she still felt what he thought there on a subconscious level. If he could control himself, even though he couldn't choose to be there, he could at least be careful and not scare her. He could go along for the ride, observe undetected, until he woke up.

Mindi stopped and looked at herself in the hallway mirror. Jeff somehow knew it had been her mother's, and she'd kept it after her father died. Mindi leaned forward and looked into her eyes as if she felt that if she looked hard enough, she might see the answer to why she had these voices and odd feelings.

Her alluring dark eyes, framed with long lashes and set in unblemished skin, enchanted Jeff. Her lustrous hair, pulled back in a ponytail, and the small gold hoops in her pierced ears added to his appreciation.

In that private place in his mind, he thought, *She's gorgeous. She could be a model!*

Mindi stepped back from the mirror. She wasn't scared, but her thoughts, clear enough for Jeff to hear, showed him she'd received the message subliminally.

Well, Mom did tell me I could be a model. Not the runway kind—my legs aren't long enough—but makeup or hair. Hmm. I sure miss Mom.

Mindi's sadness for her mom touched the same place in Jeff's heart for his own mother.

He was amazed how close their thoughts had lined up. With such an emotionally powerful subject, he really had to keep his mind quiet. He enjoyed being with Mindi. *She's a good person. I wish I could meet her.*

She stepped away from the mirror and rubbed her eyes again. He reminded himself to quit analyzing. He didn't choose to be here; this is where his dream had taken him, but he didn't want to leave.

Jeff stayed with her as she took the bus and walked the block and a half to the doctor's office. She took the stairs to the second-floor office and opened the door. A door chime announced her arrival.

Mindi looked toward the receptionist's window, met the girl's eyes, and announced herself. "Mindi Ketchem. One o'clock." She stepped up to the window.

Jeff wanted to see the date so he could see how their days were lining up. Obligingly, she looked down at the appointment book and her eyes settled on the date: Monday, July 13, 2015. She glanced at the first appointment that afternoon, and Jeff saw her name printed with care between the lines. Her doctor's appointments were on Monday, he noted.

"Please, have a seat. Doctor apologizes; she's running a

couple minutes late, but she won't keep you waiting long."

Jeff's view went gray, and he woke up, surprised that the dream ended so suddenly and disappointed that he'd miss Mindi telling the doctor about her dream that Shirley was gone.

He recorded the dream in his notebook, added that he'd discovered how better to control what she could hear of his thoughts, and made another list:

> *Hypothesis 1: These dreams still might only be manufactured by my mind—The Kelly Clarkson song: Charlie has the album. It's about dreaming and being brand new. Too coincidental. I put that in the dream.*
> *Hypothesis 2: Why am I having these dreams about real places and a woman who has a problem? Do I need to be a rescuer? What problem of mine am I trying to work out by helping someone else?*
> *Question: If I can do this analysis, why can't I analyze what's wrong with me? Do I need to talk with someone? Who? A shrink? Charlene? Dad? How could I explain it?'*

He looked at the clock, then put the binder in the bottom of his nightstand drawer, wondering what the next installment of his dreams would reveal.

CHAPTER 7

The next evening, while Jeff watched a documentary about bears on the TV, he fell asleep on the couch. He transitioned from falling to floating to again being in Dr. Ananya Singh's reception area. Jeff watched, listened, and tried to keep Mindi from being aware of his presence.

She stood at the receptionist's window. The receptionist must have said something to Mindi just before Jeff arrived. He felt a flash of uneasiness from Mindi, but only for an instant, and her newly found serenity returned.

Mindi took a seat in the waiting room and sorted through the magazines in the neat, fanned-out stack on the table next to her. She pulled one out of the middle, being careful to maintain the orderly pattern of those that remained. *People Magazine*, June 22, 2015, had a popular actress on the cover. She idled through the magazine, stopping every page or two to look at a photo or read a caption.

Ads with female models drew her interest. When she came to one, she opened the magazine wide and held the picture of the model in full view. Jeff watched as she scanned the model's face, analyzing the photo. Her gaze darted from the model's eyes to the woman's lips, then to her hair. She finished with a glance at the angle of the model's head and neck.

The evaluation complete, she turned the pages until she got to the end of the magazine, then flipped back to the table of contents at the front.

"The doctor is ready now, Miss Ketchem," the receptionist announced.

Mindi put the magazine neatly back in the stack and walked into the doctor's office. Jeff felt Mindi's comfortable familiarity with the pattern of the visits.

The doctor sat in her wingback chair, one leg crossed over at her knee, notebook on her lap with a gold Cross pen resting on top. "Hi, Mindi. My apologies if I kept you waiting."

"No worries, Doctor," she said with confidence as she sat down.

The subject of the doctor's apology suggested to Jeff that tonight's dream might pick up where his dream left off last night. Maybe he wouldn't miss Mindi telling the story of Shirley's vanquishment.

"Mindi, I've been going over my notes. I'd like to review them with you. We've already talked about this, but I like to review so that we can both agree how you've progressed with our sessions, and especially where we might place emphasis going forward. Is that all right?"

"Yes, Doctor. Fine."

The doctor summarized their past sessions. When she said that they'd met every week, Mindi politely pointed out that during one of those weeks the doctor had taken time off, and she'd had a two-week break between sessions.

Jeff noted Mindi's confidence and politeness in correcting her doctor and her aptitude for precision and detail. She had a good memory.

The doctor looked up at her and smiled. "You're right. You've been quite diligent in keeping your appointments. That's good." She then flipped to a blank page in her notebook. "And you haven't sensed Shirley in your mind since I prescribed the medication for you, right?"

"No, just in my dreams, like we talked about."

The doctor looked at Mindi for a moment, then flipped back through the notes. "Right. Now, you've had two dreams, one in which you said you couldn't hear her, the next one where you could hear Shirley and the same man talking."

"Yes, and I've had another dream since my last visit here. I want to share it today."

"Good. Now there are three dreams. Please, go on."

Mindi settled back in her chair and began. Jeff watched and listened as Mindi told the doctor the dream, beginning with Shirley yelling at her and then about his interchange with Shirley.

The doctor held up her hand to ask Mindi to pause while she finished her notes.

Then Dr. Singh said, "I'd like to go back to the beginning for a moment. Did her yelling upset you?"

"Well, no one likes to be yelled at."

"Were you scared?"

"It was only a dream. She couldn't hurt me."

"What did you say to her, Mindi?"

"Nothing. She yelled at me, never gave me a chance to say a word."

"Please, go on from where you left off." The doctor looked down at her notes and read back to Mindi, "Then he appeared behind Shirley. She turned and yelled at him. He said he didn't know what he was doing there . . ."

Mindi nodded. "Right. Shirley yelled at him again, and he just looked at her with a sympathetic, compassionate expression.

He didn't show anger and didn't seem afraid of her either. He didn't react to anything she said. He acted kind toward her, told her I didn't need her. He gave her a hug, but she didn't hug him. She just froze, like a statue. Then she dissolved—like, evaporated. He turned and looked at me for a moment, and I woke up."

Jeff had no memory of turning to look at her.

The doctor reflected on her notes for a few seconds, then looked up. "Mindi, you seem very sure of what you saw. Dreams seem to fade, yet you are very certain of what they said and what happened."

"Yes, Doctor. It's all still clear. Like I'm still there. It was real."

"Is there anything else?"

"Well, I knew I was dreaming while I was standing there facing Shirley and then watching them talk. The part I remember best is that he didn't argue. He was kind to her."

"Have you had those kinds of dreams before?"

"No. I remember thinking, *This is a dream. That's Shirley.* And that he looked and acted like a nice guy, the way he, well, the way he handled the situation."

The doctor made a few more notes. "Any thoughts about Shirley? You said you're sure she's gone. Like she's been . . . Let's see, in your notes you used the word 'exorcised.' Do you still feel that way?"

"Yes, Doctor. She was gone from my head after I started taking the pills you gave me. But now I feel, well, like I've had a terrible headache, and now my head is clear. I'm not afraid. No, that dream when she disappeared was . . ." She paused. "Like I had a laxative, and I'm cleaned out. He flushed her."

The doctor smiled at Mindi's sense of humor. "That's an interesting way to put it, Mindi."

Jeff suppressed a laugh.

"Mindi, you're still taking the medication, right?"

Mindi nodded.

"Since you say you're managing well, let's do a little test. Cut the pill in half and take half of what I prescribed. Do that for a week, then if you're still doing well, maybe we can take you off it. You seem strong. Now, if you get nervous, feel afraid, start hearing voices again, don't be shy. Increase your dose, and keep your notes on your feelings. I'm pleased with the progress you've made."

Mindi smiled. "Thank you, Doctor. Me too. I couldn't have gotten here without you."

"Let's still meet and discuss your feelings. I want you to consider continuing our sessions to address any issues you may have regarding your parents."

"Okay, Doctor. I do want to talk a little more about that, but I think I've forgiven my father."

"Good, Mindi. We'll pick up there next week. Anything else?"

As they left the building, Mindi—with Jeff tagging along for the ride—sensed her positive vibe now that her fear of Shirley was gone. Jeff thought about her goal of becoming a model. She had something to look forward to.

During the walk to the bus stop, he enjoyed being with her and wondered what was next on her agenda today. But he never found out. He awoke on the couch to a documentary on the TV—not the one about bears to which he'd fallen asleep, but one about honeybee die-offs. Apparently, he'd been asleep for some time. He straightened up, rolled his head around to work out the soreness from using the arm of the couch for a pillow, and headed into the bedroom. He'd write in his notebook in the morning, confident that he'd remember it all. He slept the sleep of the innocent.

~

The next morning, Jeff took his time trying to get everything about Mindi's last doctor visit down with accuracy. As he reread his journal entries, it felt to him like he'd watched a TV series about a young woman on the threshold of beginning a new life after a troubled start. He'd had a part, albeit a tiny part, in why Mindi felt free now. She'd done all the work. He'd just ignored Shirley's anger and given her a hug, then watched as Mindi's fears melted away. *The heroine wins her battle and, like a storybook ending, can now live happily ever after.* That last visit to her doctor was the final scene that tied everything together. *Now she's ready to launch.* Like any good story, the characters seemed real. The story was over, and Jeff felt happy for the character he'd created in his mind. With that thought, he put the notebook deep in the drawer and left his apartment.

~

For two weeks Jeff had had no free-falling dreams, but tonight he fell again in the all-enveloping gray. As he descended, he wondered again about the significance of the gray. If he was going to snap into someone's head, why not just go straight there? He was still curious about how it worked to get from 2017 to 2015 and then to occupy space in Mindi Ketchem's mind while he dreamed.

Just as that thought formed, he found himself back in Mindi's spotless apartment, sitting at her 1980s reproduction oak table, with matching chairs and seat-pads. Had it been her parent's dining room set? His virtual hand went over his virtual mouth to silence his commentary. He had to be careful. Once again, he saw with her eyes and heard with her ears. A radio or stereo played soft instrumental guitar music.

Mindi looked around and brushed her hand across her forehead.

She feels me here.

As soon as he thought that, she turned and looked behind her—a reminder for him to keep his thoughts in that private part of his mind where she couldn't hear him.

With a shake of her head, she turned her attention back to the application form in front of her, filling in her name, address, phone number.

Is this real? Not just a dream? He'd try to remember everything and look it up later. What was the application for?

If he could see the banner at the top, he'd know. She continued to fill in the blanks on the form. Then, almost like she wanted to show him what he'd asked to see, she looked up at the top of the form long enough for him to read, *Monroe Cosmetology Institute, Los Angeles.*

She's filling out an application for beauty school!

Mindi smiled. Jeff noticed that their feelings and emotions became closer the more often he visited her. He could see, hear, and smell, as well as feel the chair beneath her, almost sensing what it was like to be her. His denial of her reality faded as his interest in her as a person increased.

She finished filling out the form and checked both sides for completeness, then turned it over and signed it. Her signature had flair. The date? July 31, 2015.

I wish I could see her address.

With that thought, she turned it over and scanned the address with her finger as if checking it for accuracy.

He read it over, pausing at the zip code: 90248.

She folded the form, put it into a postage-paid envelope, and slid a cashier's check drawn on the Bank of California into the envelope before sealing it.

Mindi walked to the window and watched a couple holding hands while walking on the sidewalk. She gave a deep sigh, then smiled. *I'm going to do it!*

Jeff felt her satisfaction at the thought.

She returned to the table, sat down, and looked at a yellow legal notepad on which she'd written:

My Two-Year Plan:
August 2015:
Cosmetology school
2016:
Cosmetology State Boards
Modeling School
Headshots
Get Agent
2017:
On my way!

Jeff felt pleased that she'd set her goals. *She'll do it*, he thought. Mindi nodded.

Without planning to leave the dream, Jeff awoke. As he swung his feet over the bed and reached for his notepad, he smiled and wondered if he'd learn how to apply makeup.

He jotted down her address: 2511 Marine Drive, Apt.__, Gardena, 90248. How could he have forgotten the apartment number? The date next to her neatly written signature had been July 31, 2015. He kept writing: *Miranda J. Ketchem. Bank of California. She's going to the Monroe Cosmetology Institute, Los Angeles.*

Later today he'd find out if the school was real.

His phone dinged. A text from Charlie: *Dinner tonight? Got some news.*

He thumbed the screen, sent back a big-smile emoji and typed:

Sure, call you later?

The reply came back right away with a thumbs-up emoji in the upper right of his text.

Good, now *he* had something to look forward to today. He dressed and went to work.

~

The warm August evening on Alki Beach made for pleasant dining. They sat outside, overlooking the Seattle skyline across the expanse of Elliott Bay, and Charlie snuggled next to him as they drank their cocktails. They watched the dance of the lights from the Great Wheel, the majestic Space Needle, and the twinkle of the ferry cabin lights as they crisscrossed the bay. Other diners sat nearby, but it felt that the restaurant was just for them.

"Well?" he asked. "Are you going to keep me in suspense the rest of the night?"

She smiled across the top of her glass, her eyes sparkling with excitement. "Okay." She took another drink. "I've got a temporary assignment at our office in Santa Monica."

He set down his glass. "That's great. What'll you be doing? How long will you be down there?"

Charlene placed her glass on the table and looked away for a moment as she reached for the nachos. Balancing a loaded chip covered with nacho filling, she looked back up and poised the bite in front of him, offering it with a smile.

"Oh, maybe a few weeks." The bite disappeared into his mouth. She dabbed at the corners of his mouth with her napkin, then her eyes met his.

He worked hard not to betray anything except his support, but he didn't want to be without her for any extended period.

"That's great," he said. "What's the gig? What's 'a few weeks' mean? I'm going to miss you."

"Well . . ." She drew out her response by answering the last question first. "A lot depends on how we can organize the project. It's for a new client, and my boss told me today that I'm a perfect fit to work with the group there in Santa Monica."

Jeff nodded, both agreeing and understanding.

"Here's the serious part: it'll be a *huge* account, and they want to *super* fast-track this project. *Super* fast-track. We've got a little over two months to get it off the ground."

The extra emphasis wasn't lost on Jeff. He frowned in confusion. "*Super fast-track*," he said reflectively. "You've never used that term before."

"The client had originally planned to announce their product line next Valentine's Day," she explained. "That would've put the project on the fast track, but their production line is way ahead of schedule, and they wanted to know if we had the capabilities to meet a pre-holiday launch. Before Thanksgiving, for this Christmas.

"So our management said, 'Absolutely.' One step beyond fast-track is super fast-track. This is going to be huge."

Jeff's eyebrows rose. "Wow. Even with our products, there's a minimum of three to five months after beta testing before official release. And ours is simple. Our ads are in trade magazines and are business-oriented. Aren't their customers wholesale and retail outlets, with lots of moving parts? I don't doubt that you can, but how *will* you do it?"

She waved her hand. "They're giving me an unlimited budget. Money can move mountains. They need someone like me to head the project. I've got a great staff here, plus the whole crew down there. We've already contacted the media alerting them to a huge new client. It'll mean superb profits for them. Television, and all the internet angles such as YouTube, Facebook, Twitter, all the rest. Billboards, even Jumbotron in Times Square. The major sport venues this fall and after the New Year, Super Bowl ads . . . the works! It's so exciting. The client and my management said we'll pay whatever it takes to move this thing forward. Class A treatment."

"Wow. What a great opportunity for you."

"Aaaaaand," she said, grinning, "if it goes well—and there's no reason it shouldn't, even considering the time frame—we'll have the national account for at least two more years. And the whole thing will be *my* baby." She finished with a triumphant wave of her hands.

"I'm impressed," Jeff said, drawn into her excitement. "Will you have to move down there?" He foresaw this having a major impact on their relationship but remained upbeat for Charlene.

"No, I don't think so. Lead account managers"—she pointed to herself by waving both index fingers at herself—"choose their own headquarters, and Seattle is *my* town." Her eyes sparkled with excitement.

"That calls for a refill." Jeff caught the server's eye and signaled with his glass raised. He realized their relationship would have to adjust, but it would be great for her.

Several questions came to mind. What to ask first?

Expecting the question, she said with pride, "The account is LaDormeur Cosmetics. They're new on the scene, but they've got huge backing. For all intents and purposes, they're really, uh—" She paused for the right word, then settled for a cliché with no attempt to apologize for it. "Trendy, and New Age." She shrugged. "Of course, nobody says New Age anymore, but everyone can see they'll be huge, and fantastic for the agency, and me." She raised her glass in a mock toast to herself and added with a coy smile, "And you. What's good for me is good for you, no?" She sipped her drink, holding his gaze.

That she'd included Jeff in the toast wasn't lost on him.

Charlene wasn't usually so flamboyant—letting her ego loose like this—so some of the grandeur might have been the alcohol. Still, this was truly great news. He was proud that she wanted to share it with him.

He gave her a tender nod, raised his glass in a real toast, and said, "To the future."

She returned the toast with a nod and more eye contact, then they sampled more of their appetizer.

The combination of Charlene's excitement, the alcohol, and the romantic setting delayed Jeff's analysis of the subject of her project—cosmetics. When he did pause and give it a quick thought, he figured it was simply another coincidence, but he could examine that more tomorrow.

Tonight he wanted to continue riding the positive wave of her grand announcement. When they got back to his apartment, the passion was indescribable.

CHAPTER 8

Over a cup of coffee, yogurt, and toast for breakfast the next morning, Charlene said, "Since I'm going to be down in Santa Monica for at least a couple of weeks, why don't you come down on Friday night? We can spend the weekend together before I have to get back to work on Monday."

"That's a great idea." He considered the logistics with no hesitation. "That'll be fun. It's been a couple of years since I've been to LA."

Charlene smiled. "If you get your tickets soon, you might still get a good price." She was in full business mode.

He nodded, then leaned over and kissed her. The conversation moved on to their plans for the rest of the day together.

Toward the end of the afternoon, Charlene announced she needed all the next day, Sunday, to prepare to head down to Santa Monica. They picked up a pizza for dinner and took it back to Charlie's to eat. She assured him she'd text him when she arrived in LA and would stay in touch during the week.

Jeff went home, opened a beer and his laptop, and made his reservations. What to do with the rest of the evening? He unburied his notebook from the bottom of his nightstand

drawer, anticipating, even hoping, that he might need it in the morning. He was curious about what had been thrust upon him with these dreams and wished he could predict when he'd time travel again. The word "cosmetics" returned to the front of his mind.

Jeff didn't keep any secrets from Charlene, except this one. Everyone had a secret they'd never share with even their closest friend or partner. This one, a true enigma, was his. If he shared it, they'd lock him away tighter than someone convicted of a Class A felony.

He wondered, now that his tacit acceptance of travel into the past was mostly settled, could he travel into the future? But as soon as the thought materialized, he pushed it away. He had enough on his plate. His scientific mind was busy trying to develop the empirical data from the dreams: How long was he falling? How long did he float? How much time between visits? What was the correlation between dates and times? Sleep overtook him, and many questions remained unanswered.

~

Falling, floating. Grayness. He'd get no hard data tonight because there were no reference points while falling and floating. The time clock didn't start until he dropped in on Mindi and he joined her time scale.

Mindi sat taking notes in a classroom with a dozen other people. Young women and a couple of young men sat at tables in front of her. As before, when he dropped in on her, she rubbed her forehead, pressed her temples, and closed her eyes. A well-dressed instructor talked about color matching, skin-tone types, and a bunch of other stuff he didn't understand. He kept his mind muted so he could observe.

His first choice for an evening's entertainment wouldn't be a lecture on color. Neither, he rationalized, had been being a server at Denny's. Yet he'd learned things about a restaurant that made him appreciate the efforts of service industry workers. His knowledge of cosmetology, up to this point, had been limited to the scent of a woman's hair and the taste of her lipstick, so since he'd been summoned here, he'd pay attention.

Mindi sat alone in the back row because, as Jeff already knew, she didn't like anyone sitting behind her. Although Jeff thought in the private part of his mind, he knew she felt it. She looked to her left and right, then gave her head a shake.

Wanting to help her relax, he took a deep, virtual breath. He knew she felt it because she took a deep breath and relaxed. She looked at her watch; its little window showed *Tue 8*.

The homework Mindi needed to do before next class had been written on the whiteboard. She copied it in her notebook under the heading, *For 9/10*.

The tutor dismissed class a few minutes early, and as she and the other students stood, a gentle buzz of conversation filled the air. Mindi picked up her notebook, tucked it into her flowered book-bag, zipped it shut, and pulled it over her shoulder in one movement. As she turned to go, a young man approached. Jeff judged him to be about her age.

"Mindi," the guy said, "d'ya want to grab a soda or a sandwich in the canteen?" Before she could reply, he added, "That is, unless you have to be somewhere."

He could've been a little more confident, Jeff thought, but he didn't give off bad vibes. *This could be promising.*

Mindi hesitated for a moment, glanced at her watch, then looked back up at him. "Oh, thanks, Daniel. I do have to go. Maybe another time?"

Daniel didn't act rejected. He just smiled and said, "Yeah, no sweat." Then he turned toward the door, showing no attitude or negative body language.

Jeff sensed Mindi feeling that Daniel didn't match her type— not enough self-assurance. Mindi had learned to be cautious in all circumstances, so she didn't head toward the door until he'd left the room.

Jeff tried to analyze why he was here to witness this brief, casual interchange between them. He concluded that Mindi was setting and maintaining her standards for a relationship with a man. Dr. Singh had talked about establishing healthy relationships, and Mindi wasn't willing to settle for less. She'd give it time to find her perfect soulmate. He remembered when Charlene and he'd met. Neither of them were looking for a steady relationship, and that worked out well. Give it time.

An image of Charlene formed in his head, and he woke up back in his own bedroom in 2017 and resumed his analysis. He'd thought about Charlie, and the dream ended. Cause and effect? Was thinking of Charlene all he needed to do to end a dream?

He sat up, turned on the lamp, and wrote in his notebook: *The visit before, she'd just filled out the application for school. Now she's already in class. That's a big jump in time. July to September.* He documented the night's dream and his thoughts about what he'd witnessed, then added a note in the style of a programmer or experimenter:

Try individual name of the subject "Mindi" to start dream, and "Charlene" to end dream. Target specific destination date. If successful, test-target future dreams using same technique.

He looked at the clock, saw he could get a couple more hours of sleep, and lay back in bed.

⁓

Jeff told Craig about next weekend's jaunt to Los Angeles. Because Craig grew up there, Jeff asked where he and Charlene should eat.

Craig chuckled. "Well, I can tell you about a bunch of pizza places where if you're underage you could get a beer—if they haven't been closed down. No, I've been gone too long. Check Yelp. They'll tell you what's trendy. Plenty of restaurants there have a great view of the ocean. Very romantic." He kept his smile and added a wink.

Jeff now treated his time traveling like a hobby. He wanted to learn as much as he could of time travel and dreams. Since Charlie would be out of town a lot, he could both fill his time and get some answers. He'd done a little studying on the subject online and at the library, but he now had time to do more.

During his research, he revisited the time travel paradox. If a time traveler wanted to go back in time and kill his grandfather before his father was born, then if he was successful, the traveler would never be born. But if he wasn't born, he wouldn't go back and kill the grandfather, and if grandfather wasn't killed, he'd be born to go back and kill him, and the do-loop would go on forever; therefore, a paradox. Fiction authors for decades had used various literary devices to avoid invoking such a paradox in their stories.

If all of this was somehow real for Jeff, and not just a dream, then the pseudo-physics invented by fiction writers would be invalid. Real science wasn't much help either. Physicists said time travel, on a non-quantum basis, wasn't possible, unless wormholes or Einstein's "spooky action at a distance" were involved—and that was still just theory. Even if that kind of time travel was possible, none of that would explain Jeff's experiences.

His mind raced. If visiting someone in the past was possible, even in dreams, then what he did there could affect history, even in a limited way. Hadn't he influenced Mindi's behavior in 2015 by prompting her to enroll in beauty school? That would affect her future. What about others? If she would've done that anyway, without Jeff's prompting, his thoughts wouldn't have influenced her, right? He argued with himself again, but neither side would win.

How big a difference could his activities make on the future? Was there danger of activating the butterfly effect? Now a science cliché that originated from a facetious scientific theory and a science fiction short story. Neither were open to scientific scrutiny.

In his research, Jeff had come across the speculative science presented by meteorologist Edward Lorenz in 1961. Lorenz suggested, metaphorically speaking, that the air disturbed by a butterfly flapping its wings today (the cause) could influence a tornado weeks later (the effect).

Jeff's sci-fi interests had exposed him before to the 1958 science fiction short story by Ray Bradbury titled "A Sound of Thunder." In the story, an into-the-past time traveler inadvertently killed a prehistoric butterfly, and that act significantly changed the future, millions of years later.

Jeff's musings that he might damage the space-time continuum and change history led to him verbally admonishing himself to control his ego by saying, "Thinking pretty highly of yourself, aren't you, Jeffy-boy, that you can change the future of humanity?" He said it loud enough that someone could've heard him, but luckily, being alone in the hallway at work, no one heard. If he wasn't careful, people would think he was as crazy as he was beginning to think he was.

~

Jeff decided to experiment trying to initiate and target his dream visits. He went to sleep thinking Mindi's name. The test dreams began with the usual enveloping gray-out, falling, then floating, and his view opened onto Mindi in one of her classes. This happened twice, on different days. The experiment worked.

Each time Mindi showed she knew when he arrived by rubbing her temples and eyes. He could choose to visit her but could not target a set day or time—yet. He ended each visit by thinking Charlene's name three times.

~

On the third night of Jeff's directed destination tests, he went to sleep intentionally thinking about Dr. Singh and Mindi, and he successfully joined them in the middle of a counseling session.

"And Mindi, have you had any more dreams?" the doctor said.

"You mean dreams with Shirley and the man?"

"Do you want to talk about them?"

"I haven't really thought about them for a while. I don't know what I'd say. I'm sure Shirley's gone. I haven't dreamed about the guy again, though I think I'd like to," she said with a smile.

When Mindi said no more, the doctor said, "Carl Jung, one of the pioneers in psychiatry, had a theory of the unconscious. He saw dreams as a way for the self to communicate from one's unconscious to their consciousness." The doctor waited to see if Mindi understood.

"Wasn't Freud the inventor of psychiatry?"

"Well, he developed a lot of the techniques, yes, but Jung and Freud collaborated. Jung also studied in India, where I first studied. Much of psychiatry is based on both of their work. Anyway, I feel that your dreaming may, in fact, validate Jung's ideas. Your dreams have helped you make progress."

Mindi, liking to know how things worked, said, "So what you're saying is that in my dreams, I made up the dream guy. And he told Shirley, who I also made up, that I'm okay. And then Shirley went away."

Dr. Singh nodded. "If by 'made up' you mean they were constructs of your unconscious created to work out your conflicts, yes, I think so. I feel sure that Shirley was there to protect you, although in an aggressive way that frightened you. You worked it out yourself by having the man confront her. You said that you feel free of her."

"They worked it out, right?" Mindi said.

The doctor smiled. "I see what you mean, but not exactly. The 'they' you're talking about are actually part of you. So you worked it out for yourself." It appeared that the doctor wanted to be sure that Mindi understood that these were not external entities invading her mind.

Jeff understood what the doctor meant. He'd recently learned what the doctor had explained to Mindi while doing research on lucid dreaming. One of Jung's archetypes was the "shadow-self" which the unconscious constructs from repressed ideas, weaknesses, and fears. If we acknowledge and embrace the shadow-self, it loses its influence over us. Shirley was Mindi's shadow-self. The doctor thought that Shirley and he were both created by Mindi to play "good cop, bad cop" to help heal herself. But Jeff had come from Mindi's future—he wasn't someone she'd constructed—and when he'd literally embraced Mindi's shadow-self in their dreams, he'd reduced her power over Mindi.

Jeff mused, with a smile, that if the doctor ever knew the reality of their situation, she'd need a shrink herself.

The doctor continued, "You have made excellent progress, but I need to remind you that you may still feel vulnerable to events of your past."

Jeff's dream ended right there. He would've liked to have seen the rest of the session, but satisfied with the doctor's analysis that Mindi had made significant progress, he accepted he was done for the night.

As he finished his dream documentation, Jeff remembered other things he'd learned during his dream research, and he summarized them in his journal, along with some musings about the how or why of the mechanism that created his experiences. He wrote:

> *Jung wrote that even if one feels a "universal mind" exists, it is merely an assertion—not a fact without scientific proof. Jung also wrote of a "collective unconscious," which has been used as an explanation for the similarity of world religions shared by societies in common throughout the ages. So, if a universal mind does exist, it may communicate with us through our "collective unconscious." So is it the universal mind that's causing my dreams?*

He hoped he'd be able to verify his hypothesis at some point, but he couldn't guess how. After storing the notebook, he went back to sleep.

⁓

Jeff put in an intense workout at the gym with weights and swimming freestyle laps. He ate a salad at home while he watched the last half of a documentary on whales, then went to bed so tired that he had no thoughts of a visit to Mindi.

The dream started with a brief sensation of falling, transitioning to floating, then the grayness cleared. He expected to see through Mindi's eyes, but instead saw through his own eyes in the gray room. Anxiety followed an initial flash of disappointment, because Shirley had confronted him in the same setting and he didn't want to see her again.

He stood alone on the monochromatic gray floor, wearing the same colorless clothes. An indeterminate distance away in all directions was the horizon. Should he end the dream by saying Charlene's name? Silently, a door opening appeared some distance in front of him. A figure, backlit by a lighter gray background, walked toward him. It was Mindi. Jeff felt a knot of nervousness at the possibility of confrontation with someone he'd been—albeit unwillingly—spying on until now. He suppressed the feeling by reminding himself he'd handled talking with Shirley successfully.

She wore clean, white athletic shoes, proper length work slacks and her black Denny's uniform shirt, well pressed, with her name tag. Her order pad and two pens sat upright in her apron's right-side pocket. Their eyes met. She surveyed him as he examined her, from shoes to face. She didn't smile, but neither did she show signs of fear. He saw instead curiosity in her eyes.

Whose dream was he in? Or were they in each other's dream?

He let her take the lead, because his prime directive was to not do anything that would make her afraid. So far so good, since she showed confidence in the way she walked toward him—head up, arms relaxed by her side, taking short, ladylike steps. She stopped about ten feet in front of him. The doorway behind her disappeared.

She spoke softly. "Who are you?"

He waited for her to say more. When she didn't, he said,

"My name is Jeff."

"I've seen you before. I watched you talking with Shirley."

While contemplating whether her statement required an answer, he maintained eye contact without being threatening. He nodded.

"Why are you here?"

He wanted to be honest. But to do so, he'd have to be conversational. For now, he let her take the lead and ask questions; he would answer.

He said, "I don't know."

"Your name is Jeff, but you didn't tell me who you are." She paused. "Who are you to me? Are you a part of me?"

Truth must prevail. "I'm a friend."

"What are you doing here?"

"Visiting you."

"Have you visited with me before?"

Jeff didn't answer. He waited to see if she would repeat the question.

"I'm not afraid of Shirley anymore," she said in a matter-of-fact way. Short pause. "Were you afraid of her?" She spoke as if she expected an answer.

"No."

"Good. I think she's gone."

"Good." He smiled, wanting her to feel at ease.

"I'm not afraid of you."

"That's good, because I'm your friend."

She considered his reply while she looked into his eyes. "Why are you here?"

"I don't know. And I don't know where 'here' is." He looked around, then back at her.

"This is my dream," she said. "You were here before. And you . . ." She stopped, as if she couldn't find the words. "You were kind to her, and she went away. I wanted her to go away. You made her go away. Why are you here now?"

"I don't know. It just happened."

She tilted her head as if trying to understand. She said nothing.

"May I ask you a question?" Jeff said.

"What?"

"What day was it when you went to bed tonight?"

"Why?"

"It's important so I can answer your question of why I'm here. Do you remember what day it is?"

"What do you mean?" She looked at him, puzzled.

Jeff tilted his head forward, urging her to answer, and put his hands palms up in a non-threatening movement, indicating he wanted an answer. "Please."

She closed her eyes tight, as if to trying to remember. "I think it's September . . . sixteenth. Why?"

"What year?"

Mindi, slow to reply, said, "It's 2015. Why?"

"I, well, I ask you to trust me, and I promise I'll explain, but later."

She nodded assent and took a breath. Her eyes met his and she smiled. After the short pause, she said, "Well, friend-Jeff. I feel you're honest. You ask strange questions, but you're welcome here."

The look on her face showed she had something more to say. He waited.

She kept her eye contact with him, stood up straight, and with total confidence in her voice, she said, "And you're handsome too."

She smiled, put up her right hand, and gave a little wave. Her image dissolved into fluttering, colorful glitter.

Jeff watched it settle, but it never reached the floor.

He stood there for a moment, looking at where she'd stood. She hadn't vanished like Shirley did. She seemed to know this was a dream and wasn't afraid of him.

His view turned gray and he awoke.

~

Jeff opened his eyes, feeling astounded by what he'd just dreamed. *What? Why? How?* Unafraid, she'd answered his questions about the date, then flattered him. Or had she flirted with him? In the dream, she seemed in control. What was going on?

He took his notebook into the kitchen, turned on the light, made himself a cup of coffee, and wrote the whole interchange. Tonight's entry ended with: *Last two visits were a month later for her. Our dates are no longer two years apart. Is this significant?*

When he finished, he looked at the kitchen clock: 1:24 a.m. He realized he'd had coffee and might not get back to sleep. He had to be at the airport early. Resigned to being awake, knowing he could nap on the plane, he turned on the TV in his bedroom, prepared to watch an adventure movie until he needed to get ready and go. But he fell asleep.

CHAPTER 9

At 4:30 a.m., Jeff awoke to his alarm. He arrived at the airport feeling alert and refreshed, with plenty of time to buy a magazine at concessions. Ever since Rick's death, he acknowledged this newly acquired anxiety about flying and needed something to distract himself during the flight.

After an uneventful flight, he arrived at LAX and picked up his rental car. His phone's map program claimed a fifteen-minute drive to the address on Mindi's application. Gardena was in the opposite direction from Santa Monica, where Charlene worked, but he'd pick her up, at the earliest, at four o'clock. He had plenty of time to play detective.

Jeff hoped that Mindi Ketchem, a.k.a. Craig's cousin, might still live in Gardena. "Dream Mindi" had become very real to him, and he needed to know if they were the same person. He drove past her address, noting that the mailboxes were accessible. But would he find her name on one of them? He found a place to park half a block from her building. Many boxes weren't marked, but of the ones that were, none were labeled Ketchem. In two years rents go up, people get married, change jobs. People move on, so she might not live there now.

He felt disappointed but wondered what he would've done if he'd seen her name there and rung the buzzer. What would he have said to her when she answered the door? "Oh, hi. I met you in our dreams. I've been there with you at your psychiatrist and at your work."

Yeah, it'd be fine—after Charlie posted his bail on a misdemeanor charge of being looney-tunes.

When he got back to his car, he checked the map program on his phone. Denny's in Gardena was a few minutes' drive straight down Western. He turned into the parking lot at eleven thirty—in time for lunch.

Jeff walked in and noticed the booths and carpets were different from what he remembered. Apparently, it had been remodeled in the last two years. As he waited to be seated, he scanned the restaurant. A person wouldn't change much in that time. Maybe a new hair style or hair color, but still recognizable. Mindi wasn't there.

After he ate his lunch, his server brought the check. He looked at her name tag, made eye contact, and said, "Thank you, Jeri. Say, could you please tell me, when does Mindi come on shift?"

Jeff noticed a slight shift in her posture. "I'm sorry, sir. There's nobody named Mindi here."

"Oh, uh. When did she quit?"

Her answer continued to be businesslike. "Sir, I've been here over three years. Nobody with that name ever worked here while I've been here."

"Sorry, I must've misunderstood her name when I was in last. She's about five foot two, dark hair? Sound familiar?"

"Sorry, sir." She shook her head.

He thanked her, stood up, and met her at the cash register where she ran his credit card. He signed the slip for his fifteen-dollar lunch and handed it to her along with a five-dollar bill for a tip.

She smiled as she accepted it. "Thank you, sir. Come again."

Maybe, but not when I'm awake, he thought ironically as he exited.

Jeff was sure that Jeri had concealed the fact Mindi had worked there—and may still work there. He figured they were coached not to answer strangers' questions about other staff, for good reason. He didn't get what he wanted straight out, yet he got his answer. Jeri had earned her tip. The weekend had started well.

Jeff picked Charlene up outside her agency's office building. She bubbled with enthusiasm, regaling him with the details of working with her people and the client. She would put together a nationwide, and eventually a worldwide ad campaign for a company that had created a full line of cruelty-free cosmetics that contained no heavy metals or toxic chemicals.

"Whoa," he said. "Are you trying to sell me? I'm not a customer." He chuckled, smiling at her with affection.

"That's just it," she said. "They've developed a full line of skin care for men too." With excitement she added, "And they've got chemists and scientists that worked on the latest physiology of acne for teenagers. They're a great company."

Jeff reached over, taking her hand for a moment and squeezing it as he said, "I'm so glad it's working out for you. What's the next step?"

"Well, the list is long. I've been able to add to my staff for the campaign. We've hammered out a very challenging schedule. They still want to launch right after Halloween, to catch the Christmas crowds. And by Valentine's Day, they launch their outdoor skin care line with sun blocks and warm-weather moisturizers in time for spring break. We'll do the ad campaign for that too."

He reflected on their conversation of last week and asked, "Still no problem with the tight schedule?"

"Oh, there'll be problems, sure, but that's what my team is good at. That's why this job is so fun, even with the stress. We'll do the project in double-time—no, make that quadruple-time—to make the release date. Is that a term? Quadruple-time?" She laughed and went on, "They've got big plans, and the boss is trusting us with the whole thing. Any support I need, I've got it. Success is the only option."

She continued listing the things on her to-do list from memory. Jeff couldn't keep up and let his mind drift as he negotiated the downtown Friday traffic on the way to the hotel. He realized he hadn't been listening and tuned back in to her enthusiasm when she ended her list of tasks with, ". . . and I've been asked to help in the choices of the makeup models for the print and TV ads."

Models? Jeff tightened his grip on the steering wheel. Charlene didn't notice, being caught up in sharing her excitement.

His mind raced. As he turned on his turn signal and started the laborious chore of changing lanes, he cautioned himself: Don't jump to conclusions. It's just a coincidence and may mean nothing. But, he argued with himself, there'd been a long line of coincidences with his dreams, so why not another? He pleaded in silence with the universe for a reprieve or at least an answer to what was going on.

Charlene realized Jeff had said nothing, that she'd monopolized the conversation. She put her hand on his arm. "Oh, Jeff, I'm sorry. I've been babbling like a schoolgirl. Your flight was good? What did you do while you were waiting for me?"

Jeff returned to the conversation. He glanced at Charlene

and smiled. "No, no, I enjoy it when you're this excited," he said, deflecting the question so as not to have to account for his earlier time in LA—he hadn't expected that. "Flight was boring as it should be, because a non-boring flight might mean a disaster."

In an instant he realized an airplane crash joke wasn't at all appropriate, but she didn't react. She hadn't noticed the unintentional oblique to her dad's death. In fact, she seemed to have forgotten she'd asked what he'd done since he landed. Angry with himself for being so self-absorbed about makeup models, he changed the subject and asked about her schedule. It wasn't like him to slip up like that.

He pulled into the lot at the hotel. As they entered the lobby, he told Charlene he'd done some research and found five restaurants that each had at least four stars on Yelp, with three that overlooked the beach there in Santa Monica. All claimed to serve excellent clam chowder. Ever since they met in Seattle, they'd made a game with themselves of sampling restaurant clam chowder, keeping a list and grading them on a scale of one to ten. They'd surely continue their tradition tonight.

As they made their way to the hotel elevator, he put his arm around her waist and told her he'd need help to make a choice from the list. Ever the diplomat, he added, "Or maybe there's someplace else you've heard of you want to go."

"We'll decide," she said with equal diplomacy. "When we get you settled, we'll look at what you've found."

They chose a restaurant within walking distance of the hotel and sat on the veranda while they watched the sun dissolve into the ocean beyond the horizon. Jeff understood why so many lived down here. It could be described in one word: climate.

After they finished their bottle of wine and then their dessert, they walked back to the hotel. They'd last seen each other only a week ago, but they acted like it had been months. The passion in their lovemaking, elevated by Charlene's excitement for her job, added to their sense of being on holiday.

Later in the evening, the moonlight through the window painted the room in a soft glow that matched Jeff's mood. Charlene had fallen asleep. He reflected on the new excitement of her career and was pleased. They both had jobs they liked that paid well. Everything was ready for the next level of their relationship. As Jeff lay there, he considered when they could go shopping for an engagement ring. Things were so right.

His thoughts then turned toward his hobby of being an amateur dream detective. He'd gone to Denny's, and Jeri's answers had made Mindi even more real to him. The doctor was real. As he thought about the synchronicity of Charlie having a choice in the makeup models for LaDormeur, sleep enveloped him.

~

Jeff floated and chastised himself for thinking of Mindi's work as he went to sleep. It had probably started this dream. Where would he go tonight? The floating gave way to standing in the gray fog. A door opened in front of him and through the doorway he saw the same gray, limitless space of his earlier dream with Mindi. *This is a new way of getting here*, he thought, now looking forward to another visit with her.

Feeling compelled, Jeff stepped through the doorway. Mindi stood there dressed as before in her Denny's uniform. He walked toward her and stood about ten feet away. Her face showed no emotion.

He smiled. Whoever was in charge of wardrobe had no sense of style. He raised his head and looked into her eyes. *Those eyes are so beautiful.* He smiled again.

She blinked, tipped her head to the side, maintaining his gaze, and with no challenge in her voice, asked, "You smiled. Why?"

He was glad she'd started with a question.

"Well, first, I'm glad to see you. Second, there's so little color here. We're in a black-and-white and gray scale world." He gestured at his clothes—which were the same as before—and to hers.

She ignored his first comment and lifted her chin in defiance. "It's just a dream. Why do we need style?"

Jeff noted she knew she was in a dream.

"Are you real?" she asked in an even tone.

"As real as you are," he replied, trying not to betray the irony of himself dreaming and being in someone else's dream.

Her expression didn't change while she considered his answer for a moment. "My name is Mindi. You're Jeff?"

"Yes."

"Why are you here again?"

Another clue. She remembered the other dream.

"Where is here?" he asked.

"In my dream. Why are you here?"

His answer? A non-answer. "Because of you."

She looked at him and tipped her head. "That doesn't answer my question. Why are you being evasive?"

Jeff noted her boldness; he must be careful. "Mindi, I told you I'm your friend. I don't want to make you afraid. Are you uncomfortable?"

"Would your answers scare me?"

He chose his words with care. "You were afraid of Shirley. I don't want you to be afraid of me." As he spoke, he wished he could've said it differently, but her next statement relieved him of any anxiety.

"Shirley's gone. I told you before that my fear of Shirley is gone," she said displaying her self-awareness and self-confidence. "If she does return, I can handle her. I'm still curious about who you are, and why are you talking about Shirley?"

"I don't know. Maybe to help you not be afraid of her. It seems like it worked, from what you just said."

"That answers why you were here then. But why are you here now?"

Shirley had asked that too. How should he answer? The truth.

"To answer that question, I have to ask you some questions. Is that okay with you?"

"If it'll explain why you're in my dream tonight."

"Fair enough. First, you know this type of dream is special and has its own name?"

"What do you mean?"

"It's called a lucid dream. While you're dreaming, you know it's a dream. In other types of dreams, you don't know you're dreaming until you wake up and realize that you had a dream. With a lucid dream, you know you're in a dream while you're in the dream."

"O-kay?" She looked puzzled. "Lucid dream? What does that have to do with why you're here?"

"When you learn more about the word, it'll make it easier to talk with you about it. When you're awake, please look up the word." He spelled it out for her. "Do you have that?"

"Yes." She still looked puzzled.

"When you wake up, I want you to write a note, like Shirley wrote you a note."

"You know Shirley wrote me a note?" she said with an edge in her voice.

"I do," he replied, hoping she trusted him enough now to handle the truth. "Knowing that helped me to help you, so she'd leave you alone. I think I was sent here to help you, and I mean you no harm." He waited for her to analyze what he'd said.

She nodded slowly.

"Good. Just focus on when you wake up, you write a note that says, *Lucid dream. Jeff is a friend.*" He waited while she processed.

"Lucid dream. Jeff is my friend."

"You'll remember to write it?"

She nodded.

Jeff didn't know how waking-Mindi would respond. She'd surely remember the dream and tell Dr. Singh, but would she continue to trust him?

"Do you have more questions, Mindi?"

"No. Not right now. I have to think about this."

"Good." He gave her his most genuine smile of friendship and raised his hand. "Let's meet again another time, okay? It's time to go."

He gave a little wave of goodbye and watched her return the gesture. Then they both dissolved into glitter.

~

He woke up without thinking Charlene's name. Charlene had made coffee, and she handed him a cup. She looked great with her slender legs and the pink baby doll nightie she wore just for him.

He looked at her and thought that she, too, could be a model. It had become a habit to document his dream, but it could wait. He'd remember enough until he got back home. Meanwhile, he had other, quite enjoyable distractions to keep himself busy the rest of the weekend. Charlene approached him, placed her hands on his chest, and with one motion, rubbed her hands over his well-defined pecs and leaned in to give him a kiss.

~

Early Sunday evening, while on the plane back to Seattle, he reviewed his weekend with Charlie. The fond memories would keep him for another week. He took out a notepad and wrote the details of his dream. He'd forgotten nothing. As he reread his entry, he reflected on Mindi's innocence and determination, then restated his one overriding question about the purpose of these dreams: *Why?*

CHAPTER 10

Jeff had a great time with Charlie and had fresh information for his new hobby, but he was glad to be home. He took a quick shower to wash off the travel grime, ate a salad, and switched through TV channels until he finally changed his mind and decided to read in bed.

He went to sleep reading a library book by a distinguished PhD physicist about black holes, wormholes, time machines, and parallel universes.

He fell, then floated. The gray envelope opened up, and he found himself back in Mindi's head, watching the doctor's foot moving up and down slightly, her right leg crossed over her left.

"Mindi?" the doctor said.

Mindi looked up, diverted from her focus on the shoe. "Sorry, Doctor. I felt strange there for a moment. Like that time when I was putting on my makeup." She shook her head, rubbed her temples, looked the doctor in the eye, and said with an apologetic tone, "Please, uh, say again?"

"I said, go on," the doctor said patiently, then paused before continuing, "You'd just told me you had a strange dream last week after our visit, and you remembered it. Did you take notes?"

"Oh, yes," Mindi said, reenergized to the conversation. "Here it is." She opened the folded notepaper, singled out the top sheet, and half stood up to hand it to her.

The doctor took it, and before she could focus on it, Mindi directed her, "On the bottom half, see there?"

After reading the dozen lines twice, the doctor handed it back. "At the bottom, you wrote 'lucid dream' and 'Jeff is a friend.' That was the same man you watched talking to Shirley?"

Keeping eye contact, Mindi replied, "Yes."

"So why did you write that?"

"Because Jeff asked me to."

"Oh?" The doctor's eyebrows rose and her head tilted up. With a hint of concern in her voice, she said, "Did he explain why?"

"Well, he asked me if I knew what a lucid dream was."

"Do you?"

"I didn't then. I looked it up."

"Well?" the doctor said, encouraging her to go on.

"My dream was a lucid dream because I knew I was dreaming while I was having it. It felt like real life. I remembered it when I woke up. My dreams with Shirley were lucid dreams too, right, Doctor?"

The doctor nodded. "It seems so. Lucid dreams are not as common as our regular dreams." She paused. "Did Jeff tell you he was a friend?"

"Oh, yes, Doctor. And he said he didn't want to scare me."

"How did you feel in the dream? And how do you feel now?"

"I felt okay. I feel I can trust him. It was a dream. He couldn't hurt me. Just like you told me that Shirley couldn't hurt me. I feel so much better with the pills you had me taking. Shirley hasn't come back. I don't need to be afraid of her anymore. And Jeff also said I didn't need to be afraid of Shirley anymore." She

smiled at the doctor with a sense of pride, of accomplishment, happy to have shared her progress.

Jeff was glad he hadn't mentioned the doctor to Mindi, but he wished he'd said less to her about Shirley. Jeff hoped the doctor wouldn't think he'd replaced Shirley and caution her about his appearance in her dreams.

The doctor nodded. "That's right, Mindi. Now, let me tell you what we as doctors know about dreams. Regardless of what Jung said, what we really do know about dreams is that we don't know a lot about dreams." She paused a moment. "We do feel that it is in our dreams that our subconscious is working things out for us, filing away the day's activities, hopes, fears, longings, wins and losses, getting ready for the next day."

The doctor explained at length to Mindi about REM sleep and finished with, "Many report they remember their lucid dreams, well,"—she chuckled—"lucidly, meaning clearly."

Mindi nodded that she understood. Then . . .

~

Jeff woke up to his alarm in his own bed. He turned it off, sat up, and rubbed his eyes and face while he reminded himself that these dreams were about events that happened two years ago. Though for him, they were just last night.

He documented his dream, then looked over his notes and added: *The last dream answers questions about her ability to handle our meetings. Is it still a possibility that* my *dreams are just that? Dreams, not reality. It's all in my head. Time travel isn't possible.*

He couldn't shake the lingering doubt that these were only dreams, with no foundation in reality. On rereading the last bit, his private editorial on his activities, he considered adding how he felt about Mindi as a person, that he found her lovely, strong,

121

intelligent, charming and, if he weren't committed to Charlene, might be attracted to her. Being the scientist, the observer, he knew his notes should be complete, so he wrote: *Is Mindi just a construct of mine in these dreams? Even though she's a real person in real life, have I made her up for my dreams? Either way, I like her and feel protective of her.*

Then he clipped the pen to the notebook and put them into the bottom of his nightstand drawer. Before he closed the drawer, he wondered if all the dreaming was related to asking Charlene to marry him. Was Mindi just a surrogate for feelings for Charlene? Or was she a guardian angel who, after testing him, would let him know what he was supposed to do? He retrieved the notebook and added these thoughts to his notes. He shut the drawer. His day had begun, and he intended to make the most of it.

~

Craig asked Jeff how things were going with his family tree. Jeff told him he hadn't had time to work on it because of his visit to Santa Monica.

That prompted Craig to share. "I'm headed down there for my cousin's wedding."

This piqued Jeff's interest. Trying to remain casual, he asked, "Oh, how many relatives do you have? Do they all live in Torrance?"

Craig looked at the ceiling and listed them out loud: "Let's see, from my uncle and aunt that both passed away, they had one girl. There's my cousin that's getting married. He has two brothers, one younger, one older. And my dad's sister had two girls. They live in the Bay Area—they'll go down—and my mom and dad and my two brothers."

"You've got a big family," Jeff said. "So they'll all be there?"

"I hope so. It's fun to have the family together for a wedding, rather than at a funeral. Last time was when my uncle died a couple years ago."

Jeff had determined from Craig's ancestry chart that the dead uncle was Mindi's father and actually Craig's cousin. He nodded, agreeing with Craig's comment that family reunions should be happy. Jeff thought he had the info he wanted. He was pretty sure Mindi would be there.

"Well, safe travels, Craig. When is it? I'll be interested in hearing all about it when you get back."

"In a couple of weeks. Oh, before I forget, I'd better confirm my vacation request."

Jeff hoped Craig would bring back pictures of the family. Funny, Jeff realized as he walked back to his office, how something always dragged him back to thinking about his dreams and Mindi.

~

Jeff walked through the doorway into the gray room. Mindi was already there, looking comfortable as she stood waiting, dressed like the last time in her server's uniform.

As soon as she saw him, she said, "Hi, Jeff. I'm glad you're here. I've got some questions, okay?"

Her light, conversational tone showed him she'd crossed the threshold of comfort and confidence with these dreams and him.

"Sure. Go ahead," he said.

"Are you dreaming now?"

"Of course. Why?" If she thought, like the doctor said, that he was a construct, why would she ask that question?

She didn't give him time to analyze that further, asking,

"Where are you from?"

He hesitated. How should he handle this? But he hesitated a little too long.

"Why don't you tell me? Or are you just in my mind?" Mindi said.

"Why do you ask?"

"You said you were sent here. Where are you from?"

She listens and she's smart. "Well, it's complicated."

"How can that be complicated? I'm from California. Where are you from?"

Jeff stalled. "Where in California?"

"Gardena. So. Now I've told you. Please tell me. Where are you from?"

"I'm from Seattle."

"How do you know me?"

"I don't know. I'd never had lucid dreams before. Then one night, I'm—" He looked around. "I'm here, talking to Shirley. Now I'm talking to you." He knew his answer wasn't complete. How long could this go on?

But she seemed satisfied with his answer, so he asked if, before this, she'd ever had a lucid dream.

"Before I saw you last time, I didn't know what a lucid dream was. I've never dreamed like this and when you were here with Shirley."

He nodded.

"I thought about my doctor while I was falling asleep. About how I told her about you, and how you told me about lucid dreaming and to put your name in my notes. Suddenly, I was here. Then you showed up. You say you're from Seattle, but are you a real person or somebody I made up who says they're from Seattle?"

He smiled, somewhat relieved the question was finally out

124

in the open. "Does it matter?"

She frowned. "Again, you didn't answer my question. That's what someone says who doesn't want to answer." She watched him and waited for his reply.

He said again, "Does it matter if I'm real?"

Her eyes narrowed with irritation. Clearly, she didn't like him avoiding answering.

"Maybe. I might've made you up. You could be a dream person who I created." She sighed. "No, you're *not* real." She shook her head and frowned, her irritation morphed into disappointment.

"Do you wish I was real?" Jeff asked. "After all, this is just a dream."

She considered what he said but didn't speak.

"Whether I am real or just made up in your mind," Jeff said, "I'm still your friend. I mean you no harm, and I want you to be happy. You can take care of yourself. You know what you want." After a brief pause, he added, "You're quite competent working in the restaurant, but you want to be a model."

She shifted her weight and put one hand on her hip. "Yeah, I've made you up. Otherwise, how would you know I'm good at my job or want to be a model?"

"Sure. And I did know that Shirley wrote you a note. So why wouldn't I know that? I told you I knew about Shirley's note to you so I could help you, right?" But he wanted her to believe he was real, so he said, "What would you do if I am real?"

"Are you married, engaged, or attached?"

The direct question didn't surprise him. She had said he was handsome. Had he become an example of an ideal mate?

"Are *you* attached?" His answering her question with a question wasn't a challenge, but a deflection.

"You. Are. Very. Clever." She smiled and gave a little twist of her head. But rather than insist he answer first, she said, "No,

125

not attached."

He grinned, realizing he was enjoying the verbal jousting as much as she seemed to be. But possibly for different reasons. Her dream-self might be looking for Mr. Right. He still needed to know why he dreamed about her and why he visited her in their dreams.

She'd answered him directly. Now he owed her an answer. "Thank you. The trouble is, my answer might spoil us being able to talk."

"What do you mean?"

"Well, if I'm attached, would you still want to talk to me? I can imagine lots of reasons you wouldn't want to talk to me again." He paused, letting that sink in. "If I'm unattached, you might not want to talk to me because you may think that I come here because I have ulterior motives. Understand?"

He was sure she understood when she said, "I'm damned if you're real, and damned if you're not."

"That could be. I don't think it matters right now. Please believe me, I want to be your friend. I want only what's right for you. You're on a great path. Having overcome things that no one should ever have to deal with. You've done it all yourself and need to follow your dream."

She smiled back at him. "Thank you, Jeff. But my doctor said I constructed you, like Shirley, who was part of me. And besides, how else could you know all of what I'm dealing with, what I do and want to do, if I didn't make you up?"

Jeff just looked at her, making eye contact, and tried not to react outwardly. The question was rhetorical anyway; there was nothing he could say.

Abruptly, in contradiction to what she'd expressed previously, she said, "No, Jeff. You *are* real! You're not just in my mind . . ." She looked down at the gray floor as if trying to think all this through again, then she looked up at him, meeting his gaze. "You are a real person, and you visit me in my dreams."

"Help me understand why you think that," Jeff said.

"I don't . . . I mean . . . Well, I just feel you're a real person. I didn't make you up. I don't know how you know what you know. Or how you can be in my dream, but . . ." After a long pause, she said, "But how *can* you be in my dream?" She looked at him with hope in her eyes. "Whatever you are, I hope to see you again." Then she shook her head and dissolved into a fluttering of glitter.

Jeff knew she'd awakened in 2015. A moment later, he awoke in 2017.

While drinking his coffee, he watched the morning TV news with the sound off, and replayed the latest dream in his mind. He was sorry he'd created conflict, but it wasn't his choice to be in her head or in the gray room. He resolved to just take it as it came, try not to overthink it, and especially not to scare her. He finished his journal entry with those thoughts.

Next, he took inventory of his life. What made *his* life comfortable? His job paid well. He had a reliable car and a nice, comfortable apartment in a pleasant neighborhood. He liked his job, enjoyed the city and city life, had a great girlfriend—and a growing relationship with her—good friends, good health, and he had his family, who were healthy and happy themselves. His future included a wife, and maybe children. What else did anyone need?

Part of him wanted these dreams to be done with. Was it possible this might cause a problem, keeping the secret from Charlene? How could that happen? It didn't affect his sleep; he woke up refreshed after every dream. There was no evidence that any of this happened, except the notebook. And that could be destroyed. So there was nothing to worry about.

The dreams were like a hobby that didn't cost anything. Except that trying to figure them out used waking time to think, research, and then write about them in his secret dream journal. Nobody could imagine a hobby like this, and if they could, how would they make it happen? Should he end this virtual relationship with Mindi? And if he decided to, how could he make that happen? It felt like he was held hostage to the dreams.

But why would he want to end it? She was nice, but she had her own life in 2015. Surely by now, in 2017, she would've found a companion, and that guy probably wouldn't tolerate a dream friend. He wasn't sure Charlene would. What rational person could accept such an irrational scenario? So, Jeff wondered where he fit in. His mission was finished. What else was there to do? He shrugged and looked at the clock—time to go to work.

~

The next night, after his fall and float, he again saw Mindi's world through her eyes. This time she sat in her apartment at her kitchen table, which was an organized confusion of textbooks, notebooks, highlighter pens, and her book-bag. Light jazz played on low volume.

She looked out the window, rubbed her temples, then stood and carried a mug with a tea bag tab hanging over the side over to the stove.

Jeff watched her turn the knob that controlled the burner under the kettle. She swished the kettle to be sure it had plenty of water, then set it back down on the red-glowing burner.

She leaned against the counter opposite the stove and rubbed her temples, then turned and glanced out the window, as if wondering if someone was out there watching. Jeff sensed she felt vulnerable, and pulling the cord to close the mini blinds didn't help her feel better. The teapot's sudden whistle startled her. She jumped.

Jeff, inside her head, flinched too. *That didn't help!*

She looked around to one side, then the other, then pushed away from the counter. "Who's there?" she asked, fear reflected in her voice.

Jeff chided himself for his carelessness. She'd heard his outburst in her mind.

The kettle whistled louder. She turned off the burner, walked to the front door and confirmed it was locked and the night latch secure. When she turned around, it made Jeff's psychic-self dizzy. He tried to close his eyes, and her eyes closed in response, then flashed open again.

She went into the bedroom and said out loud to the room, "I know I heard you talking. I'm not crazy. I-am-not-crazy!"

Jeff tried to keep his virtual mouth shut, surprised that his connection with real-time Mindi was so much stronger than before. Her sense of urgency had distracted his concentration.

Again, something slipped out of his mind: *This is not good.*

Mindi swung around a full circle. "I heard you! Why are you here? You're right, this *is* not good!"

Jeff sensed Mindi's panic and then his own. He needed to leave. *Charlene, Charlene, Charlene.* It worked. The dream ended abruptly with his escape word.

Until now, Jeff had treated these dreams as if they were an interesting yet insignificant pastime. But tonight he'd negatively affected an innocent person, caused her fear, and felt her fear himself. He felt responsible and frustrated. How could he have avoided it? What lessons could he learn? He didn't want that to ever happen again and wished he could make it up to her.

Jeff struggled to be free of his emotional response and return to logical thinking. He was thinking of Mindi as a real person, not a dream-construct of his own like Shirley was for her. That's why he was so upset. He wanted to believe that Mindi was real the same way she wanted him to be real. Why couldn't they both be real? He had to find the how and why of the dreams.

There must be a scientific reason. But he'd already done the research, and no known hard science explained what he'd been doing in his dreams. Standard physics couldn't explain it, so was this beyond the boundaries of known science? What could it be? Metaphysics? He looked up the definition online and found: *The branch of philosophy that examines the nature of reality, including the relationship between mind and matter, substance and attribute, fact and value.*

More research put him in touch with the term "physical metaphysics," described as "the real nature of time, space, laws of nature, and matter." That must be the answer to his time travel dreams, right? Sure, but it still didn't answer the *how*. He kept looking. There must be an answer. After all, the antique book from Ingrid was proof that this wasn't a new phenomenon. He found links that loosely tied metaphysics to parapsychology, and he followed those threads.

Energized now, he couldn't sleep and spent the rest of the night on the internet researching parapsychology and psychic abilities. Some terms he already knew, but he was surprised to find that there were names for other things he'd experienced in his dream visits to Mindi.

The list included:

> *Clairsentience: feeling someone else's feelings, like the feelings of fear and uncertainty*
> *Clairaudience: perceiving what is inaudible*
> *Claircognizance: knowing, but not how you know*
> *Postcognition: the ability, in a supernatural way, to*

perceive past events
Astral projection: sometimes called out-of-body experiences
Telepathy: the ability to transmit or receive thoughts without words or body language

Mindi was aware of him in her head. The more times he visited, the more they could hear each other's thoughts and sense each other's feelings. Their connection was becoming stronger. All of those psychic elements had occurred in this last dream: telepathy, clairsentience, and astral projection. And the explanation for his time travel? Postcognition!

As he sat looking at his laptop's screen, his feelings of guilt increased. He considered getting professional help, but denial set in. Arguments against: I'm too busy; I've got guard weekends; I have to pick up Charlie from the airport. He had a big project at work, and he wanted to enjoy the summer. Besides, his insurance wouldn't cover more than a few visits to a psychologist. He'd be okay—if he could only stop this dreaming.

He closed his laptop, resolving to quit this fantasy dream stuff because of the stress. What he didn't know was how to do that. Tonight was one of the few times he hadn't had a good night's rest. He looked at the clock. "Crap. Tonight? It's already morning."

CHAPTER 11

No, no, no . . . Can't I take a pass on this? Jeff fell again in the gray fog-space. He hadn't felt this scared since this first happened. He wanted no more of it, no matter how much it piqued his curiosity. He tried to relax and decided he'd use his escape word as soon as he landed. That would wake him up.

Jeff floated and found solace in this comfortable part of the dream. Then suddenly, he was in the gray room with Mindi standing with her hands on her hips in the posture of solid confrontation. Like Shirley had been.

He tried to escape—*Charlene, Charlene, Charlene*—but didn't. *Oh shit!*

"Oh shit is right," Mindi said, meeting his gaze. "Why are you spying on me?"

The moment seemed to go on forever. Mindi's eyes bore into his. Her strength of will astounded him. She was stronger, more determined than Shirley.

While trying to deny the obvious, Jeff spoke as if he had been caught in flagrante delicto. "What are you talking about?"

Her hands dropped, but she continued to fume, her fists clenched tight. This wasn't the Mindi he'd gotten to know, not a kitten but an angry she-cat with spirit. His thought slipped out again. *She's pissed.*

It was obvious that she heard his thought. "Damned right, I'm pissed. You said you were my friend!" Her scowl reflected the intensity of her feelings.

He regained his composure and said out loud, "Mindi, I don't understand what's going on. I don't, uh, mean to, uh, get into—" The words wouldn't form.

Mindi finished the sentence with a snarl. "—get into my head, huh?"

He looked at her, hoping she wouldn't interrupt him again as he tried to pull himself together after this onslaught.

She has a right to be— He stopped thinking it and said it out loud, "You're right to be upset, but please, please, understand. We've been thrown into this. It isn't my choice to intrude. I go to sleep and-and . . . here I am. I've had no choice."

She started to interrupt, but he held up his hand. He had more to say.

Her body language said she didn't want to let him finish, but she said, "Go on, this better be good."

"I've been trying to figure this out since the start," he explained. "Even when I think it's over, I visit you again." He stopped, knowing he was vulnerable—a strange feeling, one he didn't like.

"Visit? Is that what you call it? It feels like you're stalking me." Her eyes burned into his. She took a breath, looking for the next thing to say.

He'd never had to defend against this level of rage from anyone before, and he hoped she'd put the anger aside and listen. When she didn't react to that, he assumed she couldn't read his thoughts anymore. *Charlene doesn't argue like this.*

"Charlene?" Mindi shot back. "Yeah, who's Charlene? You

keep saying her name. Do you get into her head too?"

Nope. She could still read his mind.

"One thing at a time, okay?" He found some strength and, not waiting for an answer, said, "I'm so glad I can now talk with you about this. I can't talk to any of my waking friends. You've got someone to talk to about your feelings—"

She cut him off. "Who are you talking about? What else do you know about me?"

I've got to be more careful.

"You're damned right you better be careful." She took a step forward.

"Mindi, please! May I just start at the beginning? I hope we've got enough time." He paused.

She stared at him.

"I'm a real person," he continued, "like you are a real person in our waking time. I've never been a lucid dreamer before, and one night I fell into your mind. It scared me. It just happened; I didn't want it."

Mindi, with a skeptical turn of her head, kept her eyes on his. She continued to listen, but her anger still showed.

"I did not, do not, want to spy on you. No, that's not the right word, but it's got to do. I got dropped into your life and have watched you without wanting to. I don't know how to control it and have had to wait until the dream ends. When it does, I wake up in my own time."

Mindi watched his face as she thought about what he said. "You dropped in?" She didn't give him a chance to answer, but he nodded. "And you watched me? Before we met here together?"

"Yes."

"Why didn't you tell me when we were here last time? I thought we were just dreaming here. Why?"

Jeff struggled to be less defensive, to be patient. "Two

reasons. First, I thought it would scare you if I told you then, even more than Shirley scared you. And second, I really thought that after we started meeting here, those other things, like last night, would stop. But it didn't. Not only that, the more times I, uh, drop in, the more closely our minds seem to be linked, and we can hear what each other thinks. That didn't happen at first; it's happening more now. It's scary for me too. You can even hear my thoughts tonight, here in this gray room. Please forgive me. I didn't hold back to be dishonest. I did it to protect you. I didn't choose any of this."

"Okay. I think I believe you. I want to believe you. You said a minute ago, you woke up in your own time. What does that mean?"

"Good." He let out a sigh. "That's on my list. I'm glad you brought it up and we can get that out in the open too." He took a breath and gathered his thoughts. "You remember these dreams when you wake up, right?"

Mindi nodded.

"Well, to the level I understand it myself—and I really don't—remember when I asked you the date and year?"

She nodded again.

"You asked what difference does it make?"

"Yes." With impatience she added, "Just tell me!"

Jeff took another deep breath. "For you, when you're awake, it's 2015, right?"

She nodded but waved her hand, urging him to finish.

"When I'm awake, I live in 2017. When I dream, I visit you in 2015, like last night. When we're here, it's *our* dreams. I don't know what the date is."

She nodded again but appeared uncertain as to what it all meant. "Okay. I hear you, but how does it happen?"

"I don't know."

135

"How do you know I'm a real person? And how do I know you're a real person?"

Jeff relaxed a little. The emotion had left her voice. She wanted to understand.

"That's a longer story. I wasn't sure at first. I thought I just dreamed you up. But now I know I didn't construct you from my subconscious.

"I'm a real person, not someone you made up in your dreams. I've got a driver's license, pay income taxes, and have a girlfriend." He watched her eyes to see if she accepted what he said. He smiled, hoping she would smile back.

She didn't return the smile but rubbed her temples with both hands and looked at him with a help-me look in her eyes.

"Please." He took another breath. "This dream might be over any moment now. I still don't know what causes it or what controls how long I stay in your dream. The last two times we were here, you left first. What I see when you leave is that your image turns into glitter. When that happens, I wake up too. I might wake up right away or move into one of the other stages of sleep, but I always wake up in Seattle to a good life . . . in 2017."

She looked at him, looking expectant, as if he would explain more.

When he didn't continue, she said, "This is a lot to take in, even for a dream. It all seems real though." She stopped a moment and looked around. "So let's say I can trust you, that you aren't like Shirley trying to control me or take me over, or . . ." She stopped. "Okay." She thought another moment, then said, "You say that when we're awake, we're living in two different years, and we sometimes meet here in our dreams, or sometimes you're in my head."

He nodded. "Yes. Yes, that's right."

"And when you're in my head, when I'm awake,

136

you're dreaming."

"Yes. Like last night." He looked into her eyes. "I'm asleep. I know it sounds weird, but I'm aware when I dream, just like now, just like when I'm awake. And you're asleep, too, but here, knowing you're in a dream. Yeah, it's weird."

"I *knew* I was being watched. But why?"

He interrupted her with a look and a shake of his head, asking her with his eyes to wait. "I told you, I don't know. It upsets me too."

Her mind seemed to be fighting the truth, and she was furious. She squirmed around like she wanted to break free of being held. "This isn't about you," she fumed. "You're spying on me!"

Jeff hoped she wouldn't wake herself up now. What if the next time he visited her, she still didn't want to understand? But he couldn't worry about that now. He waited for calm to return.

Mindi stopped moving around and calmed down. Her shoulders relaxed, her fists unclenched, and her eyes appeared more alert, back in control of her emotions.

"Mindi, you are a strong person. You and I are in a strange situation. How and why, I don't know, and don't know how to control it." He shrugged and raised his arms in submission. "It's like I'm driving a car that's skidding on an icy road and I can't steer."

She looked puzzled.

"You've never driven on a slippery road, have you?"

"No."

"Sorry, bad analogy. I'm looking for some way to tell you how—"

She cut him off. "If you're trying to tell me you're out of control, I get it. That's how most of my life has been. This doesn't help."

Jeff's empathy swelled as he looked at her. "So we understand each other. Right?" He waited, hoping this was their common ground.

Mindi nodded and tried to smile. "This is a lot to take in."

Jeff smiled back. "Please, I want nothing to happen to you. I only want to support you, not hurt you. I am not a stalker, nor do I want to interfere in your life or molest you."

She stiffened, a note of fear in her eyes.

Jeff realized he shouldn't have said that. "I'm so sorry. I know about your past, that you're trying to heal after some terrible things happened to you. It's why I'm so concerned every time—" He paused again, searching for the right words. "When I've visited you."

She stared at him for a long moment. Jeff thought she would disappear like Shirley had. But instead, she took a deep breath and relaxed.

"Okay, that startled me." With her eyes still fixed on him, she shook herself and said, "I'm better now. Is there any more you should tell me?"

"I've told you most of it already. I'm not in control when I visit. Please, just believe me. Trust me."

She frowned. "You're not in control of this? How our, uh, meetings start or end, when you visit in my head, or when we get here?"

"That's right. I have no control. I've been learning some things, though. Not much, but some. I discovered how to wake myself up, and not have to wait for the dream to end on its own when I'm in your head. I created an escape word, a way to wake myself up. It might be different for you, though. What were you thinking the last time when you left here?"

"I thought I wanted to wake up, and I did."

"Okay, that's good. When you wake up, is that when you

write about your dream?"

She'd been looking down at the featureless floor. Her head snapped up in surprise. "You know that too?"

With compassion he said, "Yes. I do."

"Oh, wow. Yes, my doctor says to write it down before the dream fades. Jeff, I really do hope if we meet here again, we might know more about why this is happening."

Her rage had passed. She now showed some trust and had addressed him by name—a signal that she thought of him as real, and not invented.

"Me too. I feel better. I've wanted to introduce myself better, but I didn't know how. I'm so sorry I scared you. Really, so sorry."

"Thank you. But I think I need to go. This is a lot to . . . to . . ."

"Thank you for listening. I needed to explain. Maybe we'll meet here again . . . ?" He raised his hand and gave a little wave.

"Sure. From what you said, we might not have a choice, right? G'bye." She turned to go and again dissolved into the cloud of glitter that disappeared before it touched the floor.

Jeff woke without his escape word. "Wow. Intense," he said out loud as he started writing in his notebook. His notes included his ongoing feelings of guilt and helplessness, and now that many things were out in the open, that he felt better. He hadn't realized how much he'd been holding in since he'd become convinced that Mindi was a real person. He wrote *Ninety-nine percent real. One percent sci-fi time travel*, then closed his notebook and went to sleep. He felt like he'd had a fever and it had broken.

～

Two weeks had passed since the last dream, and Jeff had assumed the dreams were over now that Mindi knew about him. But tonight he arrived to watch Dr. Singh through Mindi's eyes as Mindi answered a question the doctor had asked a moment before he arrived.

"No, Doctor. No more dreams, no feelings that anybody's watching me."

Jeff made sure his thoughts stayed in the quiet part of his mind. He wondered if that was really true for her. Did he drop in here *before* that last gray room talk? The dreams seemed to have always been in chronological order. Was this visit out of sequence?

Mindi rubbed her eyes while the doctor made some notes.

Jeff?

He startled. Mindi's voice was in his mind!

Jeff?

He hesitated, surprised he could hear her thoughts. *Yes? Yes, I'm here.*

Mindi's focus went back to the doctor as the doctor said, "Like I suggested last session, have you been thinking about the people you meet, customers, people on the bus or in the store, that might be the model for this Jeff you put in your dream?"

"Yes, Doctor. I've been looking for him on the street and in the stores. One guy kinda looked like him from the back, but it wasn't. When he turned around and saw me staring, what he must have thought. You know what I mean?"

The doctor nodded. "I see. You must be careful." She smiled. "Mindi, like we talked about before, I believe your subconscious constructed another personality to confront Shirley. I have discussed your case with my colleagues. Since Dissociative Identity Disorder is so rare, your case is one that I'll write up for a journal submission. Your case may help others who experience similar symptoms and triggers. We must ensure that it doesn't recur for you, no matter what form it takes. You're an independent person, with a capable personality. Please let me know when you experience anything out of the ordinary."

"Yes, Doctor. Thank you. I understand. I feel good about how you've helped me. I remember how scared I was. I don't want to feel that way again."

"Good. Mindi, you're doing very well. Now, how are you doing since we cut your medication dose in half?"

"Okay. I feel fine. Should I keep taking it?"

"That's up to you. You can take them or not. If you quit, keep the prescription. Don't throw it away. If you have an anxiety attack, or even feel a little jittery, anything strange, take them according to the directions."

Mindi left the building and walked toward the bus stop. *Jeff, if you're still there*, she thought, *the doctor said "anything out of the ordinary?" What could be less ordinary than talking to you, a man from two years in my future, in my head and in my dreams?*

Jeff chuckled. *Yeah, I'm still here. That's funny.*

Mindi stopped, leaned against a building and rubbed both temples with her thumb and fingertips. *I'm glad you're still here.*

I didn't ask to visit you today. I don't want to scare you.

She tipped her head sideways. *I'm fine. I've been thinking about us since we talked. I didn't feel scared when I felt you in my mind today, now that I know who you are.* She continued her walk toward the bus stop.

Jeff responded, *I'm glad. I never know why, when, and where I end up. It feels like I'm some kind of puppet, and someone is pulling my strings.*

It's disorienting for me, Mindi thought. *I can imagine that it's that way for you too. But I sense that I'm safe with you.*

Yes, it has been strange. I'm glad you trust me. He paused, then asked, *May I ask why you left out telling the doctor about our last meeting in the gray room?*

I think I understand why you asked, she replied. *I'll answer you, but I'm sure you understand that's* my *business, okay?*

Jeff was pleased she could set boundaries and express them. *I know, and that's why I asked if I could ask you. You're right. What you tell your doctor is none of my business. You don't have to answer. I asked because you've told her so much already and I wondered why you left it out.*

Sure, it's a fair question, I guess. Anyway, she knows I had voices in my head. I told her about my dreams—you and Shirley. So who have you told? Have you told your girlfriend?

He remained quiet for a moment, then thought, *You got me there—I've told no one. No, I can't tell her or any of my friends. This is so improbable. They'd lock me up.*

Mindi arrived at the bus stop and looked up the street. No bus.

Okay, you're right, she thought to him. *I guess it is kind of your business, too, since you've been with me at the doctor's all along.* She took a breath and rubbed her forehead and face. *Since I saw you face off with Shirley, and our meetings in the, uh, gray room, I feel better. A lot better,* she explained. *I can now go to beauty school. I'm strong enough to stop taking the meds. I didn't tell her, but when she cut the dose in half, I just quit taking them. Something good has happened. All my fears, my anger, the near-panic feelings are all gone. Maybe it's a coincidence, but all that progress is since you've been around. You're a good guy. Given me hope there are more guys like you out there. You're here to help me heal. I didn't think I could convince the doctor that you're a real person."*

Jeff said nothing. He didn't know how to respond but appreciated what she said.

Jeff, you're still there. I can tell.

I'm glad you feel I've helped you, but like the doctor said, you've done the hard part. I'm so glad you . . . Well, that you feel better.

Thank you, Mindi said.

You're welcome. Thank you for trusting me. That's something that I've worried about.

They stood in silence for a few minutes, then Jeff continued their internal conversation.

Hey, there's something else . . . Oh, there's the bus. Can we talk a little more? I'll wait while you get on and get a seat.

Sure.

Mindi showed her bus pass and sat near the back.

What do you want to say?

Every time I visited with you, I've wondered why this is happening to us. The reason, uh, the—he struggled to find the words—*universe put us together, to give you a little nudge to get you to where you are today. My job may be finished. If that's true, this might be our last visit. So I'm glad I met you.*

Mind smiled. *I hope this isn't the last time we get to talk, but if this is it, thank you for being my friend.*

You're welcome.

They remained silent as the bus traveled on its route. After all the emotion and stress of their last few visits, they enjoyed the peacefulness of each other's company.

Jeff broke the silence. *I think, maybe, it's time for me to go.*

Mindi's reply sounded reluctant: *Okay. I hope I do get to see you again. I feel like we just met, and I'll be sad if you don't come back.*

Me too, Jeff said. *We'll see if I can come back to your time. If I can't, it won't be my choice. But you'll do well. Good luck.*

Thank you.

Jeff thought, *Charlene, Charlene, Charlene.*

It worked again. He awoke. The name of the woman he would marry had awakened him. But was his time with Mindi over?

143

CHAPTER 12

Jeff had no dreams for over a week. He tried, as a test, to say her name to prompt a dream visit, but was unsuccessful and disappointed, which meant he had nothing to add to his journal buried in the bottom of his nightstand.

He'd accomplished his mission to help Mindi get past a major stumbling block in her life caused by a traumatic childhood. It gave her a push to get started in school. Jeff had been a positive part of her therapy. It had only been a few times, but he'd enjoyed talking with her in the gray room, rather than being in her head. Somewhere there had to be an answer. With those thoughts, he dropped off to sleep . . . and that night . . .

He dropped directly into Mindi's mind—no fall, and no float—instantly in her mind at her work in Denny's. As happy as he was to be there, Jeff resolved to be silent. Mindi told him before that she could tell when he was there, but he still didn't want to distract and announce his presence while she was busy. Besides, there had been none of the signs this time of her hand to her forehead, no rubbing the temples.

Then he heard her think, *Hi, Jeff.*

Hi, Mindi.

I'm so glad you're here, but I'm really busy. If you can stay, maybe we can we talk later.

I'll be quiet and just watch.

Mindi approached a booth where two middle-aged men in business suits and an attractive woman in a red-and-white flowered dress sat waiting to order. Mindi stood at the edge of the table and looked first to the man sitting to her left, then to the woman opposite him in the booth. The woman appeared younger than the two men. She returned Mindi's smile, then looked back down to her menu.

While the woman contemplated the menu, Mindi focused on the man sitting next to the woman, immediately to Mindi's right. At that instant, Jeff recognized the man as Rick. The shock of recognition made Jeff's psychic-self recoil backward, and his solid connection with Mindi caused her to lose her balance. She stumbled, and her feet started to slide.

The woman in the booth emitted a startled, "Oh!"

Mindi grabbed the edge of the table, and Rick grabbed her right arm and steadied her while she regained her footing.

"Are you all right?" he asked, letting go as she straightened up.

Though embarrassed, Mindi composed herself. She looked down at her shoes and mumbled, "I slipped. I'm so sorry. Must be something on the floor there. If one of you gets up before I can get someone to clean that up, please be careful." She smiled at all three in turn, ending back at the woman. "May I take your order?"

"Carolyn?" Rick said.

The woman looked at him, then back down at her menu.

Jeff understood that his shock at seeing Rick had transferred to Mindi and made her lose her balance, but she recovered well. Other than being embarrassed, she was fine.

Jeff had two things on his mind: First, he had to apologize

to Mindi. And second, why was he in Gardena at the same time as Rick?

As Mindi left the table to put in their orders, Jeff asked, *Mindi, can you hear me?*

Yes. What were you doing? You made me slip.

Are you all right? I'm sorry, so sorry.

Yes, but you startled me; I almost fell. Her mental voice was shaky.

That man who grabbed your arm is my girlfriend's father, Rick Thomsen. In my time, Rick is dead. Next March, he'll die in a plane crash. He must be the reason I'm here today, to see him. But why? I've got to leave and think about this. Maybe we can meet in the gray room when we can talk. I'm so sorry.

What? He dies? Mindi said. *That's terrible. Horrible. That's why you're upset. You take care. I'll be okay.*

Charlene, Charlene, Charlene.

Jeff awoke thinking about Rick. He wondered if this was another reason, or could it be *the* reason for him to be in Mindi Ketchem's mind in these dreams? But for what purpose? Rick's other daughter, Gail, had an apartment in Redondo Beach, which was near Gardena, but the woman with Rick wasn't Gail. There might be an FAA office, an airplane manufacturer, or vendor near the Denny's where Mindi works, which could explain why he was there. Rick traveled all over the West Coast—to Los Angeles, San Francisco, San Diego, Portland. Rick being there wouldn't be that unusual.

But why was I there?

What was the reason both of them were there at the same time? Coincidence? Serendipity? With all the travel into Mindi's time, it had never occurred to Jeff that Rick was still alive then. He wrote all of this in his notebook, still feeling the adrenaline of the experience. He stopped when he realized his writings might be the rantings of a crazy man.

~

He dreamed again and landed in their gray room. Mindi wore her work slacks, blouse and apron, and he was grateful that he wasn't inside her head tonight so he could see her.

They stood ten feet apart again. He smiled. And she returned the smile. Jeff felt awkward but said, "Hi. Good to see you again. How are you doing? Sorry about . . . tripping you."

"Hi, Jeff. It's all right. Thanks, though." She paused. "The guy you said had died is your girlfriend's dad?"

"Yeah. I'm trying to figure out why he and I were there at the same time. It's too much of a coincidence."

Mindi nodded. "And we still really don't know why you and I are here together. Right?" She waved her arm to include the room. "Or the times when you're here." She tapped her forehead. "This is something right off the Sci-Fi Channel for me."

"Yeah, me too."

They started their next sentences at the same time, then paused, then both said, "You first."

Jeff pointed at her. "No, you go first."

Mindi smiled. "Well, first I need to tell you I did tell my psychiatrist about our last conversation here, but I didn't tell her you were a real person. She as much as said it's all in my head, which I guess it is, since we're both dreaming. But the doctor meant it differently, of course. She told me that at first, she thought it might be my way of handling my problem, like Shirley. But the more I explained, the healthier it seemed to her. She thinks that you're not part of a split personality, not a dissociative identity problem. Besides helping me to embrace my shadow-self, she implied I have imagined you as someone

I would be attracted to." She stopped and looked down, appearing shy.

Jeff waited for her to continue. But when she looked up at him, he realized she wanted him to comment. He wasn't sure of the best way to answer her but started with the first thing he felt. "I'm flattered. I've gotten to know you, and you're a smart, sensitive person. You have all the qualities that anyone would appreciate. Plus, you're attractive, but you haven't let your intelligence and your beauty go to your head. That's rare."

She smiled as she met his gaze. "Thank you. You are a kind, gracious man. I felt embarrassed when I woke up the next morning after I told you were handsome. I suppose I blurted it out because you *are* the kind of guy I'm attracted to."

Jeff wondered if she had a crush on him. "I'm only a person in your dreams right now," he said, "although I am a real person. We've established that two years separate us. Who knows who you'll meet between now and the time you reach my time?

"You know, I've got a wonderful woman back there." He gestured with his thumb over his shoulder, looked around, and with an embarrassed look at Mindi, said, "That's silly. She's not back there. She's in 2017. She and I have been friends for a while now, and she has the same qualities I see in you. She's beautiful and smart, but not arrogant about either. I'm planning to ask her to marry me." He searched her face for a reaction. She gave him a nod of understanding. He saw no sign of disappointment.

"Charlene's a lucky woman," she said. "And that guy's her father?"

Jeff's eyes widened with surprise. "How do you know her name?"

Mindi smiled. "It first came up when we had our . . ."

Jeff finished her sentence. "Our, uh, fight? You asked me if I got into her head, too, when I compared your anger to hers."

"Yeah, I remembered that. And her name is your escape word, too, right? When you left my head last week, I heard you say her name three times, then you were gone."

Jeff took half a step forward. "Yes, yes. That's the stuff we need to talk about. I told you, I don't have any way to control when I, well, get into your mind. But using her name to escape has worked so far."

He waited a moment, but she held his gaze. He continued, "Well, you know the times I've been with you: When you've been to see Dr. Singh, when you've been on the bus, at your job at Denny's and . . . I was there while you were filling out your application for school. You want to be a makeup model like your mother talked to you about before she died."

"Wow," Mindi said. "If this wasn't a dream I could—no, I *would* call the police on you. You have been stalking me, haven't you?"

Her accusation made him feel defensive. "Stalking? That's not fair. It's not because I wanted to, Mindi, honest." He held up his arms, palms up, facing out, in a sign of surrender.

She smiled and waved her hand in dismissal. "I know." Then she said with a serious tone, "So you know what my father did?" Embarrassment laced her voice.

"Yes. I don't know any details, but I'm so sorry. And after I saw you with the doctor, I decided to do some research on my own. I learned why you may have created a Shirley to protect yourself. I'm glad you're handling it well."

Mindi's candid reply made Jeff even more sure of her internal strength. "I was screwed up for quite a few years," she said. "I lived with my father for a little while after Mom died and then moved out on my own. Then he died. I was scared of men. Couldn't get close to anyone. After years, I felt so much pain, I had to surrender and get some help.

"My father taught me about surrender when he stopped drinking and went to AA meetings. I'm working hard to forgive him. The doctor's helping me with that. There's scars, but I have to go on with my life." She paused a moment to collect her thoughts. Jeff remained quiet. She said, "I've sure told you a lot—but you already knew, didn't you?" She frowned and her lips quivered as if she might cry. "Oh, and you helped chase Shirley away by being kind to her, and not by force. That was good." She looked relieved. She searched his eyes for acceptance, then said, "Okay. Your turn," she said with a weak smile.

He returned her gaze with recognition of her pain. "Thank you for wanting me to know about you. And, yes, I did know. And I've watched some of your struggle."

He wanted to change the subject but couldn't, so he said, "I've kept a dream journal in a notebook." He quickly added, "But I'll keep it private, so you don't need to worry that I'll share it with anybody. I work with computers and software; we document everything."

Mindi gave no feedback, nonverbal or otherwise, on what he'd just said.

"Do you want to know more about me?" Jeff asked.

"Yes, please."

"I'm, well, I'm thirty-three years old. I grew up in Indianapolis. Mom passed away right after I enrolled at UW. My dad and younger brother, Mark, live back home. Dad remarried. He and my stepmom are happy. I live in Seattle, work at a software company as a marketing rep. You know about Charlene. Let's see, what else can I tell you?

"Oh yes. I'm in the National Guard. Do guard weekends once a month. I drive a two-year-old Toyota Camry. Oh, and sometimes people want to know what my sign is. I'm a Gemini, and my favorite color is blue." He considered adding that he knew Craig, but her next comment, interjected quickly, derailed that thought.

"Hey, you haven't seen me get undressed, take a shower, or anything like that, have you?"

He looked her straight in the eyes and said quickly and with firm honesty, "No." Then with compassion, "Thank goodness, no. I was so afraid that might happen. That's why I came up with an escape word—to make myself wake up, rather than put us through that. Especially since I realized you knew I was there—how you rubbed your eyes."

Mindi said, "I was worried, but I couldn't remember a time when I felt you were there when I was undressed."

Jeff kept his mind still to not betray the time in the restaurant bathroom. He didn't want to share that.

"So I hope, since you can't control yourself—" She paused, maintaining eye contact, then said, "Sorry, I didn't mean for that to sound like it did. I mean, since you can't choose when you visit, you'll use your escape word, won't you?"

Jeff assured her with a quick nod. "Yes, of course." He waited as she searched his eyes and confirmed he meant it. Then he said, "Whatever the reason all of this is happening, it seems to be steering us toward something, and that's what we need to talk about."

"Sure," Mindi said. "I hope we can meet here again. It feels like our dreams have synchronized to when we're both asleep." Another pause. "Promise me something, though. The next time you come to visit me, and it's not here, but in my head, tell me. Please? I'm grateful to know now that those feelings are you and not guys undressing me with their eyes, or worse, there's some creep stalking me. Okay?"

"Yes, I promise."

"Thank you. You said that you're my friend. I want to be

your friend too. I wish we knew what this is all about." She looked away a moment as if she had a thought. "I'll be honest with Dr. Singh about this, but leave out the time difference thing and that you are a real person. She'd put me back on meds, or give me shock treatments, or put me in a padded cell if I told her all of it. My recovery depends on me being honest with her so she can help me. I'll always be honest with you too—whether you're real or just a figment of my imagination."

"So you still have doubts that all of this is real?"

"Don't you? You might just be someone I created to help give me hope."

"Sure, I understand. I know that I'm real. And I know you are a real person too, but there's still a lot unexplained, and I guess I've still got a little doubt too. Regardless, I promise I won't betray you."

She gave him a warm smile. "Nor I, you. We can't end up in some medical journal or locked away and dissected by the CIA who'd want to use you as a spy."

Jeff laughed at that. Then his mood sobered. "How did you think of that? Damn, you're right. Okay, we'll keep this secret." He changed the subject. "Say, have you seen the glitter yet?"

"No. You talked about it."

"Okay, I'll leave here first tonight. You can watch."

She smiled. "Okay. Let's see."

He returned her smile. "Charlene, Charlene, Charlene." He watched her as he dissolved into a cloud of glitter.

He awoke, sat up and reached for his notebook. At the end of writing the night's entry he noted that she hadn't asked his last name or where he worked. He'd started to tell her about

Craig but had gotten distracted. So without her having asked more questions, he wondered if it was still possible that she was just a figment of *his* imagination, that these were really just dreams. Could it be that she thought he was just a figment of her imagination, making those details unimportant?

He finished this dream's entry with *Do I need to see a shrink to help me with this?* He stuck his dream journal back down in the drawer and got ready to go to work.

~

Charlene called in the morning and talked at length about the progress of her project. She'd been working on the LaDormeur account nonstop. She traveled less often between Seattle and Santa Monica now and spent more time down there than up north. With the willingness displayed by the media to, in her words, "jam the account into their existing schedules," she was sure they'd meet their Halloween deadline.

Jeff told her he was glad she was healthy and fit. The twelve-to-fourteen-hour days would brutalize anyone else. He commented that the work seemed to energize her.

Charlene admitted it wasn't all her work. "The money the client is throwing at this has opened a lot of doors. That's what's making it happen."

"Charlie, it takes more than just money to get people to work together toward a challenging goal. It takes talent and skill, and you've got both."

~

Jeff fell asleep wondering if he would dream tonight, and if so, where it would it take him. To the gray room or into Mindi's head? Those thoughts were all it now took to initiate his falling/floating sequence. He'd practiced this sequence so often now that all he did was think about it, and the dream would start. He still couldn't choose where he went, gray room or Mindi's mind. Tonight, the choice was once again made for them; it was the gray room.

Jeff wondered why they always stood ten feet away from each other in a featureless space without boundaries. "Why aren't we sitting down, having a glass of wine?" he said.

"Well, hey, this is our dream," Mindi said. "Why don't we imagine some chairs?"

At that instant, gray, overstuffed chairs appeared. They looked from each other to the chairs and back again, then back at each other with a smile. They sat down facing each other, dressed as they'd been before in their daily work attire. But there was no wine.

Mindi began the conversation. "Well, that's better. Comfortable?"

Jeff grinned. "What a great idea."

She nodded, made eye contact, and said, "You work for a software company in Seattle." It was a statement born of confidence, not a question.

Jeff knew that she'd been giving this some thought. His previous concerns about whether she felt he was or wasn't real were almost gone.

"Yes." He suspected the next question, but it came in the form of another statement.

"My cousin works in Seattle at a software company in the marketing department."

"Yes, I know."

"Do you know him?"

"Yes. Craig's a friend of mine. We work together, play golf, go to games. I know Barbara and the boys."

"That's reeally spooky," she said, drawing the word out and leaning toward him.

"Well, a lot of this stuff is spooky, right?" Jeff replied as he shook his head. "There've been so many coincidences like this." He told her how his dreams progressed. How, before he could see anything, he'd heard the doctor's receptionist say her name. How he saw her name tag. He told her he saw her on Craig's family tree and how he researched Dr. Singh. He mentioned the first time he was with her at work, then finding the Denny's on Google Earth, going there in person in 2017 for lunch, and trying to find her apartment—the whole private detective thing.

"You *were* stalking me." She tried to remain serious, but her eyes sparkled, teasing.

"No, no, no," he started to protest, then saw her smile. "Okay, that's funny. So when I visited you in my dreams and then the coincidences built up, then moved over to when I was awake, of course I had to follow up. Please believe me, I did not choose to spy on you. But I'm glad we met. I've watched you while you've worked on . . ."

She finished the sentence for him. "My problem? Yeah, thanks. But I haven't done it alone. You and Dr. Singh helped."

Jeff nodded. "And I'm so sorry you've had such pain in your life. I can only imagine what it would be like to be an adult orphan, both parents gone, all alone, and until now, no healthy relationship with a man."

"I don't *have* a relationship with a man," she said firmly.

"I know, but you and I are friends. No, it's not romantic, but a friendship is a relationship, right? You are pretty and charming. It won't take you long before you meet the right guy. I'm sure of that."

"I hope so. I really hope so. It makes me sad when I see

couples together, out to dinner, on a walk holding hands, and I'm alone . . ." Her voice trailed off.

Jeff nodded his head in understanding and wanted to say something positive. "You are, well, new to this lucid dreaming thing. I've been doing it a few weeks longer than you have, and to be honest, I think that you're handling it better than I did at first. You've caught on quicker than I did."

"Me too. I thought about it a lot, and now you've confirmed my cousin is your best friend in Seattle. It's beyond strange. Do you think we're being manipulated?"

"I don't know. I've wondered that more than once, but I don't know how we could find out. We just have to go with it, I guess." He shrugged.

She changed the subject. "Oh, hey, I've only seen pictures of Craig's twins. Have you met them?"

"Yeah, they're the smartest twelve-year-olds I've ever met. They give Craig and Barb a run for their money and keep them busy weekends—summer with baseball, then soccer in the fall. Craig is crazy about those boys."

"Let's see, they'd be—"

Jeff finished her sentence. "—ten years old for you in 2015."

"Oh, yeah. I'm still getting used to the two-year difference and your time travel thing."

"Yeah, that's one of the other things I want to talk with you about. I'm not sure what I can tell you about your life in 2017." He paused, waiting for her to catch up. "Craig talked about his cousins and that your mom and dad had passed away. He hasn't talked about you personally, but you're on his genealogy chart. He calls your folks his uncle and aunt, but your dad was his first cousin. Must be the age difference that he called him uncle."

She started to interrupt, but he anticipated her question and shook his head. "No, he knows nothing about all this. I haven't asked him about you or shown any direct interest in his family, let alone you, because I don't think I could explain why I'm so interested. Nobody, I mean *nobody*, knows about my dreams. Not Craig, not Charlie . . ."

"Who's Charlie?"

"That's my nickname for Charlene." He paused and glanced around, thinking her name might wake him. He didn't want to end tonight's session yet.

"What's wrong?"

"I was afraid I might end the dream by saying her name."

She smiled. "We're still here. Go on."

"I don't think I should tell you anything about the future, your personal future in particular, because if you knew stuff, it might make the future change. In doing research on time travel, I came across the term, *time travel paradox*."

Mindi frowned. "Paradox?"

"Maybe you've heard of it and don't recognize it." He told her the basics—that you can't go back and kill your ancestors before you were born.

"Yeah, I have heard about that, but I haven't given it much thought. We're not planning on killing anybody, right?"

Jeff chuckled. "No. Not hardly. But we have to be careful we don't invoke any other kind of contradiction in the order of time. There might be some things that no one should know about their future. Maybe we should leave stuff alone and not mess with it."

Mindi considered this. "So if you knew anything about what I'm going to do, that if I meet a guy or stay in LA, go to New York or Paris, anything . . . you wouldn't tell me?"

"I don't think I should. And I don't know about any of those things. Really, I don't."

She studied his face for any sign of a lie. "You don't, do you?

And you want to do the right thing and not mess things up."

"That's right. I might learn things in my waking real time in the future. Craig and I are friends—he's likely to tell me about his family. I might see family photos when I go over to his place. I just don't know. And I don't want to screw up choices you make."

"It might help me make choices, keep me from guessing what to do. It could guide me."

Jeff considered that and nodded his agreement. "Yeah. But is it my place to tell you? I'll have to watch my words when we meet here or when I drop into your head."

"Well, dropping into my head isn't a great choice of words, is it?" Her eyes shone, then her expression grew more serious. "Besides, wouldn't it be my choice what I do with what you tell me?"

He looked at her, admiring both her sense of humor and common sense. "Well, to your first point, I guess I could be more diplomatic about what I call a visit. Second, I don't want to cause a disaster."

"You didn't answer my question. It would still be my choice, right?"

This was a debate he couldn't win, so rather than risk a loss, he went for a tie. "You may be right. We'll take each issue one at a time, if we need to, right?"

"I know. I trust you and I like you. I'm becoming convinced you're as much a victim of all of this as I am."

Jeff realized she wasn't the fearful person she was when he first saw her. Shirley was gone. Mindi was enrolled in school, worked in a job many people considered beneath them, and did it with joy and efficiency.

"What are you thinking about, Jeff?"

"Just considering how far you've come in such a short time."

Mindi smiled. "Thank you, but I still feel very vulnerable, and now more vulnerable, because you and I are coming together in dreams that we can't control—and don't know why."

Jeff nodded. "Well, there's a part of your future that is my past, and I already shared it with you. It might, *might* be why we're being drawn into this."

She sat forward in her chair, a question on her face.

"Charlene's dad, Rick. He worked—well, in your time, *works*—for the FAA, and there's an office close to Denny's, so that might be why he was in your restaurant." Jeff stopped for a moment to consider. "Unless . . ." He paused.

"Go on," she said.

"Nah. Rick had a good marriage. He wouldn't be fooling around. Never mind. So why was he at your table when I was visiting you?"

"So, this is just another coincidence?"

"Maybe, but I'm not so sure. Some say there's no such thing as a coincidence, that things always happen for a reason. Of course, others think that's a rationalization to help people accept whatever happens to them. I really don't know."

"What happens to him is sad, but how could that affect us?" Mindi asked.

Jeff smiled, pleased that she wanted to help him figure this out. "I don't know. I just don't know. There's got to be a reason for the synchrony of all of us being together."

"Synchrony?"

"Kind of like a coincidence. I've got to think about it. Maybe I'll have some ideas next time we meet here. Next subject . . ." He waited for her a moment to catch up.

"Sure. What's next?"

"Please don't consider contacting Craig in your time and telling him you're having dream conversations with his friend

159

from work. Don't ask him questions about me."

"Why would I do that?" Her eyes narrowed, a defensive tone in her voice.

"Curiosity, plain and simple. And I wouldn't blame you one bit for being curious. But it might somehow mess around and cause a paradox. Maybe or maybe not anything serious, but how would we know?"

Jeff glanced down at his hands, then back up to make eye contact. "Trust me, I've had big, I mean huge curiosity itches that I wanted to scratch ever since these 'coincidences' started showing up, and I've had to keep from scratching them. Like asking Craig about you, where you live and such. But it would mean too many questions I might have to answer. So if you do need to satisfy your curiosity about me, check out my LinkedIn page. You can find out everything I want the public to know about me. That will verify I'm real. You do know about LinkedIn, right?"

"I've heard about it. It's kind of Facebook for professionals."

"Well, yes. You could have a page as a model, or even a student. It's not just for techies. Here's what I was thinking: you could set up your own page on LinkedIn and request to connect with me. No, that won't work, because if you do that, I would've seen it two years ago. Wouldn't have known who you are. But if you put your picture on your page, and I was asked to link with you, I might not have, or I might've, because you're so pretty. But that never happened. I'd remember. Regardless, I would have known about you from before I heard your name and saw your face in my dreams . . ." He trailed off. "No, that won't work. It might mess us up here."

She frowned thoughtfully for a moment, then nodded.

"I see what you mean. I can't even mail something to you through the snail mail, can I? You'd get it two years ago, right?

It'd change what we're doing now, right? By the way, thank you for that compliment."

"You're welcome—it's true. And you're right. If I mailed something to your apartment in 2017, and you still live there, you'd get it in my time, and I would be communicating in these dreams with you, Mindi version 2015, and then by mail with Mindi version 2017. Things could get all messed up with that too."

"Yeah," Mindi said. "But in 2017, I'd remember I had these dreams. It'd be old business for me by then."

"But," he said, "if we talked in 2017, telling me what we did, say, a month from your now, that's still in my future. That might have the same effect as if I told you what you did in the next two years. Because you could tell me about my future, stuff that didn't happen to me yet because I'm doubling back in time to see you. Oh, crap. This is so confusing. My job is all about logic and I'm having trouble tracking this. I need a flowchart.

"Remember, when I wake up," he continued, "you, Mindi Ketchem, are alive somewhere in 2017. And likewise, there's a Jeff version 2015, and me, here now, I'm Jeff version 2017. You, here, are Mindi version 2015. There's four of us. Actually more, because there's Mindi in 1991 when you were born, and Jeff 2021, and so on. Technically, there could be an infinite number of versions.

"It's confusing, I know. But in the real world, the timeline only runs in one direction, toward the future. Mix and match like we're doing should never happen. Except that it has. And because it has, I might screw things up if I brought back 2017 news information to you in 2015. Like who's president in my time, what the stock market is doing, what sports team wins the 2016 Super Bowl." He lowered his voice to a conspiratorial whisper, "You know, there are science fiction stories where

161

someone goes back in time and places bets based on scores he knew already. And cleans up big. But if we tried that, I'd be afraid it would invoke a paradox. The universe might not like that kind of swindle. So I think we can keep from messing up the future by keeping the number of variables low. I should never talk to my v.2015 or talk to Mindi v.2017 and same for you."

"I'm sure I'll remember a nice guy named Jeff that I dreamed about when I get to 2017."

Jeff grinned. "Thank *you* for that compliment."

"My pleasure. Say, what's your last name? I need your whole name to look you up, right?"

"Marlen, Jeffrey C. Marlen."

"Is that like the fish?"

"No, with an *e*."

"Okay, what's the *C* stand for?"

"Christopher."

She leaned forward, bringing her head down in respect. "Nice to meet you, Jeffrey Christopher Marlen. Until next time."

"G'night, Miranda Jasmine Ketchem."

Her eyes widened. "Now, how do you know my full name?"

"I saw it on Craig's genealogy chart. It's a very pretty name."

Mindi replied with a laugh, "All right, that's enough for now. I've got no secrets from you, do I?"

They were both smiling as they dissolved in a flutter of glitter.

Jeff woke up, grateful for another day and feeling unexpectedly refreshed, considering he'd sat and talked with a new friend for what seemed half the night.

He noted the entire dream in his spiral notebook. While transcribing the conversation about LinkedIn, he wondered if she'd tried to link to his page two years ago, and that's where his subconscious had her name and face for his dreams. When he finished, after he hid his dream journal in his nightstand, he searched on LinkedIn to see if she'd established an account. He didn't find one and felt relieved because if she had, he'd again believe he might've constructed her. He enjoyed visiting with her and would hate to have this new friendship dissolve into being merely a dream.

He put all those thoughts away and thought about the excitement of Charlene's return from Santa Monica tomorrow.

CHAPTER 13

When Jeff met Charlene outside arrivals at Sea-Tac, they embraced, and their kiss lasted so long that a young man passing them on the sidewalk said, with good humor, "Get a room!"

They both laughed and leaned in for another kiss.

Jeff had reservations at a fancy restaurant to celebrate her return because she'd only eaten on the run while she'd been gone, and he felt she would appreciate a sit-down dinner.

"I ate well," Charlene said, "but I sure could use some time at the gym. I'm going to seed."

"Charlie, you look great."

Charlene gave a little laugh, leaned over, and kissed him. "What a charmer. We haven't been together for a while."

Their conversation centered on the LaDormeur campaign. She told him that every idea her team had floated was treated as if brilliant.

"Jeff, they loved the idea of using mostly unknown makeup models. Even though the public might not notice, they want fresh faces for the younger market. It'll be noticed by the competition and keep them off-balance. They loved it!"

Jeff gave her a positive look, her cue to keep talking.

"We'll use a natural blonde, a Black woman, an Asian, a Native American, a brunette, and a redhead. LaDormeur wants the young women who haven't settled on a specific brand yet, and new faces should help do that. Plus, they want to encourage many to switch brands when they see the quality."

Charlene took a deep breath and continued, "LaDormeur wants to pick up a large market share that includes mature women too. So, to draw in that market, we suggested we recruit retired models not seen for a while and even women who've had no public face.

"We'll saturate the media with stills, ten-second spots, and entertaining thirty- and forty-second spots, all featuring the new, younger, older, and seasoned models. The client liked it all. They were thrilled."

"And looks like you're thrilled too."

"Absolutely. And y'know what? They want my staff and me to have input on the final choice of models. Agents from all over the country have been contacted and we've started receiving portfolios."

Jeff wondered if Mindi v.2017 had an agent yet.

"Terrific. You're going to be one busy woman. Will I be able to get on your calendar or do I have to wait weeks for an appointment?" he said, being playful.

"I always have time for you, Jeff. Always,"

"This is great, really exciting. It's what you've been working for. You've got this handled, right?"

"Yes, you're right, but one of the other things I've been fine-tuning is my team. I'm not having to do all of it on my own like some of the other programs I've had. I've got a great group. I'm relying on them pretty heavily."

The evening ended on a good note. At her apartment he

helped unload luggage and the portfolios containing the campaign materials. They both had to get an early start at work the next day, so it wasn't practical that Jeff stay over. They shared a nice, long goodnight kiss and promised they'd get together again this week.

Charlene teased him. "I'm sure I can find space on my busy calendar for you. Stay in touch."

Back at his apartment Jeff watched a bit of TV before going to sleep. Would he have another dream? No. He didn't.

~

Charlie had been putting in grueling hours on the ad campaign, so Jeff arrived at her apartment with steaks for grilling, potatoes for baking, salad, and a bottle of wine.

"What time do you want to eat? Should I start the grill?" he said as he opened the bottle of the red wine and set the cork aside to let the wine breathe, then wandered over to Charlie, who had papers and photos spread out on the dining table. He wrapped his arms around her and kissed her neck.

"Mmm," she said as he pulled her even closer. "Oh, Jeff, you're so distracting." She set down the photos, closed her eyes, and leaned back against him, snuggling in.

When she turned around to embrace him, he turned her back to face the table with a mock admonishment. "Now, now, now, don't let distractions divert you from your work." He looked over her shoulder at the pictures spread out on the table. "What are you working on there?"

"Okay," she said in a disappointed tone. "We got a new batch of portfolios by email, and I had Janice print them out because I can't look at them on the screen to compare them the way I can with hard copies." With that, she fanned out the fresh eight-by-tens, using both hands. "There's some gorgeous girls here. What d'ya think? Don't make me jealous and don't drool on them."

He leaned over and moved photos around, teasing her with ohs and ahh's. He picked up each picture and looked at the smiling, seductive, and passionate poses the women had supplied for review. His shuffling revealed a surprising photo, and he froze, staring at the image. Mindi! He tried to maintain his composure, trusting that Charlie wouldn't notice his struggle.

But of course, she did. Charlene looked from his face, back down to the picture, and back at him.

"Yeah, I was taken by her too. I've already put her in the final top three brunettes to present to the group when it's time. Let's see." She picked it up and looked at the bio on the back. Jeff tried to put his surprise at rest. Charlene read, "She's twenty-six, a little older than the rest, but she looks much younger. Her name's Miranda Madisen. That's exotic, eh? Out of an LA agency. Only a year in the business. Some local work in LA Magazine, and for the local Macy's and Bloomingdale's. Thanks for your feedback. You have good taste."

When Charlie read Mindi's professional name, Jeff realized why he couldn't find her on the internet. She'd changed her name. Was it a stage name? Had she legally changed it, or maybe gotten married? She might've changed it because she didn't want her father's name. *Nah*, he decided, *she wouldn't do that*. But wasn't the usual spelling of *Madison* with an *o*? He wondered if, when she chose her new name, she kept the *e* at the end of her last name to match the change of *e* in *Ketchem*.

He'd become distracted, so he returned his attention to the woman close-by.

"Yeah," he said as he pulled Charlie close to him, nuzzling her neck again. "I do have great taste in women."

167

Charlene kept sorting the photos, and Mindi's ended up on top of the keeper stack. Jeff stole another look at Mindi v.2017. She looked so professional and poised, even better than when he'd first seen her in the mirror in her bathroom. He couldn't stand the distraction, so he put a file folder on top of it for his own good.

In bed, Charlene fell asleep before Jeff, who had his arm around her. Her head nestled where his shoulder met his arm. He tucked her in closer and stared at the ceiling. He felt pleased that Mindi *had* made it through school and was following her dream. That's why she hadn't been at Denny's.

As he fell asleep, his mind raced, arguing with itself. Would he tell Mindi what he knew, or should he keep it from her? She'd find out in time. What harm could it do for her to know? Wouldn't it, when times got tough, give her motivation? Or, if she thought it was all predestined, would she get overconfident and lazy and screw it all up?

He didn't resolve this argument with himself. Absent, too, was any resolution by Jeff about the age-old debate between philosophers, theologians, and physicists regarding predestination versus free will. The arguments had been around for centuries, and no one was any closer to an answer.

He woke up in the morning after a dream-free night. Charlie sat on the edge of the bed offering him a steaming cup of coffee. She was wearing a smile, a T-shirt, and not much else. After Jeff left for work, Charlene would devote all day to her project. She saw him to the door, gave him a passionate kiss, held him tight and said, "Jeff, you are so patient with all the time I have to give to all of this." A wave of her arm swept toward the table strewn with paperwork and photos. "I promise we'll get more"—she gave him a coy look under her eyelashes—"quality time before I have to go back to California."

He gave her another long kiss. "I'm looking forward to it. Do good work."

When he got home after work, he straightened up his apartment and fixed dinner, then brought his dream journal up to date with Mindi's name change. He felt relieved that Mindi v.2017's future had progressed and looked promising.

Jeff didn't know if this chapter of Mindi v.2015 had closed to him now that he'd satisfied whatever the universal mind, that formal pantheistic metaphor, had planned for him. Would the dreams now stop? Could there be more for him to do—or for both of them to do? Or was this some pointless joke visited on them to humor some unseen entity?

To give him some peace of mind, he tried to accept that they were merely dreams, as meaningless as dreams are prone to be. With a frown, he closed the journal and put it in the bottom of the drawer, wondering if it might stay there until he threw it out. He turned out the light.

~

And after a quiet, brief interlude of floating in the gray, Jeff sat across from Mindi in their equally gray, overstuffed chairs.

"Hi, what's up?" Jeff said.

Mindi smiled. "Well, it works."

"What works?"

"I called you here tonight. I went to bed thinking I'd like to tell Jeff about my latest visit to Dr. Singh. And it worked—here you are."

"You sound pleased."

"Right. I am. I shared my notes about our last few meetings with her."

"I thought you told her about that?"

"Well, I did. And I've told her about the rest we've talked about too. I figured I'm paying to get help and she can't help if I'm not honest with what I'm doing and experiencing." Anticipating Jeff's question, she answered it right away. "But she still thinks you are an 'exceptionally finely detailed construct of my subconscious.' Those are her words." Mindi smiled at Jeff, her eyes bright and her chin held high.

Jeff tried to interject, but Mindi gestured for him to wait. "The doctor told me my case doesn't fit the critical multiple personality/dissociative identity disorder definition, but I'm still going to be in a paper she's writing. Don't worry, we'll be anonymous. Bottom line with my visits to her, I'm not as sick as I thought. She said about 'the voices in my head'—those were her words—that I should filter them and listen to only what is best for me, not act on any impulse. She thinks that I've made great progress. I should continue my visits, but not every week, to work on my feelings toward my parents, particularly my father. She said it would be better for me if I didn't let what had happened to me define who I am."

Jeff nodded. "That makes sense. I've done a little more research on healing after trauma like what happened to you. It said pretty much what your doctor told you, that as you heal, your ability to have meaningful relationships will increase. So I agree with that part."

Mindi smiled again. "Thank you. It means a lot that you care enough to want to understand."

Jeff returned her smile, then said, "Of course, I disagree with her that I'm not real. But . . . I agree that you should always be true to yourself."

"That's what Mom told me. Well, something like that. A short time before she died of breast cancer, she said to always trust my heart, to not be a people-pleaser." She looked away, remembering her grief.

Jeff frowned. "I didn't know how your mom died. I'm so sorry."

"Thank you." Her eyes had begun to puddle up with tears.

These dreams are so very real, Jeff thought. *Those are real tears.*

Mindi sniffed. "Well, what's next?"

"I don't know. I told you that one of the reasons this woo-woo stuff could be happening is that someone or something unknown sent me to help you decide to go to beauty school. As a bonus, I get a friend."

With a smile, she replied, "I got a friend too. You're a nice guy. Charlene is blessed to have you."

"Thank you. I feel lucky too. Now, about her dad. I've been thinking about why Rick was in my dream. Maybe we are supposed to do something for Rick, maybe to keep him from dying."

Mindi's eyes widened. "Wow. That's pretty bold." Her questions came out in rapid succession: "Do you think we could? How would we know if we should? Do you think other people do things like this, and we don't know it because everybody keeps it a secret? And what if we could do that? Would we cause a paradox and mess up time?"

"Wow. You are sharp and ask good questions. Some I never had. My answer to all of them is, I don't know. Here's what I have come up with, though. I've had to learn to relax when the dream starts. It hasn't been easy, but when I do, the falling turns to floating. And when I have questions, if I relax, the answers appear, not always right away, but they do come, or as a clue where to find them. Like when I helped you about being a model. It just happened. I was in the moment and thought the right thing."

"Okay, so you're saying we need to wait and see?"

171

"That's pretty much it. We really have no choice. Worrying about stuff that hasn't happened yet is just a waste of time, anyway. But on the other side, we do have to have some kind of plan. There's no point in me worrying that you might time travel forward to meet me."

"Where did that come from?" she asked.

"I dunno . . . Just thinking about how this whole thing works. Wondered if we traveled forward in time, where could we end up?" Jeff twisted his face into a silly look. "You know, we might have to use escape words to escape in a hurry."

Mindi was in tune with exactly what he was thinking. "Yeah, I'm not sure I want to hang out in a guy's head when he's with his girlfriend."

Jeff grimaced. "Or vice versa."

They looked at each other for a moment, thinking about the possibilities, then they both broke out in laughter.

After catching her breath, Mindi said, "It's so good to laugh. It's been a long time under a dark cloud. Thank you for being here for me."

"You know, I don't think I've ever heard you laugh. It's a nice laugh."

Wiping tears of laughter from her eyes, Mindi said, "What do you think about me sending you an email? Would it mess up the time travel continuum thing?"

"Don't know. Let's see . . . if you send me an email in 2015, I would get it in 2015. I never responded in 2015, did I? No, you don't know yet, you haven't sent it. It would not surprise me I didn't respond, because I rarely respond to unsolicited emails. This is confusing. If you sent, no, correction, if you *send* me an email, would I have even gotten it? If I did receive it, did I ever see it, or saw it and don't remember? It might've gone to junk mail or I just deleted it, or . . ." No other possibilities came to mind. He looked at her for a reply.

"Well, my father used to say, 'Nothing ventured, nothing gained.' What's your email address? Let's try."

Would it invoke a paradox? He didn't know. "Sure, let's try it. There're no butterflies at risk here."

"Butterflies? What does that have to do with anything?"

He told her about Ray Bradbury's short story, then gave her his email address.

She repeated it and added, "Check your email when you get home." She rolled her eyes and gave him a big smile. "Oh, you're already home—asleep, right?"

"Right," he said, returning the smile and smacking his forehead in mock chastisement. "This is so real, I forget this is a dream."

Still smiling, she nodded.

"Charlene, Charlene, Charlene," and he woke up in his own bed in 2017, a smile on his face in appreciation of her sense of humor.

~

Discipline at completing his journal entry prevailed. Before checking his email, he documented their meeting, including her plan to email him from 2015.

Finally, he opened his email inbox, feeling certain that he'd find nothing. Email from two years ago wouldn't have shown up in today's email. He shrugged. *Silly to think it might be stuck there.* Nevertheless, he still scrolled to the bottom of the inbox. Of course, he found no email from Mindi.

He stared at the screen, disappointed. Then he remembered the junk folder and felt foolish. He was in the computer business, yet he'd *never* checked that folder, ignoring it since he'd set up his address years ago. It had never been emptied. Click. Filed by date. The most recent stuff on top. A lot of spam. He scrolled down to get to 2015, moving backward in time through the folder. Finally he saw December 2015, November 2015, a few more clicks. There, dated October 14, 2015, was an email from MindiModel@yahoo.com. He froze. *It's from her!*

When he clicked on it, it didn't open. Paradox? Conflict? It took a moment until he realized it wouldn't open until it moved to the inbox. He moved it, then hesitated with his finger on the mouse button. It'd been in his junk folder for almost two years. That's why he'd never seen it. He clicked it open.

Hi Jeff.
If you're reading this, it means all this is real for both of us. I've thought about the logic, and you can't answer me here. I wouldn't get the email until 2017. By then, I'll know all we've done during our friendship up to your time. Who could ever forget these dreams and weirdness? Here's the thing—you might learn things about my future, at least the next two years' worth, and haven't told me. That's okay. I probably shouldn't know, like you said.
I thought about it some more. If you read this email in your 2015, because I sent it in my today, 10/14/2015, it might screw things up for you to visit me in your time. I guess I'll find out if you can't come back. Of course, like you said, if Jeff v.2015 reads it, he might think it's junk and delete it and forget about it, and you will still visit me in my head or the gray room, and we can continue our friendship. But you wouldn't be reading it because he/you deleted it. So if you're reading it now, you didn't see it until your

time. Does that make sense? Thinking about your time travel is cray-cray.

Because we've talked about the danger of changing the past or the future, I want to keep our communication the way it is now. You visit me, keep what you know about my future to yourself, if you do know something. Unless something bad happens to me in the next two years, then you could tell me so I could avoid it and not get hurt. But that might kill a butterfly, right? And upset the whole space-time continuum thing, right? Would the world blow up, or something?

I won't call Craig v.2015 and talk to him about you, and I know you won't call me in 2017. You said it might mess up you being able to visit me now in 2015, and I do so enjoy our visits. The future will take care of itself, right?

Let's limit the times when you're in my head. I'm always doing something like work, doctor, shopping, school. It never seems to happen when I have time and I'm just sitting. The best time for both of us seems to be when we're both asleep and visit each other's dreams. Let's work on that—it's the only thing I might be able to control on my end, to meet there. I'll try meditating or doing yoga to be ready.

Maybe we can figure out what this is all about. Next time you see me, I'm sure you'll tell me you got this. Otherwise, until then.

One more thing about all this and you finding me. Even with all the weirdness that felt scary at first, you've helped me be strong. Thank you.

Hope you read this in your tomorrow,
Mindi.

Jeff stared blankly at the screen for a moment before he reread it. This proved it was way more than just dreams. Mindi v.2017 was out there right now, and she knew what they had or hadn't done. But she was right. He couldn't reach out to her in his time, couldn't answer the email. She probably still had his email address, but she'd said no and her logic was, was, was—he fumbled for the right word—flawless.

His mind raced. What if they met through Charlene's work? No, that wasn't likely—unless he invited himself to some kind of interview or audition or whatever they called it. But that would never happen.

He clicked *Save Message* and put it in a new mail folder named *Dreams*. With it still on the screen, he sent it to his printer, which immediately came to life and printed something that he could now hold, tangible evidence he wasn't crazy.

After sticking the page in his dream notebook, he looked at the clock. He'd get to the office early. Beat the traffic.

All the way into work, he considered how to control getting to the gray room. He slapped the steering wheel with excitement over what that email meant to his sanity and his friendship with Mindi.

~

Jeff had been at work a full hour before Craig walked by and saw him, did a double take, popped his head in, and said, "Hey, Jeffy, you rarely get in before me. How long have you been here?"

Jeff looked up from his computer screen. "Woke up early. Thought I'd get in before the traffic demons stole some more of my time stalled on the freeway."

Craig smiled. "Move closer in. Get one of those condos down the street here, and you can walk to work."

To which Jeff replied with a smile, "At those prices, I'd have to walk because I couldn't afford my car."

Craig agreed with fake solemnity and a nod. "Grab some lunch later?"

"Sure thing." Jeff turned back to the screen as Craig left.

He stopped working for a moment and considered Craig going down south for his cousin's wedding. Would he bring back more information on Mindi v.2017? He ended his right-brained curiosity by giving his attention back to the screen, using his left brain for work.

~

That night, after talking to Charlene on the phone, he watched TV. When he went to bed, he remembered to test saying Mindi's name three times.

As he floated, he again wondered why everything was always gray. It didn't take long for a plausible answer to come to him: When he falls into Mindi's head, he's in her brain. The brain consists of gray matter. When they're in the gray room, that room is in her brain, therefore, gray. It would be hard to prove, but the idea satisfied his curiosity.

"Mindi, Mindi, Mindi," he called, then waited.

In the undefinable distance, a door opened. Through the doorway, he saw another gray background. Mindi appeared, her wardrobe different from before. She was barefoot, dressed in light pink sweatpants and a matching hoodie. He looked down at his clothes: blue plaid pajama bottoms, bare feet, and bare chest—what he'd worn to bed.

He was glad he didn't sleep in his underwear, or worse, nothing.

Mindi giggled.

"What?" He figured she'd just heard his thoughts, so to distract her attention from himself, he asked, "Why are you wearing sweats?"

"This is what I sleep in. I get cold," she replied, still smiling.

"Hmm. I wish I had my robe," he mused, wanting to cover his naked chest. Suddenly, he wore his long, plush, wine-colored lounging robe he didn't wear often—because he didn't "lounge" much.

He looked down at it, then at Mindi. "Charlene gave me this for my birthday."

"Oh," Mindi said. "Very nice."

"Thanks."

"Well, she has good taste, in robes—and men."

His face warmed as if it were his real face. She probably saw his color rising. For a moment he questioned how a dream image could blush, but then she spoke.

"I was asleep and heard your call."

"Yeah. I guess I need to be more careful with sleepwear. Say, are you falling or floating before you come through the doorway?"

"Neither. But you do, don't you?"

"Yeah. I thought about why it's always gray. I think I know. I'm falling into your brain, your gray matter. You're already in your brain, so you don't need to fall. But in our minds, it's gray in here. Makes sense, right?"

"Sure, I guess. You're quite the scientist, aren't you? You want to know how things work."

"Uh-huh. It's my job."

"I like to know too," she said.

"What did it look like before you came through the door?"

She looked around. "It's kinda like this. Maybe a little lighter."

"Yeah, I'm sure we're in our brains. I've got another question. When you wake up after dreaming here, do you wake up refreshed, or do you feel you need more sleep?"

"Oh, refreshed, I guess. I've never had a hard time sleeping or waking up, so except for the time before I started going to the doctor, it's all been good."

He nodded. "I sleep pretty well myself."

"Well, now that we know each other's sleep habits—and sleepwear," she said with another grin, "what else do you want to talk about?"

He looked around and, talking to the space, said, "Why don't we sit?" The chairs appeared, and they both sat. "I wonder if we wanted something to eat or drink, would our dream get them for us?"

She gave him a blank look.

"That's not so silly, really. I found on a blog post a guy lost weight through lucid dreaming by only eating junk food in his dreams, but not in real life."

Mindi raised an eyebrow. "Interesting. I'll keep that in mind."

"Oh, I got your email."

"Oh, good!" She grinned. "How did it show up? I kinda rambled in it. Did it make any sense?"

"Yes, it did make sense. I can tell you've been giving this stuff"—he waved his arm around indicating the space again—"a lot of thought." He explained the whole story about how he'd found it, the excitement in his voice obvious. "You realize that email shows we're both real. Not figments of our imaginations. You're real! I'm real! We're in each other's dreams, but it's not a dream, it's real."

"You're moving fast. Slow down a bit." She motioned downward with her palm.

Jeff smiled and realized he'd been leaning forward with enthusiasm as he talked. He sat back, took a deep breath, closed his eyes, and relaxed. "I'm sorry. It's been getting to be too much, and I haven't been able to talk to anyone about this, and now that I can talk to you . . . I guess it's been building up." He paused. "Sorry."

"It's all right. I feel the same way. It's as weird for me, except I have a psychiatrist to share with." She smiled.

Jeff was amazed at how mature, cool, and calm about this she was. It encouraged him to take another deep breath and say, "Now, about Charlene's dad . . ."

"Sure. First though," Mindi said, "I'd like to say that when I first saw you here, I found you very attractive. I thought someone like you would be, you know, my dream guy." She acted coy, a little like a schoolgirl, then caught herself and met his gaze with seriousness. "Your style in dealing with Shirley was, I don't know. Had real class, real maturity. That's the kind of person I want for my boyfriend."

Jeff wondered what this had to do with Rick. It sounded like she was making it about him, which made him uncomfortable. But he'd hear her out.

Mindi went on, "Now that I know you're real, well, dream real, and you have Charlene . . . and you mentioned saving Rick . . . That shows you really care about her. You want to help her with her pain." She stopped, not knowing what to say next.

Clearly she was thinking out loud, and this was something she couldn't talk to her doctor about, and he now understood what she was saying had to do with Rick.

Jeff acknowledged her with eye contact and a look of understanding. "Yeah. So first, if we are supposed to save Rick, we'll figure out a way. Second, whoever *you* meet, he'll be a very lucky guy. With the career you've chosen, I'm sure you'll have many chances to find your Mr. Right. You won't have to settle for second best."

She didn't acknowledge what he said, apparently still having things she needed to say. "I'm so curious, and I know you said you wouldn't tell me about my future, and I said I didn't want to know, but I am curious about how things will turn out. I'm not bringing this up to ask, but . . ."

Grateful she'd changed the subject, Jeff said, "I really know hardly anything about what you'll be doing. When I went down to Santa Monica and visited your apartment building in Gardena in 2017, many of the name tags on the mailboxes were missing, and your name wasn't on them. And before you and I, uh, met here in person, I did try to google your name, but I couldn't find a Mindi Ketchem. I figured you moved or got married or something, or there was just no reason for you to be on the internet's radar. I did find your father's obituary in the newspaper. I'm sorry."

She shrugged. "Thanks, but don't be. He tried to pull himself together, and he was sober for over a year. And with Dr. Singh's help, I'm coming to terms with what he did. It's no secret. I don't feel like a martyr. I am sad, but it is what it is. But as far as what you know about me, I sense you do know something about my future, but based on our agreement, you won't tell me. I also feel that what you know isn't bad, because I'd be able to read it in your face. I'm going to school now. I don't know if I'll move from my apartment. It's a nice place, so no point in moving, I guess. Denny's is a good part-time job. I can choose my schedule while I'm in school. That's about it. I admit, though, I did google you and confirmed you work where Craig works, and I know your address, or rather, where you lived in 2015. I found you on LinkedIn. You've got an impressive bio."

Jeff nodded. "I have your email, and you have my LinkedIn info. I still think it's crazy that I've ridden around in your head in 2015." He made the crazy-cork-screw motion with his finger at his temple.

Mindi nodded in agreement. "Speaking of that, I know we talked about it, but I do hope you can control that. You haven't visited me in my head lately. You said you don't control where or when we meet . . ." She paused, not sure of what to say next, but then continued, "You, inside my head, that's something different. I have to tell you again, it still makes me feel shy, or even worse, to think you might visit during an embarrassing time. I hope you understand."

"Yeah," he replied. "That bothered me too, but I'm sure I can control that with my escape words."

"And that makes me feel better." She straightened up her posture, a signal she was changing the subject. "Now, you said you called me tonight. What about?"

"Yes, and—"

Mindi cut him off. "Wait a sec, more on visiting me in my head. I have an idea. Why don't I test it, see if I can call you when I'm awake?"

"Hm." He looked up at where a gray ceiling would be. "Would that work if I'm awake?"

Mindi had the answer. "There's two years separating us right now. Who's to say if you can call me when I'm asleep, I can come here in my dream? Why couldn't you hear me and show up in my head when I call you when you're asleep and meet me here? The time-date-sleep-awake thing seems to work that way, doesn't it?"

Jeff nodded. "Yeah, I think you're right. We need to see if we can test it."

She smiled. "Thanks for letting me talk. Now, do you want to talk about Charlene's dad?"

"About changing Rick's future?"

"Yes. If we decide to help—"

He broke in, "Only if we're given some sign. And we have to

think it through. We can't do something dangerous or stupid."

"Yeah," she said. "If we get a clue, we could work together for you to coach me, or, I don't know . . . So we can know what to do. That's why I might need to be able to call you here." She tapped her temple with her forefinger.

"Why are you willing to do this for Charlene? You have your own life, and I'm sure it's pretty full."

"Because I like you, and like I said in my email, you helped to get Shirley to leave so I could go to school and move on. You got me thinking about being a model. I'd like to repay you."

"I can tell that's important to you, and I'm glad it's working out. But you don't owe me anything. It was just a random thought about modeling in the spur of the moment. And as far as keeping Rick from dying, we don't even know if that's why all this is happening."

"Right," she said. "So we wait and see. Even if nothing can be done for Rick, I hope we can still visit each other here. And if we can't, I've got your email address and I'll look you up in a couple of years." She smiled.

He returned the smile and said, "Sure, let's try it. And I've got to give this some more thought to figure out what we might be able to do for Rick. Let's call it a night, and we'll do this again soon. Okay?"

"I'm looking forward to it. G'night, Jeff."

"Good night, Mindi." As his image dissolved, he had no reason to believe that this would be one of their last visits, but he felt a little sad anyway.

Jeff awoke knowing the situation with this dreaming, meeting, and talking with Mindi was real, even though the subject was unnatural, improbable, and unexplainable. Since the logician and scientist in him required documentation, he continued to transcribe a precise accounting of each meeting, hoping to eventually find a pattern.

How could Rick be stopped from getting on a plane to keep him alive? Would there be unintended consequences? Would Rick die some other way because the universe wanted him dead? If so, it would make putting forth the effort to save him a senseless exercise?

CHAPTER 14

Jeff looked up the Los Angeles area FAA office and found the closest one to the Denny's in Gardena was in El Segundo. But the Denny's in El Segundo was closer to the FAA office than the one in Gardena, so this discovery created more questions than it answered.

~

Charlene sat on Jeff's couch, holding a wine glass and watching as Jeff cooked chicken on the grill out on the deck.

"So how's the project going, Jeff? Are you going to expand the account?"

"It's going really well." He looked up at her. "Yes, they'll sign next week. How about LaDormeur? What's the latest there?"

Charlene, with a hand over her eyes in mock distress, replied, "Oh, Jeff, you wouldn't believe how hard it is to get anyone to agree on which models to choose. People think someone is too pretty, too tall, too sexy. Too 'girl next door,' too sophisticated, too plain, too fancy, too sensuous, or not sensuous enough. Too, too, too!" She stopped and looked at him. He paused chopping the lettuce and smiled. She resumed her rant. "Too many choices!"

"Well," Jeff said, intentionally aggravating the conversation for fun, "I've got it easy when the most difficult choice we've got is which font and font size to use."

"Good thing I'm not holding that knife. I'd throw it at you right now." She smiled as she moved to the counter, stood right behind him, and gave him a hug around the waist, and kissed the back of his neck.

"Thank heaven for small favors." He put the knife down, pulled free of her embrace, turned around, slid his arms around her, and gave her a kiss. Then he held her at arm's length, looking straight into her eyes, and said, "You'll pull it all together; I know you will."

"Oh, yeah, it'll all work out. But we've got to make choices on the models soon. We've held some focus groups and narrowed the field more, and we've subbed out a lot of other stuff to boutique agencies for their creative expertise, but we've kept the model selection all in-house. I'm still in control of that."

After they'd finished eating and cleaned up, they settled down to watch the latest movie release on TV. Then they slept, with the breeze from Puget Sound blowing through the open window.

⁓

Jeff found himself in his gray dream cocoon again, falling. He expected to land in the gray room.

He heard Mindi's voice call, "Jeff, Jeff, Jeff." A pause, then it came again. "Jeff, Jeff, Jeff."

The floating stopped and he was in Mindi's living room, feeling and smelling the warm Southern California air coming

through the open door and windows. His experience of her senses was sharper with each visit.

Mindi. I'm here.

"Yes, I can feel you," she said.

He looked through her eyes into her smiling reflection in the mirror. He smiled back.

Although she couldn't see him, she must have felt his smile because she said, "I trust the smile is for me, Jeff."

You can tell I'm smiling? Jeff said. *Yes, I'm happy to be here. Is this your day off?*

"Yes. Needed to take a break from studying and thought I'd try to call you here, see if it works, and it does." Mindi moved over to her sofa, sat down, rubbed her temples and said, using her mind's voice only this time, *I wonder if you'll show up only when I call you, or if you'll still drop in unannounced.*

Don't know. We've rewritten some of the rules. He appreciated being able to just talk with her rather than, as before, having to be careful he didn't scare her, having to tiptoe through her mind.

It's good we can talk and no one can hear us, Mindi said. She paused before continuing, *Have you thought any more about Charlene's dad?*

The FAA has an office about fifteen, twenty minutes from your Denny's. But there's a Denny's closer to the FAA than yours. That's all I know so far.

Okay.

After I made you stumble that day, did you hear any of their conversation? Do we have any clues there?

No, just that their conversation was friendly. They didn't seem to be doing a lot of business talk when I brought their breakfast. Other than that, I don't know.

Please let me know if you see them again.

Are you thinking it's more than just business?

187

No, not really. Just looking for clues. Charlene told me he was a devoted father and husband. Quite a few aircraft subcontractors operate down there, though, but I don't know if his work would need him to visit them. Gail lives down there too, so he might visit her when he's down there. We may never know what this is all about, but it doesn't matter why he was there. What matters is why I was there when he was.

If I see them when they come in again, I'll let you know, Mindi said.

Well, now we know you can call me. If I do drop in without you calling, I'll announce right away. You were rubbing your eyes just now. Does this give you a headache? Should I leave? Does this make you uncomfortable?

No, you're fine. Don't leave yet. I like that you're here. It's hard to describe what it feels like to have you in my head. A little like it's just a little crowded. It's not a problem. Please tell me more about Charlene.

Why?

Well, she's important to you, and she's the reason we might be doing something for Rick. So I'd like to know about what and who's important to you.

Sure, okay. Let's see, where do I begin? Charlene's thirty-three, same as me. Graduated from U of W with a degree in communications, has a master's in advertising, and got a job as an intern at a minor ad agency in Seattle. Who she works for now recognized her talent, recruited her, and she worked her way up to being a creative director with responsibility now for the advertising strategy for LaDormeur Cosmetics.

That's some credentials, Mindi said. *Who is LaDormeur? Never heard of them.*

They're a new company. Charlene is pretty involved in getting their advertising campaign going for Christmas 2017. After Charlie's dad died, she became immersed in her work, put in really long hours. She got assigned as head account manager for LaDormeur. She and Rick were pretty close, so him dying shook her up pretty bad. That's about it. We seem pretty good together.

I understand how she felt about her dad. Even though we had big issues, I was still shook up when he died. I can relate.

I'm sorry, Mindi.

It's getting better. Yeah, his Alcoholics Anonymous sponsor contacted me. In recovery, they have to do a personal inventory of those they hurt. And what he did, well—when he . . . um, well, he confessed it to his sponsor. My father had planned to make amends to me, but he died first. His sponsor told me about the guilt my father carried with him. Do you want to know what my first thought was? It was "Good! Serves him right!" But I don't feel that way so much now. I don't know how I would have reacted if he'd lived and talked to me about it. I don't think he could ever erase the harm he did. But Dr. Singh's helping me. I'm dealing with it.

Jeff felt Mindi's sadness. *Thank you for trusting me with that,* he said. *I don't know what to say. No one should have to go through what you did.*

They watched the traffic and pedestrians out the apartment window and enjoyed the pleasant Southern California climate.

Thanks for letting me share that, Mindi said after a moment. *I like it when we can talk. I've had no male friends as an adult. My cousins, like Craig, we used to play together, but we were kids. When we started high school, we didn't hang out anymore. And in high school, I had already been—well, I was pretty messed up, so any guys that wanted to date . . . I didn't really know how to act. I always felt defensive, suspicious of their motives. And for most of them, all they wanted was sex. So I appreciate you are, well—*

—Safe? Yeah, tough to be threatened by a dream, right?

Well, no, I'm not worried about being threatened by you, she said. *But you do have a girlfriend you're committed to, someone you want to marry. I'm happy for you.* She smiled.

When Jeff heard her say that, it put to rest his concern that she might be infatuated with him. They could just be friends, with no agenda.

I think my doctor is right on one point about you, though. You've become a role model for who I want to have as my soulmate. But she's wrong that I manufactured you. Meeting you shows me that there are men out there that I don't have to be afraid of. Thank you for being patient with me.

Jeff smiled and hoped Mindi would know it.

She went back to the mirror for eye contact, and said out loud, "It's time to say ciao. I should get back to my studies."

Jeff said, *Sure, I like this. But when we meet in the gray room, it doesn't cost you any wake time, like now. See you soon. Charlene, Charlene, Charlene.*

~

Jeff awoke with a start and opened his eyes. Charlene, up on one arm, was watching him with concern. "Jeff, you were having a dream. You called my name—like you were scared or something." She caressed his forehead and then his cheek.

He sat up and faced her, then gave her a hug, held her for a few moments.

She relaxed. "You sure you're okay?"

"Yeah, I'm fine. I don't know what that was all about, but I'm okay. Really." He shook his head as if to clear it. The clock said 2:23 a.m. He'd said her name and woken her. Had he ever done that before?

"I'll be right back," he said as he got up. "Please, go back to sleep. I'm sorry I woke you. It's all right."

In the bathroom, he splashed cold water on his face, wondering why he felt like he'd been cheating on her. Of course, he couldn't tell her about the dream, she wouldn't understand. He got back in bed, cuddled up to her, and fell back to sleep as he thought of the visit with Mindi.

~

Jeff sat on the deck at Charlene's apartment and read all day. When in town, Charlene preferred working on the LaDormeur account at home. She'd go in to the office if she needed to meet with someone, but she could spend longer hours at home, work through the weekends, and get more done than working downtown.

The bonus was that Jeff could be there on the weekend. Charlene's whole team worked long hours too. The Gantt chart taped to the coat closet door showed dates and deadlines with different color horizontal bars and the overlapping trail of activities that represented the project.

Later that afternoon, Jeff removed the cork from the chilled bottle of wine with an exaggerated flourish, filled the glasses with a generous amount, and handed one to her. Holding the glass in one hand, Charlene stepped over to the Gantt chart and traced individual critical paths with her free hand, running her finger from the top of the chart and examining each activity's expected date of completion. After letting out a satisfied sigh and taking another swallow of the wine, she turned and gave Jeff a quick peck on the cheek. Then she crossed to the table and started spreading out photographs. "C'mon over here, please. I need some help."

He joined her at the table. "What's up?"

Eight-by-ten glossies of exquisite young women covered the

table. He had seen them before, including Mindi's, which sat there in plain view.

"What do you need?" he asked as he stepped closer and scanned the photos, trying not to betray his interest in his friend from 2015.

Charlene looked at him from the side. "I need a beauty pageant judge to help make choices. We've got a shortlist. We need to make it shorter. Give me some feedback to help narrow these down to two of each type: blonde, brunette, Black, Native American, Asian, and, uh . . . Yes, that'll be enough for now. We got the girls with red hair selected already."

"Charlie, you're putting me in a difficult position," he said, inspecting one photo, then another.

"What do you mean?"

"There's only one beautiful woman I'm interested in. You. You want me to choose from other beautiful women you're parading in front of me like you're a cat-house madam?" He chuckled.

She elbowed him in the ribs.

"Ow!"

"You deserved that. But, of course, I'm flattered . . . Nice try trying to stay out of trouble. I'm serious though—I could use your opinion. Your choice is not the final one, but like I said, I need feedback from people I can trust. Remember, women are buying cosmetics for themselves to be feminine, to feel at their best. And men enjoy the benefits of their efforts, so a man's opinion counts, okay? Now help."

"Okay," he said. "This is the final round, best two out of . . . How many of each type are here? Hmm." He picked up each picture and moved it under the desk lamp, but the lighting wasn't that good. He turned on the overhead light. "That's better."

One by one, he set the headshots aside, taking the job seriously. He pulled two out of the discard pile and reconsidered,

trying not to make any sounds indicating yea or nay, or by what standards he made the choices.

When he finished, he looked back over his choices. Mindi, of course, was among them. He wished he could tell Charlene the side-story of him and Mindi conspiring to keep Rick from getting killed. But it would sound bizarre. Why? Because it *was* bizarre.

He came back to the moment, looked up at Charlene and asked, "How did I do? Did I pick any your team picked?"

She looked over his selections and nodded. "You have superb taste. Those you picked are pretty close to what the team and I picked. Few of us chose all the same models, except one. Everyone picked her." She pointed to Mindi.

Jeff grinned. "Like you said, I have good taste." After a short pause, in a low, soft voice, he added, "How else can I be of service?"

Charlene turned, gave him a passionate kiss, and in a voice laden with desire said, "Oh, Jeff, you can be of service in sooo many ways." She took his hand and led him into the bedroom.

~

Jeff hadn't heard from Mindi for a couple of days, and he wanted to talk to her, although he had nothing in particular to talk about.

In the light of day, with real-world reality firmly in place, Jeff still had a small twinge of doubt of whether the dreams were real. But he easily dismissed them when he remembered the email. That was pretty conclusive evidence. The real Mindi Ketchem, Craig's cousin, was now known professionally as Miranda Madisen. The dream books said lucid dreamers eventually confuse reality with the dream. Was that true for him? Absolutely, because for him it *was* reality.

193

He still wondered if the dreams were to play some role regarding marriage to Charlene. When could he pop the question to her?

His dad's homily came back to him: *If you don't know what to do, do nothing. The answers will come.* Following his dad's advice had always worked for him. He would try to be patient.

That night, Jeff fell asleep to another fall in the gray space, realized it, stopped the fall as he relaxed, and then floated. He heard Mindi call out his name.

Then instantly, with no walk from the doorway, there he was, standing in front of his gray chair, facing Mindi, who already sat in her gray chair, a serious look on her face.

"What?" he said, eager to find out why she had called.

"Hate to break it to you, but I think your discarded hunch might've been right," she replied.

"What hunch?" Puzzled, he settled into the chair, trying to get comfortable, but he now expected bad news.

"They came in yesterday. Rick and Carolyn."

"You said that like they're a couple." His eyebrows lifted.

"They are."

"Why didn't you call me yesterday? And how do you know her name?" Questions formed in his mind faster than he could ask them.

"Remember, he said her name when I took their order that first time we saw them? But there's another way I know. I'll explain."

"Go on."

"I didn't call you last night because I was so busy at work, and then I had to go to a class. When I considered our weird time difference, I figured it wouldn't matter until next March, right? Aren't meeting times flexible considering the distance? I hope that's okay." She paused, waiting for validation.

"Of course, you're right. I forget there are different rules here."

"They weren't in my section, but I kept an eye on them. They were acting all lovey-dovey." She saw the pain on Jeff's face. "I know how you must feel. It made me sick to see her dad fooling around like that, too. After they left, hand in hand, I cleared their table for the other server. Stuck down between the seat cushions was a red envelope." Mindi paused a moment, watching his face.

He nodded for her to go on.

"I snagged it and put it in my apron. They'd already left. No one saw me. I looked at it later at break. I wanted to call you then, but like I said . . ."

"No worries."

"He'd written her name at the top of a mushy friendship card, and at the bottom he'd written, *So happy I met you*, then signed it, *Love, Rick*."

"Crap," was all Jeff said at first. Mindi remained silent, giving him space. Then he said, "The guy's a creep after all. Then he dies, devastating his wife and girls, and we're trying to figure out if we should save him." Jeff thought for a moment, then said, "Even if we can keep him alive, would he keep cheating on Mary, hurt his family anyway?" He frowned. "What should we do? Why is this happening to us?" He saw on her face the same confusion he felt. "Thanks, Mindi," he said. "We've got to think about this."

Mindi nodded. "It complicates things, for sure. We might still do something, but what? I feel so bad for Charlene."

"Thank you for caring and for staying alert and letting me know. Charlene will never find out—I'll never tell her. She doesn't need to know." To close the subject, he said, "I'll have to think about this some more." He sat there, shaking his head for a moment, then said, "So how are your classes? Is everything else going okay?"

"Oh, everything's fine. I'm not doing much except school. Working shorter shifts at the restaurant. That's it for now." But she wasn't finished with the conversation about Rick. "Are we still waiting for some kind of a clue or sign?"

He studied her face for a moment and understood how sincerely she wanted to help. "Well, yes, maybe. But that card is pretty good clue pointing us to *not* doing anything, don't you think?"

Mindi nodded.

"So we still have some time before his flight, in your time, to find more clues," Jeff said. "We'll talk again. Darn it, I wish things weren't so serious." He tried to smile, then he stood. Mindi returned his smile, then Jeff said, "Charlene, Charlene, Charlene."

As his image dissolved, he saw Mindi watching him, a sad look on her face.

Jeff woke up and stared into the dim light of the bedroom. Then he sat up and transcribed the details of his conversation with Mindi, his mind racing with the problem he'd been handed. He wrote his editorial comments in the notebook.

I can't discuss this with Charlene. She can't know her dad cheated on her mom. She's still grieving. And how would I tell her how I know? Even if I could explain the dream thing, she'd think I'm being cruel. If we were to save Rick, would it change my relationship with Charlie? Am I being selfish? We've got a good thing going. If he lives, would Charlene still pour herself into her work like she did after he died? Will Mindi still get these breaks? Would Charlie even get the LaDormeur account? If we don't at least try to save Rick, will I feel guilty? Should Mindi even be involved?

He stopped, looked down at the notebook in his lap, and considered that he would eventually have to burn the notebook. Charlie could never see it. Then, as had become his habit, he stowed the dream journal in the bottom of the drawer and slid it closed.

He sat, his head in his hands. "Damn. Damn, damn, damn. Why do I have to know this? Why me?"

As he headed into the kitchen to make coffee, an inner voice, his own inner voice, answered his question with a question: *Why not me?*

Back in high school, he'd been concerned with a problem between one of his friends and another student who was a bully. Jeff had talked it over with his father, and when his father asked if the issue affected him directly, Jeff had said no. Dad's advice, in the form of a question, resonated in his mind: *Then is this any of your business? Do you think you should get involved?*

The question in Jeff's mind now was, With Rick and Carolyn, what business was it of his? From deep in his mind came the answer. *I don't know. Wait and see.*

CHAPTER 15

Jeff's phone rang. The caller ID indicated "Charlene." He answered, and she said, "Jeff, I need you right now. Do you have time to come over?"

"Charlene, what's wrong?"

"Not over the phone. I need someone to talk to. Tonight. Please?" She had to be back in Santa Monica for an important meeting tomorrow and needed him now.

"Of course, Charlene. I'll be right over."

Soon after, Jeff and Charlene walked together in silence along the beach while dozens of other people enjoyed the view of the sun following its nightly descent beyond the waters of the Sound.

"Mom called last night," Charlene said in a somber tone.

Jeff looked over at her. She gazed down at the fine pebbles scattered with broken bits of crab shells and seaweed. "And?"

"Mom wanted to pack some of Dad's books from his office at home. A letter fell out of one of the books."

Jeff knew intuitively that the letter represented bad news. He remained quiet.

Charlene continued, "She read the letter to me over the

phone. Dad had written it shortly before he died. He addressed it to Mom, and in it he admitted to being unfaithful. He'd had an affair that was over, and he was sorry. He said he had no right to expect to be forgiven, but because of his love for her, he had to confess and was willing to accept whatever decision she might make for his being unfaithful to their vows." Another long pause. "The letter was unfinished, unsigned."

Jeff squeezed her hand lightly in solidarity. He assumed the letter was about Rick's affair with Carolyn. It would probably affect any attempt he might make to alter Rick's future.

"Mom is devastated. She loved Dad. She said she had a flash of anger, was glad he was dead, then immediately felt guilty for thinking that. She wasn't going to tell Gail or me, but she had to tell someone, and she called me first. I don't know if she'll tell Gail. Poor Mom, if only she hadn't found that letter . . ."

They walked with their heads down, contemplating the news.

"Mom said she'd accepted his death, had shed a lot of tears, and a divorce would've been painful had he lived. I asked her if she would've divorced him. She said she didn't know. How could she know now?"

A few more yards along the beach, they turned around and started walking back toward the parking lot. Jeff remained silent until they reached the car. As he opened the door for her, he said, "Charlene, I can't imagine the pain your mother must be going through."

"She's reliving news of the crash. The closed casket funeral without his body, the three of us crying, holding each other up, her loneliness, her listening for his voice and his footsteps. Now she has to process this. Damnit! Damnit to hell!"

They drove to her apartment in silence. Before he parked the car, she said, "Please, just let me out. Thanks for being here tonight. I needed to talk, but now I need to be alone. I've got to get ready for an early flight tomorrow. Is that okay, Jeff?" She leaned over and gave him a kiss. "Thank you."

"Sure, sure, I understand. Call me." He watched her go up the walk and, following his habit, waited until she'd gotten into the building before pulling away. The confluence of sadness and concern for Charlene resonated through him.

If he'd had any residual doubt about his dream world with Mindi being real, it was gone now. What might it mean if he and Mindi still tried to interfere with history? Would it make any difference now if they kept Rick from dying, with his unfaithfulness revealed? There were no guidelines, no rules, no instructions for something like what he and Mindi were considering.

～

"Mindi, Mindi, Mindi," Jeff called out. He waited suspended in the gray void, then suddenly, once again, he found himself in their gray room approaching the chairs. As he sat, she walked in. He watched her, admiring her confidence.

"What's up?" she asked. "This is a real treat to see you so often." The look on his face told her that this would be a serious conversation.

"Hmm . . . Got some news on our mission, if that's what it is. Charlene told me something we should consider before going any further with trying to save Rick. Another data point."

She waited, hands folded in her lap.

"Charlene found out today that her dad had been having the affair. But not from me," he was quick to add. "And it shocked Mary, her mom, who told Charlene that it had ended between Rick and . . . what's-her-name?" he said in a harsh tone.

"Carolyn," Mindi replied.

Jeff knew he hadn't forgotten her name. He hadn't wanted to say it because he was angry.

"How did she find out?"

Jeff shook his head. "I can't imagine how that must hurt so many months later . . ."

Mindi remained quiet.

". . . to reopen the wound of his death and then to open another wound."

Mindi nodded, understanding. "So we need to rethink saving Rick?"

"I think so, but we need to talk about it some more. At the very least, it complicates things."

"Hmm, I like a good puzzle, but not if I'm in it," Mindi said.

"Are you still seeing your doctor?" Jeff needed to change the subject.

"Yes."

"Have you brought her up to date on our conversations?"

"Yes, I told her everything except me sending you an email and me finding you on LinkedIn. She doesn't know you're real."

"So you thought it best to leave that out?"

"Yes, same reason you haven't told Charlene about your dreams."

"You and I have done nothing wrong. I'm not cheating on her. I just don't want her to think that I'm crazy. If I did tell her, hell, I don't know what I'd tell her, or how. I'd have to figure out just what to tell her of this extra-natural friendship."

"Whoa, big words. What does *extra-natural* mean?" Mindi said playfully.

"It means about the same as *supernatural*." He chuckled. "But it doesn't get used that much. Both mean that science hasn't figured it out yet. Extra-natural sounds fancier; supernatural is clichéd. Either way, I don't want her to have me committed."

Mindi nodded. "I feel the same. The doctor is sure I'm dreaming about a fantasy nice guy, setting a standard to find Mr. Right."

He smiled. "Fantasy nice guy. I like that."

Jeff told her about visiting the bookstore and the book Ingrid sold him. He paraphrased the passage to her about lucid dreams. "Dreams are a gift from the universe. We dream and meet other souls to awake with a loving memory of the journey." He smiled again and looked directly into her eyes. "That's what I feel about being able to meet here with you."

Mindi smiled back. "That sounds so sweet. I hope I can see the book sometime."

"I'd like to share it with you."

"Oh, one thing about my therapy," she said, "I've cut back on seeing Dr. Singh to once a month. I've been having trouble working it in around school and work. With all I have to do to get through beauty and makeup school, I may even cut back on some shifts at the restaurant. After I finish makeup school, I'll start my modeling classes. I've still got money from my father's life insurance—it'll stretch if I'm careful. Then, well, I trust I'll be successful at being a model."

"Speaking of that," Jeff said, "I've been meaning to ask you, why did you decide to get a cosmetology-makeup certification if your goal is to be a model?"

"Yeah, it's a lot of extra work," she replied. "But I think I can be a better model if I know all the working parts of the business. And I won't be a model forever. I could work at a cosmetics firm or run a modeling agency doing marketing, management, or even do hair when I age out. It'll look good on my resume. See?"

"Smart girl. Sounds like a great plan, well thought-out."

"Thanks."

"Well," he said with resignation, "let's talk about Rick now that Mary found that letter. It seems less likely we could give Rick and Mary another chance, but let's say we did. You know what that might mean, don't you?" He raised an eyebrow.

Mindi gave a puzzled frown.

Jeff realized he'd started out in the middle of an idea.

"Let me back up a bit. Changing his future might mean a change in other people's lives too. Ours in particular."

Mindi's frown deepened at the changed tone of the conversation. "What are you talking about?"

"I was there to support Charlene when Rick died. If Rick hadn't died, Charlene might not have used her work as a distraction from the loss of her dad. They'd been close, even closer than Rick was with Gail. It's possible her career wouldn't have taken off like it did if she hadn't been so driven."

"I don't understand. Why be concerned about her job? She wouldn't have lost it, right?"

"No, you're right. But if he hadn't died, her career might not have developed like it did. She threw herself into it, worked long hours to take her mind off it. Now she's being rewarded for all that effort."

"Ah, all right," Mindi said with hesitation.

Jeff guessed she still didn't quite see his point.

"Maybe this will help. I'm concerned about *your* career here too. Charlene might never have been given a chance at the LaDormeur account without all that extra focus on her job. This is important. So important that I need to tell you I've seen your headshot from your agent in 2017. You are in the running for 'Brown-eyed Brunette Caucasian' for the LaDormeur advertising campaign."

He watched her as she absorbed the information, then went on, "Charlie asked my opinions on the models under review. When I saw your photo, I knew right then that you made it through school and had an agent. I really liked the photo, but I wasn't alone," he was quick to add. "Everybody, I mean *everyone* else in the agency, including Charlene, likes you too. I saw the list. You made the final cut. You might get the job!"

Mindi gasped and leaned forward. "No way."

"Yes way." He started to speak again, then stopped himself and kept his expression impassive. *She's a smart woman. It'll come to her.*

After the initial excitement faded, she stared at him. Then it hit her. "If she's not leading the campaign, there's a chance I might not get chosen."

Jeff nodded. "But we don't know you wouldn't either. It might be destined for you anyway. Or something even better might come along instead. How would we ever know? But this one is real, very close to happening for Mindi v.2017."

He remained still, watching her eyes as she thought it through.

"No, Jeff. Giving Rick and Mary another chance is bigger than me. But . . ." A long pause passed as she thought. "There's you and Charlene. If we change things, you two might not become a couple."

Jeff just looked at her. He hadn't even considered Charlene and him. Jeff and Mindi both froze, each considering the rewards and consequences of their decision.

Finally, Jeff said, "But this is bigger than me too. We have to do this together. If we decide to save Rick, it would be you that would do the physical work. I'd be along for the ride in your head, of course. Alexandria, Egypt, is a long way to travel. You, uh, we can't go there on a lark. This isn't a James Bond movie where we can go jet-setting around the world and spill a glass of red wine on a white dinner jacket to make him miss his flight." He watched her face, then added, "And it could even be dangerous, too."

Mindi shook her head, looked at him, and frowned. "The first problem is to decide to do something. Then we might not be able to find a way. Or find a way and not make it work, or find a way, and it works, but it really screws up everybody's future. Right?"

"Yeah. This is like the thought experiment for decision-making that we had at a company seminar. It was about a runaway streetcar trolley, where if you do nothing, five people you don't know will die. But you can throw a switch to change where the trolley goes and save those five, but one other person, your friend, will die instead. Your friend would live if you let the other five die. What do you do? How do you choose who lives and dies?"

Mindi, still frowning, said, "But if we do nothing about Rick dying, the world in 2017 goes on the way it is now in your time. If we interfere—if we can interfere—other things might or might not happen. The chain of events could spiral out of control." She shifted in her seat. "What about this? If we save Rick, how do we know that Rick and Mary will stay together? Mary might be so hurt she can't stand the sight of the guy. Things might not turn out the way we want them to, even if he doesn't die in that crash."

Jeff's shoulders slumped. "And what if he survives and doesn't tell Mary he's having an affair, keeps having the affair, or has another affair? Who lives happily ever after? So many possibilities. Maybe we shouldn't play god with this. Accept what has already happened in my time. Accept that's the way it's supposed to be. People are on the path toward accepting his death. You and I might still have some mission to complete, but maybe not this one. What right do we have to change history?"

Mindi opened her mouth to speak but stopped herself when

Jeff continued, "My trolley-death analogy doesn't fit. It's only two choices. In our scenario, there are a lot more choices, and perhaps an infinite number of theoretical outcomes. Maybe I have already completed my mission. I gave you the nudge on your path to your career and helped you lose Shirley. I can sleep guilt-free." He paused, laughed, and shrugged his shoulders. "If you can call this sleeping. Seriously, though, I shouldn't involve you in deciding other people's fate."

Mindi looked at him and spoke with compassion and sincerity. "Jeff, your goal is to relieve the pain of someone you love. That is the most generous gift anyone could give someone. It's why I can be your friend. Mom told me, 'To have a friend, be a friend.' You were a good friend to me. You want to do right by Charlene and Mary. Because we are friends, if this is something you need to do, I'll help you do it, no matter what the consequences."

Jeff smiled. "That is so sweet and generous. Thank you. You're so good. I wonder if we might get another sign. We might trip over a clue. Until then . . . you know what we have to do?"

"We wait and see," she said.

He laughed. "You sure have a way of making things simple. You said in four words what it took me a whole paragraph to say." He started to get up to end their meeting.

"Wait, Jeff. One more thing. You said you didn't want to reveal my future for fear that somehow I might sabotage my chances, somehow mess things up. What you told me tonight about LaDormeur will make me work even harder. I'll be sure I earn whatever chances I'll get. Thank you so much."

"I like that. Thank you for telling me that."

Together they said "Ciao," and both dissolved into a flutter of sparkling glitter.

~

Three days later, Jeff fell asleep and began to dream immediately. He walked through the portal door into the gray room, complete with chairs, but no Mindi. He looked around, and as he sat down, the opening in the opposite wall appeared.

Mindi walked in, smiling and looked directly at him as she sat down. "Hi, Jeff. Glad you called," she said as casually as if it were a telephone call.

"Hi."

"Any new insight about what we should be doing with— this?" Mindi's arms spread to indicate the space.

Jeff shook his head. "No. There are no new clues, but I have given this a lot more thought. Here're the data points: Mary found the letter. Rick is dead and buried. The girls have grieved and have another dose of pain that I'm sure they'll work through. In our universe, I don't think any of that can be undone, no matter how hard we may try."

Mindi nodded. "We can talk about that. But first, what do you mean by 'our universe?'"

"There's a theory in physics of multiple universes, or the 'multiverse'—parallel universes that each contain their own Ricks, Jeffs, Mindis, and all. Let me answer that in a minute. First, though, whatever we do that may affect Rick dying would mean changing the past I already know. I don't think that can happen. There's only one choice—to accept the outcome that's already happened. It's the law of entropy."

Mindi frowned, puzzled, and shook her head slowly.

"Entropy is movement toward a state of chaos," Jeff explained. She gave him a blank stare.

"Okay," Jeff said, "if a glass drops on the floor and breaks, it can't be unbroken. Broken is a state of chaos, which is the opposite of an unbroken glass, which is in a state of order. But it's a one-way street. So if right now the glass is unbroken, there is the possibility it could be broken, so we're careful to keep it safe. But if it falls on the floor, it becomes broken and can't be unbroken. There are many choices: protect it to keep it unbroken, or break it on purpose, or an accident happens and it breaks. Several choices mean several paths into the future. When it breaks, one path is taken and there's no going back. But with any path taken, there are now other paths, other chances for other choices up ahead. Even with the broken glass. Throw it away, recycle the pieces or let them stay there on the floor. But it can no longer be protected from being broken because it already is."

He paused for Mindi to absorb that. She gave him a nod.

"For us, it's a matter of perspective. The perspective of where you are in time. It's whether you are there before something happens or after something has happened that makes a difference in the paths available to choose from. Your future, in 2015, could be changed for a lot of things because they haven't happened yet for you. For example, before you'd decided to go to modeling school, you were at a crossroad. You had a choice which path to take, school or no school. But time has moved forward, and now that path is already set because you decided to go to school, and you've started, in part, because of me. You had the choice to quit school until I told you your agent sent your headshots to Charlene, and that has now locked in your path forward.

"I broke the glass by telling you and you cannot *not* finish school. If I hadn't seen that you're in the running, it could have been possible to quit school. But not now. I thought a lot about this, and I created a bubble in time by being here. I didn't do it on purpose. But it's a done deal."

Mindi nodded slowly while maintaining eye contact. "But

I don't want to quit school, and I won't quit school, because I know that when I finish I've already succeeded as Mindi v.2017. Right?"

"Right. That's good, because you can't. Our universe won't let you, for lots of reasons." Jeff grinned and made a fist-pump motion acknowledging her success. "You're going to be a model. And if not for LaDormeur, then for someone else.

"Okay. Now, do you still want an answer about what is 'our universe?'"

"I'd kind of forgotten I asked, but, well, yes, I guess I do. The answer can't be any worse than what you've already covered, can it?"

Jeff threw his head back and laughed. "Well, it might be worse. But what I said before might help this next part make sense. The multiple universe theory in physics suggests—doesn't prove, it's just a theory—that there are, uh, lots of copies of us somewhere. Like I mentioned before, maybe an infinite number of us exist in an infinite number of separate universes.

"Each of those lives go in different directions at each and every one of the infinite number of crossroads. In some universes, there might be major differences from ours, or some might be subtle. There've been, and will continue to be, an infinite number of crossroads and choices, because there are billions of people alive now, and billions that have lived who will or have made an infinite number of choices in an infinite number of universes. The whole subject of infinite is pretty overwhelming, and difficult to get your mind around."

After taking a breath, Jeff said, "You and I are in 'our universe,' and have no way to cross over into another one, unless . . . we mess with our choices in a situation like we have here where you try to quit school when you can't, and it would kill the butterfly. The universe gets screwed up and creates some kind of a cross connection to another universe to try to get things back into equilibrium, which might then screw us in some way. So bottom line, it's good you want to stay in school. It's safer."

Mindi grimaced. "Well, I'm kinda sorry that I asked. I already second-guess myself enough. Now I'll wonder if anything I do is the right thing. So what do we do now?"

"I don't know. But one thing's for sure, we don't save Rick."

"Okay, *that* makes sense."

"One more thing, and then I think the physics lesson can be over. The one-way street thing affects us in another important way, and it's why we can't talk to the other Jeffs and Mindis. If—"

Mindi interjected, "I think I understand why I shouldn't talk to Jeff v.2015 right now. I could somehow change your meeting Charlene and even change what you've done until now with me because Jeff v.2015 would have advance knowledge of us meeting. He might check his junk email and . . ." She looked at Jeff and smiled. "And if *you* talk to me in . . . That is, if you call and talk to Mindi v.2017, it will mean we wouldn't be able to visit like we are now, right? We can only talk with one of each of us, right? If we involve our other selves, even by accident, we can't switch back and forth. This is a one-way street, too."

Jeff looked at her in disbelief. "Yeah, you do understand, don't you? Hell, *I* don't even understand all the consequences of what we're doing. The paths that might change or disappear forever. We have to be careful."

He smiled and nodded his affirmation, then the conversation gave way to a simpler and more comfortable set of questions.

"Now, about school," Jeff said. "Is it going okay? How's work?" He almost asked if she was dating but thought he'd save it for another visit. Then Mindi's response gave him a hint that her answer would've probably been no.

"I'm really, really busy because I'm taking a full load at

cosmetology school. One of the sections is a little tough, but I'll make it through. I've cut my hours at the restaurant to make it easier to take day classes. The night shift tips are not as good, though. What about you?"

"Oh, things are good. The clients are easy to work with, and the new projects keep things interesting. My team is great."

"Is Craig on your team? I've been meaning to ask, how is he?"

"Oh, he's fine. The boys keep him on his toes. Craig took a vacation for his cousin's wedding. We haven't talked recently. He left for Chicago right after he got back from Gardena." *Oh damn!* Jeff stopped as he realized what he'd just said. They'd just talked about learning about the future, and he'd completely ignored his moratorium on telling her about a future that might involve her. He'd added, or removed, he couldn't tell which, another crossroad.

She looked puzzled. "I'm . . . I'm not that cousin, am I?" Then she added, "Can you tell me which cousin?" She grimaced, closed her eyes, and covered her face with her hands.

Jeff guessed she felt if she hadn't asked, he wouldn't have slipped, but the fault wasn't hers. "Oh, Mindi, I'm sorry I said anything. I told you I wouldn't . . . I let down my guard." A long pause allowed him to figure out how to back out of the problem he'd caused.

"I truly don't know which of the other cousins is getting married, and I didn't ask. Of Craig's family, I just know you and his wife and kids. I don't even know any other of his, uh, your family in California." He knew that if she replayed the conversation in her mind later, she'd know by the way he phrased his answer that she wasn't the cousin getting married.

"That's fine. I'll find out soon enough." She paused. "Well, in a couple of years."

"I'm sorry. That wasn't fair for me to do that to you, or to the, uh, universe."

"Jeff, no, it's okay. It can't be serious. You don't think it will change where the sun comes up, do you? We haven't blinked out of existence, have we? No dead butterfly," she said with a smile.

"You're right. I'm sure it's less critical than me telling you you're in the running for LaDormeur." He gave her a weak smile, extending his apology. "I've got to be more careful and not slip up like that."

"And I should be more careful with the questions *I* ask," she said, accepting her part of the responsibility.

Jeff nodded. "Let's move on. I'd like to run something else past you, if that's all right?"

"Sure, Jeff. What?"

"Well, with us not taking on a mission to save Rick, it still seems that maybe I should be using . . . Well, maybe I'm supposed to take this, this talent I've got and visit other folks and be like a . . ."

"Yes?"

"It sounds kinda arrogant when I say it out loud." He waited a moment, but with a nod of her head, Mindi urged him to continue. "I could be a mentor, a guide, a friend. Give folks a little push without them knowing. Give help from the sidelines, so to speak. I don't know. It sounded better in my head last night. Now it sounds sort of silly." He felt his face warming in embarrassment.

"No, no, no. That sounds really noble. What got you thinking about this?"

"Like I said, we were going to help Rick and Mary, and now there's a . . . a void. And I guess me being alone more recently, with Charlene so busy . . . Well, things were getting really close with Charlene about the time I"—he tried to be careful choosing his words—"first visited you, and she started working on the cosmetic account. She works on it more than full time . . . We still talk. Everything's fine. We're still friends. We haven't fought. She's just been so . . . busy."

He realized he felt vulnerable and readjusted. "I guess I've had more time on my hands lately, and I could spend it working on this." He waved his hand to indicate the gray space.

Mindi leaned toward him. "Are you two really okay?"

"Yeah, we're fine. I was going to ask her to marry me. I want to take her to pick out a ring. But LaDormeur came up, and she's giving all her attention to that." He felt compelled to say more. "I'm really glad. It's great for her career, gives you a chance to have a great gig. But it's gotten in the way of moving our relationship forward like I'd like to."

He recognized the beginnings of self-pity and said, "It'll wrap up soon. She'll be finished. I'm good at rolling with the punches. I'm pretty self-sufficient, but—"

Mindi held up her hand and stopped him. "Hey, if you ever need to talk, let me know. I'm here to listen and give feedback." She waited for him to look up at her. "Do you want some feedback now?"

"Sure. Yes. Please."

"You and Charlene have a good thing going, so wait this out. Don't worry. You've said yourself that once the product line launches, she'll be freed up. Meanwhile, keep yourself busy with this new, um, hobby you've, I guess, been given. Right?" She waited a moment before going on. "Tell me, what are you thinking of doing next?"

"Sure. So I tried a little TM a few years ago, and I've been studying up on astral projection, out-of-body experiences, telepathy and lucid dreaming . . ."

"What's TM?"

"Transcendental Meditation. It's a structured way of

meditating. Also there are books, DVDs using hemispheric-synchronization, or hemi-sync for short, for the brain for out-of-body experiences, OBE for short. That's what you could call what we're doing right now, visiting someone somewhere else while not in our bodies. But I want to learn how to control it. To go where and when I want." He stopped to see what her reaction would be.

"I get it. Go on."

"Well, since I, uh, we already do this, could I do more? Visit others in their gray rooms?"

"And . . ."

"If I figure out what they need and gain their trust, give them the nudge they need to make things better for themselves, or their families, or even the entire world. Kinda like a spirit guide, you know?"

"If we think about it," Mindi said, "you did help me, but I already knew I wanted to be a model. I had already started helping myself by going to the doctor. You gave me a gentle push, and yes, that got me started. But if you'd tried to get me to do something I didn't want to do, you may have done harm, or at least, wasted your time and energy if I'd resisted or ignored you. Right?"

"I don't want to hurt anyone. I'd be careful."

"Have you tested this?"

"No. Only thinking about it. First thing is to visit someone else. If I can even do that . . . Well, if it works. Have to test it."

Mindi nodded. "You'd have to be really careful. Someone who's on a ledge—you might push them off, make them crazy. Look at how I was until I trusted you."

"I know. The whole thing seems pretty complicated, and it might not even work. But it gives me something to think about. It's only a hobby. I'm glad we talked."

"Me too. I'm glad you trusted me to talk about it. Just be careful."

"Yes, I guess it could get really serious. I'd have to know when to stop, or not even start. You haven't said it, haven't even hinted at it, but I know I'd have to keep my ego under control. Just do good, not harm anyone." He paused a long moment, thinking. "Do you think you could help me?"

"I'm happy to help. I don't know how, but I'm here for you. Keep in mind, the scientists that invented nuclear energy only wanted to explore science and do good. Look what happened. They invented the bomb, and that genie will never be back in the bottle."

Jeff's enthusiasm waned. "I don't plan on inventing an atom bomb. But if I could help just one person." Jeff looked down, then back into Mindi's eyes.

Mindi said, "You are a good person, a good friend. Now, you like to make lists, so how about this? One: see what you can do to expand, sharpen the skills. Two: see who, if anybody, you can visit; see what you might be able to do. Three: come and talk to me before you do anything besides visit and explore. How's that sound? You said we could be a team. I'll do my part, okay?"

"Sure, thank you. That sounds good."

"Anytime. Is there anything else?"

He shook his head. "No."

"Practice, explore. Then let's talk again."

"Thanks. This was good. Time to say good night?"

"Yeah. Till next time. Ciao."

He awoke, the conversation still fresh in his mind, thinking, *Sure, what harm can it do to visit someone else?*

CHAPTER 16

Jeff finished his meditation in the morning before going to work. He knew that after he meditated—every day lately—he felt more relaxed and invigorated. He'd always enjoyed work, both challenging and mundane tasks, but he now approached his projects with even more vigor and interest.

He still felt left out of Charlene's life, but no matter how distracted or tired she sounded, he approached each phone call with her, or their now infrequent dates, as a new event with no expectations, good or bad. He had no resentment and no fears.

As soon as the LaDormeur account was up and rolling, he'd resume the plans he'd been making to propose, and they would pick out an engagement ring.

Before retiring after a superb day at work, he used his headphones and a binaural sound recording to stimulate an out-of-body experience. Jeff was trying everything, except drugs, to start a lucid dream he could control. The rest, he was sure, he could take care of as it came up.

There hadn't been any visits with Mindi in the gray room since they last talked about physics and made the decision not to save Rick. Nor had he dropped into her mind.

After several nights of dream-free sleep, it happened without trying. He was falling again and felt sure that Mindi had called him. He relaxed and floated in the gray nothingness for a short time, then the lights and sound came on inside Denny's.

Mindi? he called mentally.

She didn't answer, and he realized he was sitting in a booth, not waiting tables. The eyes through which he watched looked up and saw the server approach the table. He saw the server's name tag, "Mindi."

He saw Mindi's face as she said, "Welcome to Denny's. May I take your order?"

Mindi poised her pen on the order pad, looked at each person in the booth, then stumbled. The man sitting to Jeff's left took hold of Mindi's arm to steady her as Jeff's host said an urgent, "Oh!"

He was in Carolyn's head! *How could this be?*

"Are you all right?" Rick said, letting go of Mindi's arm as she regained her balance.

"Must be something on the floor there," Mindi said. "If one of you gets up before I can get someone to clean that up, please be careful." She regained her composure, smiled, and making eye contact with Carolyn, said, "May I take your order?"

Jeff's view changed for a moment as Carolyn looked at Rick, then back down at the menu.

Rick spoke, a one-word reminder she should order. "Carolyn?"

Carolyn glanced up at the man sitting across from them, then back down at the menu. "I'm so hungry, Rick. Hmm . . ." Eventually, looking up at Mindi, she said, "Two eggs, over well, bacon, crisp, whole wheat toast, no butter . . . and a small orange juice. Thanks." She closed the menu and handed it to Mindi.

Jeff watched Mindi look at the man across from Carolyn. Rick gave his order and when finished, reached under the table and clasped Carolyn's hand. Jeff felt Rick give it a little squeeze, and Carolyn returned the gesture.

Jeff was angry that Rick had cheated on Mary, but kept his mind quiet because Carolyn could hear him if he didn't. She let go of Rick's hand and massaged her temples. Jeff noted she wore no ring on her left hand.

Rick said with concern, "Are you all right?"

"I'm fine, just a little headache or something coming on."

Jeff knew he had to leave now. He'd seen all he needed to and this confirmed he could visit others besides Mindi.

Charlene, Charlene, Charlene.

Jeff awoke, stared at the ceiling, and reviewed the events he'd just seen. How could he be in two minds at the same time and place? Was this just a normal dream and his subconscious playing tricks on him?

No, it's real. But the rules changed. Known science didn't apply to any of these dreams, anyway. His dreams until now made little sense, and this visit into Carolyn made even less sense. He'd built a basic understanding of how things worked on the surface, and now he'd have to adjust to a new pattern of what might happen when he went to sleep.

He got out of bed, sat in the low light of the living room, and concentrated on his breathing for a few minutes to help quiet his mind. It also helped him to relax when he wrote the details of the dream. After he finished his entry for the night, he paged back and reread the description of the visit where they'd first seen Rick and Carolyn. The two scenarios matched.

~

The next night, after his meditation, he climbed into bed with specific thoughts of Mindi and decided he should visit her in the gray room. He needed to control the destination. Every dream now was practice directing the dreams. As he began to float, he called, *Mindi, Mindi, Mindi.* To his relief, in an instant, he was walking toward the chairs and smiling at her.

"Well, hello," she said. "I've been looking forward to catching you up on my progress."

"Good to see you too," he said with enthusiasm. "You first."

"No, no, no," she countered. "You called me."

"Well." He sat down and felt the seat beneath his virtual body in the virtual chair. "Here goes. I've been meditating and doing OBE exercises. And had success." He smiled as he paused, hoping she'd urge him to continue.

It worked. Mindi said, "Go on, don't tease."

Though pleased he'd created some suspense, he'd also distracted himself. "Sorry. Where was I? Yeah. Well, I'm sure you remember when you, with me along, first saw Rick with his girlfriend . . ."

"Yeah, I nearly fell."

"Yes. Well, last night I leapt—"

"Leapt?"

"That's what they call it in an old TV series called *Quantum Leap.* It's about a time traveler. Scott Bakula's the actor. His character *leaps* into other people's lives and takes over their minds. He tries to do some good or fix something. The problem, though, is he keeps trying to get back to his real time but can't. Each episode is a leap into a different person, in another time, for a new problem. But he can't get home."

"Wow. I'm impressed." Her sarcasm was obvious. "I wish I could do *my* homework by watching TV. I'm sure that tells you what you should be doing." She took the edge off the sarcasm with a heartfelt look into his eyes.

"I'm crushed," he said with a mocking gesture, his hand on

his chest, head lowered. "No, it's true, there's not a lot of science there, but it gives me a vocabulary. So I get my guidance where I can. May I go on, Your Honor?"

"Sure." She laughed. "I meant nothing by that. And really, I'm kinda impressed you're taking this 'being careful' thing seriously, trying everything, and talking to me. You're here to ask for my feedback on what you should do, right? So tell me, besides being a couch potato with a TV remote, what have you been up to?" Mindi spoke playfully.

"Besides work," Jeff replied, "which is great, I'm still spending a lot of time trying to figure out the science of these . . ." He looked away while he searched for the right words. "These talents we've got."

She waited, leaning toward him slightly, interested in what he would say next.

"We know there's nothing on the internet about time traveling dreams, but I found a lot about psychic phenomena. People have been interested in this stuff for years. Some of it is what you and I've actually done."

She nodded. "Does it help make any more sense of this?"

"It might. Okay, I told you about *Quantum Leap* to set the stage for telling you about my dream, my leap last night . . ."

"I'm all ears, Jeff. Quit stalling." Another smile.

"Last night, I leapt into Carolyn's head."

"Huh? Really?"

"Yes. I didn't ask to do it. It happened, spontaneous and strange. It's more strange than anything we've done so far, because I was in her head that same time and day, the same instant, at your Denny's, as when I made you slip."

"What?" Mindi's eyes widened. "You were there in her head while she sat in the booth, and you were with me when I took their orders? That's, uh, improbable."

Jeff nodded. "Yeah, I know. We're immersed in the improbable every time we dream, though, aren't we? This just ramps it up a few notches."

"Yeah. Go on. You've got my attention. What happened?" Mindi said.

"I saw you slip, Rick grabbing your arm, your recovery, you warning everyone to be careful, and watched as she ordered—"

Mindi finished Jeff's sentence, "Bacon and eggs, over well, whole wheat toast, and a small orange juice."

Jeff looked at Mindi with his mouth open. "Wow. I know you have a good memory, but how do you remember that? That's incredible."

"It's what I do. It's a gift that served me when I had to memorize all the bones and muscles of the head and face for my cosmetology class. Oh, and her toast was dry, and bacon crisp. Speaking of my cosmetology class, I'm going to get my certificate for makeup stylist too—the full program, hair, makeup, and nails. That way, I'll always have something to fall back on."

"That's terrific, great plan." He stopped for a moment. "That memory thing, that's kind of scary. But impressive."

"Sorry to interrupt. What else?" Mindi asked.

"Not much. Rick and she were affectionate with each other. I couldn't stand it. I escape-worded it out of there. It felt way too weird."

"What are you going to do now?"

"That's why I need to talk to you. I'll wait and see if I visit her again. If I do, I'll ride around, try not to scare her, and see what it's all about. It's not my choice, but it must have happened for a reason. Remember, I'm not in control."

"So you still think there's someone else arranging this?" Without waiting for an answer, she said, "Okay, sounds like a plan. I like that you're doing more research. What else can you do? And I prefer the word 'visit' rather than 'leap.' Leap sounds so, so harsh."

"I'll try to watch my words," Jeff said. "I'll practice my skills. Gurus and new-agers have been messing with this stuff for years. When I look at what we've done from a practical point of view, I thought this whole dream thing was just about me helping you. I've done that, so why are we still coming here, still lucid dreaming? And you're still involved too, or you wouldn't be here, right? I'm trying to think about how you're supposed to use your lucid dreaming. I can't help but think there's more to it than giving us something to write about in our dream journals. What do you think?"

"I agree."

"So up to now, I'm the only one that travels into other people's heads. But until you time travel and visit others, I can see you helping me in the background. At least as an adviser, being a sounding board for me to talk all this out and give me honest feedback. Are you in?"

"You mean like meeting here and talking it out? Sure. I can do that. It sounds easier than leaping into other people's heads." She laughed. "There you go—you've got me saying leap."

Jeff winked at her. "See, one syllable is so much easier to say than two."

Mindi smiled. "You seem excited about all of this. It's okay, but you're going a hundred miles an hour. May I suggest you meditate on this some more?"

Jeff nodded. "I will. And I'll report back to you, Sensei, on whatever happens, what I can come up with."

She tipped her head to the side indicating non-understanding.

He caught on immediately and said, "Sensei?"

"Yes."

"That's a martial arts teacher, a master."

"I like that, Jeff. It sounds noble."

Jeff stood and gave a bow from the waist. "Your highness."

"Now that's a tangle of metaphors." She waited a moment, then asked, "Is it safe for you to tell me how the ad campaign's going? And is everything still okay with you and Charlene?"

"To answer both your questions, things are going well. She's been busy—really busy. We get together whenever we can. I understand the demands. I picked up dinner for us the other night. We ate at her place. First time I'd seen her in a couple of weeks. It's all good."

"Good, Jeff. I'm glad."

"Thank you. I'll let you know if there's anything new." He waited. She nodded, and he said, "Ciao."

"Wait, not yet. One more question," she said. "You said a few minutes ago, 'Until I do this time travel and visit others thing.' Do you think I can do what you do?"

"Yeah. I did say that. It's occurred to me you took to all this lucid dreaming stuff even quicker than I did. Anything's possible, so maybe you can. I dunno. We just wait and see."

"Okay, I get it. Something to think about." She stood and gave a little wave. "Ciao." Then her image dissolved as before.

He smiled as he awoke in his own bed. "That went well," he said aloud to no one, then he wrote in his journal. His day had begun.

~

It just happened—he hadn't tried to visit Carolyn again. He dropped in as she cleaned up in a kitchen.

The TV played the background, tuned to a news report, but Jeff couldn't make out the details. She wiped the counters, put things away, and when she opened the door beneath the sink to hang up the dishcloth, he smelled green onions in the garbage bin. Now, besides being able to feel touch, see, hear, and sense his host's feelings, he could also smell.

He was connected to Carolyn's mind and felt what she felt. She looked around the kitchen and things were to her liking. She nodded, a movement of finality, then crossed to the cupboard, took out a wineglass, and then opened a bottle of white wine from the double-door refrigerator. She twisted the partially inserted cork, poured herself a generous glass, and took a sip. Jeff savored its bouquet and realized that his senses with this host had developed even more. He added taste to his list.

He wished he could see the wine label, and she lifted the bottle and looked at it, as if to show him. After corking it, she put it back in the fridge, then picked up her cell phone, turned off the kitchen light, and glided into the living room. With the wineglass set on a fancy coaster, she picked up the TV remote. Her eyes scanned the room. Jeff noticed she shopped at Ethan Allen or Roche Bobois for her furniture. The room, nicely decorated and neatly arranged, reflected excellent taste and a generous budget.

Her phone announced a text message. She muted the TV, opened her phone, and clicked on the text that had just arrived—from Rick.

Jeff frowned, and Carolyn rubbed her eyes with her free hand and gave her head a slight shake. Jeff vowed to conceal his thoughts better. He was there to watch and learn.

The date on her phone said Monday, November 9. Jeff read the message along with her: *Be down for a week, starting this weekend. Want to get together?*

She went back into the kitchen, took out her calendar and opened it to November. One entry for her tomorrow, the tenth, was written in neat script: *Lunch with Kate—call Joanne?* She picked up a pencil and drew a line across from Friday thirteenth through Friday twentieth and wrote *Rick?* She then returned to the sofa, picked up the phone, and into the text window typed, *Sounds great. Call me*, followed by a heart emoji.

Carolyn set down her phone, turned up the volume on the television, and for the next half hour, channel surfed, never watching over five or ten minutes of, alternately, a cooking channel, shopping channel, home improvement channel, and back again.

Jeff mentally dozed, wondering when to use his escape word to leave Carolyn's mind. And if his mind fell asleep from boredom, when he woke up, would he be in 2017, or still with her? He sat mindlessly with her until she dozed. The wine was likely the culprit. Would she go to bed soon?

She got up and began to ready herself for bed.

Uh-oh, he thought to himself and kept his mind quiet while trying to decide whether he should go. Her bedroom was furnished in the same luxurious style as the living room. She'd done well for herself. When she started to disrobe, he decided he'd seen enough and in a mental whisper said to himself, *Charlene, Charlene, Charlene.*

But Jeff didn't leave. Carolyn looked around and moved her head as if to focus on something she thought she'd heard.

He needed to go. Jeff tried again, more forcefully. *Charlene, Charlene, Charlene!*

He awoke, lying in his bed thinking that Carolyn had reacted to his presence the same way as Mindi. Another data point. He had to be careful he didn't drive her crazy.

As usual, he documented everything he saw that night in the journal, plus a written reminder: *Why Carolyn? Must talk to Mindi again.*

The next night, Jeff wanted to visit with Mindi. Instead, after he fell asleep, he found himself back in Carolyn's mind. She was in the shower. She stepped out and started drying off.

An internal debate ensued. Should he leave now? It didn't feel right. But he'd arrived here for a reason. Should he stay and find out what it was? He felt conflicted.

Carolyn, in response to Jeff's lack of care in trying to mask his worrisome thoughts of being there with her naked, opened the bathroom door and listened, as if trying to discern if someone was in the house. Jeff tried to shut off his mind. He felt the chill of the cool air on her skin as she dried off.

He didn't think of himself as a voyeur, but he was a man who appreciated seeing an attractive woman, especially naked. This was from a different point of view, though. Carolyn looked around again, clearly puzzled at having an indistinct voice in her head.

Jeff turned his attention to figuring out why he was there. He still hadn't been able to stop his thoughts. *Am I being tested? If so, I've failed.* He smiled to himself.

She shook her head, another cue for Jeff to control his thinking. With the voice in her head quiet, she continued toweling herself off, looking at her legs and feet one at a time, balancing herself on one foot, then the other.

As uncomfortable as Jeff was, he couldn't help but notice and comment, in the quiet part of his mind, that she had nice legs, but that she should be more careful with her razor. She had nicked herself.

As if in answer to his thought, she noticed it. She blotted the cut, then looked at the little blood stain on the towel. Jeff felt her frown. She finished, and with Jeff watching, admired herself in the mirror. He'd leave this part out when reporting back to Mindi.

Jeff heard her think, *No wrinkles on my neck—good.* His senses were becoming more synchronized with his host's. She wrapped the towel around herself, grabbed a smaller towel and went to work on her highlighted hair.

That wasn't so bad, Jeff thought. Except it reminded him that he and Charlene had had none of those enjoyable personal moments lately. He missed Charlene.

She dressed, then went back into the bathroom to do her hair and makeup. Her cell phone chirped and then chirped again. She raced out of the bathroom, pausing for a quick moment to admire herself in the full-length mirror. Jeff tried to distract himself by remembering that Rick was a creep to cheat on Mary with this woman.

Her cell phone chirped again, demanding attention. The date banner read November 13. He'd visited Carolyn his last night, but a week in her time had passed. Interesting. Seeing the caller ID announced "Rick," she accepted the call.

"Well, hello," she said in a seductive voice. "I was hoping this would be you."

"Hello, beautiful. I've missed you," Rick said, and then he summarized their plans for the evening, and after dinner, coming back to her place.

Jeff thought, as Carolyn disconnected the call, that if there was an *adult* part of the evening, he would use his escape words to wake up before it began.

Rick texted when he arrived at the curb. Jeff felt Carolyn's anticipation as she opened the door of the rented Cadillac, sat down, and leaned across and kissed Rick. Jeff felt uncomfortable. Carolyn fastened her seat belt, and Rick pulled away from the curb.

Jeff had seen enough for tonight. *Charlene, Charlene, Charlene.*

However, before his view went gray, he heard Carolyn say to Rick, "What? What about Charlene?"

What Jeff didn't hear was Rick replying, "I didn't say anything."

CHAPTER 17

Jeff woke up early with his mind full of questions. The main one was why did he visit Carolyn? It couldn't be to confirm they were having an affair, that fact was well established. So was it to get Rick and Carolyn to end the affair? Why? Wasn't that already a done deal, too, because of the letter that Mary had found? Why did he need to be involved?

His dad's words resonated again: *Wait and see. The answers will come.*

Maybe he was supposed to keep Rick from writing the letter so that when Rick died, the secret died with him. Then Mary and the girls wouldn't have to endure that added pain. Jeff's mind was conflicted. *No, that can't happen, because the letter's already been written and found.*

When Charlene talked to him about the letter that Mary found, she didn't say if it indicated how the affair ended. Maybe it was through his efforts that they broke up, and his decision wouldn't be based on free will but that he'd be the instrument of predestination.

Jeff's mind worked quickly. If he got Rick and Carolyn to break up, and Rick wrote the letter, did that make Jeff responsible for Mary's pain when the letter was found? If he left it alone and there was no letter, would the secret die with Rick? *No*, Jeff's mind reminded him. *The letter's already been written and found. Be patient, wait and see. The answers will come.*

His mind continued to whirl with questions, possibilities, realities, and consequences. He started to doubt himself again, thinking that maybe what he'd told Mindi was wrong and maybe they could change the past and the future. After all, he argued with himself, what he told her about changing the past and the future was just theory—or even less, just speculation—based on thought experiments and never tested. Maybe *they* were supposed to test it.

No. If there were a scale of improbability, stopping Rick from being on the airplane on March 11, 2016, would be far harder, if not impossible, than changing the history of the letter that Mary had found. Could he stop it from being written, or once written, keep it from being found? Or maybe he was supposed to keep Rick and Carolyn together so that the letter wouldn't be written in the first place.

Why did he need to be involved?

Wait for the answer.

Jeff cursed how his mind worked. His ability to see multiple causes and outcomes in his business tormented him with the time travel problem: a dead future father-in-law and letters hidden away in a book on a bookshelf.

His thoughts rolled on. But if the future could be changed, what about other crossroads? Could a one-way street be made to go the other way? If Carolyn ended the affair with Jeff's help, would that start a series of decisions where Rick didn't confess, but he tried to rekindle his marriage with Mary and they took a second honeymoon vacation? *Someone else does the investigation in Egypt, so Rick isn't on the airplane and doesn't die on the return trip. Or . . . he takes Mary on his trip to Egypt for a vacation after he finishes his work, and she, too, dies on the return flight.* His mind quickly circled back to the conclusion that neither of those would happen. Rick was already dead. Mary wasn't dead, and she found the letter.

Jeff still wanted a good outcome from all his mental manipulations. He realized he was fighting the logic by trying to mold the facts to meet his desires. But his mind still went full throttle. Who's to say that the negative consequences he suggested to Mindi would actually happen? Maybe everything would ultimately work out better for everyone if Rick lived somehow. His and Charlie's relationship would still blossom. Charlene would get the LaDormeur account. Mindi would become a successful model with LaDormeur. It could happen. Couldn't it?

Wait for the answers.

Despite his father's wisdom, Jeff's thoughts raced on. *The affair did end. Rick's letter confirmed that.* His thoughts had come full circle. Was Jeff the reason it ended? Would it end anyway, without him? How was he supposed to know what to do and when to do it? He had no answer, and he didn't want to wait. He continued to figure out the logic of something that was ultimately not logical. None of the dream time travel visits he and Mindi had been living were logical. This left Jeff sorely conflicted. He always had answers, and logic provided them, but here, he could find no traceable logic. Self-doubt had, until now, never been one of Jeff's character traits, but he had it now. His abilities with deductive reasoning always served him well. He wasn't depressed, but he sure was sorry he didn't have the answers. But still, he wanted them. He had no instructions for any of this. The computer programs his company wrote always had documentation, quick start guides, and a troubleshooting matrix.

The admonition to wait and see that had repeatedly appeared in his mind repeated again, but no longer in his voice. His father's voice, sounding as only a parent's lesson can sound, said, *Son, wait and see. The answers will come.*

Lying there in his bedroom, staring up at the ceiling, another question occurred to Jeff: Could being actively involved in the breakup satisfy—Satisfy who? Jeff didn't believe in a supernatural, unseen, omnipotent, omnipresent being who played chess with everyone's lives. He admitted he was beginning to feel like he was being shown something substantial with these dreams and out-of-body experiences. But what was he supposed to learn? What was he supposed to do?

Ingrid's book didn't talk about a god, capital *G* or even a lowercase *g*. Nothing in the book implied anything more than a generic universal mind, of which all minds, including his mind, were a part. The same theory that Carl Jung had.

Ingrid's book told him that through acceptance, one could find peace. That, at least, gave some direction, a little comfort. It suggested that he trust his intuition and have faith that everything would work out, even if he didn't know how. Just thinking about that book gave him serenity. He took solace that he had other tools to help him: his father's words and Mindi's words, so curiously similar. His dad had said, *Wait for an answer. You'll know when the time comes.* And Mindi's shorter version, *Wait and see.*

He made a thorough entry in his dream journal, including the part about watching Carolyn get dressed, and ended that entry with a promise to himself to wait for the answers to come. After two cups of coffee, he finished the day's journal entries and got ready for work.

Jeff texted Charlene: *Thinking of you, xxoo.*

Several hours later, mid-afternoon, the phone dinged. He

looked at the text, obviously typed quickly from Charlie: *Hi been busy will call u.* The ad campaign must be putting a lot of pressure on her. He wished he could help but knew that quiet support was best.

~

After work, he stopped at the local tavern. He hadn't been there for weeks. He ordered a beer on tap and sat and studied himself in the mirror behind the bar. How had all this become such a bizarre hobby? The books said that lucid dreaming could be a problem when the line between dream and reality got blurred. The line now wasn't blurred; it had ceased to exist. Added to that, the border between 2015 and 2017 had also dissolved. In a word, his life had become bizarre.

He finished his beer and signaled the server for another, as well as the bar menu. He ordered the tavern's special burger and fries. When he'd finished, he walked out into the delicious autumn evening. The beers had muted some of the anxiety over what decisions to make. An artificial serenity settled on him.

This is the strangest hobby anybody's ever had. One good thing about it, though—it doesn't cost a dime, and I still get a good night's sleep.

He got home at 8:16 p.m. without receiving a call or text from Charlie. He stared at the phone in his hand for a moment. *Should I call?* He let it go. She'd always been considerate of him. The night was still young; maybe she'd call later. If not tonight, then tomorrow. He turned out the light at ten thirty. But his thoughts returned to the disappointment he felt at not having heard from Charlene.

To distract himself from those thoughts, he visualized himself at the gym tomorrow after quitting time, working off the night's second beer and the huge plate of fries. He slept without dreaming.

~

The next night, his falling dream routine resumed. Destination: Carolyn. When he arrived, her TV was tuned to Sports Center Scorecard. That was strange. Carolyn didn't seem like the sports type. When he heard her speak, it sounded different from before, then he immediately saw her across the room as she walked toward him, holding a beer. The hand that took the beer was a man's. He'd leapt into a guy! Was it Rick? If not, who?

Carolyn sat and snuggled next to him. Jeff felt it as he put his arm around her and pulled her into him. The man's left hand had no wedding ring.

After a bit, the man said, with an English accent, "I need go to the loo."

That wasn't Rick. The man, with Jeff aboard, untangled from Carolyn's cuddle, kissed her quickly, then stood and turned toward the bathroom. Jeff could smell Carolyn's perfume.

The man entered the bathroom and closed the door. As Jeff watched him pee, the guy let out a soundless, yet pungent fart. Jeff was sorry that his senses were closely linked to his host's. Once done, the guy washed his hands and dried them. Finally, Jeff got a look at him when he looked in the mirror, confirming it wasn't Rick.

Jeff resisted passing judgment on Carolyn, though it was clear she was playing it free and easy. That was none of his business. But why did he need to know that? Jeff made a decision. He didn't need to stay here. *Charlene, Charlene, Charlene.*

Jeff awoke thinking he really didn't want to be in the middle of a soap opera. He loved Charlene and wanted to protect her, but right now, he didn't know how any of this could protect her, if she even needed protecting. Most of this dream stuff lately had become a diversion, especially since Charlene had been gone. He now enjoyed the rush of doing something totally out of the ordinary and having a problem to solve. Heck, all he had to do was go to sleep. But the situation had changed into a bad drama where he didn't like the script and already knew the story's ending.

He transcribed the dream with all its details, including that he'd looked down at someone else's penis and was forced to smell the remnants of what the guy'd had for dinner yesterday. He added: *This wasn't as much fun tonight.*

~

While he was at work, his job helped him stay detached from his extracurricular musing about his dreams with Carolyn, Mindi, and time travel—so long as there were no triggers during the day to drag him back to the past. It was when he wasn't thinking about his work that the lack of contact from Charlene occupied his mind.

After work he went to the gym and repeated his routine of weights and swimming followed by a long meditation in the sauna. He drove home feeling cleansed and ready for a good night's sleep.

But when he retired for the night, sleep didn't overtake him, and he lay in bed wondering why he felt anxious.

The dream books said that lucid dreams could reduce anxiety, but that was while the dreamer was in the dream. So that wasn't the issue. He did have a healthy concern about doing the correct thing dealing with his dream characters and didn't want to make a mistake and cause anyone pain or fear. He had a hunch that things would work out the way they were supposed to with his latest visits with Carolyn. But he still wanted to do the right thing, whatever that might be.

He had a new friend, Mindi, and the feeling of success at having helped her over a hurdle in her life made him feel good, as did the time he'd spent with her. The only bad part was that he couldn't share the story with anyone. If he was anxious about anything, it was how and when he should propose to Charlene. She hadn't been in touch lately, and he missed talking with her.

He really wanted the committee in his head to quit serving him doubt and the possibility of regret. Specifically, he just wanted it to shut up. There would be no answers to his question tonight. He lay awake watching as car headlights traced patterns on the ceiling and the walls of his darkened bedroom—until he finally fell asleep.

As if the universe intentionally obliged him with a diversion from *his* personal relationship issues, back he went in time to witness someone else's personal relationship. There, in Carolyn's mind, he listened to a phone conversation with Rick.

"Rick, so glad you called. Where are you?" She and Jeff listened as Rick explained that something had come up. He wouldn't be able to make it down this afternoon and would be back down next week.

"I'm glad you called this morning," Carolyn replied. "I was waiting for your call. I can't say I'm not disappointed, but I understand."

"I really am sorry," Rick said. "Disappointed too. I miss you. I'll make it up to you."

"Okay, no problem. Just call me when you know and we'll make plans then."

Rick agreed. The call ended.

Carolyn rubbed her temples with the fingers of both hands

and looked at the clock. "I'll call Will," she mumbled to herself, then she scrolled down to Will's name in her directory and started the call.

"Hi, Will. Hey, you said to call anytime. I had plans with one of my girlfriends this evening and something came up, and she had to cancel. I hate to waste a good open evening. I've got some steaks in the freezer. How about I defrost them, bake potatoes, and make a salad? If your evening's open."

The voice on the other end, upbeat, said, "That'd be great, Carol. I was wondering what to do with myself tonight. Why don't I pick up some wine? See you about . . ." He waited for her to finish the sentence.

She did. "Say, about six thirty? Two bottles?"

"Yes," he replied cheerfully. "See you later; looking forward to it."

Jeff didn't want to have to wait until six thirty to find out who Will was, but he wasn't the guy from the other night. Will had no accent.

Carolyn pranced into the kitchen and pawed through the contents of the freezer. "Here they are," she said as she scraped frost off the steak labels, then set them in the sink to defrost. She glanced in the crisper drawers, took inventory, and satisfied, returned to the living room to watch TV. A jewelry infomercial was in progress.

Jeff knew he wouldn't enjoy watching late-morning TV with this woman. Without hesitation, he said to himself, *Charlene, Charlene, Charlene.*

~

Carolyn looked around, rubbed her forehead, and thought to herself, *Why do I keep hearing Rick's daughter's name?* But the commercial ended, another show started, and her question was forgotten.

Jeff awoke and documented his dream.

Why leap into Carolyn's head and meet her boyfriends? Is it to tell me that she isn't as dedicated to Rick as he is to her?

Maybe, he thought, it was to convince her to break it off with Rick. If getting Carolyn to break it off didn't work, then was Plan B to get into Rick's head and get him to quit seeing Carolyn?

Just like Dad had said, he had gotten the answer. It was decided. Jeff could make the hosts hear him. They knew someone was there, but they didn't know who he was. He would be the voice of their conscience, like Jiminy Cricket was to Pinocchio. But he needed to visit Mindi to run the plan by her.

Jeff's day job was thoroughly engaging. He and his team resolved a difficult issue, and their department head rewarded them with dinner—paid for by the boss—at a local restaurant. After the celebration, Jeff decided a light workout at the health club would cap his sense of accomplishment for the day.

When he got home, he got the call he'd been waiting for. Feeling elated, he answered right away. "Hey Charlene!"

"Hi, love," she replied. "I apologize for not calling or texting you. It's been crazy. My best assistant found out she was pregnant and slipped off to Vegas for a quick wedding to make it legal—Lord knows why. She left us in the lurch, so we've all had to pick up the slack. I'll be moving a rep from another account over to my team—my choice—but it will take my boss talking to his boss, then we'll have to bring him up to speed."

Jeff commiserated. "Oh, honey, I am so sorry. What have you been eating? Off the ptomaine wagon, I bet? How's the weekend looking for you? Can I cook you a real meal, make you feel you're on vacation?"

"Oh, Jeff," she replied with regret in her voice. "That sounds so good, but I have to go over to LA to give another pitch at LaDormeur headquarters, with everybody together at one time. I've given them each, at different times, different parts of the program. Now they want it presented all together and for the big brass. They've already approved all the print ads, though. Major pubs will have the ads in next quarter's issues. Vogue wanted to scoop the other mags, so our ad will be in their current issue. Make sure you check it out. It has your girl in it."

"Who's that?" he asked, although he knew who she was talking about.

"The pretty brunette."

He replied with a scoff in his voice, "They're all pretty."

"Don't be coy. I saw you sneaking extra peaks at her headshot when you helped me sort. I met her at a shoot in LA. She's as nice as she is pretty. She's a little older than some of the other girls, and her maturity makes her even more attractive—that stuff gets through. I think it's her eyes. Anyway, we're working on getting all TV, cable, and internet spots wrapped for the Christmas crowd. We're getting two months' work jammed into two weeks, but my crew's great. We'll get it done. But . . ." She paused for effect. "I've been burning the midnight oil as well as delegating as much as I can, even though Carrie flaked on me. We'll still make the deadlines, I'm sure, but it'll be close."

Jeff whistled. "You'll get it done. But remember, all work and no play makes Charlene a dull girl."

"Oh, Jeff, that's so clichéd," she said cheerfully.

"Yeah, but you burn the candle at both ends, you end up a drip," he quipped.

She laughed. "That's enough, Jeff. You only get two. Enough about me. You doing okay?"

"The boss took us out for dinner tonight. We did a great job on a tough task. Plus, we picked up a new account, and it'll be an easy start-up. I've been eating well, working out, getting plenty of sleep, and reading." He hoped she wouldn't ask what he'd been reading. He didn't want to explain about Ingrid's book and have to come up with another title. He was keeping enough from her now. He didn't want to lie.

Obviously tired and distracted, she didn't ask but did say, "Glad you're taking care of yourself. I miss you. If you text me, and I don't answer, it's not because I'm ignoring you, just busy. Take care, we'll talk soon."

"So glad to hear from you. Glad you're doing so well. I miss you too, love. Bye,"

She clicked off.

He plugged the phone into the charger and went to bed.

~

The falling, floating, and grayness had become quite familiar. He'd been having these dreams every night for the last week. Why so much so fast? First the vision went on and then the sound. He was back in Carolyn's living room. She was drinking a glass of wine again. The TV was on, but muted. Streetlights shone through the open living room window, and cars passed by, their sounds also filtering in. She'd just finished a phone call and placed the phone on the cushion next to her before taking a sip of wine, leaving remnants of lipstick on the rim.

His mind wandered to what Carolyn did for a living. Although not important to his mission, he was nevertheless curious. She obviously lived large, at least on the surface. She had plenty of friends—boyfriends and girlfriends. Yet her calendar had told him nothing about business appointments or where she might work.

Jeff hadn't visited with Mindi and gotten her feedback on

what he should do. Like other leaps, he didn't know why he was there, but he'd always learned something useful, so he figured he had all night to find the reason. He soon realized that wasn't true. Her eyelids were getting heavy from the wine.

He'd learned, after all these leaps into their minds, that if they weren't distracted or engaged in something, they could sense he was there. Sometimes they'd hear his thoughts directly if he wasn't careful. If he thought quietly, they'd react to what he thought and act as if it were their idea. Also, he was becoming, with each visit, uncannily sensitive to their moods, thoughts, feelings, and all their senses. It seemed that Jeff plugged directly into their brain stem.

Tonight, he rode around with Carolyn as she turned off the television, closed the windows and patio door, and prepared to turn in for the night. When she undressed, Jeff was grateful she didn't look in the mirror. She got a black T-shirt out of the dresser drawer and shook it out. The large LA Raiders football helmet covered the front of the soft, well-worn, shirt. It had to be at least twenty years old. *Was it left there by a past lover?* Jeff mused.

After she pulled it on, she looked down and lovingly rubbed her hands over the helmet. Had she heard his thoughts, or was that just a coincidence?

In the bathroom, she cleaned her face with facial cleanser, and Jeff realized he'd come to one of the crossroads he'd talked with Mindi about. His dad had said to wait for answers. He had waited and intuitively had the answer now to suggest to Carolyn that she and Rick quit seeing each other. If she didn't want to do it, she wouldn't. Mindi said you can't make someone do something they don't want to do.

Now, as she looked to confirm she'd gotten all her makeup off, Jeff was ready to set the hook. He would take control. In the most stern, parental mind-voice he could muster, he said loud and clear, *I have to break up with Rick.* Jeff waited. She kept staring at herself. Then again, Jeff said with more emphasis, *I have to break up with Rick!*

Did any of that register? Could she be so narcissistic that all she could see were her eyes and couldn't hear the voice in her head? After another moment of wiping her eyelids, she stepped back, closed her eyes, shook her head, then opened her eyes, looking down. After a pause, she turned on the water, tested it for temperature, and washed her face.

It didn't seem to have worked. Did the wine get in the way? Should he try again?

While drying her face, she looked at the mirror, then leaned on the sink and gave her image a verbal lecture. "You've got to break it off with Rick. He'll break your heart. He's married. He'll never leave her. And you know you'll hate how you'll feel if Rick's girls ever learn he cheated on their mother."

Jeff's virtual mouth hung open because she'd said so much more than he'd prompted, given a complete soliloquy. Clearly, the seed was already there, and he'd just watered it and made it grow. Anything that happened next would be the universe's responsibility.

Time to leave. *Charlene, Charlene, Charlene.*

Jeff heard Carolyn think, *Yes, and Gail too.*

Awakening in 2017, Jeff thought, *Mission Accomplished!*

CHAPTER 18

The next night, after Jeff's successful visit to Carolyn, Jeff's dream routine put him in the mind of someone sitting in an office.

What? Where am I? Disappointment flooded him. If he traveled anywhere tonight, he wanted to talk with Mindi.

The man typed a report on a desktop computer. Jeff's dad's homily came back to him again. *Wait. The answer will come.*

After reading the text on the screen, Jeff realized he was with Rick. The information on the computer was technical, about stress tests on an airframe. Jeff sensed they were in the Federal Aviation Offices in a suburb south of Seattle, not too far from Sea-Tac Airport. Had this leap into Rick happened because he'd considered visiting Rick as an alternative to getting them to break off the affair? But Carolyn had made the decision. So why be here?

Jeff felt profound sadness. At first he thought it was from himself, knowing Rick would die next March. But after a few moments, Jeff realized the sadness was emanating from Rick's mind alone.

What had made Rick feel sad?

Rick saved his document, picked up his cell phone, and looked at it as if to make a call. Instead, perhaps in response to Jeff's silent question, he pressed the icon for text messages, found the string labeled *LA1*, and pressed it. Jeff saw a message from Carolyn. Rick read it again.

Rick. It's been great, but I think we shouldn't meet any more. You are a wonderful guy, but our relationship won't go anywhere— you've got a wonderful family. We must let it go.

Jeff felt anger. She broke up with a text message! Was it his anger or was it Rick's?

Rick closed his eyes and rubbed a hand over them, then massaged his temples. Someone passed by in the hallway. Rick looked up and turned the phone face down. No one entered the office. Rick deleted the texts, then opened his email and typed in the search window, *LA1*. A chain of emails appeared, and he deleted them. He went to his trash folder, sent the contents to cyber-nowhere-land, and last, opened his contacts folder, chose *LA1* and pressed *Delete Contact*. The phone asked, *Are you sure?* He selected *Yes*.

Satisfied that his job was done, Jeff planned to leave Rick's mind, but intuition suggested he wait. Rick got up from his desk, walked over to where his suit jacket hung on a hanger behind the door, and pulled a single folded sheet of paper from the inside pocket. He closed the office door, then sat at his desk, spread the paper flat, and read it.

> *Mary,*
> *This is hard for me since we've been married for so long, but I feel I have reached a crossroads in my life and must be honest with you. I have met someone else with whom I feel I can be happy and who I want to spend the rest of my life with. I love the girls*

very much, and now, rather than later, I must stop deceiving you, and we must divorce. I will . . .

The letter ended, unfinished. Charlene had said the letter Mary found wasn't finished, but this wasn't the letter that declared the affair was over and asked for forgiveness. Jeff wondered sarcastically, *Doesn't this guy ever finish a letter?*

Rick pulled his shredder from under his desk and put the letter in the shredder's slot. The machine signaled its purpose with a whirring and grinding. The letter, intended to end his marriage of thirty-five years, became confetti. Feeling conflicting thoughts, and likely feeling Jeff's presence, Rick rubbed his forehead again. He tried closing his eyes for a moment, hoping he could clear his mind, then sat upright in his chair and took a deep breath.

On a blank sheet of a yellow business pad, he wrote the date, followed two lines down by:

Dear Mary,
What I am going to say is going to hurt you, but I must bare my soul . . .

Jeff's first thought was *Isn't this little dramatic?* But he understood that Rick's mood compelled him to do something, even if it turned out to be the wrong thing. He read on as Rick continued to write:

. . . to you. I have been unfaithful to you. I had an affair. It has ended. I fear that with this knowledge, you may not forgive me, yet I humbly ask your forgiveness of this most serious betrayal of your faith in me. My guilt is without measure. We must talk

about this, if only for the sake of the girls. I admit, I am being a coward not giving you this news in person. I will accept your decision . . .

Rick stopped writing. Jeff felt it had to be the pain from the breakup and built-up guilt that prompted Rick to write this letter. Jeff wished Rick hadn't written it.

He had to try, even though Mary had already found the letter, but he screamed in his mind anyway, *NO, RICK! YOU MUST SHRED THIS ONE TOO!*

Rick jerked his head toward the door like he'd heard someone, but he didn't honor Jeff's plea.

Again Jeff yelled, *SHRED THIS LETTER! NOW!*

Rick flinched but again ignored the voice in his head. Months later, his widow would find this letter, and it would reopen and add salt to the wound caused by Rick's death thirty thousand feet above the Mediterranean Sea.

Jeff had done what he could. He'd encouraged Carolyn to break up with Rick, but he'd failed to keep the letter from being found. Were Jeff's actions to encourage Carolyn to end the affair predestined?

If he hadn't gotten her to break up, would Rick have ever revealed his transgression and prevented the additional pain in 2017 from the found letter? Jeff would never know because time was a one-way street. But Jeff had a new data point that validated that the past cannot be changed once it has been lived.

Charlene, Charlene, Charlene.

Rick looked up from his computer and thought fondly of his daughter.

Jeff was falling again and expected to awaken in Seattle in 2017.

~

For the second time that night, his dream-self, seeing only gray, wondered where and when he would land next. After the short, familiar floating, he walked through the gray room door and saw Mindi walk through the door opposite him. They walked to their chairs, which now sat closer than before.

To say that they were pleased to see each other would be an understatement.

Mindi began. "Well? What do you have to report, mind traveler?"

Jeff replied immediately. "I'm glad I'm here. I needed to tell you what's been going on."

"Whatcha got?" She sat down.

Jeff filled her in on the visits to Carolyn, how he influenced Carolyn's breakup from Rick, and Rick shredding the request-for-divorce letter. Jeff told Mindi he was absolutely sure that they couldn't change history, that the "guilt" letter was destined for the bookshelf.

"Do you think I did the right thing? I wasn't able to consult with you first."

"Yes. I'm sure what you did was right."

"Thanks. You know, because of all of this we've been doing, I've learned more about free will and predestination. Philosophers and theologians have argued about it for ages. If things are predestined, it doesn't matter what we do. We are controlled by the hands of some unseen force or guidance. If things happen based on free will, our personal influence does matter even though we try to make our own choices.

"So I'm still not sure that I exercised my free will when I encouraged Carolyn to break up with Rick. Did she use her free will to follow through and send her text? So was it predestination that they broke up? If so, was I the instrument that made it happen? If so, it pokes a hole in the whole free will thing, doesn't it? I thought I'd made the decision, but we already knew that they would break up, so . . ."

He leaned forward, put his elbows on his knees and held his head in both hands. "Mindi, I don't know. I hope I did the right thing. But . . ."

"Of course you're having second thoughts," Mindi said, "but like we talked about before, no butterfly died, so there's probably no more harm done. I don't think we need to worry about consequences, because you already knew they'd broken up. It was a done deal before you got her to break it off with Rick." Mindi waited for him to sit back up and look at her, then she said, "Here's what I think. You told me that Charlene said that Mary hadn't dated since Rick died. Maybe finding that letter is what it will take to help her find closure and begin the rest of her life."

Jeff smiled. "If that happens, then it was the right thing to do."

Mindi gave him a quick nod and a smile, confirming that everything would be all right.

"The real test of whether I have any value with what I can do with this out-of-body stuff is if I can do good in real time, where I don't already know the outcome."

Mindi nodded. "Yes, I agree. But you already did that."

"What? When?"

"I've given you credit for helping me go to school. And here's why: You didn't know I would go to school to become a model when you suggested it, right? I'll give you a pass on the Rick-Carolyn thing because, as you said, it had already happened, and you knew it because of the letter. But you're the one that got things started with *my* future."

Jeff shrugged. "I guess you're right." He sat up straight, his expression relaxed.

"Good. Jeff, I don't think you would ever intentionally hurt anyone. You're a good soul. You'll always try to do the right thing."

"Thanks."

"What do *you* think about free will versus predestination?" Mindi asked.

"Sure. I've thought about that. It feels like we don't always get to choose the situations or influences in our lives. Those influences may be predestined. But don't we have free will on how we act on those influences? So to answer your question, I think it's a combination of both free will and predestination. Like, when we're born, it's predetermined we're going to die, but it's up to us to choose what we do until the end. So, yeah, a combination of both. What do you think?"

Mindi gave a small nod. "It makes sense. I agree." She paused a moment, then said, "Okay, what's next?"

Jeff sighed. "Good question. I started out on this part of the adventure with the intent of . . ." He let out a little chuckle. "I mean this facetiously, of course—saving the world. Yet I've only seen Carolyn and her boyfriends. Did I do any good there? Where will the next leap take me?"

"Speaking of leap," Mindi said, "I watched a couple of episodes of *Quantum Leap* last week. You got my curiosity up. Rather cool concept. Sam Beckett leaps into people in the immediate past to change history, but he becomes those people. Then the actor, Dean Stockwell, as Al the hologram, helps him. It's a shame we can't do the hologram thing. Anyway, I can see why you picked that as your, uh, pattern."

Jeff chuckled. "Well, there aren't many choices for a role model, you know. And I really hope we don't copy that. Beckett gets stuck in the system and can't get back out. But, like me, he doesn't seem to get to choose where he goes. Luckily, my leaps are not as complicated as his either. That's a good thing. Besides, you're a much better looking assistant than Al."

Mindi grinned. "Well, thank you."

"You're welcome. And thank *you* for helping me with this, whatever *this* is."

"Jeff, I have to say that you telling me about Charlene having my headshots has helped me plow through school when it's been tough going. There's so much to learn. I'm grateful you told me."

"That's good." Jeff sighed. "Very good. I'm glad you're using that like a goal rather than a gift. I projected onto you what my first reaction would be for information like that when I was in school. I'd have said, 'Cool, now I can party more!' You're more mature than that."

"I doubt you would've been a slacker at all. Actually, I work harder, making sure I'm worthy of it all. You would've done the same."

Jeff felt himself relax. He hadn't realized the stress he was carrying about having told her, worrying that he might've screwed things up. Now he was excited to share more, he blurted out, "Oh, what the hell, I can tell you."

"What? There's more?"

"Yes. Charlene told me that the next issue of Vogue has your photo in it. You made it, girl! I'm proud of you, and you haven't even finished school yet."

She bolted to her feet, excited. "Really? Vogue? No!"

Jeff nodded, enjoying her enthusiasm. "Yes!"

"That's so great. You've seen it? Could you show me?"

Jeff said nothing.

"No, I guess there's no way you could show me. I wish I could thank Charlene. I can't thank her, but I can thank you."

She sat back down.

Jeff smiled. "No, I haven't seen it. She just told me tonight on the phone before I came here. I'll pick up a copy tomorrow. But I don't know any way to show you. Remember, for you it hasn't happened yet, but barring anything really weird happening, it will. You're welcome. I expect to see more of your work. It's so cool that I know a model who's on the pages of Vogue."

"Well, if it's to be, it will. And regardless of what happens in my future, between now and then, I know I'll remember you if we eventually meet."

Jeff frowned. "Wait. What do you mean? Regardless of what happens if we eventually meet?"

"Oh, I just mean if whatever this is stops and we can't meet here, or I can't call you to meet me, that you've become an important person in my life. I know, uh, well, you know what I mean," she finished, embarrassed.

"Oh, Mindi, what can I say? If I were to see Mindi v.2017 tomorrow, it would be even better than meeting you here in my dreams."

They both stood as if to leave, but before Jeff could say anything, she took two steps forward, put her arms around him and hugged him. Jeff hesitated a moment, then put his arms around her and returned the hug. He could feel her arms around him and his around her, and her warmth. This was the first time they'd touched each other in their dreams. It felt as if it were real life, not a dream. It was another breach in the barrier between lucid dreams and reality.

They moved apart simultaneously. Mindi said, "I hope you don't mind, Jeff. I wanted to show you I really do care about you, and that I'm still really concerned about you gallivanting around, leaping into other people's heads, trying to save the world."

Jeff started to reply, but Mindi held up her hand. "No, no,

no, I know you don't think of yourself as some knight in shining armor riding off to defeat all the bad dragons of the world. I know you have a good heart and mean well in what you might accomplish. Just be careful. I don't know what could happen, but I'd hate to get to my future and not find you there. Okay?"

He smiled. "Mindi . . ." He was speechless. Jeff gathered his thoughts and finally said, "Until next time. I'll meet you here if I get any more news. I appreciate your input, really. And thank you for the hug—I needed that. It felt good." He looked directly into her eyes. "Ciao."

"Ciao, Sir Knight. You are a prince among men." Their images dissolved.

It took Jeff extra time to document every detail of the night's dreams. His clear memory amazed him, and the conclusions he and Mindi had come to and their discussion of free will and predestination pleased him.

After finishing in his journal, he fell asleep and awoke fully refreshed and grateful that a burden had been lifted.

~

Two days passed without further lucid dreams, and Jeff figured he might be finished with his missions. But on the third night, he again fell in that familiar gray envelope. Where would he land? He hoped it wouldn't be with Carolyn again.

The gray gave way to Rick's office.

At first Jeff felt frustrated, then he accepted he was there for a reason. He mentally sat back, resigned to watch Rick, who was answering emails. It was like watching scenery go by while riding in a car. Eventually, Rick closed his company account and opened his personal email account. Rick's eyes settled on an unread email to him from a doctor. Jeff's connection to Rick was so strong that Jeff knew it was from an oncologist. Rick had been copied into the email. The primary addressee was Rick's internal medicine physician, and the subject read: *Test Results: Richard Thomsen.*

Rick's lab tests had been run last week, and the results were available at the center's online portal. He clicked on the link, thinking that the results would be negative—otherwise why would they send a copy to him? The report appeared on the screen, and Rick's attitude sobered, as did Jeff's. The test results were positive for pancreatic cancer.

Rick phoned his doctor's office. The receptionist, as expected, told him the doctor was unavailable. Would he like for the nurse to return his call? Rick said, "I just saw my lab results. Would you please have the doctor call me as soon as possible?" She indicated that she'd give the message to his nurse. Rick repeated his request, "Please have the doctor call me as soon as possible."

"Yes, sir," she replied.

He disconnected and set the phone down, then stared at the computer screen for a long moment. "Death sentence," he said softly. His head snapped toward his office door, fearing that someone could've heard him. He got up and shut the door, then returned to his chair, leaned back, closed his eyes, and suppressed a sob. The phone's ringtone announced an incoming call.

He sat upright, gathered himself and answered, "Hello, this is Rick Thomsen."

Rick and Jeff listened as the doctor's nurse said, "Mr. Thomsen, the doctor is with a patient right now, but should be free within a half hour. I want to tell you that the doctor received your test results, and he has you on the list to call you right away. I see the other doctor's office also sent them over to you. Is that why you are calling?"

Rick answered with a clipped yes.

"I see. Usually the doctor calls his patients when their test results come in. This looks like a breach of procedure."

Rick, continuing in a flat manner, said, "I understand. I'd like to talk with the doctor as soon as possible." He added with emphasis, "Please."

"Yes, Mr. Thomsen. I assure you I will give him the message."

Rick ended the call without thanking her.

Jeff sat there with Rick, in silence, of course. Even if he could talk to Rick, what would he say?

Jeff experienced Rick's agonizing fear of the diagnosis and impatience while waiting for the doctor's call. He heard exactly what Rick was thinking: *I can't tell Mary or the girls.* A pause. *I have to tell Mary.* Pause. *And the girls.* Another pause. *How do I tell the girls? Don't jump to conclusions. Wait till I talk to the doctor. Things might not be that bad.* Denial was setting in.

Jeff understood Rick's default to denial, the beginning stage of any grieving process. He tried to stay detached, but Rick's grief saturated his mind. Jeff wanted to get out of there, but his intuition said to wait. He stayed there, quiet, in a corner of Rick's mind.

Rick's phone rang, the doctor returning his call.

"This is Dr. Jamison. My nurse told me you called."

"Well, Doc, I understand I wouldn't normally learn my test results until you called me."

"That's right, Rick. This is unusual. What did you learn?"

"I've got pancreatic cancer."

"Yes. I'm sorry. Do you have any questions?"

"I don't understand most of the terms. What does it all mean?"

"Rick, I'll give it to you straight. Tests indicate stage 4. The CAT scan showed it may have spread to the liver, but we have to do more tests. You need to come in so we can talk about treatment alternatives, depending on what subsequent tests reveal, to tell how far it may have progressed. Then we can begin treatment. There are some good websites to help you understand. I'll send over a list. Look at them before our next visit. Make a list of questions. Rick, many people live many years with chemotherapy and radiation. You will have time to play with your grandchildren."

Jeff had heard enough. This was between the doctor and Rick. It was hard on Jeff, too, because he knew, and not because of the cancer, that Rick would never walk Charlene down the aisle. Rick would never play with their kids.

Charlene, Charlene, Charlene.

Jeff awoke, but not refreshed as usual. Being with Rick had drained him. The clock said 1:30 a.m. Jeff paced around the apartment, but he needed to get more sleep before work tomorrow. Back in bed, turned toward the window, his mind busied itself processing what he now knew.

Rick never told his family about the cancer, otherwise Charlene would have told him. The news died with Rick.

Jeff couldn't fall asleep, so he took his journal into the kitchen, fixed himself a cup of herbal tea, and transcribed the dream. The writing served as a catharsis, unburdening his mind of the pain he had empathetically drawn from Rick. When he was done, he fell asleep, only somewhat relieved of the responsibility he'd been given.

CHAPTER 19

The next morning Jeff received a text from Charlene: *Staying extra day here to see Gail, then San Francisco with client and then home [heart emoji]*

To his delight, she rang later in the morning.

"Hey," she said, "the project's a little ahead of schedule, and I'm exhausted from all this work. I need a holiday to recharge before we do the final push to the finish. I can delegate before I leave. They can call me if they need me. Could you take some vacation days so we could get away?" They loved the coast, and she suggested a visit to the Olympic Peninsula. "Maybe three or four days? What do you think?"

Jeff felt elated. He missed her. Some time alone would be fantastic. "Great idea! I'll check with the boss and we'll talk later."

~

Jeff got the time off. He met Charlene at her place early in the day, and after breakfast, they set off toward the Washington Coast and the Hoh Rain Forest. They planned to drive further north to Neah Bay to watch the waves and the eagles, and then walk out to Land's End at Cape Flattery. They'd finish the loop back to Seattle through Port Angeles, Sequim, a ferry ride from Port Townsend to Whidbey Island, and then back to the mainland.

Jeff was excited as a schoolboy to see Charlene. It had been quite a while since they'd had quality time together, and this would be a perfect opportunity to open the subject of marriage. He'd rehearsed the reasons: they were both launched on their careers and had saved up some money. They could buy a house.

After driving south on Interstate 5, they turned west on the more peaceful highway toward the ocean before turning north on the coast highway. Charlene commented several times about how hectic LA was: the freeways, the crowds, the pace. She filled Jeff in on her visit with her sister. Gail was dating someone, and they had talked seriously about marriage.

"That's great. How do you feel about that?" Jeff asked.

"Oh, I'm happy for her. From what Gail said, the guy seems like a good fit for her. I'm glad she's found someone who really cares for her." Nothing more was said on the subject. Jeff was disappointed that Charlene hadn't brought up the subject of marriage for them. But he would use Gail's upcoming engagement as a springboard for their conversation. Jeff fantasized about a double wedding. After a couple of days of nature walks, peaceful drives, and holding hands, the mood would be perfect.

On the last day of their holiday, they did a little shopping, then stopped for some wine, shrimp cocktail, and fresh sourdough bread with garlic butter at a little bistro on the waterfront. It was a good setting and a great time to bring up the subject that had been burning in his mind for weeks.

"Say, about Gail getting engaged . . ." He paused, trying to ease into the subject.

Charlene frowned. "What about it? I don't know any more than what I told you. What do you mean?"

Jeff was sorry he'd started out being circumspect. He shouldn't have been so coy. Time to be more direct.

"Well, truth is, I've been waiting for a good time to open the subject of us getting married. I want to propose."

Her eyes widened in surprise, and something in her expression told him this conversation might not go in the direction he hoped. *Easy, Jeff,* he told himself. *Hear her out.* He waited.

She held his gaze, studying him to see if he was serious. Her expression changed to confusion.

"Jeff," she said with hesitation. "What a surprise. We've been real happy when we're together, but I didn't . . . I hadn't . . ." She stopped to search for the right words. After regaining her composure, she continued with more confidence, "This catches me totally off guard." She looked out over the water, then back at him.

Jeff watched her face, letting her find her thoughts, and tried to not read anything other than surprise into her reaction. He nodded sympathetically, implying she could go on when she was ready. This was not a battle to be won, merely a conversation about a serious subject. He hoped her initial reaction wasn't a prediction of where this conversation would end up.

"Jeff . . ." She took a sip of wine, then picked up her seafood fork, stabbed a small shrimp, swirled it in the cocktail sauce, placed it between her lips, and chewed.

After swallowing, she continued with, "Jeff, I don't really know what to say. You don't seem impatient for an answer, but you are serious, aren't you?"

Jeff nodded.

"Have you given this a lot of thought? You're not just, uh, reaching out with this because I've been gone?" She put the fork down, took his hand, and looked at him, waiting for an answer.

"You know, even though neither of us have talked about

being in love with each other," Jeff replied, "I certainly feel that way about you. We both respect and support each other as friends—good friends. We have so much in common, especially great respect for each other and each other's feelings, wants, and needs. Isn't that a solid foundation for love that will last a lifetime?"

He searched her face, hoping for a positive answer.

She kept holding his hand but treated the question as rhetorical, making no effort to respond.

So he went on, "I have thought about it, been thinking about it a lot, even before LaDormeur came about. I admit I have missed you, and I totally understand the demands on your time, energy, and attention. I can share you with a career and trust that whatever my career has in store for me, you'll do the same." Another look into her eyes, and he knew what she'd say, but he hadn't finished.

"Charlene, I love you. That's why I want to ask you to marry me." He gave her hand a slight squeeze.

She withdrew her hand a little and sat there for a few moments. After a sigh and another sip of wine, she cleared her throat and said, "Jeff, I think it's too soon, really. I just can't . . ." She shook her head. "No, Jeff. Not now."

Jeff frowned, disappointed. He had at least expected something like, *Let's think about it.* Obviously, he'd miscalculated.

"Okay," he said.

"I can see you're disappointed," she said. "I know you well enough to know when you're sincere, and you are . . . You are precisely the kind of man I would marry."

"But . . ." He waited.

"Yes, Jeff. But . . ." They both knew what would've followed that word, and it didn't need to be said again. She'd given him her answer.

They sat in silence and finished their wine and snacks.

Eventually, Jeff said, "Really, Char, I had hoped you might be in the same place as me about this. I do feel that two people, us, can have an intimate friendship, enjoy each other's company without a binding commitment. I don't take your lack of enthusiasm for marriage as a rejection of me. You're just not ready . . . yet."

She placed her hand on his knee, moved over and gave him a kiss, which he returned.

"Jeff, we're great together. Can still be great together. It's just that I'm not in the same place as Gail. I'd really hate to lose you as a friend and lover. But I can't make a commitment like that now. My brain is just so full . . ."

Jeff helped Charlene down off the stool. He left cash for the tab on the table and they left the bistro.

Jeff put his arm around Charlene's waist, pulled her close, and as they started down the sidewalk, he said, "Charlie, I'm so sorry. I really hope this doesn't dampen the rest of this trip."

She shook her head, looked over at him, and smiled.

Jeff hadn't considered she would say no. He'd misread the cues he thought he'd been getting from her. He felt anger and wasn't sure where it came from . . . Was it because he felt misled by those cues, or angry with himself for being so arrogant about his certainty that she would say yes?

His ego wasn't bruised—too much. *There's nothing to feel guilty about. It's an honest mistake.* Yet even though he hadn't gotten the answer he wanted, he felt relieved to have asked what he'd been wanting to ask for so many months. He would accept her decision. But of course, he was disappointed. Very disappointed.

"Thank you for being honest," he said, working hard at keeping his disappointment hidden.

She acknowledged him with a nod and reached down and

drew the hand he had around her waist a little tighter. "Thank you, Jeff, for understanding."

They walked in silence, listening to the seagulls singing out to each other again and again while performing their aerial ballets in front of the creamy bouquet of clouds suspended in the bright blue sky. The serenity of the moment was how Jeff wanted to remember the holiday.

They arrived back in their city amid all the commuters on the Interstate, each one jockeying into position to achieve some illusory goal that afternoon. Jeff deftly negotiated the traffic as he drove back to Charlene's apartment. Their conversation included just where on her deck they would hang the colorful windsock she'd purchased at a little shop on the beach. They ignored the shadow of the subject he'd brought up during that otherwise perfect, luxurious afternoon overlooking the water.

Charlene's phone rang just as Jeff shut off the engine in front of her apartment building. She answered the call and engaged in a conversation about prints and proofs, approvals and signatures.

She looked over at Jeff and mouthed, "I'm sorry," then got out and walked around to the trunk, phone perched on her shoulder.

Jeff indicated, with hand signals, that he'd get her suitcase and other bag. He shut the trunk, locked the car, and followed Charlene up the walk. She continued to finalize plans of some phase of the ad campaign while Jeff set down the bags, reached out for her keys, and unlocked the apartment door.

She walked inside and he followed her with the bags and waited patiently as she said to the caller, "Joyce, I'm just getting in. I'll have to get the file and call you right back, okay?" She ended the call, put her arms around Jeff's neck, and gave him a passionate kiss. He returned it, pulling her close. When they broke free a moment later, she looked him in the eyes and said,

"Jeff, what a wonderful weekend. It got Southern California out of my pores. Thank you so much." She smiled and gave him another kiss.

He stepped back, gave a theatrical bow at the waist, and said, with flair, "At your service, milady. T'was my honor, indeed." He dropped the medieval show and looked her in the eye. "You're headed back down south soon?"

"Don't know. My plan was to get some more work done up here. I'll have to see."

"When you go, please let me know you got in safely."

She affirmed with a quick nod, and as he turned to leave, she headed for the table stacked with files.

~

Jeff smiled as he drove home. It felt good to know exactly where things were in the relationship. Even though his goals for the future had changed, he was sure that their relationship would continue on as it had before. Their friendship was strong and the refused proposal was just a small bump in the road to be put behind them and soon forgotten. He enjoyed the views over the city and ignored the traffic. He'd be okay.

~

Jeff's familiar dream introduction embraced him. Again, he found himself back with Rick, who was sitting at a desk, but not at work, unfolding a page of note paper.

Must be his home office, Jeff thought.

Rick looked up, as if in answer to Jeff's unspoken inquiry, and looked through the French doors into the adjacent kitchen and the living room beyond. Mary watched TV, the top of her head visible as she sat on the sofa.

Rick looked down and reread the unfinished letter about the affair that Mary would eventually find. Rick's phone rang and he answered. The date on the phone indicated that almost a month had passed since he'd learned he had cancer.

The caller was from the FAA Accident Investigation Division. Their Go Team had been activated. "Proceed immediately to Borg El Arab Airport, in Alexandria, Egypt."

The FAA investigated incidents with airplanes operated by United States carriers wherever they occurred in the world. Rick would be working with the EAAID, the Egypt Aircraft Accident Investigation Directorate, with whom he'd had contact before. Since there'd been no fatalities, but major equipment damage, this would be for routine documentation of a non-injury incident, possibly caused by either ground crew error or equipment failure. It should take less than a week.

The caller said, "You leave tonight. Flight arrangements have been made as usual."

Rick cursed under his breath as the call ended. He looked back down at the paper and refolded it in thirds, then in half, and looked around the office, considering where to hide the letter.

Jeff knew it would be futile, but he had to try anyway, so he pushed his thoughts to the front of his mind and said as forcefully as he could, without yelling, *Rick, shred the letter! You must shred the letter!*

But Rick got up, crossed to the bookcase, selected *The Complete Poems and Songs of Robert Burns* from a shelf above his head, and put the letter inside before returning the book to its place. Jeff could only guess that Rick's intent would be to either finish it or shred it upon his return. Perhaps he planned to think more on it while he was away.

Jeff recognized the irony that no other person on earth

would ever see: it was Robert Burns who wrote the now famous line, *The best-laid schemes of mice and men gang aft a-gley.*

Rick went into the living room and told Mary he was going to Egypt that night.

She met his gaze and said with understanding, "You can sleep on the plane. Call me when you can." She smiled at him and turned back toward the TV.

Jeff felt the tenderness of Rick's thoughts as the couple made eye contact. Rick seemed to have made peace with his infidelity and cancer diagnosis. Based on his own knowledge of the future, Jeff was sure that Rick hadn't told Mary about his cancer.

Having seen all he needed to see of this little vignette, Jeff thought, *Charlene, Charlene, Charlene,* and left Rick's mind. Jeff wondered if Rick had heard his daughter's name.

At 2:14 a.m., Jeff awoke from the dream knowing that Rick's pain would be over within a fortnight for him, but the rest of the family's pain would just be beginning. Jeff had witnessed Rick's last time with his wife. Once again, he was enveloped in Charlene and her family's pain.

The apartment was chilly. Fall had arrived. Because yesterday had been a warm day, Jeff had left the windows open when he'd gone to bed. The brisk marine air now filled the apartment. He got up and closed the bedroom windows, then documented that evening's dream, including Rick's tenderness for Mary.

Ready for sleep, Jeff wanted to bring Mindi up to date on this latest dream, hoping he would visit her in the gray room tonight, but it didn't happen.

~

Jeff woke as the sun was coming up, disappointed that he hadn't visited Mindi. Though he felt better than when he awoke earlier,

he still felt the effects of Rick's emotions. He fixed a cup of coffee, took it back into the bedroom, and reread his journal entry from late last night. Reading it only reinforced the feeling of sadness he felt for the Thomsen family.

Jeff was eager to get some fresh air and a little exercise, knowing it would do him some good, so he tossed the journal in the nightstand drawer and shoved it closed. He would take advantage of this beautiful day, go out to the golf club's driving range and knock out a couple of buckets of balls to clear the cobwebs from his mind.

Jeff had accepted that Charlene wasn't ready to get engaged and had forgiven himself for bringing up the subject during a stressful time for her. He was sure that if he gave the relationship plenty of time, even though she didn't want to consider it now, she'd eventually want to tie the knot. The future would take care of itself. Considering his experience with time travel the last few months, the irony of *that* thought was not lost on him.

Charlene had been busy putting the final touches on the ad campaign, so Jeff invited her over and offered to cook dinner again. While sitting side by side on Jeff's sofa, working their way through their second bottle of wine, Charlene announced the LaDormeur account was still on schedule to be publicly announced at the Halloween-themed, client-centered gala party on Halloween night in Seattle.

With exaggerated Hollywood flair, she said, "Everybody, absolutely everybody, has gotten invitations. Everybody from LaDormeur will be there, including their board of directors. All of our people will be there, of course. I've still got to choose my costume." She put her hand on his arm. Their eyes met and she said, "And you will be there too? Right?"

"Of course. Wouldn't miss it for the world. This is big. I definitely want to share it with you." He chuckled. "I'll be sure to take some business cards. There might be a chance to pick up a new client."

Charlene slapped him playfully on his arm. "Oh, you wouldn't."

"Oh yes, I would. But I'll be good."

"Oh, I know you will. You know, I'll have to flit around, so you might have to fend for yourself now and then while I schmooze with the client. You're self-sufficient. You'll be okay with that?"

"Absolutely. For you, anything." He smiled, and she returned it. The rest of the evening was as delightful as ever before.

They'd been asleep for a while when he awoke with a start, sure he was falling, but there was no gray background. He was still in his bed next to Charlene. He hoped he hadn't awakened her, but she purred peacefully in her sleep and didn't stir as he got up and paced out to the kitchen to get a glass of cold water. He sat in the dark and reflected on how the last few months had been. It was 4:37 a.m.

That rough patch he and Charlene had had on the Peninsula had smoothed out. Things were back to the way they were before he proposed. Mindi was in school. They'd accepted their limitations with Rick's problems. Jeff's job was secure, and he was happy. He returned to the bedroom and slipped back under the covers and into a restful, dreamless sleep.

~

The next morning at the office, Jeff finished filling out his annual performance reviews. He acknowledged the incongruity that he worked in a software-based business that still required written forms.

Before he could begin to work on something else, Craig

plopped down in the chair across from Jeff and set a return-from-travel gift on his desk.

"For you, m'lad. Don't eat it all at one sitting, but it sure is good with beer. They call that Chicago Style Popcorn. Who would have thought about cheddar cheese and caramel popcorn in the same bag?"

After his cousin's wedding in Gardena, Craig had had to travel back to Chicago for work, so he and Jeff hadn't seen each other, except once in a video conference call with him and the team.

Jeff looked at the bag, then back at Craig. "Thank you, Craig." He wrestled with the adhesive tag to open it.

"So, did ya get over to Wrigley Field?"

"Absolutely. Last game of the season!" Craig exclaimed. "Cubs swept the Pirates in the series. Last game they slaughtered them 17–3, score more like football than baseball."

Jeff smiled as he pushed popcorn kernels into his mouth. "Anything else going on? No problems getting the system going? Say, this is good, thank you."

"No, no, went smoothly." Craig paused. "Except for the heat and humidity, it was like a vacation."

"Speaking of vacation, how was the wedding?"

"Beautiful," he replied, sounding uncharacteristically sentimental. "The bride, Katherine, was gorgeous. And my cousin looked . . . Well, let's say, the couple could've been the models for the figures on the top of the cake." He smiled.

"Any pictures?" Jeff asked. "Worth a thousand words." He hoped Craig would have photos that included Mindi. If so, he'd get him to talk about his cousins, aiming to get current personal information on her.

"Oh," he said, dragging out his phone. "Hang on a sec." He opened *Photos* and started scrolling, then handed the phone to

Jeff. "Swipe left—there's a bunch."

Jeff obliged. First, the groomsmen at the bachelor party. Photos of the groom's parents, Craig's aunt and uncle. Craig explained, now looking over Jeff's shoulder, who some people were. The groomsmen in their tuxes. Jeff scanned through the photos, moving quickly past ones Craig dismissed as friends they knew as kids, a few he didn't know, assuming they were the bride's family. Jeff stopped at the picture of the bridesmaids as a group. All the women were lovely in their matching dresses. They all could've been models, but Mindi stood out above the rest.

Jeff swiped quickly through individual photos of each of them in close-up, keen to get to the one he wanted to see. When he found it, he stopped and drank in her image.

"Yeah, she's gorgeous, isn't she, Jeff? That's my cousin Mindi. She's a model, can't you tell? Sure, I know, most models are leggy, and she's petite—but there must be a place for her in the business." He paused. "Hey, buddy-boy, that's my cousin you're drooling over. Besides, you're taken. I don't think Charlene would appreciate what you're considering here. Move on before you stain my phone," Craig said with a chuckle.

Jeff didn't move on, nor did he laugh. He stared at the lovely woman in the photograph. She was truly striking, beautiful. Emotions stirred in him, but before he could examine them, Craig continued, "She's single. And didn't even bring a plus one. Tough to accept that she hadn't landed some guy, the way she looks, and she's every bit as nice. Lots of class. Which is strange, because when we were kids, she was a snotty little brat. Lost touch with her, though, after her mom died. She turned out well. Said she's got an agent and is getting gigs, one a big cosmetic company. Every guy, even me, wanted to dance with her—she's a fantastic dancer. Anyway, move on, there's more to see."

Jeff continued scrolling, and Craig's voice faded into the background as he played back everything Craig had said. Jeff thought back over the times he and Mindi had talked in the gray room, and the hug she'd given him.

Craig took the phone back, and Jeff absentmindedly ate more of the popcorn. "Got to get back to work," Craig said. "Some phone calls to make. How about we get together for beers if you've got time this weekend, or maybe next?"

Jeff snapped to. "Sure thing, Craig. I'll call you. And hey, glad things went smoothly in Chicago, and thanks for sharing the photos of the wedding and the popcorn. This is good stuff."

Jeff tried to get back to work but couldn't get over Mindi's pictures, all dressed up for her cousin's wedding. And she was alone? That made him a little sad, since he'd hoped she'd have found someone by now. He wanted her to be happy. But part of him, although he didn't want to admit it, was glad.

CHAPTER 20

Charlene was busy with the upcoming public launch of LaDormeur's advertising campaign. It would take place at the Fairmont Olympic Hotel. "A truly grand venue for the Halloween Masquerade Ball," she announced to Jeff. He asked her what his costume should be.

"Oh, Jeff, I really don't know. I haven't even figured out mine yet. I'd say, be dashing, very dashing. You're worth it."

He looked online for something that wouldn't cause sweat to run down his back and into his underwear. Something not too cumbersome that wouldn't keep him from mingling comfortably, and he didn't want anything encasing his head.

A flash of inspiration came when searching on the internet for *dashing men's Halloween costume*. His idea for a costume that he could assemble with little effort included the tall black—and comfortable—riding boots he already had. With a few careful purchases, he'd be all set.

~

Jeff hadn't had a falling dream since his last visit with Rick.

Apparently, the subject had been put to rest. He frowned that he'd let the bad pun cross his mind, and as he fell asleep, he had no further thoughts of dream visits to anyone.

But soon he realized his dream sequence had begun again. *I hope this one will be fun.* His mood had been light lately, and he visualized a personalized caricature of a carnival barker who set the wheel of chance spinning saying, "Round and round Jeff goes. Where Jeff stops, nobody knows."

The answer was revealed when the gray cleared, and the lights and sound came on back in Mindi's apartment. Two weeks had passed since he'd last visited her.

"Jeff, you're here!"

His disembodied mouth formed a smile.

"Hi, Mindi. Did you call me? I didn't intend to visit you like this. Anyway, glad to see you. That's funny. I can't see you, and you can't see me. Please go over to the mirror—I'd like to get a look."

At the mirror in the hallway, a smiling Mindi said, "Yeah, I get it. I can only imagine I'm seeing you."

"Is anything wrong? Otherwise, why not the gray room?" he asked.

"I just wanted to share that my final grades from beauty school came in the mail today!" She clapped her hands in glee and walked over to the dining room table.

A sheet of paper lay next to its envelope. She focused on the sheet, and Jeff read that she'd received 99 percent on her final written exam, *Excellent* was her practicum grade, and her instructor had commented, *Great student, wish there were more like her.*

"What's left now," Mindi said, "is for me to pass the state boards. That's two more exams, and state practicals. Then I'll be a fully licensed beautician."

271

Jeff shared in her enthusiasm. "That's great. What's after that?"

In rapid-fire phrases, Mindi said, "Makeup school. To learn secrets of cinema and models' makeup. Then modeling school. I don't know which school yet. I've got some brochures. I'll figure that out soon."

"What's today's date for you?"

She picked up her phone and showed him the screen. *April 24, 2016.*

Jeff thought for a moment. "You told me it takes sixteen hundred hours." He did the math on virtual fingers. "That usually takes—"

She finished the sentence for him. "—ten months, but I did long days, doubled up on some classes and finished just shy of eight months." She took a breath. "They asked me if I wanted to go that fast, that they'd seen other girls burn out, but I told them I was motivated."

"Well, I guess so," he said. "You were driven, weren't you? Great going. But why did you put it in overdrive?"

"I put in the application to school in July, got accepted right away, but my program's classes didn't start until mid-August. I was already a couple of months into the program when you said I'd be in the running for the LaDormeur campaign. That was the motivation I used to finish early. After the state boards, I'll do makeup school and then I'll have to get at least some of the modeling classes finished. Next, I'll have to fast-track getting an agent and get some work for my portfolio. I had to do it this way. I calculated I wouldn't have had enough time for the headshots that you and Charlene will see—uh, have seen." She laughed. "I have to tell you, I told you so!"

"What about?"

"About when you told me my future. I'm sure that classified as the predestination you talked about."

Jeff shook his head, then realized he needed to say it. "I don't understand."

"If you hadn't told me about my chances of being in Charlene's ad campaign when you did," she explained, "I wouldn't be ready. So you had to tell me, see? That's why I needed to share this."

Jeff said, "You were right. That's good to know. So when we choose to do something, the choice might really be controlled by something else. So much for free will. But I won't give up on the concept, though. This is so great. I'm so proud of what you're doing."

"Thanks. I've been hitting the books pretty hard. I just didn't have time for us to get together. And you've been busy too, right? You never called."

"Yes, I'm sorry. Now, you're in April, I'm in October. You're closing the gap. Only a year and a half difference now. That's interesting, not just because it's happening, but because we still have no way of knowing the mechanics of it."

"Do you think we ever will know?"

"I don't know." Jeff paused a moment. "Oh, I need to share something important. Since the last time we talked, I leapt into Rick on the day he found out he had stage four pancreatic cancer."

Mindi gasped. "Oh, Jeff. The poor man."

"And I was there when he got the assignment to go to Egypt. In your time now, Rick's plane has gone down. I was a little worried that I might end up on the plane with him when it went down. I'm glad I wasn't."

"That would have been . . . strange," Mindi said. "Could you have been hurt? I don't want to think about that." She gave a shudder that Jeff felt. "I saw the news about the crash on TV and felt so sad. But how was it for you, being there when he learned about the cancer?"

"I was completely exhausted when I woke up after that leap.

I'm pretty sure, though, that when he left Mary for the last time, they were in a good place together. I tried to get him to shred the letter, but the universe had other plans—confirms that we can't argue with fate and change the past."

Mindi took a moment to absorb this information, then said, "He never told them about the cancer?"

"I don't think so. Charlene never mentioned it. If she'd known, I'm sure she would've told me."

"Doesn't she have a right to know?"

"Probably. But I can't tell her. It would raise questions that could only be answered if I got pumped full of Thorazine. And what good would it do? It would just cause more pain and questions. There's enough extra pain with that letter that opened a wound big enough to fly an airliner through, no pun intended."

"I agree. But it's one more secret you have to keep."

"Yeah," he said with a sigh. "I'll just add it to the list. I wish I could figure out why I needed to know about Carolyn, the letters and his cancer. It doesn't make sense."

"I've thought about why you had to nudge her to break it off. She might not have done that without you. Because it was over, he at least tried to make amends. What if Mary had found out about the affair from someone else after he died? That might have caused more pain than the letter.

"Jeff, you did what was right. You've got so much going for you: a good job and an attractive, smart, talented girlfriend that you'll marry someday."

Jeff flinched, and Mindi felt the jolt.

"What was that about?" she asked in concern.

He didn't reply.

"Jeff, what did I say that made you jump?"

He remained silent.

"Hey, if you're still there, do I need to remind you, we're

friends? Friendship is a two-way street. You've been here for me. Now, what did I say that was wrong?"

"Nothing."

"Jeff! What are you not telling me?" Mindi scolded him.

"It doesn't involve you."

"Well, my friend, I know something's up now. Tell me." It wasn't a request but an order. After another moment of silence, she added, "Please."

Jeff sighed. "Okay." After a virtual deep breath, he told her about how he'd proposed and that Charlene had rejected his proposal. "I'm pretty much over it. We've gone back to the way we were before with no expectations. We haven't dated anyone else, and I don't think we will while we're together. Everything's fine."

"Do you love her?"

"We're really comfortable with each other. I'm patient. She'll change her mind in time. I'm all right."

Mindi waited a few moments to see if he had any more to say, but he remained silent. "Thank you for sharing that," she said. "You needed to tell someone, and you haven't shared this with anyone, have you? You've been stuffing it, right?"

He said nothing.

"I asked a question and can't see your face, so please say something."

He still didn't respond.

"Hey, I should have been a dentist. Getting you to talk is like pulling teeth."

She heard him chuckle, but still he said nothing.

"If you're embarrassed to be vulnerable with me, please don't be, okay? Okay?"

He felt her compassion and knew it was genuine and strong. Being inside her head with it felt comforting.

He sighed once more. "You're right. I haven't told anyone. But her not accepting my proposal hasn't changed anything."

He hadn't admitted it to himself, but something wasn't the same. The excitement of her accepting his proposal and then looking forward to getting married was gone. But they were still together. The relationship, as before he proposed, was exactly the same.

Jeff changed the subject on purpose. "I'm so glad you shared your success with me. You've earned everything coming down the line for you, and I want you to call me anytime, every time, you need me, or want to share something like this with me."

"Of course, Jeff, and I expect the same from you."

"Thank you. Really, thank you so much. I do feel so much better after sharing that with you. I probably should go now. Ciao."

"Okay. Ciao. See you soon."

~

When Jeff woke up, it took him a moment to realize that he hadn't said Charlene's name to end the dream with Mindi. Was his new escape word "Ciao?"

Before meeting Mindi, Jeff had never had a woman friend that hadn't been a lover. After that visit, he felt so much better. She was a friend who had called him on his stuff and not taken sides. Even if the only takeaway from all these dreams was to have her as a friend, it was worth it.

The clock said he only had an hour until the alarm would go off. While drinking coffee, he entered their dialogue and his feelings into his dream journal, then he opened his laptop and checked a national newsfeed. Nothing exciting there beyond the standard junk. He then checked his email inbox, and on top was

one dated April 25, 2016, from MindiModel@yahoo.com.

She sent it last night. No, she sent it his last night, but it was actually the day after, her time, of his latest visit with her, a year and a half ago. He frowned. How was it he'd not seen that one before? It made no sense. He opened the email.

> *Jeff,*
> *I hope you get this, that it didn't end up disappearing. I really am glad you could drop in so I could share my good news. And that you could share with me what's going on for you. I'm sorry it's not working out the way you planned, but there's time. It will all work. Since you can't email something going back in time, I think I can assume, if you could, you'd send the same back to me I send to you now. So . . . You're welcome, for when you thanked me for wishing you good luck, and thank you for you wishing me good luck.*
> *Ciao for Niao. Mindi.*

NIAO means "not intended as offensive." Why would she sign off that way? *That's weird.* Jeff puzzled over what she meant by that.

Then it hit him, *Now I get it!* He laughed out loud. "Ciao for NOW! Clever girl." He was disappointed that he couldn't answer her email. She wouldn't get it until his today, a year and a half after she sent this one.

Wait a minute! Because she sent it in 2016, he should've already seen it when he found her first email. And because of the sent date, it should have been at the bottom of all of his unread emails in his inbox. But it wasn't. It just arrived today, and it was on top. He briefly looked for a logical explanation to the email's arrival, but there was none.

He shrugged his shoulders. It was part of his new normal. It didn't need a rational explanation—it is what it is. If there *were* any answers, they would come.

His cell phone rang. A client in Atlanta. After handling the client's issue, he left for the office. It was a good day.

CHAPTER 21

Jeff pulled into the parking garage at the Fairmont Olympic for the LaDormeur Masquerade Ball as the crush of invited guests began to fill the hall. He straightened his costume then remembered to get the sword from the back seat of his car. Charlene had arrived early that day to coordinate preparations. He expected it would be a marvelous evening.

The hall had been decorated well beyond the black and orange crepe paper and bobbing-for-apples decorations of a neighborhood Halloween party. This was a Beverly Hills-quality setting in the hotel's Garden Room that had a full wall of windows, floor to ceiling, which overlooked downtown Seattle to the north. The evening being clear and crisp, the city's skyline sparkled against the sky. Jeff sensed the anticipation of the evening.

Charlie had told him during one of their conversations, "They've hired a designer for the hall who's done major stuff for movie studios and theater opening night parties. It will be spectacular."

She was right. The décor was amazing. He stood at the entry, first focusing on the life-sized, ghostly trees placed all around the room—each over ten feet tall, fashioned from black entwined tinsel, draping down as if to grab passers-by. Little orange lights subtly twinkled among the dangling, dark, moss-like branches.

He looked up at the dozens of suspended ghouls in dark brown and black robes gazing down with eerie, lighted eyes. They actually moved around as if surveying the crowd mingling below.

Male servers dressed as vampires moved efficiently through the room. The female servers wore frayed, flowing witches' robes, pointed hats, and pointed-toed shoes. Guests were dressed as skeletons, pirates, astronauts, ghosts, prisoners, multiple cartoon characters, and more.

He admired the costumes as he scanned for a familiar face. He was arrayed in the dashing garb of a King Arthur-era nobleman—black, highly polished boots, faux leather breeches, and a matching tunic dramatized with a crest of red, gold, and deep blue on his chest. Stylized golden lions stood on either side of the crest, which was topped with a black and gray bird of prey, wings spread, looking outward as if to attack.

His wrist gauntlets, in silver-gray metal, ended in black fingerless gloves, and the imitation red velvet cape, cut to just below the waist, swirled dramatically as he turned. The authentic short sword, borrowed from a coworker, hung on a leather belt on his left hip, and a gold crown completed the costume. The mask covered only his eyes, leaving his nose and mouth free. He'd searched relentlessly online to find one he could push up and away from his eyes without detracting from the crown.

For comfort's sake, the sword would have to go as soon as he could find a place to secure it safely, but first, he had to make a suitable impression on one particular person.

He continued to scour the crowd to find the one he'd most like to awe and finally achieved his goal. Charlene stood talking with two others, a man, obviously dressed as Count Dracula, his costume miraculously tasteful with detail that included incisors appropriately marked with blood. The other, an older woman with black hair perched atop her head, wore a dress with blossoming sleeves—probably a Lady Tremaine costume, Cinderella's evil stepmother.

Charlene looked glorious in a full-length, champagne-colored, close-fitting 1930s-era dress. Her character was Claudette Colbert or Jean Harlow—he'd have to ask her which. The dress was chaste in that it covered most of the skin on her body, except for her lovely arms, bare to the shoulder. However, the dress left little to the imagination as to the shape it covered, and the material flowed with the movement of her legs, hips, and torso as if it were one with her body. Her long blond hair flowed equally exquisitely, styled to match the era of the dress.

Jeff wondered when she'd found the time to get her hair done. He approached her from behind and paused a short distance from the group. Lady Tremaine's eyes widened with appreciation, and Dracula and Charlene turned to see the object of her attention.

Charlene's eyes widened to match those of her conversation companion. She drank in the image Jeff had created, beginning with his crown, stopping for a moment at his eyes, with a private acknowledgment of their shared intimacy, then enveloping each part of his costume with an advertiser's eye for detail. She scanned his torso, legs, boots, and the cape, which he pulled away to display the sword. Her eyes met his again, and she smiled her approval. He approached the group and she introduced the head of her agency, Dracula, and Lady Tremaine, the president of LaDormeur.

After the introductions, Jeff bowed at the waist, remaining in character to the end of the bow. He stepped forward, gently taking the hand of the lady in a most gallant fashion, and next offering his hand to the count. Then, demonstrating that he and Charlene knew each other, he leaned forward and they exchanged a Hollywood double-cheek kiss. He then stood back and offered generous praise for Charlene's efforts for the party. She accepted the compliments with grace. Another guest, costumed as a salmon, approached. Charlene excused herself and spoke with him briefly, then others in various costumes joined her, and the crowd quickly consumed her.

Jeff spoke with the two who were key to Charlene's business success until they too, were spirited away to mingle with other guests.

Time passed quickly as he walked around with his glass, occasionally meeting up again with Charlene and being introduced to other key players in both organizations, the client and the agency. Jeff guessed that the room contained well over three hundred elaborately dressed revelers. Many kept their masks on, and he was glad he'd chosen a mask that allowed him to remain in character without the associated discomfort—unlike the guy who'd come as Shrek with a huge silicone mask.

When Jeff finished talking with Shrek, poor fellow, he glanced across the room and recognized a face who was completely out of place here—like seeing your white-coat-wearing pharmacist at the theater in evening attire. In an instant his mind made a quick identification, and he gave a wave. They moved toward each other.

Jeff reached out his hand. "Craig, I sure didn't expect to see you here. Hey, great costume, a pirate. Nice choice. I'm glad you're here." He leaned in toward Craig and said quietly, "But how did you get an invitation?"

"I'll explain, just a second." He scanned the room, looking

for someone. "Ah, there she is." Jeff turned to see where his friend was looking. Craig explained, "She had no escort, and was obligated to be here, so she asked me, and I said, 'Of course.'"

Mindi.

She'd been speaking with a small group nearby, and when she heard her cousin's voice, she excused herself from the conversation, turned and looked, paused a moment, then closed the distance to the two men with a smile on her face and in her eyes.

Mindi v.2017 in person completely entranced Jeff—she was exquisite in her costume. Somehow, he maintained a professional posture, but his mind reeled. Their eyes met in recognition.

She's so lovely! Their gazes locked.

Craig, the gentleman, in proper etiquette style said, "Jeff, you remember the pictures of my cousin's wedding? Mindi was one of the bridesmaids." He looked over at Mindi, then back to Jeff. Neither looked at him. They were totally focused on each other.

Jeff accepted her offered hand, which he took in perfect medieval fashion, and said, "Yes, Craig, I do remember." He glanced at Craig. "I don't think I told you. I recognized her from the modeling agency headshots that Charlene brought home for this ad campaign."

"Ohhh . . ." Craig said. "That's why you kept staring at her photo on my phone—you recognized her."

Jeff returned his gaze to Mindi. "Yes, indeed, I did. I truly am so glad to meet you in person, Miss Ketchem. This is very much a pleasure."

Mindi's eyes twinkled, noting his reference to her real name. "Well, Mr. Marlen, the pleasure is all mine. If you wore armor, I would know you were a knight." She looked up at the crown. "But no, you must be a prince."

Jeff smiled, acknowledging her reference to their conversation in the gray room. "Well, then, a prince I shall be. Yet I can also be a knight, as noblemen frequently were."

Mindi smiled and tipped her head sideways in agreement.

"And if I may, m'lady," Jeff said, "you appear to be—am I being too bold to say, representing Snow White?"

Mindi laughed. "You certainly are quite—charming."

Craig looked from one to the other with a confused expression, trying to figure out what was going on with their back-and-forth talk—odd for two strangers who'd just met. And he hadn't used either of their last names in his introduction.

"You, sir," Mindi said, "are far more adept than my cousin here. I had to explain to him who I was. You identified me right away." She looked up at Craig and smiled as she bumped her shoulder onto his arm, a teasing move betraying the familiarity of relatives who'd grown up together.

Craig, looking a little uncomfortable, checked their drinks and, seeing Mindi was without one, said, "What are you drinking, cuz?"

"White wine, thank you, Craig."

He left quickly, as if keen to escape.

Mindi turned her attention back to Jeff, waited a moment for Craig to be out of earshot, then said, "I'd hoped you might be here. I met Charlene down in Santa Monica and easily put two and two together."

"I'm . . . It really never occurred to me you'd be . . ." Jeff said sheepishly. "I didn't even think . . . I guess I should have known . . . How silly I didn't consider . . ."

Seeing he was uncomfortable, she placed her hand on his arm. "No worries, Jeff. It's okay. Poor Craig. I bet our banter confused him. By the way, I worked out the timeline. For you, you saw me just last week, right? For me, I haven't talked to you in—a year and a half. I've really missed visiting with you. The last time we talked was when I graduated beauty school. I did try to call to you several times since, hoping to get you to come to our gray room. I admit, I was disappointed. When they gave us the schedule for this PR party, I was excited and couldn't wait to get here to see you. I am so glad you're here tonight, so very glad." With a warm smile, she added, "Tell me you weren't snubbing me."

"Oh, Mindi, no. I'm sorry, no. I wasn't ignoring you. It must have felt that way to you. A year and a half? That's so long." The look on his face was clearly apologetic. "I was looking forward to visiting you in the gray room this week . . ." The difference in perception from his time travel still had him off-balance. "I-I-I just saw you last week. I didn't think . . . I've been swamped with work. I'm sorry. I didn't even consider you might be here. I was going see you this week . . ."

"It's all right, really. I've been busy with school and, now, working. I admit, I really missed not talking with you. I realized that your whole ability to time travel had run out and your visits were over—but somehow I knew we'd meet again." Mindi's eyes lit up. "And now we're here and we can talk in real time!"

Jeff smiled. "How you must have felt when I didn't . . . But yes, it's so good that you—that we're here now. I hope we have some time . . . How long will you be in Seattle? Oh, hey, here comes Craig." Jeff wasn't used to feeling so awkward, or so elated, even though his confidence of earlier in the evening seemed out of reach.

Craig handed Mindi a glass of white wine.

"Thank you, Craig." She raised her glass in an acknowledgment toast.

Craig looked at each of them. "Well, what are you two talking about? Advertising, cosmetics, software, or the Seahawks?"

Mindi, with a straight face, replied, "No, Craig, nothing so pedestrian. We were discussing the quantum physics of time travel, wormholes, and the consequences of unanticipated paradoxes created when one's consciousness moves quickly back in time, and then another's life moves forward at a normal rate." She smiled directly at Jeff, which helped bolster his confidence.

Craig's expression turned blank. He blinked.

Jeff had difficulty suppressing a laugh and turned it into a broad smile.

Mindi looked back at Craig. "No, actually, I was asking Jeff what one should do in Seattle. This is my first visit here. Sure is a lot quieter than LA." Returning her gaze to Jeff, she said, "I'll be here for a week." She looked from one to the other in anticipation of one of them offering to be her tour guide.

Craig jumped in with, "Well, if you want to go to a kids' soccer game, the boys are playing early Saturday morning. I'll check with Barb, see what else we could put together."

"Why don't I talk with Charlene?" Jeff said. "I'm sure there's something going on at The Seattle Rep, or perhaps the Paramount. She might be able to get tickets."

Mindi, with the grace and style she'd already displayed, said, "Well, gentlemen, I'm sure a lady in Seattle will not be ignored." Her gaze shifted to someone behind Jeff.

Jeff turned to see where Mindi was looking. Charlene approached them, and Jeff moved aside to let her into the group.

Charlene said, "So, Jeff, I see you've met Miranda Madisen in person. I remember you were quite taken by the picture her agency sent over." She turned to Mindi. "Jeff helped me vet the huge number of portfolios from agencies when we first got started. Yours was one of those he selected."

Mindi dipped her head to Jeff, acknowledging the implied compliment. Though they stood together, Jeff and Charlene never touched each other, betraying nothing of a personal friendship, let alone intimacy.

Jeff diverted the conversation away from himself. "Charlene, of course you know Craig?"

Charlene nodded.

"Craig is Mindi's cousin," Jeff continued. "You're second cousins, right?"

Craig and Mindi nodded.

"They grew up in Gardena. He's her escort for the evening."

Charlene offered a hand to Craig—a mere formality, since she'd known Craig as one of Jeff's friends for some time. "Of course. Craig, how is your lovely wife?"

"Oh, she's fine. Thank you for asking, Charlene. She's watching the boys this evening while I enjoy this great party. I'm glad Mindi asked me to accompany her."

Mindi told Charlene, "I'm staying at Craig and Barb's and taking some time off. I asked these two where things might be happening here in Seattle, and Jeff said you might have access to tickets for a show."

Charlene looked at Jeff, one eyebrow raised in query. Embarrassed, he said, "Yeah, uh, I thought we might be able to go as a group"—he waved his hand around, indicating them all—"and show Mindi some Seattle hospitality."

"That would be splendid," Charlene said. "Let me see what I can do. I should be able to arrange something. Perhaps dinner and a show?" A group of three people approached and whisked Charlene away with an apology. She nodded and flashed Jeff a warm smile as she left with the others.

Mindi turned to Craig. "Nice to know people in high places, huh? You got great friends." She indicated Jeff with a nod. Craig looked from Mindi to Jeff and back, but said nothing.

A group of four other women—their appearance indicating

they were also models in the ad campaign—approached Mindi and asked her to join them. Each of them gave Jeff more than a subtle examination and indicated their appreciation with smiles and twinkling eyes.

Mindi took Jeff's hand in both hands. "It was so very nice to finally meet you. Thank you for whatever part you played in helping me be here tonight. And I truly hope we meet again this week. I'll leave you in Craig's good care." Her smiling eyes locked on his for what seemed to Jeff a long, glorious moment, then with a glance at her cousin, she said, "Craig, could you please text my phone number to Jeff, just in case Charlene gets tickets or something?" Before she left, she said, somewhat breathlessly, making direct eye contact with Jeff again, "Ciao, for now."

Craig leaned close to Jeff. "Well, she certainly is taken by you. A knight? A prince—charming, indeed."

That broke the spell. Jeff, turning to Craig, in a most diplomatic way said, "Your cousin is truly beautiful, and charming."

Craig nodded, and he and Jeff watched the five models walk away. "If Barb knew what I was thinking right now, she would castrate me."

After a hearty laugh, they turned and headed toward the bar.

The evening continued with the proper amount of mingling and concluded with a fabulous sit-down dinner and a generous, but not overwhelming number of short speeches introducing the key players in both organizations, the client and the agency. Soon, LaDormeur would be a household name, with the public clamoring for their products.

As Jeff drove home alone from the party, he reflected on how his life would now return to normal. His mission with Mindi had been a success. She'd grown from a fearful woman to a successful model and credited him with helping her. Though pleased about that, he felt sad that there'd be no more dream visits to their gray room. Mindi v.2015 would no longer exist in his reality, except as a warm memory. Their v.2017 friendship would now most probably be limited to emails and text messages. So many parts of his life wrapped up in just one evening.

CHAPTER 22

The next day, Jeff didn't feel like working. He forced himself to sit down at his computer and review the error messages generated by a client that had been beta testing their latest program.

He'd replayed the previous evening several times, primarily Craig's comment. "She is certainly taken by you." Jeff hadn't had romantic feelings toward Mindi, aside from acknowledging that she was truly an exquisite woman. Knowing her history, he couldn't imagine making a pass at her. He felt guilty just considering it and quickly dismissed it. The dream books, and Ingrid's book, now rested in his bookshelf at home to gather dust.

His cell phone rang. He looked down at the caller ID, picked up the phone and said, "Good afternoon, Charlie. I thought you might sleep in. What a great party! The décor, the dinner, and speeches."

"It wasn't all my doing," she replied. "The client had a big hand in the party last night, but yes, I'll take credit for getting the puzzle pieces put in place. I've got a great team. Everyone's getting bonuses. But that's not why I called." Then lightly, "How about I pick up some takeout, something light like salads, and bring them over to your place tonight?"

Her suggestion caught Jeff off guard because of the recent infrequency in their dating schedule. It did, however, represent the casualness of their relationship, so he accepted, and they arranged a time.

~

At seven thirty, Jeff heard a slight tap at the door, then it unlocked. Charlene entered and set her key on the kitchen counter. She looked at Jeff with a smile and set down two sacks—one with the salads and the other with two chilled bottles of white wine. She unpacked the salads and he opened the wine while they engaged in the gentle banter representative of their relationship.

Jeff detected something in the mood of the room, but no red flags—no green ones either, though. The subdued nature of their interaction he attributed to the end of the massive adrenaline rush of the last few months that had culminated with the successful gala last evening.

As they ate, Charlene debriefed for Jeff her conversations with management after the event ended yesterday evening. The client was ecstatic.

Then she suggested they clean up and go into the living room where they sat facing each other, Charlene on the sofa, him in his mom's wingback chair opposite her. He looked at her expectantly, now on alert.

"Jeff, I have to be totally honest with you," she began, then stopped as if she expected some kind of reply.

He obliged. "Charlie, you were honest. I know you're not ready to talk marriage. I've accepted that and am happy we've got the relationship we have . . ." He tilted his head forward, looking at her for confirmation from under his upraised eyebrows.

"Jeff, you were so sweet at the bistro. I was so impressed that you had the courage to even open the subject, and even more so, I was impressed that you didn't make a scene when I said I'm not where you are. You accepted my clumsy response like a perfect gentleman. I've known guys whose egos would have run away with them and who would've tried to make me feel guilty, thrown a tantrum that would make a three-year-old's seem tame. You were . . . amazing."

Jeff shrugged off the praise. "Then what do you mean, 'totally honest?' About what?"

She leaned forward, elbows on her knees. "Jeff, I don't do things like I'm going to admit to you that I did. It's not who I am, but in this case, I'm glad I did."

"What are you talking about?" His brow furrowed, he looked into her eyes for a clue. *Has she met someone else?*

"I wasn't going to say anything to you about this, ever. But after what I witnessed last night . . ."

On high alert now, Jeff said, "What?"

"The last time when I stayed over, after you fell asleep, I read your dream journal." She leaned back as if he might fly into a rage.

Jeff only stared at her. He couldn't process all at once the consequences of what she'd just said. He could only ask, "Did you read the whole thing?" Then things started to fall into place, but he wasn't sure yet how he felt about her knowing. He had to hear her out. His voice remained even as he said, "Okay, go on."

The confidence that Charlene first displayed when starting the conversation seemed to wane. "Jeff, you are so dear. Knowing what I know now, and what kind of person you are, after how you reacted to my refusal . . . and the things that you know, I don't know how you knew them—not sure I can explain what's in your journal—but . . . Well, it's what you do know, and how you dealt with knowledge of Mindi's past, with Carolyn, with my dad's issues, and with me." She finally took a breath and finished with, "You are incredible." Her eyes met his, asking for understanding.

"Well, thanks. But you don't think I'm crazy?"

"When I first started reading it, of course I did. Then I remembered that you'd asked about my dreams and mentioned yours that day at lunch. As I read on, of course I thought you were just having really crazy dreams, but the more I read . . . I still can't believe any of what you did is possible. But of course it happened. It certainly must be real. But if anybody else ever got ahold of that . . ."

Jeff said nothing, and Charlene continued, "It all seems so improbable, but I now think . . . I keep going back and forth, and I keep coming up with the fact that I know you're not psychotic. Okay, lucid dreams are still unknown territory and time travel is impossible, right? But not for you. You did it. No, I don't think you are crazy. But I'm surprised *you're* not crazy now after all you went through. And then there's Mindi."

Jeff flinched at the mention of Mindi's name this second time.

She saw it and said, "It's okay, Jeff, really. Please—let me finish."

He nodded, then said, "But first, how did you find the notebook? I kept it hidden in the bottom of the drawer." Before she could answer, he replayed writing his last entry. He'd been in a hurry to get to the driving range, and just dropped it in the drawer, hadn't buried it. *Clumsy idiot!* He gave his head an angry shake and said, "I screwed up, didn't I?"

Charlene didn't answer. "I woke up. I hadn't been asleep long. You were fast asleep, and I tried not to wake you. I was looking for a tissue, hoping I didn't need to get up and get one, so I looked in the drawer. When I opened the drawer, the notebook was right on top. I saw my dad's name in your handwriting. I know it was wrong—a person doesn't read someone else's diary—but I had to see what it said. I read that page, and then started at the beginning of the notebook. It took me a while. I'm sorry I was nosey, but like I said, I'm really not. It's confusing."

"Okay." Jeff thought about what she'd said and accepted the facts. "What's done is done." He sighed. "Please, go on." He waited, wondering what the consequences would be now that she knew.

"Jeff, I turned you down on getting engaged because I'm not in love with you." Anticipating an objection, she added, "Please wait. I love what you do for me, I love what we've done, I love it when we're together. You're a generous lover and so much fun to be with, so creative and sensitive, and you're so kind and patient with me. We've made a good couple. You'll make an excellent husband and, someday, a fantastic father. But that's just it. I didn't think—don't think I'm ready to make that kind of commitment to you, or anyone now. I've got my career and it's breaking wide open. There's no reason to rehash that conversation from before, and knowing you, I think you've worked through it and accepted where I am."

Jeff nodded and waited, knowing she wasn't finished.

"Knowing what I know now, even though you said you love me, I don't think you are 'in love' with me." She searched his face for a reaction.

But Jeff's expression didn't change. His mind was busy processing her words.

"You said you couldn't figure out the reason you got involved with Dad, Carolyn, and her boyfriends, and why you had to be in Dad's head when he wrote the letters to Mom, and then found out he had cancer."

Jeff leapt out of the chair. His eyes, locked on hers, were full of pity. "Oh, Charlene, I'm sorry you had to learn all of that. You weren't supposed to . . . I didn't want you to . . . I'm so sorry." He sat down slowly, his eyes fixed on her.

Her shoulders slumped. "I know you mean that, but I do know it all now. I can't un-know it. I contacted the doctor, and they released the information to me. It's all true. And you were never in my parent's home, but you described it perfectly.

"There's more that convinced me what you did was real . . . You wrote in your notebook about Dad and Carolyn days before Mom found Dad's letter. The date's in your notebook. You even knew what book he hid the letter in. I never told you that. So for you to know all of that, you must be some kind of . . . I don't know what to call it, a mystic? You really did do all of that, didn't you?"

Jeff nodded slowly. Charlene's posture expressed his own pain—shoulders folded forward, head lowered.

When she looked up, she said, "I am sorry that you had to experience all that pain that he, that we, all went through again. And how you tried to protect me, to have considered how to do what you did to keep it all from me, to save me, to save us from more pain. I'm not angry you withheld it from me. But I know now that I needed to know all this. That might be, at least in part, why this all happened to you—to us.

"You and Mindi considered trying to save Dad's life and had to abandon the idea because you realized it would've been impossible. I thank you for being willing to try. Thank you so much." Her eyes filled with tears of gratitude. She wiped them away and waited for him to say something.

He didn't say a word.

"So much of what you did is just who you are," Charlene said. "That you were embarrassed to be there when Mindi was using the bathroom, and having to watch Carolyn get undressed, and that you didn't want to be there when Dad and Carolyn had sex. Most men would at least be tempted to have that kind of experience. You were so mature. I think you're incredible, and you deserve so much."

Charlene sat up straight and wiped her eyes again. "My career will take up so much of my time. That would be cruel to you. God forbid, our children would surely suffer. I would be inaccessible. We would all become miserable. As much as I would try to take care of all my family's needs, I don't think I would be very good at it, at least not anytime soon.

"If I wasn't working at what I love, I'd so hang onto you and make sure I fell in love with you." She paused, then went on quietly, "No, that's not right. You can't make yourself fall in love, but I would certainly love everything about you, as I do now. But I can't, I won't, take advantage of you like that. That would be dishonest. It would be a gross betrayal of your trust."

Her words were painful to Jeff at first, but as she explained, his compassion rose for what Charlene must have gone through as she read the journal.

Charlene said, confidence returning, "I think the ultimate *why* it all happened is so we could get here, tonight, to this point in our relationship. You wrote in the journal that you didn't know why you had to do all those things with Dad and his girlfriend, and you speculated on predestination and whatever was making you have those dreams. Like I said, I believe one reason is so I could know the truth, and the other is so that you can move on and be truly happy. The reason you had those dreams is so you could meet Mindi. But not just to help her with her problem and then to help her become a model . . . It's

296

all right there in your journal."

Jeff said, "What are you talking about?"

"It became clear to me when I saw you and Mindi talking together at the gala. You've fallen in love with her, and I'm sure she feels that way about you. She can't say enough good things about you." Charlene took her phone out of her pocket, thumbed it awake, and went to her text messages. "Here's what she said in a text to me this morning." She read out loud. "Thanks again, Charlene, for your confidence in choosing me. It means a lot to me. And you are so very lucky to be with such a great guy like Jeff. I'm impressed."

When she looked up at Jeff again, she said, "That statement, plus what I know from your journal and watching you two last night—it's clearly written between the lines." She paused, then commanded him, "Read between the lines, Jeff. I have to let you go." She managed a hint of a smile and Jeff recognized the supplication in her eyes, it was important to her that he understand.

Neither of them said anything for a long moment. The fog had lifted, his view cleared. She was right, of course—the dreams had all been progressing directly to this point.

Wait for an answer, his father had said. His father was right. He had the answer to his question, "Why?"

He tried to find his voice. "Charlene. I, uh . . . you—"

"No, Jeff. Please. Don't say anything. Here." She reached into her jacket pocket, pulled out an envelope and handed it to him. "Two tickets to the Rep on Saturday night. Take Mindi on your first date."

Jeff glanced at the envelope in his hand, then looked at Charlene with an unspoken question in his eyes.

"Don't worry, I'll talk to Mindi. I'm having lunch with her tomorrow. I'll explain what, and how I know and tell her I've stepped away."

She stood, urged him to stand, and gave him a hug. She turned, picked up her purse, and left. Her key remained on the counter.

He watched her leave without saying a word.

The door closed.

CHAPTER 23

Mindi met Charlene for lunch downtown. Mindi thought the meeting would be about another job for the agency, but was surprised to find that Charlene knew about the dreams.

Charlene explained how she found the journal and read how Mindi's and Jeff's friendship had grown over the months. She concluded by saying, "Mindi, I've decided to end my relationship with Jeff."

Mindi froze. A look of sadness swept over her face. "Oh, Charlene, no." Then Mindi frowned, leaned forward and said, "Am *I* responsible?"

Charlene's face displayed her sincerity as she shook her head "No, not in the way you might think. Let me explain. Jeff and I had never talked about our future, let alone getting married. Jeff is so sweet, but he misinterpreted signals about where we were in the relationship. I certainly didn't mean to mislead him. That's on me and this is my decision alone. We had a good time together, but I'm not interested in settling down like that. I told him, and I meant it, it would be dishonest of me to let him think I might change my mind about getting married. I'm okay with my decision, and I'd like to think he is too—or soon will be."

"What do you mean by that?"

"I know he was more than disappointed that I didn't accept his proposal, and he's sorry he left his journal for me to find. But I did find it. It's quite clear to me that there's something mysterious, maybe even magic, about the way you two met. His journal shows he's very fond of you. But I'm not jealous. Or angry. Jeff is very smart and fiercely loyal. I'm proud to know him."

Charlene paused, took a sip of coffee, looked up at Mindi, and said, "How do you feel about Jeff?"

The directness of the question surprised Mindi. "Well, I . . . Uh, Jeff is a friend. We're friends . . . What are you saying, Charlene?"

"I'm answering your question about what I meant when I said Jeff would 'soon be okay' with me ending the relationship. I'm saying that now you can make up your own minds and see where things may lead for you two. Those dreams happened for a reason.

"Mindi, if Jeff and I were to stay together, his loyalty to me would be total and without question. I sense you're an honorable woman and would never interfere in another's relationship. Jeff and I don't have a future. Now I'm out of the picture. Need I say more?"

Mindi shook her head in disbelief, then said, "No. I understand."

When they'd finished eating, Charlene wished Mindi much luck with her career and told her genuinely she looked forward to working together on future ad campaigns. Mindi thanked Charlene for the lunch, and they parted with a hug.

~

Since Mindi was already downtown, she found the bookstore where Jeff had bought the dream book from Ingrid. The little bell announced Mindi's arrival, and she felt the transformation that Jeff had described when he'd entered the store. In the far corner of the store, a woman Mindi assumed was Ingrid sat talking quietly with two conservatively dressed women in a quiet nook nestled near a window beyond the bookshelves. Upholstered chairs sat around an antique coffee table draped with a multicolored, crocheted tablecloth. On the table sat delicate, yet mismatched china teacups and saucers, a plate of scones, antique napkins, and a ceramic teapot. The door closed; the bell tinkled again.

Mindi wandered among the shelves, taking time to read the titles on the spines of the old books. Many were shelved traditionally upright, but some lay stacked one atop another, forming de facto bookends in the middle of a shelf. Mindi marveled at the esoteric agglomeration of titles, many of which appeared very old. Their leather covers, cracked and lined with age, sat nobly on the shelf. She'd never seen so many antique books.

As she emerged from one of the aisles, she came into full view of the group. Ingrid turned, met Mindi's eyes, and acknowledged her with a nod, then turned to the others, and in a soft voice, said, "Please, excuse me a moment." They nodded, sipped their tea, and returned to their conversation.

Mindi, already at ease in the pleasant, incense-laden atmosphere, relaxed even more when Ingrid offered her hand and introduced herself. "I'm Ingrid, my dear. Is there something I may help you with or answer a question?"

"Thank you. A friend mentioned your shop, and I wanted to see if there might be something here of interest." Mindi glanced around to show she'd like to continue browsing.

"May I ask what he said in particular that interested you?"

Mindi's gaze met Ingrid's smiling eyes with curious surprise—she hadn't told Ingrid the gender of her friend. A lucky guess? Perhaps.

The corners of Ingrid's mouth showed the start of a smile which matched the twinkle in her eyes. "If you could give me a few minutes while I finish speaking with my friends"—she nodded toward them—"I will answer any questions you may have. If, of course, you have the time. Please do browse. Treasures abound." Ingrid waved her hand toward the next aisle as if to tell Mindi where her answers might be found.

Ingrid then turned and glided back toward the table. In one even movement, she picked up her cup and saucer, settled onto the chair, and offered her ear to a question one of the women asked.

Mindi watched Ingrid return to her friends, then entered the indicated aisle and resumed her perusal of the shelved volumes. She found subjects she'd not seen in the other aisles. Books in these shelves, she found, were titles she hadn't realized she might be interested in—not until she saw them.

When she saw a title that piqued her interest, she pulled it from the shelf and checked the copyright page. She found: *Telepathy, Genuine and Fraudulent* by W. W. Baggally, c. 1917; *The Law of Psychic Phenomenon* by Thomson Jay Hudson, c. 1893; *Clairvoyance and Occult Powers* by Swami Panchadasi, c. 1916; and *Clairvoyance and Thought* by L. W. de Laurence, c. 1916. And then she looked at more modern texts, such as *Dream Telepathy: Experiments in Nocturnal ESP* by Krippner, Ullmann, and Vaughan, c. 1973. Mindi, amazed at the sheer number of volumes, wondered how she might choose which would serve her best.

"Did you find anything of interest, dear?" Ingrid said in a

soft voice as she approached Mindi.

"Oh," Mindi said, pleasantly surprised by Ingrid's approach during her quiet excursion into the occult. "Oh my, yes. I see so much here—one couldn't read it in a lifetime." She turned to face Ingrid and again met the woman's patient gaze. "Are you the owner of the shop?" Mindi asked.

"Yes, I am. And you are?"

"I'm Mindi."

"What a lovely name for a lovely girl."

Mindi smiled, at ease. "Well, thank you. My friend mentioned he'd come here and found . . ." She paused, wondering how much to tell.

Ingrid waited a second for Mindi to continue, and when she didn't, she said, "Yes, Jeff chose a wonderful book on dreams. I trust he has enjoyed it. No doubt he shared it with you."

Mindi, startled again at Ingrid's knowledge of her friendship with Jeff, said without thinking, "How did you know . . . ?" Her sentence remained unfinished.

Ingrid merely tilted her head, indicating that no answer was necessary nor would one be offered. "Are you interested in telepathy or astral projection?"

Mindi composed herself. "Well . . . Well, both, I suppose." Clearly no secrets could be kept from this woman, although she felt confident that Ingrid meant no harm.

Ingrid indicated for Mindi to precede her to the end of the aisle. As she passed by Ingrid, Mindi found the woman's slight smell of patchouli comforting. Ingrid followed her and, at the end of the aisle, motioned toward the chairs and table where the other ladies had sat—now empty.

"Would you like a cup of chamomile tea?" Ingrid said.

Mindi, further comforted by her hostess's friendliness, and without checking her watch, said, "Thank you, that would be . . . nice."

Ingrid excused herself for a moment, but before she left, she handed Mindi two books taken from the bookshelf. Mindi looked at the spines. She'd seen the books on the shelf a few moments before. They weren't hundred-year-old antiques like many of the others. Nevertheless, they would be vintage. The first, *Dream Telepathy*, had a copyright of 1973. The other was written during the war years, in 1943, by early psychic researchers L. Johanssen and K. Travis, titled—unimaginatively—*Astral Projection in Dreams*.

She opened the worn leather cover of the book on astral projection and saw on the flyleaf an undated inscription written in formal, flowing cursive:

To Helen,
I trust we will meet once again in our dreams.
Love, Martin

What was Helen and Martin's story such that it compelled such a message of endearment and a wish to "meet in their dreams?" How had this book come to be in this quaint bookstore? Mindi wondered, had Helen cleaned out her bookshelf? Had the book been loaned, never returned, to its owner, and found its way here? Or had Helen passed, her family having discarded it, not realizing its import to the departed? Mindi would never know. Her imagination, however, played with their inferred romance and compared it with her own nascent relationship.

She'd just turned to the table of contents but hadn't begun to read when Ingrid reappeared with refreshments: a fresh teacup, the teapot with hot water, and a plate containing two scones, all balanced on an ever so slightly tarnished silver serving tray.

As she poured the tea over the tea bag in Mindi's cup, she asked, "How is that book, my dear?"

Mindi looked down at the book, then looked up at Ingrid as

she sat. "I haven't gotten past the inscription. You must see a lot of interesting history pass through your shop."

"Oh yes, and just as that book addresses the mysteries of dreams and travel into others' lives, many of those mysteries are never solved, merely savored—some recorded, and many more lost to time. You're wondering who Helen and Martin were? I am afraid that's a mystery that will never be solved."

Ingrid's depth of awareness continued to awe Mindi. "Well, yes. It is intriguing to get a snapshot of people and never know their backstory."

Ingrid smiled and lowered her head in understanding. "Have you any questions that perhaps I can address? You did come in here to do more than satisfy mere curiosity, did you not?"

Indeed, Mindi, now more than merely curious, wondered how Ingrid knew so much about why she was here. But it spoiled the illusion if one saw behind the curtain while a magician did a trick, so rather than be ill at ease asking how Ingrid knew of Jeff and her, she decided to get to a more important point.

"Well, my friend and I have been having some interesting dreams, and not just one or two, but a series of dreams that have taken place over a couple of years." Mindi reflected on how that sounded but knew she wouldn't have to make further explanation, that somehow Ingrid knew.

Ingrid nodded. "And you have concerns about why these dreams are occurring? Or are your concerns about their effect on your well-being?"

Mindi realized this woman had accepted the role of adviser as well as bookseller. "Well, both, I guess," she replied, "but primarily the first. Why are they happening, and how? It's been going on for a while, so I'm not really concerned about my sanity, but others might be, if they found out." She let out a short, nervous laugh, which was met with another warm smile of understanding from her host.

Ingrid nodded at the book on Mindi's lap. "That book may be of some help. What you're experiencing has also interested others for some time. Enough people have had similar, let's say, adventures over time that there have been, even many years ago, attempts at serious research into the same questions."

Mindi glanced down at the book and considered her next question, then said, "Ingrid, you seem to be interested in subjects well beyond the reality that exists out there." She motioned toward the window. "I had hoped to meet you and see if there might be answers to my questions. Could you tell me if I, er, we should be afraid of the consequences of the events we witness? Are we tampering with things that could be dangerous?"

Ingrid took a sip of tea, washing down a small bite of scone. "I am not qualified to speak to the danger. I feel that whatever is guiding my actions here in this world is, at the very least, benign, and I prefer to believe it is, in fact, benevolent. We seem to never be given more than we can carry. However, the burden sometimes may feel unwieldy. But confidence in our own ability will help us carry the load. So to answer your question, there may be more negative consequences of failing to accept the tasks presented, rather than what may seem, at first, a path to failure. Danger, if I may, is subjective, just as beauty is in the eye of the beholder."

"What do you mean 'whatever is guiding' our actions?" Mindi asked. "Do you believe in a god?"

"Oh my, that is a direct question." Ingrid looked away as she considered her answer, then looked back at Mindi. "We may never know, will we? As limited as our minds are to know the truth—and there may be many truths—and as short as our time here is, I'm certain there are things we can never understand. What I do know is that there are many wonders, from something

306

as simple as my ability to beat back darkness with the flick of a light switch to the joy of the miracle of a newborn child. So much is beyond our limited minds to understand. Humankind have invented all-powerful beings to satisfy the void in our ability to explain these wonders. I attempt to obey unnamed and unknowable universal truths so I may be at peace to have serenity. With serenity, I can assist others to be at peace amid the noise and confusion of the world."

Mindi smiled. "So we don't know?"

Ingrid returned the smile. "Well said, my dear. In short, that is true. I certainly don't know. And further, I do not make believe."

They'd been alone in the shop and had just finished their tea when the little brass bell above the door announced a young man and woman as they entered. Ingrid turned toward the entrance, stood, and, before she moved toward the front of the store, said to Mindi, "Please excuse me a moment."

Mindi set her cup down, hesitated a moment, then picked up her handbag and stood with the books clutched in her hand.

Ingrid acknowledged the couple, then looked back at Mindi. "Will you be wanting either of the books?"

Trusting her host's choices, she replied immediately, "Oh yes, both. What do I owe you?"

They completed the transaction and made their farewells, Ingrid saying she felt sure they'd meet again.

~

Once outside, it seemed to Mindi that passing through the doorway had broken a spell. Had her conversation been another dream? Yet in her hands she held books wrapped in brown paper and tied with string, proving it all had been, in fact, reality. She looked forward to sharing her experience with Jeff.

~

The evening was unseasonably warm, yet characteristically drizzly for early November in Seattle. Jeff and Mindi dined together in a lovely covered garden-courtyard restaurant under the care of attentive servers and the assured warmth of patio heaters.

After they dined, they attended the play at the Seattle Repertory Theatre.

Pride and Prejudice, a timeless story about falling in love.

The evening was a dream come true.

CHAPTER 24

After having spent the last week with Mindi, Jeff sat alone at the kitchen counter in his apartment and gazed lovingly at the page taken from the latest issue of Vogue magazine which graced the door of his refrigerator. The ad showed Mindi gazing innocently, yet subtly seductively, at the camera, the LaDormeur makeup perfectly applied. Her smile was just for him.

While he looked at the picture, he remembered sharing the wonders of his adopted State of Washington with her. They'd taken the ferries across Puget Sound to Bremerton and then Friday Harbor, driven up to the mountains through Snoqualmie Pass and its falls, and then over to Ginkgo Petrified Forest in Eastern Washington. After seeing the natural wonders, they'd toured the Museum of Flight near the old Boeing Airplane Company plant in nearby Tukwila, had dinner at the top of the famous Space Needle, then taken a ride on the Great Wheel on the Seattle waterfront. Mindi had been amazed at the diversity of landscapes and the lack of crowds compared to her home in Southern California. Their time together had the pure charm of a fairy tale come true.

Jeff took her to the airport for her return flight to LA. They hugged for a long time in front of the departure gate, yet it never seemed long enough. He handed her the carry-on bag and looked down at the airport carpeting, feeling like a spoiled child not getting his way. Other passengers carved a path around them.

He'd bought himself a ticket so he could accompany her to the gate and see her off. Mindi had teased him about the extravagance but said, with sincerity, that she understood and was glad he was there.

"I'll call you when we land," she said, lifting his chin with her fingers and looking into his eyes. "When this photo shoot is done, I'll have some more time off. We'll figure something out."

"I know. If the dreaming still works in real time, it'll keep me until . . ." His sentence remained unfinished as he stood up straight and tried to display his normal self-confidence.

She smiled. "I'll talk to you later. See you tonight, right?"

"Yeah, I'll call to you, like before. Meet you there." *I hope*, he thought.

The PA system crackled. The announcement broke their spell. "Final boarding for Alaska Airlines, Flight 404 to Los Angeles, Gate C5."

After one more quick hug, she stepped up to the boarding agent who scanned her pass, then glided through the doorway toward the airplane. Just before she disappeared around the curve of the jetway, she turned and threw him a kiss. He'd smiled and returned the gesture, but noted his apprehension as she left to return to her work in LA. She was flying on a 737-800, which had had a superb safety record since it launched in 1994, yet the memory of Charlene's dad's death last year still lingered.

Jeff remained true to his long-standing habit, instilled by his father, of seeing someone to safety. He remained in the departure lounge, saw the plane taxi to the end of the runway, and watched until well after rollout as it headed south and disappeared into the clouds.

With Jeff's reminiscence over, he glanced at the kitchen clock. He took one more loving look at the picture of Mindi, turned off the lights, and headed toward his bedroom.

Of course, nothing was certain, but he trusted that they would meet once again in their dreams.

ABOUT THE AUTHOR

Born to a military family, Joe has lived and traveled worldwide, earned a Business/Psychology degree, and chose the Pacific Northwest of the United States to settle, raise his family and pursue his careers—first in telecommunications, then environmental, health and safety education. His interest in science fiction blossomed in his teens while doing research for an essay for a class assignment. The mystery of what takes place in our minds while asleep, during meditation, and yoga provided the foundation for his *Between State* series.

A NOTE FROM THE AUTHOR

If you enjoyed this book, I would be very grateful if you could write a review and publish it at your point of purchase. Your review, even a brief one, will help other readers to decide whether they'll enjoy my work.

If you want to be notified of new releases from myself and other AIA Publishing authors, please sign up to the AIA Publishing email list. You'll find the sign-up button on the right-hand side under the photo at www.aiapublishing.com. Of course, your information will never be shared, and the publisher won't inundate you with emails, just let you know of new releases.

Read on for a sneak preview of the second book in the *Between State* series

OUR CALLING

THE BETWEEN STATE
BOOK TWO

CHAPTER 1

For the second time that night, Jeff felt the familiar sensation of falling and floating in his gray-fogged dream. He'd just said goodnight to Mindi. Had she called him back? Was he going to see her again? They'd never had two visits to the gray room in one night.

But it was not to be. When his vision cleared, Jeff stood in an open-sided building with a corrugated metal roof, seeing through the eyes of a host. The man's shirt clung to his skin in hot, humid, still air that smelled of chemicals mingled with the earthy smell of the jungle. Sweat ran down the man's face and neck.

Tools, gloves, beer cans, soft-drink bottles, and empty cigarette packs lay scattered across a nearby worktable made of scrap lumber. A young man, an *indígena*, barely old enough to shave, dressed in torn work pants and a faded green T-shirt, handed Jeff's host a small bundle, a little larger than a softball, wrapped in white cloth. He then shuffled back out into the bright sunshine. Jeff estimated that the bundle weighed a couple of pounds.

The man's calloused hands were the color of tarnished

copper. He pressed the putty-like ball into a thick metal mold about the size of a fat paperback. The mold had holes drilled in its sides and was lined with a coarse white cloth, which Jeff's host folded over the top of the putty-like material. He placed a thick steel plate on top of the ductile mass and centered the ram of a hydraulic press on it. As the host pumped the press's handle, the ram pushed down, forcing a milky liquid through the holes and onto the dirt floor. When the press ceased moving and the liquid flow stopped, the man removed the steel plate along with the pins that held the corners of the mold together and removed the pressed block. He placed it on a ceramic plate in a microwave oven, set the timer, and pushed *Start*. The microwave hummed. As the block spun on the turntable, the man took a crumpled pack of unfiltered cigarettes from his shirt pocket, lit one, and discarded the match. Jeff hated the taste of the cigarette smoke, but he endured, obligated to watch the scenario into which he had been dropped.

The timer signaled the end of the microwave's cycle, and the man retrieved the white brick and placed it on a balance scale. He grunted in satisfaction, wrapped the block in plastic film and stacked it with dozens of others like it.

That's cocaine! Jeff shouted inside the man's mind.

The man heard him.

The startled host looked first at one, then the other of two men working in the building. "*¿Quién dijo eso? ¡Yo sé qué es esto! Y, ¿quién de ustedes habla inglés!*" Who said that? I *know* what this is! And—who of you can speak English?

He looked from one worker to the other. Both returned his puzzled look. One shrugged and turned away. The other replied, "*¿De qué estás hablando?*" What are you talking about?

Jeff's host said, "*Alguien dijo en inglés que esto es cocaína.*" Someone just said in English that this is cocaine.

The other worker frowned at him. "*Estas escuchando cosas, amigo mío.*" You are hearing things, my friend.

Jeff felt no guilt for the confusion he'd created. Because of the heat, humidity, cigarette smoke, and discomfort of watching these people, he called out his original escape words to force himself to end the dream, "Charlene, Charlene, Charlene."

It didn't work. He was still there, the humid air holding him hostage.

"*¿Quién es Charlene? ¡Esto no es gracioso!*" his host said in anger. Who is Charlene? This is not funny!

Wrong escape word, Jeff thought, then used the correct one. *Ciao!* he shouted in his mind.

Before Jeff left, he felt the man's head jerk up as he repeated it, but as a question. "*¿Chao?*"

Jeff awoke and lay in his bed for a few minutes before he arose and documented the dream in a new notebook—his old one safely locked away.

The clock said 4:35 a.m. *This is crazy*, he thought to himself. *Is it the start of a new adventure?* "No!" he said aloud. He didn't want another "adventure."

Then curiosity tempered his fit of pique. *Where was I? South America somewhere?* He wished he remembered more of his high school Spanish.

It was too late to go back to sleep for just an hour, so he made coffee and googled "cocaine manufacture" on his laptop. "Well, Jeffy ol' boy, it looks like you've been south of the border," he said quietly to himself.

He learned more than he thought he wanted to know. During the second documentary about drug labs in Colombia, he watched the laborious steps of turning coca leaves into cocaine using gasoline, acids, bases, and time-consuming, sweaty, arduous labor—and just as in his dream—saw the bricks molded, dried, wrapped, and stacked.

When was that? Did I time travel or was that real time?

He added a footnote to his journal entry that his senses—smell, touch, taste, and hearing—were more acute in that dream than ever before. He'd felt the oppressive heat, humidity, and cigarette smoke.

Mindi's smiling face looked out at him from the page, cut from a Vogue magazine, that he'd stuck on the refrigerator door. Jeff smiled at the picture and shook his head. "I can't wait to tell you about the crazy dream I had."

ACKNOWLEDGMENTS

My special thanks to the following for their invaluable input and feedback, without whom the story would never have been completed:

Gratitude is extended to Delaney Dallas, who gave the early manuscript a thorough examination and offered superb suggestions, among many other issues, regarding the balance in the development of the characters.

Many thanks to Enoch and Brandi Freeman, beta readers who I found through Fiverr and who provided both extensive encouragement and valuable comments to ensure the story met the standards of quality and taste for which I was striving.

Thank you to Anthony Bianco, whose performing arts education, training, and experience provided valuable input on the structure of scenes to move the story forward. Ant, your consistent encouragement and positive vibe made it possible to carry on until completion.

Many thanks to my friend, my brother-from-another-mother, Randall McKinney, for his support and affirmation that the journey was worthwhile and to ensure that I didn't do or say something stupid.

To my editor, Tahlia Newland, I offer thanks for her skill and particularly her patience in ensuring both the prose and sentence structure could tell the story the way I intended.

And to my wife, who showed unlimited patience and tolerance with me sequestering myself alone, as writers must do, in my "writer's loft," and who provided continuous, unconditional love, support, and encouragement.

BIBLIOGRAPHY

Al-Khalili, Jim. *Black Holes, Wormholes and Time Machines*. Florida: CRC Press, 2012.

Jiloha, Ram C. "Relevance of parapsychology in psychiatric practice: A rejoinder." *Indian Journal of Psychiatry* 54, no. 3 (2012): 297–9. https://doi.org/10.4103/0019-5545.102462

Kaku, Michio. *Physics of the Impossible*. New York: Random House, 2008.

LaBerge, Stephen, and Rheingold, Howard. *Exploring the World of Lucid Dreaming*. Toronto: Ballantine Books, 1990.

Lin, Steven. "The Five Stages of Sleep & Brain Wave Cycles." Accessed April 23, 2022. https://assets.cdn.thewebconsole.com/S3WEB8659/images/Dr-Steven-Lin---the-five-stages-of-sleep-and-brain-wave-cycles.pdf.

London, Jack. *The Star Rover*. New York: Random House, 2003.

Monroe, Robert A. *Journeys Out of the Body*. New York: Crown Publishing Group, 1977.

Morley, Charlie. *Lucid Dreaming Made Easy*. California: Hay House Inc., 2015.

Nunez, Kirsten. "Lucid Dreaming: Controlling the Storyline of Your Dreams." *Healthline*, June 17, 2019. https://www.healthline.com/health/what-is-lucid-dreaming#how-to-experience.

Oura. "What are the Stages of Sleep?" Oura Ring, Accessed April 23, 2022. https://ouraring.com/blog/sleep-stages/.

Peters, Brandon. "What Is a Hypnagogic Jerk and What Causes Sleep Starts?" (March 2022) https://www.verywellhealth.com/what-is-a-hypnagogic-jerk-and-what-causes-sleep-starts-3014889.

Raduga, Michael. "An effective lucid dreaming method by inducing hypnopompic hallucinations." *International Journal of Dream Research* 14, no. 1 (April 2021): 1–9. https://doi.org/10.11588/ijodr.2021.1.71170.

Vonnegut, Kurt. *Slaughterhouse Five*. New York, Dial Press, 2009.

Voss, Ursula, Romain Holzmann, Inka Tuin, and Allan J. Hobson. "Lucid Dreaming: a State of Consciousness with Features of Both Waking and Non-Lucid Dreaming." *Sleep* 32, no. 9 (2009): 1191–200. https://doi.org/10.1093/sleep/32.9.1191.

Watt, Caroline. *Parapsychology: A Beginner's Guide*. London: Oneworld Publications, 2016.

Wells, Herbert G. *The Time Machine*. New York: Bantam Classics, 1982.

Wikipedia. "Metaphysics." Accessed April 23, 2022.
https://en.wikipedia.org/wiki/Metaphysics.

Wikipedia. "Parapsychology." Accessed April 23, 2022.
https://en.wikipedia.org/wiki/Parapsychology.

Yetman, Daniel. "What Is Hypnagogia, the State Between Wakefulness and Sleep?" *Healthline*, October 26, 2020.
https://www.healthline.com/health/hypnagogia.

Printed in the USA
CPSIA information can be obtained
at www.ICGtesting.com
CBHW031204160724
11666CB00030B/142